THE LONG WAY AROUND

DOUGLAS CAVANAUGH

Copyright © 2020 by Douglas Cavanaugh
Copyright Office of the United States of America

ISBN 978-0-985-4684-3-9

All rights reserved. No part of this book may be reproduced or used in any manner without written permission of the copyright owner except for the use of quotations in a book review.

This is a work of fiction. Names, characters, places, and incidents either are the product of the author's imagination or are used fictitiously. Any resemblance to actual persons, living or dead, events, or locales is entirely coincidental.

First paperback edition February 2020

Cover design by Kyle Krier

Kirostar Publishing:
Into Hell's Fire – July 2012
The Long Way Around – February 2020

All inquiries: croauthor@yahoo.com

Reader ratings and reviews are welcome at your favorite online bookstore.

Dedication

This book is dedicated to the memory of three great Americans and proud Iowans. These men were the only American World War II veterans I ever knew personally. Each survived the war and returned to their home state to thrive in their rural communities.

* * * * *

Harold J. Neiers (August 30, 1916 – July 11, 2011), Cascade, Iowa. Harry and his family lived next door to my mother's family as she grew up.

During World War II, Harry served in the 104th Infantry Division, known as the Timberwolves. Unlike the two veterans featured in *The Long Way Around*, Harry did not participate in the Battle of the Bulge. He was wounded in Holland before the Battle of the Bulge took place, and was awarded a Purple Heart for the injuries he received.

Harry was a huge sports fan, particularly of the professional teams from Chicago. He was an original Chicago Bears season ticket holder and attended most home games from the 1940s through the 1980s. He told me how he'd drive to East Dubuque, Illinois, to catch the midnight train to Chicago the night before gameday to see Dick Butkus and Gale Sayers play at Wrigley Field. I have many fond memories discussing the Chicago Bears, Cubs, and Iowa Hawkeyes sports teams with Harry on the hanging swing on the Neiers' front porch.

Paul A. Ryan (December 13, 1916 – October 06, 1998), Washington, Iowa. Paul was my father's uncle, my grandmother's younger brother.

Paul served in the Army Air Corps during World War II. He was a sheet metal mechanic who patched up Allied planes that had been shot up by the Germans. He was stationed in North Africa, Sicily, and Italy.

Paul lived in the same rural Iowa community as my father's parents, so in my youth, I got to know him well. He always enjoyed when my gang of brothers came to visit from Davenport. I can remember one particular summer evening in the 1970s when he and my father drove the lot of us around the Iowa countryside in the bed of his pickup truck. What a thrill for a city boy!

James A. Ryan (July 30, 1919 – March 10, 2006), Marengo, Iowa. Jim Ryan was Paul's younger brother, my grandmother's youngest brother.

Jim enlisted in the Navy during World War II (1942-1945), where he served as an electrician third class aboard a submarine chaser in the Pacific Theater. In addition to seeing action in New Guinea, the Philippines, and Okinawa, the ship on which he was stationed participated in the initial landing in Japan.

As a result of time and distance, I didn't know Jim as well as I did his older brother, Paul, while growing up. I do have some excellent memories of visiting him and his family on their rural Marengo farm during pheasant hunting season during my teen years and early twenties.

* * * * *

As often happens in life, the accomplishments many elderly friends and relatives achieved during their lifetimes go underappreciated by younger generations. It seems inexperience and the distractions of youth too easily obscure full recognition of what older folks had to endure decades before. Sadly, it may be long after those elders have passed before they are rewarded with the appreciation they genuinely deserve.

I regret not having spent my time more efficiently with each of the men above when I had the chance, yet I'm grateful for having the opportunity to know each in the time we shared. Even now, I would enjoy discussing their experiences during the Great Depression and World War II with them, and how they transitioned into post-war America. And I'm sure each would gladly tell me all I wanted to know. In the end, I'll always have the memories and the honor of having known these men, and for that I am truly thankful.

Prologue

*Strawberry Point, Iowa
Tuesday, October 19, 1993, 3:30 a.m.*

The crisp night air cut through me as I scurried outside with my coat draped over my shoulders like a cape. The lawn's frozen grass crunched under my weight with each step, and the driveway pebbles moaned beneath my boots as I neared my truck. I had a full load of hunting equipment cradled in my arms. I laid my bow case carefully in the truck bed and tossed the less valuable accessories onto the passenger seat. After starting the engine, I left the vehicle idling while I scraped the frost from the windshield. Then I hurried back into the house.

I sat at the kitchen table with my head in my hands. Resting between my elbows was an untouched glass of orange juice, a toasted bagel, and a cup of black coffee, which was quickly cooling. *What in the world had I been thinking?* The question was rhetorical, as I already knew the answer.

When the alarm clock had buzzed thirty minutes earlier, it had taken several attempts for me to roll out of bed. About a month ago, I'd devised a plan to wake each day before dawn, figuring if I rose at the same time every morning for several weeks it would get easier. In hindsight, it was obvious I'd been too optimistic, and that I'd underestimated the challenges my plan would face after the nights grew longer and the outside temperatures dropped accordingly. I suppose I should have known better, as waking early has been difficult for me ever since I could remember. The only thing making it tolerable now is the reason I'm doing it, my main passion in life—deer hunting. Or, more precisely, bowhunting for white-tailed deer.

To anyone unfamiliar with country living and the outdoor recreations associated with it, the difference in hunting techniques demands distinction, as almost every deer hunter who prefers the archery style over the more common method of walking through the woods with a shotgun in hand will testify. Bowhunting is considered an art and science to those in the know, quite like a fly fisherman would tenaciously defend his chosen fishing method over a traditional cane and bobber. The bowhunting season is an annual event I've enjoyed with great delight ever since my father took me on my first hunt when I was still in grade school. This year's season is in full swing.

My name is Ryan Meyers, and I am the youngest member of my family to hunt deer with a bow and arrow. I may also be the last member to do so unless God grants me the good fortune of marrying, and then raising a healthy son who enjoys the outdoors as much as I. The reason I may be the final family member to do this is because I am an only child, and my parents, Randy and Rita Meyers, are both dead. They died six months apart when I was fifteen years old.

I'll never forget the day my dad, a heavy smoker since his high school days, met me at the front door with a blank stare on his colorless face as I returned from school one afternoon. It was the kind of expression I'd never seen before. The kind someone may see only once or twice in their lifetime, if they're lucky. It was the sort of expression that makes a person instantly aware something is terribly wrong without a single word having been spoken. When I asked him what the problem was, he told me he had lung cancer, and that it had spread to his pancreas. His funeral was just five weeks later. My mother, who had been battling ovarian cancer for years, didn't have the strength to carry on alone. She died six months after my father.

The same day as her funeral Mass at St. Mary Catholic Church, I moved in with my grandfather, Conrad Doyle, and before long, he became my legal guardian and savior. I'm not the first person to describe my grandfather as some sort of hero, though, because my Grandpa Conrad has never been shy about lending a hand to anyone in need. Besides me, he's been a knight in shining armor for dozens of people over the years. It seems my grandfather has a special knack of rescuing people from the brink of disaster, usually just in the nick of time. And though his character is notoriously imperfect, his timing is impeccable. Somehow, he always knows how and what to do exactly when something crucial needs to be done. From what I've heard around town, it's always been that way. Seeing the acts of goodness of which the old man is capable helps me to ignore the nasty traits he carries, and I manage to tolerate his surly behavior. I've always attributed those obnoxious qualities to his tough upbringing and difficult childhood.

My grandfather came into the world the son of a dirt-poor, sod-busting farmer who spent more time in his barn with a bottle of moonshine whiskey than in the fields tending his crops. In fact, my Grandpa Conrad once told me that by 1933, when he was just eleven years old, he was practically running the family farm single-handedly as the Great Depression wreaked havoc across the country. He quit school the same year, woke at daybreak to milk the cows and feed the pigs, and never finished his chores before noon. It wasn't until after the fields had been harvested each autumn that he got to enjoy his youth, time he mostly spent wandering around the surrounding timbers hunting deer.

On many occasions, he told me how he had to learn how to outsmart the best local hunters, because by the time he had a chance to hunt, the deer were extra skittish from others who had already shot at them and missed. This was at a time when deer hunting was generally done by squatting in the thickets or lurking around tree trunks. As a result of the difficult hunting conditions, my grandfather taught himself how to find the most likely spots a deer would pass, to blend in with the scenery, and lure prey in his direction. After discovering that other local hunters were using bows and arrows instead of shotguns and buckshot to harvest deer, the technique instantly captured his interest.

He worked odd jobs and saved for a couple years to buy the first specialty bow and arrow outfit available at the time in his part of the state. It was an early Bear Products Company model on sale at the grand opening of Iowa's inaugural Sears and Roebuck outlet in Mason City in 1936. Each day the following summer, he propped a dozen bales of hay on top of one another, made a cutout of a large buck out of old newspaper, and took target practice for hours before making his bowhunting debut the following autumn.

THE LONG WAY AROUND

Minus the seasons he missed while fighting in World War II, every subsequent hunting season since has ended successfully for him. It is an unrivaled state record.

Conrad Doyle is my late mother's father. He is probably the most celebrated deer hunter in Iowa history. In many ways, he's a state legend. The fact my father loved bowhunting nearly as much as my Grandpa Conrad is probably what attracted my mother to him. My father and grandfather didn't have much else in common though, and the two rarely agreed on anything else. In truth, the love of bowhunting for white-tailed deer was about the only mutual interest the men shared. That delicate bond, enhanced by the respect my father had for my Grandpa Conrad's hunting expertise, was strong enough to keep them civil with one another when he was alive, even though my father never really liked his father-in-law and everybody knew it.

Recently, my grandpa's days in the tree stand have come to an end because of his failing health, not because of his lack of desire to be in the forest. Even in his late sixties, he could still outhunt men half his age, but the wear and tear on his body as a result of life's struggles had finally caught up to him. It wasn't until he was seventy however, that the thought of permanently retiring his bow entered his mind. That year, on the season's opening day, he was stricken by a bout of gout so crippling he couldn't get out bed until one o'clock in the afternoon. But sure enough, by three o'clock, he was in his tree stand, where just before quitting time, he took one of the largest bucks recorded in the state that year. Since that incredible performance, a full year has passed, and he hasn't hunted once.

Nowadays, he's confined to a bed in the county hospital, where he impatiently waits for me to visit him each evening, all the while spewing insults at the nurses and barking curses at the television to help pass the time. I always notice how his mood changes for the better the instant I arrive, how he livens up like a neglected houseplant that's been given a glass of fresh water. I can almost feel his spirit surge as I describe the highlights of my day's hunt to him. Then, through his glossy eyes, I can see his brain working feverishly as he sifts through the details of my report in search of strategic flaws or proven alternatives for me to try. And God pity the doctor or nurse who shows up to check on him while we're discussing tactics. Grandpa Conrad isn't known for his diplomacy, and he isn't shy about telling anyone what he thinks if his train of thought is interrupted. Around town, Conrad Doyle is as infamous for his lack of civility, according to his mood at any moment, as he is famous for his big heart, acts of kindness, and humble generosity.

I love my grandpa enormously and turn to him for advice about life every chance I get. And my Grandpa Conrad puts me before all else in his life, too. In my nineteen years, I've never had anyone I could depend on like him. That is why I feel so helpless about the condition he's in. I suppose to everybody else it appears obvious that his days are numbered, and it must seem like I'm the last person on earth to recognize it. Others might think I'm in denial, but I'm not; I just can't bring myself to show my feelings. I do realize his life is nearing its end, and as a result, mine is about to change forever. And though I've been able to hide my insecurities about my future, I dread to think about what will happen to me without him to guide me through life's most difficult times.

He's the last family member in my life I've been close to from the beginning, and I'm about to start the next phase of it without him.

Chapter One
Life Will Never Be the Same

Cedar Falls, IA
Wednesday, September 15, 1993, 10:00 a.m.

The facility didn't appear as intimidating on initial inspection. In fact, from the outside, it barely looked like a clinic at all, and it was difficult for the young woman to take seriously. Something about the structure's style and color scheme seemed odd compared to the image she'd been expecting. At first glance, it resembled a converted doughnut shop or a renovated gas station from the 1970s, and if it weren't for the large sign across the front announcing the services provided inside, she might have thought she was at the wrong address. To her satisfaction, the parking lot was mostly empty, but she could clearly see the lights on inside, confirming that she had arrived on time for her appointment. The young woman took comfort in knowing she wouldn't have to wait in line. The only thing she desired more than discretion was for the task to be completed as soon as possible.

The walk from her car to the clinic entrance seemed to take forever, even though she had overcome most of her anxieties after scheduling the consultation last week. It was a potent relief. Little had changed with her physical state since then, except for a growing fatigue and some slight nausea in the mornings, so there was little other choice than to meet with a professional, get examined, confirm or refute her suspicion, and then make a final decision before it became too late. From a bystander's perspective, it might appear as simple as that.

Internally, however, her mind was in a constant state of turmoil because her future wasn't the only one in question. The fate of others was under her command, and if her concern was justified, she would be forced to choose an outcome that would be impossible to suit everyone. She opted to use the word 'suit' because there was no perfect way out of the predicament. She hated the position she was in, a position she'd vowed never to find herself in a thousand times before. Yet there she was, between university classes, walking through the entrance of the local Planned Parenthood Center for an initial consultation. Still just eighteen years old, she wore faded jeans and a cotton pullover with the letters UNI stenciled in purple on front. Her long, amber hair was pulled into a ponytail.

Once inside, she approached the front desk, her shoulders drawn back and head held high with dignity. But her pale face and the cold sweat collecting on her brow were dead giveaways to the emotions she was feeling inside. The front desk assistant explained the routine and placed a clipboard holding a questionnaire on the counter for her to fill out. The college freshman wondered how many other girls had been through this same drill over the years and based on the expressionless face of the assistant seated in front of her, she presumed there had been plenty.

She took the paperwork to a waiting room chair to check the boxes and answer the questions, and when she'd finished, she returned it to the front desk and reclaimed her seat. There she sat, waiting for her name to be called, staring at the posters on the wall, and wishing for the entire experience to be over.

Chapter Two
My Nightly Visit

Mercy Hospital
Oelwein, IA
Wednesday, October 20, 1993, 7:10 p.m.

"Remember, Ryan, stay away from the great big heifers!" my grandpa warned, his voice louder than necessary. "A woman who starts out fat never gets any thinner."

My grandpa was in a foul mood almost all the time now, as if being cooped up in the hospital for the last several weeks had aggravated him so much, he was determined to make everyone else around him miserable as well. He was using the term for a female cow deliberately and spitefully. He was being mean. The unprovoked attack was directed at an overweight nurse who was removing a dialysis needle from one of the many distended veins in his forearm. Of course, I was embarrassed, but not as much as I've been at other times over the past few weeks. I knew if I tried changing the subject, he would have sensed my motives and escalated his harassment to the point where tears would have been shed. There was little I could do except sit in my chair looking uncomfortable and plot how to repair the damage afterward. I'd become an expert at apologizing on the sly since the end of summer.

"I mean, they might start out thin," he continued, "but women don't know how to cook homemade-style like your grandmother could. These days, a woman will just stick some frozen piece of processed garbage in the microwave and call it dinner. Then, a few years later, after all that grease has clogged up her husband's arteries, she'll cry about why his health is so bad. And that's exactly why these very same women are so damn fat, too! Before they know it, all that blubber in their bellies is flopping over their waistlines forcing them to wear those tacky polyester slacks and causing their knees to rub together when they walk. And once a woman balloons up, she can never reclaim her figure—never! The sight of all the obese women wobbling around these days is a national disgrace, I tell you," he proclaimed, his free arm flailing. "No, don't get fooled, son, because they're all the same. The hell they aren't," he stated with a final wave of his hand, as if intending to stop me before I could offer a rebuttal.

While he rested in his pajamas, I noted how frail my grandpa's physique had become over the last several weeks. His muscles had atrophied from lack of exercise, at least that's what the doctors had told me, and he had lost several pounds as a result of that. His face had narrowed, and the excess skin sagged now more than ever. His thin, gray hair, which he had worn close cropped ever since his military days, had grown out. Of the half dozen strands that were combed over his crown, two wisps were standing up wildly from the rest.

After the nurse left to make her rounds, my grandfather simmered down and his demeanor softened. But the calm didn't last long. A Samsung television sitting on a bureau near the foot of the bed was turned on with its sound muted. CNN was showing footage of fighting taking place in ex-Yugoslavia. The scenes of artillery shells tearing up some village in Bosnia caught my grandpa's attention.

"Well, would you look at those barbarians? I knew after Tito died it would be just a matter of time before those Slavic savages were at each other's throats. More senseless misery the world doesn't need," he said in disgust. He then picked up the remote control and switched channels. Before I could ask who Tito was, CBS Sports was showing on the screen. A World Series game was scheduled to begin at half past seven, and a pre-game interview with one of the participants was underway. The player being questioned was wearing a red and white pin-striped Philadelphia Phillies uniform, had long scraggily hair, and a scruffy, goatee-style beard.

"Aw, for crying out loud! Now I have to look at this clown? Another disgrace," he snarled. "Why couldn't this guy catch a haircut and a shave before appearing in a nationally televised interview? Tim McCarver ought to bash that bozo over the head with his microphone. Off-camera, I hope he tells him that his sixty-seven Cardinals could've easily whipped his team of bums in four, all the while being paid a pittance compared to the salaries the jokers on his team make. The next thing you know, these second-rate athletes will be appearing as prison convicts, sporting tattoos, earrings, and only the devil knows what else. What the hell has this country come to?"

I didn't respond to his outburst, which may have partially been directed at me. My grandfather was a staunch St. Louis Cardinals fan. I root for the Chicago Cubs—a point of contention that keeps our relationship competitive, but always friendly. After the interview ended, the room fell silent.

"So...have you heard from her?" he asked me.

"Heard from who"

"Who the hell do you think I'm asking about?" he fired back. "That little girlfriend of yours who has your head all screwed up."

"You mean Mary?"

"Of course, I mean Mary. Why else would you be moping around so much like you've been?"

"I just have a lot on my mind lately, Grandpa. Mary is only one of the things that have me down," I said.

Instantly, his disposition changed toward compassion. "Hey," he said in a gentler tone. "Don't worry so much, Ryan. Everything is going to be fine. You're a sharp kid, and you have a good head on your shoulders. I'm real proud of you. When they carry me out of here all stiff and cold, I'll be leaving you with so much money you won't have to work for at least a decade. But I know you're too smart to travel down that road. If you've really learned all that I've been trying to teach you, I'm sure you'll make the best choices in your life. Before long, you'll have things sorted out, hopefully sooner rather than later. For now, just concentrate on finishing your education, get a steady job, keep the farm rented out and maintained. Before you know it, you'll be coaching your own grandson how to tackle the tough decisions that life will throw his way. And believe me, the choices he'll be making in his lifetime will be far more difficult than the ones you'll have to make in yours. It seems nowadays, intelligent decision-making has become a full-time job all by itself," he said with a sarcastic sneer. "In any event, I'm leaving the deeds to the house and farm to you in my will, and enough gold bullion to see you through another Great Depression, God forbid another should happen. You know where it's all stashed and how to cash it in when needed without alerting Uncle Sam—just like I taught you, right?"

I answered that I did. My grandfather was quiet in deep thought for a few seconds.

"But do me a favor; try to save plenty of coins to pass on to your kids. And be sure to tell them they were a gift from me, okay?" he asked in a self-satisfied, almost silly tone. The next thing I knew, his manner changed again, and he was pointing a gnarled index finger at me. "Now listen carefully, son. I don't know exactly when, maybe in a decade or two, but the way our government handles its finances, trust me, those coins are going to be extremely valuable one day. And remember, you can invest a little cash in the stock market now and then if you want, but never forget…" He stopped and tried to lean closer to me. "Wall Street is run by a bunch of goddamn crooks. They have a license to steal, and those greedy bastards will rob you blind if you're dumb enough to let them. Next to politicians, bankers are the lowest form of life in the world. Far lower than lawyers. So, you can speculate a little in stocks if you want, but never put more than play money into the market. Aside from that, a divorce is the only other thing you'll have to worry about as far as your financial future is concerned. If you're inclined to get hitched, then you better find a good woman whose mind won't be polluted by all the garbage she'll see on television. That's what I thought you had with young Miss Mary. But women are funny creatures, often easily influenced by others, so you can never really be sure," he said. He nodded his head twice in the affirmative, as if to reassure himself that he had explained his point effectively. Pondering this a bit longer, he added some more insight. "Barring those obstacles, you're going to have a fantastic life. Much better than mine was, that's for sure."

That was the first time I'd ever heard him refer to his life in a negative manner. He was a hero, my hero, and it surprised me that it came out of his mouth.

"What do mean, Gramps? You've achieved more success and

done far greater things in this world than ninety-nine percent of all the people I'll ever meet or know. How can you say your life wasn't something special?" I asked. I considered that his hospital stay was the reason for his pessimism.

"Look, son, I grew up in a different world. That much you already know. There were some good things that came from growing up in my era, like helping people in trouble. For me, that's always been natural. It comes without difficulty. But I suffered a lot early in my life. The Great Depression destroyed my childhood, and after my twenty-second birthday, I was dodging mortar rounds and sniper fire in the European Theater. The best years of my life were stolen from me, and it didn't end in Belgium. After I returned to Iowa, it took nearly another decade for me to collect myself, for my nerves to settle down enough I could sleep through the entire night, if you know what I mean."

In truth, I didn't. I had no personal knowledge of anyone who had experienced real combat fatigue. I did know a guy from my hometown, Loren Johansen, who had returned from the Gulf War, and to me, he seemed fine, like he had never seen a day of fighting when, in fact, he had. I simply imagined it was because his involvement wasn't nearly as stressful as the action my grandfather had seen at the Battle of the Bulge. I never noticed anything peculiar about Loren's behavior, but I remembered him telling me of others in his unit he described as being psychologically damaged forever. If my grandpa had been affected that way, I never would have guessed it. In fact, my grandpa and I never really discussed that part of his life. When I was younger, I recall asking him once about his experience in World War II. I'll never forget the reprimanding look on my mother's face as she changed the subject before my grandpa had a chance to answer. After that, I never brought the topic up again. I thought about asking him now but decided to wait for a better time.

"Hey, Ryan, enough about me. My fate is sealed. Let's talk about you and solve your problems while I'm still kicking," he said with a cackle. "Maybe you haven't noticed, but because of the stress you're under these days, I decided not to press you about your future…until now. You know damn well you can't spend the rest of your life hunting deer and escaping reality. What plans have you got brewing?"

"Nothing has changed since we discussed it last time, Gramps. If I had to say right now, I'd probably choose to go to Palmer College down in Davenport. I'm thinking about taking the pre-requirement classes in Cedar Falls."

"Still want to be *choir*practor, do you?" he said, mispronouncing the title like so many other seniors in the area do. "That's something to start with anyway, a direction to head in. Sure, why the hell not?" he added. "I suppose you ought to go visit Doc Oestermann's office over in Oelwein. He has a new doctor working for him, not much older than you, an Irish kid who's supposed to be top notch. Tom Flaherty, I believe his name is. Go chat with him. I'm sure he'll fill you in on the program, if that's really what you want to do."

"You know Dr. Oestermann was the only one who helped my knee after I twisted it in wrestling camp before my senior year. All three orthopedists who examined it wanted to operate. Doc Oestermann fixed the problem with his hands in just a few visits. I was very impressed, so yes, I think that's what I'd like to do," I told him.

"Now don't get bent out of shape, son," my grandpa said, deftly switching subjects, "but since you brought it up, there's something I want to ask you."

I had enough familiarity with my grandfather's sly tactics of introducing touchy topics into our conversations to not be agitated about what I was about to hear. His sneaky style caught most people off guard, but I'd learned to defend against his shenanigans better than most.

"Have you given any more thought about pursuing your wrestling ability at the highest level? You know you'd still be welcome to wrestle for Dan Gable down in Iowa City."

"Grandpa, you know the University of Iowa never offered me a scholarship, or even tried to recruit me. I never even met Dan Gable, just some assistant coach's assistant somewhere down the chain of command. And he didn't offer me anything either," I said.

"Sure, he did, son. You just didn't hear it because you weren't listening. You know those were delicate times, and the wrestling team coaching staff had to handle the situation with great care. They had already committed to bringing that hell-raising Garner kid aboard, and your wrestling ability slipped under their radar until you showed them what real talent looks like at the state tournament. That performance absolutely knocked their socks off, I guarantee it. They just couldn't run over and offer you a scholarship they'd already promised to someone else, especially after all the extraordinary nonsense that Garner kid has put them through. There's a certain protocol in place for those types of scenarios. But Gable wants you, son, don't think for a second he doesn't. And you're still eligible."

"Grandpa, you have to know something," I said, training my eyes on his. "I've been thinking to quit wrestling for good. I don't really enjoy the sport anymore. I know I had a great run, but I hardly have the pedigree of a Dan Gable recruit. I mean, Brian Garner lost only three times in his entire high school career."

"Okay, so you lost six times your final year, but not once because you were outwrestled. Now you listen to me and listen well. I watched every one of your matches, and as I remember it, you were outhustled twice and lost the others only because your concentration was off—your head wasn't in the match. I could tell you were distracted, and I sensed you were going to lose before the ref blew his whistle. Your biggest problem, son, is that you're too good of a kid. You don't have a killer instinct, just like your father never had. And don't get me wrong about him. I always thought your father was a good man even though we had our differences, but he was always too damn weak in situations that required—no, demanded—strength and decisiveness. Believe me, we had plenty of good guys like him fighting in my unit in Belgium, and not one of those poor bastards survived to see the war's end. Ryan, you have all the skill in the world to excel at that sport: the natural strength, quickness, reflexes; balance and endurance; and most important, the mental dexterity to defeat anyone at any time. You proved it when you defeated that Garner kid down in Des Moines. For crying out loud, you were two steps ahead of him the whole match. You made him look like an overhyped rookie. No, son, I don't agree with your assessment at all," he said. "The only thing you lack is the killer instinct to finish an opponent as quickly and efficiently as possible.

Unfortunately, I'm not sure that trait can be taught or otherwise acquired. However, I'm certain Dan Gable would love to try to instill it in you. If it can be done, he'll be the one to do it."

I didn't want to talk about it any longer, so I said, "I'll think about it some more."

"Well, don't drag your feet forever. Your window of opportunity is closing as time passes," my grandpa remarked. And he was correct. "Right now, you're a shooting star that's still bright white, but it won't stay this way forever. This is one of those decisions that take great strength to make, Ryan, exactly the kind I was talking about a little while ago. Dig down deep, son. Weigh it out in your head and in your heart. Then make a definitive choice. I don't want you to have any regrets later on down the road. What you choose to do or not do during this next year could have major ramifications for the rest of your life. I need to be sure you're thinking like a man and not a boy. Understand?"

I understood, but dreaded the position I'd put myself in. I could see the level of seriousness in my grandpa's eyes, and I knew how important this conversation was to him. I couldn't help thinking how if Coach Timmerman had never asked me to help with his undermanned wrestling team I would have never been in this spot. What started as a favor had come back to haunt me. Of course, I had no idea at the time that in only two years I would develop into one of the best high school wrestling prospects in Iowa, a state famous for its wrestling prowess.

Chapter Three
Down in Des Moines

Veteran's Memorial Auditorium
Des Moines, Iowa
Saturday, February 20, 1993, 8:30 p.m.

The 1993 Iowa High School state wrestling tournament award ceremony had been organized in haste as a result of complications with the Iowa Public Television network's broadcasting schedule. Though extremely popular among Iowa sports fans, the event is not prevalent enough among the general public to broadcast live on any of the major network affiliates. Therefore, IPTV traditionally fills the void and televises the event each year, allowing the participants' families and the state's high school wrestling fans to watch the competition from the comfort of their homes.

When I stepped onto the platform to receive my medallion, I hardly noticed the camera crew pointing the lens directly at me as I scanned the crowd for my Grandpa Conrad and my girlfriend, Mary Kelleher. They'd driven together through a late winter blizzard to watch me wrestle, even though earlier that day I'd pleaded with them not to because of the treacherous roads. Both said they wouldn't miss this match for the world and ignored me completely. By now, I'd changed out of my drenched wrestling singlet and into a dry T-shirt and shorts worn under my team's black and yellow sweat suit. When the presenter announced my name as the state champion, the eruption from my cheering fans was electrifying, as nearly the whole town of Strawberry Point, and much of Clayton County, had braved the risky driving conditions to support me in what was billed as the state's most momentous high school wrestling matchup of the last thirty years. By the time the first place medal had been hung around my neck, I had finally found Mary in the crowd. She was standing on her tiptoes, arms stretched to the rafters, and screaming at the top of her lungs with her face painted in our school colors. I couldn't help but grin. When I looked to her right, I saw my grandfather standing rigid in a military posture saluting me like he had done in his army days decades ago. As our eyes locked, he snapped his salute forward, relaxed his pose, and stood tall with pride beaming on his face.

The platform I'd been directed to stand on was in the center of four others. I was on the highest podium, and the one on my right was a tier lower. On it stood the tournament's runner-up, Brian Garner, the opponent I had just defeated to win the championship title. Hailing from Oelwein, a town located not so far from mine, Garner was the heavy favorite to win the championship, and he had stood where I was standing now for the last two consecutive years. Though I never looked in his direction during the ceremony, I thought I heard muffled sobs coming from him between the cheers of my hometown supporters.

The road to the championship had gone smoother than expected. All my matches throughout the district and regional qualifying rounds had ended in easy victories. I had been paired against some of those wrestlers before in other meets, and I knew the strengths and weaknesses of most before facing them in the state tournament. When I studied the abilities of the other contenders in my division with whom I was unfamiliar, I had seen little to be concerned about, and I was able to beat each of them without difficulty. That's the way it had gone for me right until today's championship round, which matched me against the most formidable wrestler in the entire tournament. I can't recall how many times I was asked if I was nervous in the hours leading to the starting whistle. Everyone knew the force I would be facing, and few believed me when I responded I wasn't worried at all.

What my supporters failed to recognize was that I was under no pressure to win; I had nothing to lose, and everything to gain. On the other hand, my opponent had it all on the line. His entire high school wrestling career, as astonishing as it was, all boiled down to this final match. One last victory would solidify his legacy alongside those of the greatest high school wrestlers in the state's history, and I was the final challenger standing between him and that distinction.

THE LONG WAY AROUND

But what others didn't grasp, and what I managed to keep hidden, was the fact I am a better wrestler than he, and only I, and perhaps my Grandpa Conrad, knew it.

In the waning minutes before the match, I sat with Coach Timmerman and we discussed the strategy he'd devised for my success. I listened carefully to his directions, but I dismissed a lot of his guidance, which mostly focused on avoiding Brian Garner's strengths. Garner, in my coach's opinion, had no weaknesses in his arsenal. He did not think my strengths were enough to dominate, or even neutralize, my opponent's so he concocted a purely defensive plan that stressed the need for me to accumulate as many points as possible. Granted, this was my specialty, and I agreed that avoiding a prolonged engagement was in my best interest, but contrary to Coach Timmerman's opinion, I thought my adversary was vulnerable. No wrestler is unbeatable all the time, and even though Garner's skills were as flawless as his record, I was going to have three, two-minute periods to discover his weaknesses and exploit my findings. In fact, I thought I could win outright so long as I didn't get snared in his power game.

In order to succeed, I needed to capitalize on my findings instantly and impose my will without hesitation. I suspected the biggest Achilles' heel Garner possessed was overconfidence. Because he had been so domineering throughout his career, and since he had pinned most of his challengers in the opening period, I believed his defensive skills from an inferior position were likely untested. After studying videos of his previous matches, I thought he would struggle to avoid being pinned by another highly skilled wrestler. It was impossible to know for sure, however, because every match in the videos had ended so quickly in his favor. But I doubted he'd ever faced another wrestler of my caliber. I concurred with my coach's plan of avoiding a power match and collecting points, but I was equally sure Garner expected that strategy and had been coached to counter those objectives. What he wouldn't be aware of is that I am both more physically agile and mentally quicker than he, and the inch and a half height advantage and longer limbs I possess would work in my favor, too.

When we met in the center of the mat, Garner and I shook

hands, and then the referee blew his whistle to start the action. For a short time, we circled head-to-head in a feeling out process. The period passed quickly with little to show either of us had dominated the other. After a successful takedown by Garner and an escape by me, the first period ended with the score of two to one in his favor.

At the start of the second period, I decided to make my move. Because I'd scored only one measly point thus far, I had little momentum to build on. I planned to test my theory about his vulnerability to an aggressive attack as soon as possible. Now was time for me to put all my cards on the table and see how he handled the pressure.

The period started with me down on my knees, and after a brief struggle on the mat, I escaped his superior position and hustled to my feet, collecting another point and evening the score at two to two. Then, just like we had done much of the first period, Garner and I slapped each other's hands away and circled in a clockwise direction, testing each other for an ideal moment to strike. Then it happened. My instincts took over and I shot forward for a clean takedown. There was a fierce tussle on the mat. The action occurred so fast I cannot recall the exact details, but after a lot of push and pull, the next thing I knew Garner's shoulders were pinned flush to the ground. When I heard the thunderous slap on the mat near my head, the ref separated us immediately and the match was over.

I sprang to my feet, undid my headgear's chin strap, yanked it off, and flung it skyward. Then I threw my right fist in the air and jumped with joy. I had defeated the reigning champion, and by pinning him, I had made a statement, leaving no doubt of my wrestling superiority. The crowd went wild. Coach Timmerman and the other wrestlers on my squad bolted onto the mat and hoisted me in the air. My exhilaration was immeasurable, and for the next twenty minutes, my being ran solely on adrenalin.

Later, after all the commotion had settled, I went back to the locker room to shower, change, and prepare for the award ceremony. I sat alone on a bench, relaxed, and let the occasion sink in. As I reviewed the victory several times in my mind, a disturbing truth suddenly came into my thoughts. The epiphany was difficult to believe, especially considering its timing, yet it was impossible

THE LONG WAY AROUND

to deny. My wrestling season had just ended in the most glorious fashion, and I didn't care. More importantly, I doubted I would ever care about it again. The reality was stunning.

I decided to carry on through the award presentation, enjoy the positive energy while it lasted, and then forget about the sport forever.

Chapter Four
The Reunion

Oelwein, Iowa
Saturday, October 23, 1993, 4:15 a.m.

After my truck engine had warmed and the cab was toasty inside, I drove down the lane leading away from my grandpa's farmhouse. I turned left toward Oelwein on County Road W18, which is in the opposite direction of the area I intended to hunt. Last evening, I'd agreed to pick up Tim Ross, my best friend, at the KwikMart gas station near the town's business district. Oelwein is the largest town in the county, though oddly enough, it isn't the county seat. Nonetheless, it is the home of the local nightlife, and as a result, Tim had made plans to meet some friends and then stay awake until I picked him up to go hunting. That way, he'd informed me, he wouldn't need to drive home after drinking and risk having an accident or problems with the police. Though his strategy wasn't as wise as staying home and getting some sleep like I'd done, it was a sound one for Tim's way of thinking, even though it required me to get up thirty minutes earlier than usual. But he and I have been pals since elementary school, so I agreed. I was confident he would be waiting with a smile on his face when I arrived.

* * * * *

Tim had almost fallen asleep when his watch alarm beeped its annoying tone to rouse him. He was at Andy Ludlow's apartment, which was just around the corner from the KwikMart. Tim, Rory Meeks, and Ryan had been part of an inseparable group back in high school. Andy was a fringe member. Of the bunch, only Rory had left to attend college after graduation. Standing six feet, five inches tall and weighing two hundred and forty pounds, Rory had accepted a scholarship to play tight end on the University of North

THE LONG WAY AROUND

Texas football team, even though he did poorly on the college aptitude tests and despised football's rigorous workout schedule. He left Iowa for Texas before the rest of the college freshmen, and we hadn't heard a word from him since early August.

Tim and Andy had been out shooting pool, throwing darts, and drinking beer until closing time at a local sports bar called Ramsey's. At two o'clock in the morning, just after last call, they stopped for a slice of pizza at the KwikMart do-it-yourself kitchen, and then walked to Andy's apartment. Andy's rental was a rickety loft above one of the storefront buildings lining Main Street. The apartment's living conditions were shoddy, but the monthly payment was cheap, and since it was positioned near Oelwein's nightlife district, it suited Andy's criterion for an ideal rental. Pizza in hand, the pair entered the building's small foyer and climbed the musty stairwell to the second story living quarters. Once inside, they watched a college football game on ESPN that was being broadcast live from Hawaii. At halftime, Andy passed out on the couch. Nearly falling asleep himself, Tim jumped to attention when his alarm beeped almost an hour later. He put his shoes on hurriedly, then shuffled down the stairs and out the door in a daze. An unexpected, cold wind slapped at his face when he stepped outside and made him contemplate if he'd packed enough clothing for an all-day hunt.

On his return to the KwikMart, the alcohol began leaving his system and obvious signs of a hangover became apparent. A cold sweat broke out across his shoulders and neck, a growing headache crept toward his skull from the back of his neck, and his throat was raw and burning from shouting and laughter. He didn't relish the thought of sitting in a tree stand all day with a hangover, so he entered the KwikMart intent on buying supplies he'd used to alleviate similar symptoms in the past; a packet of aspirin, a large bottle of water, assorted junk food, and a tin of chewing tobacco, which he thought would help him make it through the day. As the heavy, glass door swung closed behind him, he didn't notice the brand-new Dodge pickup truck pull next to a gas pump outside.

Tim recognized the guy working the cash register. The two had gone to different high schools but were vaguely acquainted. The lack of traffic kept the night shift attendant in a constant state of boredom, and he was happy to see a familiar face. Tim acknowledged him, and the two chatted casually as he moved down the aisles. As he shopped for supplies, he collected the items he considered vital for the day's hunt in his folded arms. These items included several sticks of beef jerky, a jumbo packet of peanut M&Ms, three prepackaged fruit pies, a bag of unshelled pistachios, and a pack of batteries for the flashlight he used on the walk through the brush to his tree stand. He stopped at the coffee maker, topped off four large disposable cups, and put them in a cardboard carrying tray. After securing their lids, he stuffed two handfuls of milk and sugar packets into his coat pockets, and then walked to the counter to pay. When he plopped the items next to the tobacco can the cashier had waiting for him, the KwikMart door flew open. As Tim reached into his inner coat pocket for his money, he was forcibly pushed aside.

"Out of my way, shorty, I have a buck to kill today," said a goon about the same age wearing camouflage clothing.

After catching his balance, Tim looked squarely at the individual who was invading his space. Before overreacting, he studied the situation more carefully.

"And you, night owl," said the broad-shouldered thug to the cashier, "hurry up and take my gas money before I reach across the counter and ring your neck."

The cashier swallowed hard, punched the register, and said in a shaky voice, "Twenty-eight dollars."

Returning his attention to Tim, the tough guy looked him up and down, and then scoffed, "Do you have something to say, little boy?"

Unsure at first, Tim soon recognized him beyond a doubt. Disguised behind a five-day beard and insulated clothing making him appear heavier than he was, Tim knew the guy's build, and voice. It was Brian Garner, the local wrestling hero, hothead, and known menace. Not wanting to back down entirely, he said, "I'm going hunting and I'm in a hurry, too. I'm going to pay now."

The college wrestler took hold of the bag of M&Ms on the counter and whipped it at Tim's head. The yellow bag crashed against his ball cap and tore apart, spilling the multicolored chocolate marbles it contained and sending them ricocheting around the

THE LONG WAY AROUND

storeroom floor.

The cashier shouted, "Hey! Enough, or I'll call the police!"

* * * * *

I drove my truck into the KwikMart parking lot exactly on time. I was expecting to see Tim standing out front leaning on the ice machine like we had arranged on several previous occasions. This morning, however, he wasn't there. I parked to the right of the front door and noticed a decked-out, all-white Dodge Dakota truck idling with its parking lights on as I got out. I opened the KwikMart door and stepped inside, taking care not to slip on the colored balls rolling across the linoleum. The instant I looked up; I knew something was awry.

Standing at the far end of the checkout counter, I saw Tim, his face red and his shoulders flared back. In front of him, with his back to me, was a brawny guy about my size and age. I knew at once trouble was brewing. I prepared myself mentally for a fight, but I wanted to know better what the problem was before acting. Casually, I walked in the direction of the altercation and asked, "Hey, Timo, what's going on?"

Not wanting to take his eyes off my friend, the guy with his back to me said, "Better stay out of this, buddy, or you might get hurt."

I didn't know what to say, but knew I had to say something. "You think so, huh?" I answered, with the only thing that came to mind.

The guy turned slowly with a mocking grin on his face. I thought he was ready to take a swing, but he changed his mind when he recognized me. As if a light had switched on, his facial expression softened, he relaxed, and acted as if he hadn't been part of the earlier ruckus. I realized at once it was my old wrestling foe. I also knew he wasn't expecting me to be the one standing there, and had it been anyone else, he probably would have pummeled whoever was in my place. From our past encounter on the wrestling mat, it appeared I had earned his respect, yet I didn't want to test its depth. He sloughed off the others in the store as if they weren't even there and started talking to me like we were old pals.

"Hey, Meyers, what are you doing up so early? I heard you were living in Cedar Falls these days," he said. I knew he was being disingenuous.

"No, I'm still around. I might start school at UNI next year, though. For now, I get to spend my time deer hunting. Enjoying life a little longer before things get serious," I said.

Garner cocked his head upward and said pretentiously, "Oh, that's right! Now I remember. You're the lucky dog who's been allowed to hunt Metzger's Slough. How did you manage that? I heard there were some monster bucks up there. I wouldn't mind trying that land out myself."

His pupils appeared to be dilated. They almost seemed black and were encircled by a thin blue ring. From where I was standing, he seemed to be studying my face for a sign of approval. I sensed where the conversation was being steered, and I changed its course at once. There was no way I was going to share my good fortune with this clown.

"Yeah, that's right. Old Man Metzger is allowing me to hunt his property. It was just good luck, nothing more than that. We better get going now. Have to get set up before daybreak," I said, waving to Tim, who had just finished paying for his things. "Let's get on the road; there are a couple of big bucks waiting for us." As Tim passed me with his hands full, I held the door open for him, and then looked back at Garner. "Old Man Metzger always waits for us, to escort us onto the property," I lied. "See you later."

Garner didn't respond, just turned around to pay for his gas. A minute later, Tim and I were back in my beat-up Chevy S-10 heading out of town. A quick look at my watch showed we were several minutes behind schedule. Knowing there would be few police out this early hour, I gunned the engine a little more than usual and tried to make up the lost time. I didn't notice the headlights following us far in the distance.

* * * * *

Brian Garner knew exactly where the small truck was headed. He had been to Metzger's Slough too many times before to be worried about losing the taillights in the darkness. Besides, just before he'd moved to Iowa City last August to begin college, he had followed Ryan to the slough and stayed close enough to figure out where he had put up his tree stand.

The new Dodge Dakota he was driving was a gift his father had given him when he signed the letter of intent to wrestle for Dan Gable at the University of Iowa. His entire senior year, Brian had fantasized about driving a white Dodge Ram, but his father balked at buying him the larger, more expensive model when he'd lost the state championship match last February. Despising the unfavorable outcome in Des Moines and placing full blame on Ryan Meyers for having to drive the downsized model, he was not about to let his rival gain the prestige of bagging the largest buck in the state without a fight. He had decided that, even if meant poaching a record deer in the middle of the night from Metzger's Slough and dragging it through the forest to his truck in the dark, he was going to capture the glory Meyers was otherwise certain to attain.

Chapter Five
Red Grange Lives

Rural northeast Iowa
Saturday, October 23, 1993, 4:55 a.m.

"**S**o why does everybody call him Red anyway?" Tim asked, spitting tobacco juice into an empty coffee cup. "I thought he was an aboriginal or something."

Maybe it was the early hour, or maybe highway hypnosis had set in, but I needed a few seconds to figure out exactly what my friend was asking me. "You mean albino, Tim. Aborigines are indigenous people from Australia," I finally answered.

"What does indigenous mean?" he asked, sleepily. "And what's with all the fancy words so early in the morning?"

I should have known better. As good a guy as Tim is, I doubted he would know the word's meaning even later in the day, so I tried a different angle. "Aw, you know. They're the original people who lived in Australia before the English took over. Like the Indians here in America."

"Oh, yeah. I saw that on the Discovery Channel once. They have them in New Zealand, too. Right?"

"Of course, they do," I answered without a trace of doubt in my voice. I didn't have a clue, but I didn't think Tim would suspect otherwise.

"If he's all white, why do they call him Red?" he asked. "I mean, is it some sort of play on words, like Redd Foxx or something? I saw that name on the beginning of *Sanford and Son* on the Nickelodeon channel once. Now if they called him Redd Deer, then I'd understand. But I never heard anybody call him Redd Deer, just Red Grange. So, what's a Red Grange anyway?" he asked before spitting again.

Chewing tobacco was Tim's latest obsession. He said it gave

him an adrenalin rush and helped him get moving in the morning, but it was obvious he didn't really enjoy it. I think he started using it to make him feel manlier. The trouble with Tim was that even though he had just turned nineteen years old, he still looked like a sophomore in high school. He had a baby face and hadn't filled out his frame yet. This made him feel like people never took him seriously, and it bothered him more than he let on. I supposed his new tobacco habit was his way of compensating for the fact he rarely had to shave. In many ways, though, he was still a kid, and having a tobacco can ring showing on the back pocket of every pair of jeans he owned was hardly a disguise. Even though it's a filthy habit, it's one that doesn't stink up my truck like cigarettes would, so I tolerate his spitting.

"Tim, it's not *what is a* Red Grange, but *who was* Red Grange? With all the television you watch, you mean to tell me you never saw highlight reels of Red Grange on ESPN in the middle of the night?" I'd already presumed he hadn't.

"Never heard of him," he answered with a scoff.

"Red Grange was one of the greatest running backs in NFL history. He even played for the Bears. You of all people should know that," I said, knowing how big of a Chicago Bears fan he is. "Does the name ring a bell now?" I sipped at my coffee through the hole in the cup's plastic lid.

"He must have played before Walter Payton, or I'd have heard of him for sure," he said. A few seconds passed. "I thought some guy named Gale Sayers was the greatest Bear running back before Walter Payton."

"Well, according to my grandpa, Gale Sayers was, and always will be, the greatest. But to men older than he, who I've heard him talk with when I was younger and who all dead now, Red Grange was the best. Are you sure you never saw the black and white highlights late at night?"

"Nope. I don't like to watch black and white sports programs on television. They make me crazy. Old movies and TV shows, too. I can't stand them. Though I guess I do like to watch reruns of *The Beverly Hillbillies* and *The Andy Griffith Show*," he said after a moment of contemplation. He spit into his empty coffee cup again. "The question remains, Ryan. Why do they call this buck Red Grange?"

"It's because the nickname of Red Grange the football player was The Galloping Ghost. They called him that because of his elusive running style. This gigantic buck we're after is called that because he's an all-white, *albino* deer, not an aboriginal," I said with a laugh. "And because he's so difficult to hunt that nobody's ever gotten a clean shot at him. He's there one second and then, poof, gone the next. Just like a ghost." I snapped my fingers crisply for effect.

"Nobody's gotten a shot at him *yet*," he said.

As I steered my truck along the winding county road, I thought about things that hadn't entered my mind for a long time. Previous hunts, high school parties, and my old girlfriend. A worn-out song from a Seattle rock band was playing on a radio station based in Waterloo. The seasons were changing, and time was quickly passing. Recollections that seemed so vital to me just a short time ago were becoming distant memories. It wasn't long before Tim brought up the most famous subject from our high school days.

"Hey, tell me again what it felt like at the moment," he said excitedly. "I mean, pinning that beast down in Des Moines? Holy cow! I'd have given anything to have seen it."

I didn't want to come off as cocky, so I kept my answer short and told him the truth, like I always had before when he asked. "It was a thrill at the moment, but it didn't feel much different than pinning the rest of them."

"You know, before we graduated, I never once missed a wrestling match of yours, but I'd have skipped all of them just to see what you did to him down in Des Moines. *Gee whiz!*" he said with a howl.

* * * * *

Brian Garner had been a one-man wrecking crew in his four years of high school wrestling. He was built for the sport, had been trained to excel at the sport since preschool, and many say he was purposely bred for the sport. His father had been a state champion wrestler in the mid-1970s and had manically coached his son about the intricacies of wrestling since he was two years old. By

THE LONG WAY AROUND

the time he had reached the eighth grade, high school coaches from around Iowa said he could have won the varsity high school state championship at his weight division if the commission had allowed a rule change granting him permission to participate. As a prep star, he lost only three matches in his entire high school career, and two of those losses came at the hands of opposing seniors when he was just a freshman. Both of those seniors went on to win state titles the same year in different weight classes.

The third defeat was delivered to him by me in our first and only meeting, at the Iowa State High School Wrestling Tournament. It was probably the highlight of my young life. Looking back, it's hard to say why that was, but for the following three months before graduation, I enjoyed celebrity status in my school and throughout my county, whether I wanted the attention or not. That was a major difference between me and Garner; he had been a small-town superstar for nearly his entire life and had grown accustomed to the fame. He craved and demanded it. And he received all that he wanted. Another difference was how we handled our popularity. I always kept a low profile.

In contrast, by the time Garner had begun his junior year, he was out of control. Fights erupted whenever he was around, incidents requiring local police involvement were commonplace, and late-night parties with drugs and alcohol with students from the nearby, larger cities were frequent. Based on his wrestling success and reputation, which brought his high school and hometown into the state limelight, local officials overlooked many red flags, and while doing so, they created an insatiable monster. Garner's father, the Fayette county commissioner, made certain no legal ramifications resulted from his son's misbehavior, but it took a visit and several phone calls from the University of Iowa's Dan Gable to be sure his star recruit's image remained untarnished. Around town, however, the damage had been done, and by the time Garner graduated from Oelwein High School, most people in the area knew to steer clear of the dangerous troublemaker.

Since he had joined the University of Iowa's wrestling squad as a freshman, his fame had now grown throughout the entire Midwest. He still had four years of eligibility remaining, and if his wrestling career continued in the direction it went in high school, he would soon be recognized across the nation as the best collegiate wrestler in the last thirty years. Behind the scenes, however, Garner's troubles were amplifying, and everyone knew he was a loose cannon—a time bomb ready to explode. Rumors began circulating around the University of Iowa campus of him being questioned for beating his girlfriend, but the story never made it into the newspapers. A fight in a downtown Iowa City nightclub resulted in four members of the university wrestling team being arrested. Garner was rumored to be one of the wrestlers detained, but his name was never released to the public. The young grappler knew that if he kept winning wrestling matches and began setting Big Ten conference records as expected, he would be untouchable until after graduation. Until then, he planned to have as much fun as he wanted, and nobody would stop him.

Now, he was home in Oelwein on a deer hunting weekend, and all the locals were on guard.

* * * * *

"Hey, have you heard anything from Mickey?" Tim asked as we neared his drop-off point, just southeast of Elgin. It was a sensitive subject, and a question only he could get away with asking. He even stood a good chance of receiving an answer. "I mean, you haven't mentioned anything about her for a while. I thought maybe you knew something and were holding out on me."

"No, Tim. Nothing. Not a word," I lied. In truth, I had tried to call her twice over the last few weeks. Both times were unsuccessful, and neither of the messages I left on her answering machine were returned. "Why? Have you?"

"How would I ever hear anything? I've been out in the middle of the forest for the last month," he said with a grin.

"I know you have, Tim, because I've been with you. So why did you even ask?" I snapped, half-seriously. I've known Tim since grade school, and I doubted he had a bad bone in his body. That's why I believed his inquiry to be sincere.

"Aw, you know, Mickey is a cool girl. I liked her as your girlfriend. She didn't try to change you, and you didn't change when she was around. I almost liked you better after you were together than before," he answered with a laugh. He spit into his cup again. "And she seemed like it didn't bother her when I was around so much, like I was part of the team when I really wasn't. You aren't going to find that quality in many women from here on out I think."

After I thought about that statement, I decided Tim was right. Though he had barely graduated from high school after taking only the easiest classes and had never had a real girlfriend of his own, he was always surprisingly accurate about how life works, and how it probably would work in the years to come.

"I mean, seriously, Ryan, Mickey's special. I was sad to see her go," he added emotionally, as if she had died and gone to heaven.

"Tim, she's only an hour's drive away in Cedar Falls if you ever want to visit her," I said. "Give her a call. I'm sure she'll be happy to hear from you."

"That's not what I meant. I was trying to say that I was sad to see her break it off with you. I think she was the only girlfriend you'll ever have that will allow us to be best friends without limitations."

I didn't say anything after that, just kept driving. Tim was probably right again.

* * * * *

Mary Beth Kelleher was my girlfriend during most of my senior year of high school. I'd known her all through grade school and junior high, but I'd never thought much of her until our senior year. Tim had always called her Mickey, a play on the name Mick Kelleher, a utility infielder who played for the Chicago Cubs teams we watched as kids. Mary never stopped him from calling her that, though I knew she didn't like it. She thought too much of Tim as a friend to make him stop but would have drawn the line if anybody else had called her that.

I never called her that because I like the name Mary just fine. There is something honest about it. To me, it seemed everything about Mary was traditional and refined, including her name, just the way I like it. While other girls in my class with trendier names like Tiffany, Brittany, and Haley used to tease her about her name, I found it attractive and polished; a time-tested name that suited her easy-going, straightforward personality.

Mary was a late bloomer in every way. At sixteen she had lost her braces and, at seventeen, had suddenly become a knockout. With emerald green eyes, sandy-red hair, and a flawless complexion with a skin tone that gladly soaked up the sun, Mary could have been the prom queen at any high school in the state. At least, all my friends thought so, anyway. More than that, she was smart, nice, and hadn't lost her small-town charm. But what I liked about her most was that she was uncomplicated.

Mary knew a lot about sports, too, and that's what attracted me to her at first. When I lost interest in wrestling after high school, she lost interest in it too, along with most other sports. But we didn't lose interest in each other, and the summer after graduation was the best time of my life. It seemed like it would never end, until one morning this past August, it did. When Mary left for college that day, she left with the promise nothing would change between us and that she would return every weekend. But only a few weeks passed before my calls weren't returned and reasons like studying and dormitory life began to occupy her time. Had deer hunting season not started to help keep me distracted, my emotional state would be much more volatile, and I would be in worse shape than I am right now. As it is, I spend far too much time thinking about her when I sit in my tree stand.

"What gives?" Tim asked. "Do you suppose she has a new boyfriend already?"

"Maybe. I guess I'll never know at this point. I mean, I can't be driving to Cedar Falls to spy on her. Not with my grandpa in the hospital, and not in the middle of hunting season," I answered reluctantly. "Look, Mary is going to do what she's going to do, and I can't change that."

Sensing annoyance building in my mood, Tim changed the subject. "Are you having any regrets about not going to school this fall? I mean, you had scholarship offers from practically every college in the state that has a wrestling program. Even from the University of Northern Iowa. There's still time, you know. You could go if you want."

"I'm thinking it over, Tim. But I won't go to college if I don't

THE LONG WAY AROUND

know what I want to study. And I'm still unsure if I want to wrestle anymore. Besides, I have to take care of my grandpa."

"Okay, but it will be a huge waste of talent if you don't. You're a better wrestler than Brian Garner, and you proved it. I mean, he has a great future in front of him—they treat him like a king in Iowa City—and he's an idiot. I realize I'm stuck here forever. Those are the cards I was dealt. But you, with your brains, ability, and personality…I can only imagine how far you could go. Just think about that."

"Yeah, I'll think it over," I answered, not sounding too convincing. I knew in my heart now wasn't the time.

We reached Tim's drop-off point, a low-maintenance county road that passed through a farm only three miles from where I would be hunting at Metzger's Slough. Tim would have an easy walk through an unpicked cornfield before reaching his tree stand in a cluster of timbers famous for its deer activity. We agreed for me to pick him up at the same spot at noon and then get some lunch in Elgin. It was the same schedule we'd been using for the last few weeks, and the routine had become tradition. After Tim got out and took his hunting equipment from the back of my truck, I wished him luck in bagging a buck and sped away.

Chapter Six
A Difficult Decision Must Be Made

University of Northern Iowa Campus
Cedar Falls, IA
Wednesday, September 22, 1993, 1:30 p.m.

The knock on the dorm room door was firm but subtle. Mary Kelleher force herself off her bed to open it.

Her tears fell only sporadically now, usually at some random moment or after some arbitrary thought triggered a spontaneous outpouring. But whenever an outburst occurred, she took great care to conceal it. Typically, during one of these eruptions, she managed to collect herself in a hurry and put on a facade convincing enough to keep her secret hidden from anyone other than her best friend.

She hadn't eaten much since learning the test results the week before, partially because of morning sickness, but mostly because her appetite had disappeared as a consequence of the constant knot in her stomach. Her mind had been working relentlessly. The ramifications of her situation needed to be sorted out, and her options had to be thought through thoroughly. All she wanted to do was sleep, and the fatigue was the result of stress and depression rather than a by-product of her pregnancy. She felt safest in the private refuge her dorm room provided.

She stretched out on the bed's bottom bunk after letting her guest in.

"You know, Mary, you're going to have to eat eventually," said Doriana as she closed the door behind her. "C'mon, let's go grab some lunch in the cafeteria." A true friend, Doriana was determined to get some nutrients into Mary's body. "They don't stop serving lunch until two o'clock. There should still be enough time to get something light."

"No. I'm not hungry. Besides, I must study for an exam," Mary

THE LONG WAY AROUND

lied. "Maybe later."

Undeterred, Dori said, "Now is a good time to talk…if you want. I don't have to work until five, and the next two hours are wide open for me. We don't even have to go anywhere," she added. Dori rolled out a chair and sat next to the computer desk.

Doriana Schebler had been Mary's best friend since grade school. During their sophomore year in high school, the girls decided to attend the University of Northern Iowa (UNI) together after graduating. Back then, both agreed that receiving a degree from UNI was the best chance to escape having to spend the rest of their lives living in rural Iowa. For the next two years, they studied hard, tutored one another, and pushed each other to perform better in order to maximize their chances of being accepted for enrollment. Their strategy and hard work paid off wonderfully. Not only did the girls get excellent grades, both received tuition scholarships to help minimize their academic expenses. All went as planned until the beginning of their senior year, when Mary fell in love with their high school's star athlete, Ryan Meyers. That relationship didn't affect her collegiate ambitions or her friendship with Dori, but at times, it did interfere with her study habits and made her reevaluate her priorities.

"When do you plan to tell your parents?" Dori asked, uncertain of the proper timing to pose such a question.

Dori was the type of friend every mother hopes their daughter has in life—intelligent and hardworking, and her questions were always sincere, direct, and intended for the best interests of her friend. Dori was a personable girl, with a burly physique that was a great asset on her family's dairy farm. Not only proficient in performing the heavy work that farm life requires, she was business-minded and always found creative ways for her parents to cut expenses and increase revenue. But as much as she enjoyed helping her parents run the family business, she wanted more from her future, and was determined to find a change of lifestyle. She'd never had a boyfriend, yet, and was disheartened because of that. She blamed her miserable love life on the small town where she lived and the lack of suitable partners in the area. Besides earning a university degree after four years of study, she also secretly hoped to find a husband. In the meantime, she devoted her energy supporting her best friend, whose life had recently been turned upside down.

Just as Mary thought to answer, a spontaneous flow of tears poured from her red, swollen eyes. To hide them, she turned on her bed and buried her face deep in the pillow. She had already asked herself that question a hundred times over the last few days and hadn't come up with a credible answer. There were too many variables to consider at this point, and depending on her final decision, she thought it was best for now that only she and Dori knew of her pregnancy. As she cried, an intense fire burned within her mind as she remembered how hard she had worked to get to this point of her life. She bawled even harder when she thought about her parents, her father in particular, and how he had worked every extra hour of available overtime at the local John Deere factory over the last three years in order to save enough money to permit her to live on campus without having to go into debt or take a part-time job. She also remembered how her mother took every opportunity to shuttle the girls back and forth to Cedar Falls from their rural community during their senior year to ensure the transition went without a hitch.

Suddenly, it all became so clear; the unconditional love her parents had given her that she had taken for granted on so many occasions, and the sacrifices they'd made solely for her benefit, affording her the chance to choose her future on her own terms. All of that was in jeopardy now, and she'd barely left the starting gate. In a sudden explosion, she rose from her pillow and pounded it repetitively with her right fist. More tears streamed down her puffy cheeks and she buried her face back in the pillow and cried some more.

Dori couldn't think of anything useful to say, so she sat quietly until the moment passed. After Mary's sobs subsided, she rolled the chair to the side of the bed, put her hand on her friend's back and rubbed it gently. "It's going to be okay. You'll see. In fact, one day you'll look back and regret feeling so terrible now. You'll be elated. Just know this, whichever choice you make, it's going to be fine." Mary didn't respond. When she finally stopped crying, Dori braved the next question in her mind. "Are you going to tell Ryan?"

THE LONG WAY AROUND

Before Mary could offer the answer she was thinking, tears refilled her eyes and another intense crying spell ensued. This time, feelings of her first great love consumed her emotions. Ryan was the boy she had always dreamed of finding. She had secretly admired him throughout her teen years but had always considered him too aloof when he was just exceedingly shy. She realized this only after they'd become close, and even more after she'd learned of his difficult teenage years. How he managed to stay positive through all the personal tragedy he'd suffered in his young life was an inspiration to her. And how easily good grades came to him in school was an added attraction. But more than that, it was how he handled his celebrity status and all the attention his athletic achievements brought during their senior year that earned him her highest respect. To her, he was perfect—always a gentleman and hard worker.

And her parents loved him, too. She didn't even mind the enormous amount of time he spent in the woods hunting deer in the fall. She understood that was the recreation he loved most, a part of his life that was never going to change, so she had no choice but to accept it gracefully. What else could she do? But it was his unselfish acts of kindness, not only for his ailing grandfather, but to most who knew him that was the final attraction that had won her heart. Ryan was the biggest catch in their school, and she wanted the love she felt for him to last a lifetime.

"No!" she snapped. "Ryan must never know anything about this. Not until I've decided what I'm going to do. It may be that he never knows at all. You must promise me you'll never tell a soul. Promise me, Dori. Not one word to anyone!"

"Okay, I promise. But don't you think he should know?" she pressed a little harder.

"Don't you think I've been thinking about Ryan all this time? With his grandfather's future looking so bleak, I don't think he could handle this surprise. I mean, he's so confused he can't even decide if he wants to go to college when practically every university in the Midwest has offered him a scholarship. He is so stressed out about the thought of losing his grandfather that a shock like this could ruin his future," Mary said.

"But don't you—" Dori started.

"No!" Mary interrupted. "Ryan isn't going to know anything about this. Not now, and not ever. It would crush him. I don't want to be in contact with him anymore. I just couldn't face him again."

With that, Dori realized the direction of Mary's thinking. "Then you've decided for certain. You already know the path you're going to choose," she said as a statement, not a question.

"I think so," Mary answered.

"You better talk to your parents," Dori warned. "This is too big a crisis for us to manage on our own. I think they will help guide you through this more rationally. Remember, your best interests are in their best interest. And, yes, they'll be stressed and probably freak out for a while, but they can help guide you better than me. Please, Mary, talk to them," she said, rubbing her best friend's back some more. "Promise me you'll tell your parents."

Consumed in tears, Mary didn't answer.

Chapter Seven
Metzger's Slough

Rural, northeast Iowa
Saturday, October 23, 1993, 5:20 a.m.

The early morning air was brisk and chilly. For someone not as used to it as I've become, it might even be considered bitingly cold. It didn't bother me much since I've been out in the woods every day for the past month and adapted to the falling temperatures gradually. The change from summer to fall was slow and easy, but I knew if I didn't bag a buck soon, my internal thermostat would have to readjust in the coming weeks as the days grew shorter as autumn turned to winter. That's the transition in northeast Iowa people usually have the toughest time with. When winter strikes this part of the state, it usually hits with a vengeance. The cold alone can take your breath away. Even on this October morning, there was already a stinging windchill, and I could feel the cold hit me in a way it hadn't for a long time.

After I dropped Tim off, I steered my pickup back onto County Road X19. While Tim was traipsing through some cornfield in the dark, I drove another three miles toward Metzger's Slough, near a town named Elgin. When I reached the turnoff leading to Old Man Metzger's private driveway, I put my truck into neutral and rolled silently down a winding slope that levels off in the Turkey River Valley. In complete darkness, I came to a stop at the spot where I'd been parking for the past several weeks; a widened shoulder of a gravel road that receives almost no traffic before noon. After killing the engine, I got out and eased around back to take a leak near the tailgate. The Armada, an irregular-shaped row of limestone bluffs which form the western bank of the Turkey River, was just close enough to block the blustery gusts that would have made my task much trickier had the huge rock outcropping not been there.

DOUGLAS CAVANAUGH

While taking care to not to spray my boots with urine, which could reveal my presence to any potential prey later, I shifted my eyes through the darkness and looked for signs of life. Because of the nasty weather and early hour, nothing was stirring, though I supposed any creature with the good sense God gave it was still tucked away in the thicket enjoying the final hours of quiet before daybreak. That's what I was hoping for, anyway. There would still be plenty of time for me to climb a series of barbed-wire fences, cross a frosty bean field, and then slip through the frozen forest undergrowth in order to reach my destination without alerting any deer of my presence. Deeper in the slough, in the direction I intended to go, it was certain to be less windy, and I took that into consideration before choosing my path.

Today, I decided, I'd hike a different route than the one I'd taken in the previous days. This time, I would take the long way around, figuring that if I moved directly into the wind on the high ground and chose my steps carefully along the bluff's narrow shoulder and through the woods beneath it, I could reach my tree stand without alerting any prey with sharper senses of hearing and smell than my own. That is one of the biggest challenges of deer hunting with a compound bow. There is very little forgiveness for strategic miscalculations, and even less for gross incompetence. And like many other things in life I've learned from my grandpa, time is a valuable commodity that shouldn't be wasted. After all, who wants to sit in a tree in the cold, wind, and dark for hours on end with little chance of harvesting a buck because of poor planning or sloppy execution?

After organizing my gear, I applied some deer scent to my clothes, locked the truck, and scampered into the ditch through the darkness with a jolt of excitement dancing in my thoughts.

* * * * *

Metzger's Slough would be considered a deer hunter's paradise even during the worst possible hunting conditions. It is a two thousand-acre parcel that hosts multiple funnels that attract deer from dozens of neighboring farms. The land is legendary among deer hunters, many of whom claimed to have lost enormous bucks with

THE LONG WAY AROUND

record-sized racks from the nearby farms over the years because of slough's unique layout. Countless escape routes abound, and every wily deer in the surrounding timbers is likely aware of each one in the event it ever feels threatened. But what makes the property most alluring is the fact the slough has been off-limits to hunters, and the general public, for as long as anyone can remember. In fact, the initial parcel of hardwood timber was purchased by the Metzger family in 1856, just ten years after Iowa was accepted as the twenty-ninth state in the Union, and six years prior to Abraham Lincoln's signing of the Homestead Act of 1862. In that year, several newly arrived Metzger family members added a neighboring one hundred and sixty-acre parcel each, and the property expanded every decade thereafter, making Dieter Metzger's landholding inheritance one of the largest in the state.

Year after year and decade after decade, hopeful hunters from near and far have solicited permission to enter this private sanctuary hoping to reap one of the mammoth bucks believed to roam its hills. Two of the most recent brutes rumored to wander the area, Red Grange and King Charlemagne, are famous throughout state. In fact, King Charlemagne, if his existence could ever be confirmed, would stand an excellent chance as being not only the biggest deer in Iowa, but quite possibly the largest in the country. Despite this, Dieter Metzger, the last known descendant of the original German family who immigrated to the region not long before the beginning of the Civil War, has held firmly to the position his ancestors kept for generations and has forbidden deer hunting on the premises as a matter of principle. Over the decades, local politicians, lawyers, doctors, businessmen, and other prominent citizens have visited Old Man Metzger, each arriving hat-in-hand only to be turned away with varying degrees of civility depending on their approach. It's even been rumored at different times over the decades that Ernest Hemingway and Al Capone each came calling to the Metzger residence seeking permission that was never granted from past family members.

So how is it that I, a mild-mannered, nineteen-year-old misfit from Strawberry Point, received the go-ahead to be the first hunter allowed on the land in one hundred and thirty-seven years? It might be that the stars recently aligned in an unusual configuration over the past few months, or it could have been the superb job I did painting Dieter Metzger's barn last summer. But I suspect the chief reason is because my Grandpa Conrad, who fought alongside Dieter during World War II and saved his life at the Battle of the Bulge, knew just the right words to coax permission out of Dieter. Favors like life-saving don't come cheap, and since Grandpa Conrad is lying in the county hospital with his lifespan shortening with every breath he takes, Dieter's window of opportunity for payback is quickly closing. Leave it to my crafty grandfather to pin Dieter's back to the wall and tighten the screws while his guard was down. Old Dieter never stood a chance, and I'm certain his distant relatives have been grumbling in protest about his decision to allow my presence ever since. To me, it doesn't matter. I consider the opportunity to be an honor and intend to handle my good fortune with great care. I certainly don't want Dieter Metzger to suffer more torment from his decision than he has already. On the outside, I keep my mouth and emotions in check. On the inside, I am ecstatic, and can barely hide my joy.

Chapter Eight
Dieter Is Saved!

Fayette County Hospital
Oelwein, IA
Tuesday, August 10, 1993, 3:30 p.m.

The hospital room door opened little by little, after first having received three feeble knocks against its laminated surface. A stone-faced man in his early seventies entered the private suite. He was tall, his shoulders were square, and his posture was notably straight for his years. The man's hair was pure white and its thickness, except for a visible crease in the scalp above his left ear, was remarkably full. His eyeglasses had wide, bifocal lenses set in hard plastic rims that were made sometime during the 1970s. Though he entered unhurriedly, it wasn't because of poor mobility, but because he wished to remain silent in case the patient he came to visit was sleeping. In his left hand he carried an issue of *Iowa Game and Fish* magazine. The visitor set the magazine atop of the daily edition of a local newspaper, the *Waterloo Courier*, which lay folded and unread on the bedside stand.

Conrad Doyle's eyes opened gradually. He had not been sleeping because of medication, but rather because he was bored, and napping was the only thing he could do to pass the time until the next round of tests was scheduled to be performed. When he realized he had a visitor, a terrific smile spread across his face.

"Hello, Dieter, am I ever glad to see you!" he said through dry lips. "Have a seat, Sergeant. How the hell are you?" he added in a lively tone. Since receiving honorable discharges at the end of their Army days in early 1946, Conrad had referred to Dieter by his last official rank. Conrad maneuvered himself into a more upright position. "You can stay until they ship me out in an hour or so. Excuse the tubes, needles, and all the other gadgets sticking out of my arm. That sort of comes with the package these days."

"Hello, Conrad," Dieter said. "There's a nasty rumor circulating that your days are numbered, so I thought I'd drop by and have a look for myself. To tell you the truth, I wasn't sure what to expect to see when I got here. You don't appear to be in such bad shape. I've seen you looking worse than this," the spectacled visitor said with a knowing smile. "What's the real story? Is it as grave as I've heard?" he asked more seriously. Dieter flipped the light switch on and pushed the only chair in the room closer to Conrad's bed.

As the fluorescent lighting flickered on, Conrad said, "It's not good, Dieter. It's not good at all. In fact, it's really bad. You know, since that Mauser round took out my good kidney in Belgium, I've had to cope with the defective one I was born with and all the grief it's given me over the years. I've been nursing that rotten bastard along for the last decade or so, and now the doctors are telling me it's about done for. Maybe only twenty percent of it is still functioning. The tests say it'll probably shut down over the next few days, and you can imagine what that means. A transplant at my age isn't in the cards, so I'll need dialysis until the end. That's pretty hard on an old fart like me. I doubt I'll make it to Christmas."

"I'm sorry to hear it, Conrad, especially since you and I are the last of the World War II vets left in these parts since Tom Barnes died last winter from pneumonia," Dieter said. "Of course, you heard the Delaney brothers passed on the year before," he added out of habit. "How long has it been since we've seen each other, anyway?"

* * * * *

Remote Ardennes Forest near St. Vith, Belgium
December 22, 1944, 3:45 p.m.

A heavy, wet snow had been falling off and on since the night before, but the artillery shells, rockets, and mortar rounds being fired over the same period were far more consistent in their timing. Dieter Metzger and Conrad Doyle, the last of their twenty-man platoon who hadn't been killed or captured, hadn't eaten anything for three days. It was now almost a week after the beginning of Germany's grand offensive in the Ardennes Forest, and the GIs

THE LONG WAY AROUND

had been too busy fighting to hold their positions or running for their lives to worry about food. Though there was abundant snow around for them to melt and drink, they used what was left in their canteens so as not to disturb their present hideout, a makeshift lean-to that was keeping them mostly sheltered from the nasty weather. They were tucked inside an overgrown pine, the largest in a cluster of more than two dozen they'd inadvertently stumbled upon. To their benefit, they'd discovered the shelter in the middle of a heavy snowstorm, which covered their tracks leading to it as it fell. However, the men couldn't be certain if the fresh snow had buried their boot prints entirely, so they alternated turns on guard duty. After nearly three hours of relative calm, they decided that if they didn't disturb the snow stacked on the branches above, their hiding place would remain intact for the rest of the day. Feeling momentarily secure behind enemy lines, they debated the odds of breaking through the massive buildup of German military after daylight had disappeared.

The men were cold but not yet frozen. Their supplies were gone, and the weapons they had on hand were inadequate for the escape attempt they were planning to make. Their standard issue M1 Garand rifles had run out of ammunition three days ago, and they'd reluctantly discarded them in favor of their .45 semiautomatic sidearms for their retreat through the woods. After spending all the rounds in his, Dieter had been left defenseless for a day until he scavenged another .45 pistol found next to a US Infantry NCO who was lying dead in the snow. That pistol was down to its last two rounds of ammunition, but he took comfort in knowing he would have something to use while attempting an escape. Conrad's pistol had four rounds remaining, so the soldiers divvied the ammo equally between them, leaving each three rounds with which to fight.

Another factor working in their favor was that both men were wearing protective rubber overshoes on top of their combat boots. When their One Hundred and Sixth Infantry Division had received orders to relieve the battle-fatigued Second Infantry Division and hold a twenty-three-mile stretch of remote forest in southern Belgium, the two hundred troops in their company were expecting the assignment to be slack. Many of the less experienced soldiers in their unit had elected to forego the burden of wearing their protective footwear for the lax duty. Conrad, however, had warned Dieter the day before the Germans attacked to make sure he was wearing his while in the field.

"I've had too many bad experiences hunting deer with cold feet in the frozen hills back home. Don't argue with me!" he snapped when Dieter had questioned the necessity of his advice.

Just a day later, those who weren't wearing their extra foot protection would either live or die in regret of not having them on. Since their unit had been so unsuitably dressed for such harsh winter conditions, the native Iowans knew the night temperatures might kill them before the German military could, so they didn't intend on staying holed up much longer. At different times, both feared hypothermia was setting in, and there was no possibility of starting a fire to warm themselves and dry their uniforms. Nevertheless, the risks associated with an escape attempt during daylight hours made the idea of running for safety futile and was quickly dismissed.

On December 16th, seven days earlier, a massive German tank and infantry force had blasted through their company's frail defensive positions in a surprise assault. As far as Conrad and Dieter were aware, the SS division that attacked had either captured or killed everyone in the vicinity except for them, leaving the GIs stranded, virtually defenseless, and on the run. All through the shelling on the first day, including the earliest hours when their positions had been overrun by German tanks, a constant drizzle had been falling from an overcast sky.

Conrad and Dieter had shared a hillside foxhole nearly a hundred yards from the closest members of their platoon, and more than five hundred yards from the muddy logging road leading back to company headquarters in the Belgian village of St. Vith. When the German offensive turned into an onslaught, the men ran blindly through the forest with tank and artillery shells exploding all around them. In the frenzied chaos of the retreat, they soon lost track of all reference points, including the church steeple in the village where their unit commanders had set up as base. Now, after being lost and on the run for almost a week, and with fresh snow falling by the minute, the soldiers had become acutely aware of the severity of their predicament. Their situation couldn't be more dire. They were unfed, ill-equipped, and inadequately dressed in the middle of a prolonged winter storm deep behind enemy lines. Complicating matters, they had no way of knowing how far the rest of their unit had fallen back, or if the One Hundred and Sixth Division was still intact.

The soldiers agreed that since their whereabouts remained unknown by the Germans, movement during daytime hours would be foolhardy. Increasing the importance of traveling at night was the fact that even if they were able to break through the German lines undetected, there was a high probability of being killed by friendly fire after reaching the Allied positions because of the poor visibility created by the nasty weather. Waiting for nightfall to attempt their escape was the only sound choice, as darkness would conceal their movement, and the glow of the flares, tracer fire flashes, and mortar explosions would guide them in the direction they needed to go. In the event their pine tree shelter was discovered beforehand, the men had decided to surrender, with hopes that Dieter's limited German language skills would be enough to keep them from being shot on the spot by their captors.

Under the huge conifer, Conrad rested on a mattress of fallen needles and whispered to Dieter, "How did we get into this mess?" Dieter didn't answer right away. Sitting on top of his helmet, he anxiously watched for trouble to appear from a peephole he'd tapped through the snow. Their company had been so inadequately prepared for winter conditions that the gloveless Dieter was forced to clench his pistol as tightly as possible with his numbed right hand while warming his curled left one with his hot breath. Although the soldiers belonged to the same unit and shared the same circle of friends within it from the beginning, they'd first become acquainted with one another solely because they were both from Iowa.

While riding on the troop train en route to basic training in South Carolina, Conrad was surprised to learn during roll call somewhere in Kentucky that there was another Iowan on board. He was further stunned to find out the other enlistee was from Elgin, a town less than thirty miles from his rural Strawberry Point address. At the time, Conrad had just turned twenty-two years old. Dieter was nearly two years younger. Back home, they knew nothing of each other's existence, as Conrad left the family farm only occasionally. Dieter had been to Strawberry Point just once, passing through on a church outing to the nearby Backbone State Park. The route through the southern United States they were now traveling was the farthest either had ever been away from home, and each took solace in knowing someone familiar with their world was aboard.

After a full minute passed, Dieter whispered his reply. "I'm here because I joined up to fight the Nazis. You're here because you're an expert marksman."

"Just because I fired a shotgun a few dozen times before the war began doesn't make me a sharpshooter, for crying out loud," Conrad hissed back. "When I told that recruiter I like to hunt deer with a bow and arrow, I didn't mean for that chicken-brained pencil pusher to stick me in an infantry unit. What kind of arithmetic is that anyhow?" he said, red-faced.

Dieter peered vigilantly through his spy hole in the snow. He'd had this conversation with Conrad repeatedly in the past and enjoyed provoking the same response he'd already heard several times before. Just as he was about to crack a grin, something caught his attention that rattled him. He motioned to Conrad to stop talking. There was still enough light to clearly see the figures standing at the edge of the pine tree grove about sixty yards away. It was a gathering of three men, all wearing German uniforms. The shape of their helmets left no uncertainty about it. The soldiers were standing in a half circle with their backs to the wind. All three were smoking cigarettes, and the soldier in the center was doing all the talking. It appeared as if he were holding a map and giving orders to the others. He was the only one in the group wearing an all-white field jacket and carrying a Sturmgewehr 44 assault rifle from a strap slung over his shoulder. The other soldiers presented in uniforms of mixed colors and sizes. The lanky man to his left was wearing a woolen trench coat too short for his height, and the shorter soldier to his right was draped in a uniform that was at least a full size bigger than his underdeveloped frame.

Conrad instantly sat up and tapped a second spy hole through

THE LONG WAY AROUND

the snow with his pistol barrel. Dieter calculated there was about an hour left before darkness would dominate, and the Americans debated whether there was enough time for the German unit to press forward. On the spot, they devised a contingency plan in case their original one had to be scrapped. They knew making a run for it right now was the worst option because they had little idea about the size of the force they would be fleeing, and less of an idea about which direction they would need to run to escape.

*****

"What do you suppose they're up to?" Dieter whispered to Conrad. "It will be dark soon. You don't think they are planning any maneuvers this late, do you?"

"I doubt they chose that spot just to have a cigarette break. The Krauts fight on a different schedule than we do. Remember what time it was when they hit us with the opening barrage on the first day?"

Though it had happened only a week ago, Dieter struggled to recall the details. "Morning sometime," he answered. "I remember seeing the first Panzer just after breakfast, around seven-thirty I think."

"It was earlier than that. The first shells started exploding at daybreak. The Krauts were on the move at dawn. Don't be surprised now if they're ready to move at dusk. Time is not on their side, and they have to strike when the iron is hot. Let's go over our options again in case we're forced to make a break for it sooner than expected."

Just minutes later, a fearsome clattering from tank treads, combined with the disturbing sound of churning diesel engines, could be heard in the distance. The terrifying noise grew steadily, until there was no doubt what was heading their way. An entire German Panzer unit, followed by several half-track troop transports, was climbing up the only road in the valley. Their pace was slow and steady, though the ice and snow caused infrequent hindrances to the unit's progress. When Dieter saw the SS officer in the center begin to wave his arms at the convoy, and then scurry down the hill, he and Conrad were alerted to what was coming.

"Waiting until nightfall is no longer an option. We have to get out of here immediately," Conrad said. "The only remaining question is do we take off through the back door and loop around, or do we take out those two Krauts, grab their weapons, and flee before the officer returns?"

Dieter was thankful to have Conrad beside him. He was less inclined to make such drastic decisions on a moment's notice, but time was not to be wasted. "Our footprints through the snow will give us away if we take out the Krauts. Let's slip out the back."

Voices could be heard shouting in German through the trees. The Panzers had found their way to the rendezvous point, left the road, and were grinding their way up the snowy slope toward the pine tree patch. A small column of infantry had exited the transport trucks and were trekking up the paths the tanks had made in the snow. The SS officer began retracing his footprints uphill toward the recruits he had left behind. It was then the two waiting German soldiers noticed a rustling coming from the largest pine tree in the center of the cluster as snow and ice began crumbling down around it. Demands to halt soon rang out.

* * * * *

While exiting their shelter, Conrad and Dieter tried desperately not to disturb the snow-covered branches, but it was useless. As soon as the first limb moved, the snow toppled and created a miniature avalanche. Loose icicles pinged against their helmets, and chunks of hardened snow landed inside their coat collars, chilling their necks and spines. Conrad left first and Dieter followed in his footsteps in a reckless attempt to put some distance between themselves and the German soldiers. Like flushed rabbits, the GIs sprinted frantically through the trees. As the pair reached the edge of the pine trees opposite the Germans' position, they became aware of two revelations. The first was the sound of machine gun fire directed at them from a Panzer in the distance. The opening bursts were poorly aimed by the tank's gunner, who was having trouble locating his targets. The bullets hit only random branches and landed innocuously more than twenty yards to the right of the Americans, who realized the Nazis did not have them in their sights.

THE LONG WAY AROUND

The second revelation was the discovery of a church steeple on the horizon a short distance away. A quick study confirmed it was in the center of a small village that bore no resemblance to St. Vith, the village where they had spent a few days before digging into their foxholes on the hill. It was now a certainty that their bearings had been scrambled during their hasty retreat several days ago. With the rattling treads of the Panzers closing the distance, the GIs had precious little time to analyze the situation.

"Whose army do you think is running the show over there?" Dieter asked between gasps. "There's sure to be a sniper up in that church tower. If it's held by the Germans, we'll never make it across the open field to the nearest farmhouse."

"Regardless of who's in control, it will be difficult to distinguish our uniforms in this weather," Conrad answered. "Even if the village is held by the Allies, we may not make it there alive." He considered things for a few seconds. "Why would Panzers be planning to attack a village it already controls? No, I think the village is one of ours, and if our boys are expecting an attack, they won't be asking many questions before firing. This is it, Dieter. We must gamble now, and our odds aren't good. If we can make it across that open field without being mowed down, we have a chance of getting out of here alive. If we stay here any longer, the game is over for sure."

The gunfire fell closer to their hiding spot.

"Let's get the hell out of here! Move out!"

* * * * *

With the threatening sounds of the tanks closing the distance, the Americans bolted into the open in the direction of the village. Conrad was leading the way. There was no time to consider what they would find when they got there. The drifted snow in the barren field was much deeper than expected, and the men had all they could do to keep from falling as they hustled toward perceived safety. To maintain his balance, Dieter made several well-timed bounds over the white, windblown mounds. He tried to stay in Conrad's footsteps, but after several near stumbles, he gradually veered off course. By the midway point of the run, Dieter was almost twenty yards behind and ten yards to the right of Conrad's path. With adrenalin pumping through their systems, neither man heard the Panzer stop at the tree line nor spin its turret in their direction.

* * * * *

Dieter had been trying desperately to catch up to Conrad since drifting off course around the sprint's halfway point. Plowing through the knee-deep drifts had fatigued his muscles, and before long, cramps developed in his calves and dragged on his progress. While he concentrated on realigning with Conrad's path, he was totally unaware of the commotion taking place behind him. When the seventy-five-millimeter tank shell exploded just ten yards to his left, a piece of shrapnel crashed into his skull, lifting him off his feet and leaving his body crumpled in a heap. His helmet had absorbed the brunt of the impact, but the vicious wound to the side of his head left him unconscious and bleeding profusely.

During their flight, Conrad sensed Dieter had fallen behind but he hadn't stopped to check the exact distance. When the screeching whistle of the incoming shell grew louder in his ears, he fell down in the snow instinctively. When he looked up to assess the damage, he saw Dieter, almost twenty yards behind, curled on his side in the snow. Conrad hollered at him to get up and keep moving but Dieter didn't respond to his calls. Conrad rose to his knees. He could clearly see blood spread on the snow around his friend. Nearing exhaustion, he made his way to Dieter and was aghast at what he saw. It appeared the entire left side of Dieter's scalp had been ripped from his skull. Through the blood, Conrad could see the bone and noted that it had not been shattered.

With no chance to perform first aid, he inhaled deeply, then heaved his friend over his shoulder, determined to push through the drifts in the direction of the nearest shelter.

* * * * *

Conrad made slow progress. With Dieter slumped over his shoulder, he knew he was vulnerable but couldn't risk jarring his friend and exacerbating his wound. As sweat poured from his brow, Dieter's blood trickled down onto Conrad's overcoat. Conrad began reciting the Lord's Prayer aloud as he shuffled forward. He was nearing the house and thought he would reach it soon if those shooting at him continued missing their mark. Surprisingly, they had stopped after an initial burst. When he got to within twenty yards of the barn, a single rifle shot rang out from behind. Almost instantly, he felt a searing jolt in his back beneath his shoulder blade and just to the right of his spine. The pain buckled his torso backward, and Dieter's heavy mass caused Conrad's legs to give way. Both men fell onto the snow as chaos broke out.

Conrad heard machine gun fire pouring out from the farmhouse and barn, aimed toward the tree line he and Dieter had just fled. Barely able to raise his head, he looked from the corner of his eye and saw several American GIs firing Browning .30 caliber machine guns across the open field from the windows and doorways. Under the cover of gun fire, four American soldiers with red crosses displayed on their helmets rushed to the fallen GIs and carried them out of the crossfire.

Once behind the old, stone house, they were placed on makeshift stretchers and moved to the village's far side, where a column of troop trucks and ambulances were lined up ready to evacuate.

*****

Fayette County Hospital
Oelwein, IA
Tuesday, August 10, 1993, 3:38 p.m.

Conrad thought it over a while, and then answered, "Oh, about eight years, I suppose. I think we last saw one another at the VFW in Manchester back in May of '85 for the fortieth anniversary celebration of VE Day. Sure, it was. We drank some beers and had a good chat. Of course, that doesn't include telephone conversations we had last summer concerning my grandson painting your barn. How'd the lad perform, anyway? Were you satisfied?"

"As a matter of fact, I was. He worked like a horse every day," Dieter answered. "My barn has never looked as good as it does now. I even hired him to pick up rocks in the fields afterward, paid him a nice bonus besides."

"Good for you, Sarge. Ryan's a great kid, and I'm real proud of him," Conrad said, before coughing to clear some phlegm from his throat. "What's that you put on my nightstand? You didn't have to go and bring me flowers. Or is it a box of chocolates?" he teased.

"It's just some reading material to help pass the time in here. I figure you know more about fishing and hunting than the guys writing the articles, but you may find an interesting article or two and enjoy looking at the pictures. I'll bring some more magazines in a few days if you'd like. Believe me, when I heard you'd quit hunting a while back, I suspected your health was deteriorating. I couldn't imagine any other reason than that to keep you out of the woods. It always seemed to me that you just belonged out there."

Conrad managed a wide grin. "Yes, that might be so. And my grandson is the same. There must be something about the solitude, being surrounded by nature, and the mental challenge and thrill of the hunt that runs in our veins. My God, did I hate to see those days end. I fought hanging up my bow as long and hard as I could, believe me."

The room fell silent, as if both men were simultaneously thinking about how fast their lives had passed, how much longer before their lives would end, and all they had accomplished and left unfinished.

"Sarge, are you still being pestered by people wanting to hunt the slough?"

"No. Not so much these days. It was much worse twenty years ago. I think by now people already know the answer, so they no longer bother asking."

Conrad spoke openly. "Sarge, what is the point of keeping folks out? So what if you're the last direct descendant of the original immigrants who wouldn't allow hunting on the property. It's no longer their policy, it's solely your own. You know damn well that you could be the one lying in this hospital bed counting down your final days just like I'm doing now. As soon as you are dead and cold, your distant relatives will auction off your estate, the slough included. They won't give a hoot about what your ancestors thought about hunting on the property. And not only will the new owners hunt the land, they will probably grant the entire property's hunting rights to the first stranger willing to pay the highest price. You're fighting a losing battle, my friend. Times have changed, and people don't stand on principle anymore. It's all about who offers the highest bid. The hell if it isn't," he said with the wave of his hand he was known for. "And stubbornness won't change the direction things are headed either, Sarge. It might delay them a bit, but in the end, it won't stop them. The best you can hope to do is to neutralize the situation and use that to your advantage."

Dieter remained silent. The truth Conrad was telling him had already crossed his mind, and now he was hearing it from someone whose opinion he held in high regard. "How do I neutralize the situation then, Conrad?"

"You take the magnetism out of the place, castrate the legend your relatives unintentionally created."

"I would have done it years ago if it were so easy," Dieter said. "*How* do I do that?"

"You do it by leveling the playing field with the neighboring properties in the county. Once the slough has been hunted and its celebrated status has been dismantled, hunters will realize there is no special reason to covet the land. The parcel's glamour will diminish, and the legend will fade with time."

"But what if your plan backfires? What if the legends are true? What if the slough *is* home to the magnificent deer the hunters crave?"

Conrad was silenced momentarily. A few seconds later, he asked, "Have you seen any of those deer personally, Sarge? I mean, I was always curious, but had too much respect for you to ask to let me snoop around. Have you seen one yourself?"

"Never. Not once. Of course, you know I'm not a hunter. I haven't fired a gun since being decommissioned from the Army. But because of that, I never had a reason to search the place, either. I've never really understood what all the fuss is about."

"Well, don't you think it's about time to send someone in there to find out? We can learn fast if the tales are true or not. Only then can you decide how you want to deal with your estate in the future, God forbid you should find your health on the ropes like mine is now. And if the tales are true, well, I imagine your property's value will skyrocket. There are thousands of deer hunters with enormous bank accounts in this country. Most wouldn't mind paying a king's ransom to have sole hunting rights to the slough if you could prove it is as tempting as the legends say."

Dieter remained silent, in thought. It was as if he was mentally prepared to advance with the plan, but a lifetime of refusing hunters permission had been engrained in his psyche for so long he couldn't bring himself to consent. Conrad gave him a nudge when he felt the time was right.

"Look, Sarge, we've been through a lot together. What I'm telling you is coming from the heart. You have no direct kin to will the property. There is no reason for you to wait. In fact, waiting at your age is counterintuitive. The estate taxes the IRS will levy on you alone is reason enough to figure out the best way to handle this as soon as possible. The moves you make or do not make right now will be vital to your financial self-interest later on. Let me send my grandson, Ryan, into the slough to see what turns up. I'll coach him every step of the way. What he finds will determine the financial strategies you'll need to implement in the not-so-distant future. I'll make sure he does things properly. The whole process will pass smoothly, and you won't feel the slightest amount of regret, sorrow, or grief. Nor will you feel you have to explain yourself to anyone, either. What do you say? Should I get the boy prepared?"

Dieter sighed deeply. "Have the lad consult with me regularly. I won't be tagging along with him, but I want regular reports of what he finds. I'll check in with you every so often, depending on how you feel, to go over the details. Conrad, I greatly respect your judgment in matters such as this, and I'll want your advice every step of the way. Can I count on the two of you for absolute secrecy from this point forward?"

Conrad's laugh was more spirited than his ordinary chuckle. "Well, we can *try*. But I can't guarantee it. There aren't too many legends around this part of the state, Sarge, and you know how fast gossip spreads through small towns. Why? Is that a deal breaker?"

"No, I suppose it isn't. But I'd dread having any more publicity around my place than necessary. The last thing I want is a bunch of snooping, tagalong deer hunters trying to weasel their way onto my property. And God forbid if Ryan bags a monster buck. The press will be hounding me all winter."

"We'll have to worry about that if it happens. In the meantime, I'll need some time to coach the boy and research some information that will suit both of your needs. He'll be coming to visit in a couple of hours. If you give me the go ahead right now, I'll break him the news when he gets here."

Dieter took in a deep breath. "I consent. Let's see what's in there."

Over the next few minutes, the men reminisced and made small talk about their Army days. As the discussion ended, Dieter shook Conrad's free hand and thanked his old friend several more times. The men arranged their next meeting, and Dieter left feeling confident he had made the right decision.

Chapter Nine
The Set Up

Metzger's Slough
Rural, northeast Iowa
Saturday, October 23, 1993, 6:08 a.m.

I was breathing heavily by the time I reached the tree in which I'd mounted my stand last August. My lungs seemed to be affected more than usual this time of year, partly because of the cold, partly because I was carrying extra supplies, but mostly because I hadn't trained seriously since June and was clearly out of shape. After taking a short break to scout around, I climbed fifteen feet up a large American elm that had survived a blight that had nearly decimated the species in the area over the last decade. Once on board, I sat peacefully, relaxed, and concentrated on taking in air. Scaling the makeshift ladder in the dark had been no easy feat. It had been too late in the season before I'd realized the scrap lumber I'd used to make the rungs weren't thick enough and didn't leave adequate surface area for the soles of my hunting boots. This made my climbs challenging. When I'd installed the steps two months ago, I'd been wearing tennis shoes and jeans. Back then, I was in much better shape, the weather was nice, and I had been working long, hard days painting Old Man Metzger's barn. I remembered hoisting myself up this tree with little effort at all one Sunday morning after Mass. It was easy and fun at the time, but even then, it made me wonder how difficult it must have been for my Grandpa Conrad when he was still actively hunting only a few years ago. Now, I was the one who felt like an old-timer, especially with the extra burden of my bulky coveralls. I decided right after I'd bagged this season's trophy buck, I'd start training again.

Nineteen years old is too young to be lazy and useless. I thought of the words my Grandpa Conrad hammered me with almost daily. *Wake*

THE LONG WAY AROUND

up early, do something productive, and then take a break later. I still don't know if he considers deer hunting productive work or unproductive recreation, but he knows I do a lot of it and he never complains, so I plan to keep doing it until he mentions it.

After fastening myself to the tree with a harness, a safety precaution sensible bow hunters use to prevent falling in case they doze off or lose their balance, I moved my supplies to a spot that would be the least obstructive in case I needed to adjust my position in a hurry. To a nonhunter, a detail like this might seem trivial, but it was a cardinal rule in bowhunting, and one my grandpa has stressed over and over since my first hunt with him when I was in the seventh grade.

"Get settled in right away," he told me at the time. "Secure your shit in a spot where it won't wiggle in the wind or disrupt your line of fire. More big bucks have been lost in the two seconds it takes to draw an arrow than in the hours of planning it takes to place a stand correctly," he said, an intense scowl on his face.

Back then, those were powerful words for an impressionable thirteen-year-old boy to absorb. I took them seriously, and I couldn't have been prouder. He was talking to me as if he considered me a man, the way he talked to everybody *except* me, because my mother, possibly the only person in the world who held any sway over his character, wouldn't allow him to swear in my presence.

After a thirty-minute wait in the dark, signs of daybreak began to show. The sky lost its grisly black tone and a bluish hue was creeping in. I supposed that far above the slough where my truck was parked, I might be able to see a dozen yards or so into the forest. Not here. Metzger's Slough clings tightly to the night and is unwilling to surrender it easily. I calculated another forty-five minutes would need to pass before I'd be able to see more than twenty feet in front of me, so I shifted my weight to the right for a more comfortable position, zipped my camouflage coveralls to the top, lowered my brown and green speckled facemask, which blended perfectly with the elm's jagged bark, and waited for daylight. As I sat in solitude, I listened, thought, and enjoyed the tranquility—exactly as I had been doing almost every day since the beginning of October.

Chapter Ten
The Crescendo

Metzger's Slough
Rural, northeast Iowa
Saturday, October 23, 1993, 6:58 a.m.

Faint beams of sunlight began filtering through the barren branches of the tree I was in, which until a few days ago had supported a canopy of brittle, yellow leaves. The sun's heat finally began absorbing into my insulated clothing, warming my torso and making the wait in the wind much more bearable.

Once the sun rose above the eastern bluffs, the ice-glazed grass on the cow pasture that sloped down to the slough began to thaw. Several more hours of brighter sunshine, however, would be required to melt the frozen leaves and twigs buried deeper in the undergrowth.

Seated high in the elm, I pressed my back against the trunk and gyrated my spine against the bark to scratch an itch between my shoulder blades, taking care not to disturb any nearby branches in the process. My butt was beginning to ache on the skimpily padded seat, and my feet and toes began to tingle from lack of circulation. It was an annoying sensation I'd become accustomed to over the last few weeks, especially since I'd begun wearing two pairs of socks inside my boots to counter the falling temperatures. Grandpa Conrad had always stressed the importance of keeping my feet warm in the tree stand. He often said they were the most susceptible and warned how cold feet could cut a hunt short. It had only taken one bad experience during that first season to learn that he was right, and it was a lesson I've never forgotten since.

I was old enough to know better at the time, and because I was aware my grandpa knew just about everything there was to know about deer hunting, I should have heeded his advice. Yet,

THE LONG WAY AROUND

I didn't want to tell him why I was home so early that day after only two hours in the stand, so I intentionally avoided him after my premature return. Of course, he deduced the reason easily, but didn't chew me out like he would have anybody else. Instead, he continued reading the morning paper in his recliner. Later, at the breakfast table, he said, "Some things are better learned the hard way," or something to that effect. Then he was kind enough to leave me alone. "Lessons learned the hard way last longest," he told me the following morning when I was preparing to leave for that day's hunt. And that was the end of it.

I felt the urge to pee again and regretted drinking the second cup of coffee Tim had brought me from the KwikMart. Peeing was a time-consuming task that required a potentially dangerous descent from my perch, and then making a two-hundred-yard trudge in the dark through thick brush to reduce the chance of my whereabouts being discovered by every deer in the area. Having my position revealed because of coffee-scented urine would be inexcusable, and a pee break also meant missing valuable time in my stand during one of the day's peak hunting periods. This prospect wasn't too appealing, so I decided to hold it for a while longer and stay put.

In hindsight, that decision changed my life forever.

I heard a muffled, grating noise coming from the scrub brush on the slough's far end about sixty yards away. The sound was subtle, peculiar, and unfamiliar. It somewhat resembled a metallic reverberation and was unlike anything I'd ever heard in the forest in my six years of hunting. The source of the sound was undeterminable, as there were no barbwire fences or gates in the area that may have been rustling in the breeze. The possibility of a stirring raccoon or a skunk on a late season forage were less probable causes. After I'd spent several minutes listening to the unusual buzz, it suddenly stopped and didn't return. I estimated where the sound had originated and made a mental note to check the area at the end of the hunt. It sounded as though it had come from a gap between two limestone bluffs, which must have been thousands of years old. Those bluffs formed a wedge along the river that opened into the Metzger property. At that point, a coppice of maturing cottonwoods and an almost impenetrable patch of thorny briar and sumac jutted outward from an area heavily laden with birch trees. As a result of nature's dynamics, a slender deer funnel had been created that appeared to be little used.

When I'd scouted that particular point last summer, I saw no obvious signs of deer activity in the vicinity except for a single, faded antler rub on one of the smaller trees in the bunch. After further study, I'd decided the marking was probably several years old. Nevertheless, the overgrown path running alongside it looked too compelling to ignore based on the strategies my Grandpa Conrad had taught me. In fact, it was so enticing I decided to follow my instincts and place my stand in the tree I was in right now.

Improving the layout considerably, a second funnel on the ravine's opposite end ran parallel with this one. Both trails led to a central group of white oak trees, which were still dropping acorns. Grandpa Conrad always stressed the importance of placing my stand near an oak tree, and acorns of the white oak variety were the type deer preferred most as far as he was concerned. That tidbit of information solidified my decision. This grove of oaks provided an ample source of food likely known by every deer in the region, and if the wind cooperated, both corridor openings were within range of my bow and arrow. The tree I was in offered clear views of each path leading to the fallen acorns. All combined, my choice was a solid one.

There were obstacles working against my strategy, however. For instance, an unpicked cornfield, which I hadn't noticed last summer, was now clearly visible and located in close proximity. There was another deer trail showing more obvious signs of recent use leading to the edge of that food source, which was at least two hundred acres in size. Through my binoculars, I could see the corn stalks were top-heavy with drying ears of corn, exactly what every whitetail deer in the state craves this time of year. For the time being, the available grain would offer any hungry deer an unlimited supply of food and afford it easier accessibility, superior protection, and better escape routes than the acorn patch I'd chosen to hunt. Undoubtedly, this would play havoc with my strategy, and the circumstance left me debating where to concentrate my efforts. With no other experienced hunters of Metzger's Slough to consult, I decided to rely on my instincts, and contemplated what my grandpa would do if he were with me. "Always take control of the situation, Ryan," I remembered him lecturing me time and again over the years. "Think things through thoroughly, draw an intelligent conclusion, make a logical plan, and then follow your plan. Don't let the circumstances dictate for you, son. You're the boss. Think like a boss, and then act like a boss," he instructed. And that's exactly what I'd been trying to do ever since.

With that in mind, I figured the corn would be picked one day soon. The acorns, on the other hand, would last through the winter, so that was the food supply I wanted to direct my attention to considering that any deer currently bypassing them in favor of the grain would surely return after Old Man Metzger's tenant had harvested the corn. This quandary was just one example of the many challenges a bow hunter will face each season. In a way, deer hunting is almost like a chess match. I was now involved in a waiting game, a simple matter of time, which I had plenty of these days.

How short of a wait was a remarkable surprise, as only minutes later, while I was again debating whether or not to climb down and relieve myself, I heard footsteps rustling over the frozen ground coming from the same direction as the strange sound I'd heard minutes ago. This crunching differed substantially from the earlier reverberations, and I sensed in my bones that a deer was heading in my direction. The hunch I'd had concerning my positioning, it appeared, had been correct, and I celebrated internally. My heart rate jumped as a result, and my toes stopped tingling. My breathing quickened, and I desperately tried to subdue it in order to prevent condensation from blasting through my face mask and compromising my position. I forgot all about the nagging urge to pee.

Steadily, I reached to my right, lifted my Jennings bow, and removed an arrow from its case. I pulled back on the bowstring until it locked into place, an invaluable feature which allows an archer to hold their aim for an extended period without fatiguing the muscles in their shoulder, arm, and hand. Unable to resist the temptation to practice my aim, I shifted my hips and rotated my shoulders a few degrees to the right. Then, taking care not to disturb any branches, I directed my bow sight at a single golden leaf dangling from a birch tree about twenty yards away. After reinforcing my confidence, I swayed back into position to watch and listen. Soon, the sounds coming from the thicket lessened and any subsequent movements were barely audible. Every now and then, however, I heard mischievous snorts coming from the far side of the brush. I was certain they were released by a large buck, and it seemed as if it was pleased with the cache of acorns it had found and was daring any competitors to challenge him for his bounty.

On a couple of occasions, I thought I could see the deer's hot breath rise above the brush after mixing with the chilly morning air. Based solely on instinct, I concluded there was absolutely a buck on the other side, and I tried to define its silhouette from more than forty yards away. My intuition told me it was a huge one, too, and if the beast showed itself, even briefly, it would be within range of my arrow. I was an accurate shot from that distance, but the line of fire had to be clear, and one of the buck's vital organs would need to be exposed before I would dare to fire. Without both of those factors in place, I'd risk losing it to the wilderness if it escaped without being mortally wounded. That is an unnecessary gamble I'm never willing to take, so instead of shooting blindly through the brush, I elected to identify it clearly and wait for an unobstructed view of its heart, spine, or lungs. I was determined to resist being overanxious and decided to sit tight until the animal wandered closer. Adrenalin now rushed through my veins, and perspiration seeped from my pores. When my heart started racing, I inhaled three times and then closed my eyes for a few seconds. After a fourth deep breath, I opened my eyes, hoping to have a view of the brute and count the tips of his antlers. Stories I'd heard other hunters tell of the monstrous bucks lost to Metzger's Slough began swirling around in my mind.

"Patience is key for deer hunting," I recalled my grandfather telling me on my first hunt. "If you've chosen a proper location, practiced your archery aim well, and mastered the ability to control your nerves, the only thing left to screw up a successful hunt is a lack of patience. And I'm not talking about the hours spent waiting in a tree for a deer to appear. I'm referring to the moment of truth. That's the vital period of time required to allow the deer to move into the ideal position for a clean kill shot. That window of opportunity might open and close in mere seconds, son, so don't be early, and don't be late. Trust me; you'll know when it's time to release the arrow."

Through daybreak's evolving shades of gray, I spied a segment of the buck's antlers and watched as the tines intermingled with the brush. Once, I was able to catch a glimpse of its full rack when it lifted its head and chewed. When I tried tallying the points, my efforts were thwarted by the continuous motion and frequent disappearances. One thing was certain, the deer was enormous, and likely bigger than any I'd ever encountered. My excitement level surged as thoughts of taking the largest buck ever recorded in Iowa state history and all the glory associated with that distinction filled my head.

The deer strolled a bit further along the tree line, just enough to allow me a glimpse of its head through the thicket. As it advanced, I was awed by the magnificent sight before me. Standing in the clearing, the enormous buck turned and faced me. The tan fur around its head and shoulders was beautifully offset by a brilliant area of white under the neck that extended all the way up to its chin. A coal-black nose and two dark eyes simultaneously revealed a picture of fierceness and tranquility. More astoundingly, the beast's massive rack far surpassed the dimensions of all others I'd seen taken by hunters in the area. I counted sixteen points on my first try, but the animal's erratic movements left me uncertain if some had been counted twice or missed altogether.

Before I could make a second effort, the buck lowered his head to forage more food. Then it flipped its nose skyward, gave a snort, and looked in my direction. It stood perfectly still, staring, smelling, and listening. I didn't sense its unease was directed at me, but it was clearly showing concern about something coming from my direction. I was confident I could not be seen from this distance in my camouflage attire, and equally certain I was not the cause of its alarm. I had little choice but to stay still and let the scene play out. If the buck advanced just a few more yards, I would be able to size it up in its entirety. Suddenly, it bounded away from the acorn patch and returned to the protection of the derelict trail. I lost track of it as it moved through the heaviest brush leading to the neighboring cornfield. In order to reach his intended destination, I knew it would have to leave the cover and cross an open field of scrubland. When it finally made its move, I suspected it wouldn't dawdle. I'd have to be ready to act.

As it neared the edge of the forest, a bright ray of sunlight broke through the drifting clouds and shone directly on the buck's upper flank, exposing its powerful physique for an instant. All at once, I realized the significance of the spectacle before me. The great deer was none other than the mythical King Charlemagne. Overcome with exhilaration, I began to tremble.

*****

Veiled behind camouflage clothing, Brian Garner was resting on one knee under a pin oak tree about one hundred yards uphill from Ryan's position. Before leaving for Iowa City last August, he'd covertly come to explore Metzger's Slough after hearing his nemesis had been granted permission to hunt the property. After a lengthy search, he'd found where Ryan had mounted his tree stand. He'd also found a perfect spot from where to spy on him. Today's hike through the darkness to his current position had been painstakingly slow. Keeping quiet so his old wrestling rival and every deer in the area wouldn't hear him had been challenging.

Until a couple of hours ago, Garner had intended to hunt his usual hotspot near another town. When he'd unexpectedly run into Ryan and his buddy at the KwikMart, he changed his plans and decided to follow Ryan to Metzger's Slough to investigate for himself what secrets the hollow kept hidden. Along the way, he strategized how to profit from his decision, and quickly realized the difficulties he would have explaining himself if he was found trespassing, since no other hunters besides Ryan were permitted on the land. Yet, he figured he could remain concealed long enough to observe Ryan with little risk of being caught. He decided to bring his bow and arrows along in case he was lucky enough to surprise a trophy-sized buck that he could kill and sneak out later that evening. Mostly though, he hoped to see Ryan harvest a smaller deer early

THE LONG WAY AROUND

in the day so he could hunt the property in solitude the rest of the weekend without risk of anyone discovering his presence.

Just as the sun began to break through the morning gloom, he reached his hideout. He regretted being upwind of Ryan's position. He knew if his scent was picked up by any deer below, it could affect the likelihood of it advancing to within Ryan's range. Nevertheless, his hiding place was wholly shielded from his adversary, and if he used his binoculars, he could survey the identical zone Ryan was hunting. Brightening matters further was the fact that if any buck passed from his left, he was confident he could hunt it without drawing Ryan's attention. And if he were offered a clean shot, he could kill the deer quickly, efficiently, and almost silently. Once he had marked where it fell, he could return after dark to drag it from the property. He could then load it on his truck, tag it, transfer it to the farm he usually hunted, and claim victory. No one would ever know the truth, and the glory of bagging a record buck would be his. The thought made him smirk a little, but a much broader smile stretched across his face when his fantasy progressed into reality.

He heard thrashing in the brush about fifty yards in front of where he knew Ryan was sitting. Ever so carefully, he lifted his binoculars and began scanning the timbers. A gigantic buck emerged from the thicket. He'd seen pictures of many trophy whitetail deer over the years, but he estimated this one to outweigh all the others he'd ever laid eyes on. Blending into the oak tree shadows, Garner could clearly see King Charlemagne grazing on acorns from over one hundred yards away. He supposed the buck was not yet visible to Ryan from that angle, yet he knew his rival was an experienced hunter and likely aware of the deer's presence. The sight of the massive beast was almost more than Garner could stand. He decided if Ryan missed his chance, or if he could get himself within range of the mighty buck, he would take it for himself and worry about the consequences afterward. As he shifted his position to get a better view, a dead branch in the undergrowth snapped under his weight releasing a crack just loud enough for the deer to detect. Garner froze, fully aware the animal had been startled by the noise.

* * * * *

After nearly a full minute of standing in silence, the great deer relaxed and appeared ready to return to resume feeding. When it began to drift back toward the acorns, its immense form alternately disappeared and reappeared as it pushed through the heavy cover. At one point, as I saw its head and neck rise above the branches, it stopped abruptly, flipped its ears in my direction, and lifted its nose as if it had been alerted to danger. I could see the deer was agitated, as it diligently tried to identify the source of concern. With each passing second, the buck became more nervous, though I could sense nothing extraordinary that might induce such a defensive reaction.

I did notice, however, that all the chickadees and finches, which had been freely chirping in celebration of morning's arrival, instantly fell silent. In fact, it seemed as though the entire forest around me, which had been coming to life as the sun climbed higher, reverted to eerie silence. With my view of the great deer obstructed, I had no choice but to watch, listen, and remain as quiet as possible.

Chapter Eleven
The Main Event

Metzger's Slough
Rural, northeast Iowa
Saturday, October 23, 1993, 7:02 a.m.

By the time the last songbird had stopped singing, King Charlemagne was noticeably agitated. He had given several telltale signals of his intention to flee, yet he remained stationary, standing wary and alert. I watched as he continually rotated his head left and right and flipped his ears from side to side. It seemed as if he wanted to take flight but couldn't decide which direction was safest to run. Instead, he lingered and continued studying the area with great concern. His dark eyes peered out from between a birch tree's buggy whip-like branches and the denser brush he was hiding behind. He lifted his nose frequently and inhaled the morning air, while his ears strained to hear through the curled leaves rustling in the breeze.

Itching to know the cause of his distress, I struggled to suppress my urge to investigate until after the entire event had played out. After a few more anxious moments, I sensed the huge deer had reached his limit, so I readied my bow in case he haphazardly bolted in my direction. Just as I positioned myself in case a clear shot became available, all hell broke loose in the forest.

As he had likely done thousands of times before, King Charlemagne raised his forelegs and prepared to break out of the sumac and into the open. But as his powerful hind legs thrust upward and his body gained momentum, he was stopped midair by an incredible force that slammed him to the ground. After regaining his senses, the gigantic buck righted himself and swung his menacing antlers in the direction of what had smashed him so viciously. I noted how quickly the deer's instincts had switched from flight to fight, and was impressed by how, almost instantaneously, he had determined to thrash whatever had assailed him. I couldn't imagine what beast could produce the power required to bring down the enormous deer so efficiently. Even with my senses keenly focused, I was unable to see the creature that was engaging with the mammoth deer in mortal combat.

Based on the fighting style King Charlemagne was using, it appeared as if he was either struggling to keep up with his attacker or having trouble locating it during his counterattack. Through the brush, I could see the buck kick his hind legs in rapid succession, before swirling his body in a crazed, figure-eight pattern in a chaotic attempt to strike his enemy with his antlers. With the frantic sounds of breaking branches and snapping twigs echoing throughout the slough, nearly a minute passed before the uproar turned into the ghastly sounds of a wounded animal moaning in agony and fighting for survival. Now consumed with a growing fear for my own safety, I relaxed my grip on the bow and lifted the binoculars hanging around my neck, determined to watch the spectacle in the woods play out.

I scoured the tangled forest for the spot where the battle was being waged and followed a trail of destruction—shaking shoots, falling leaves, and trampled underbrush—in order to zero in on the action. Frustrated at having to incessantly readjust my binocular lenses, I finally caught sight of King Charlemagne deep in the thicket. He was now stationary, with his chest lowered near the ground and his huge white tail raised high in back. By leveraging his back legs, the buck was attempting to reverse his position, as if he were resisting an incredible vacuum that was trying to pull him forward. During the battle, King Charlemagne released a gruesome, guttural wail reminiscent of one a heifer cow might make while birthing a calf. A fountain of blood gushed skyward and splattered the nearest birch tree's white bark with bright red drops. In an instinctive act of self-preservation, King Charlemagne writhed and reeled, and finally broke free from the grip that had been trying to drag him forward.

Once free, the dazed buck changed strategies and decided to run away from his opponent. Though I could see only fragments of his gigantic frame plowing through the brush, a ruby-colored mist was clearly visible shooting upward from a wound in his neck with every stride. Spellbound by what I was watching, I remained transfixed, still clueless as to what was mauling the remarkable deer.

* * * * *

When the skirmish in the timbers began, Garner missed its opening salvo. After having his whereabouts given away by the dead branch that snapped under his weight, he'd stayed still and hesitated from bringing his binoculars to his eyes. Upon hearing the tremendous thrashing in bushes that ensued, he no longer worried about his secrecy. An incredible fight was underway, and he wanted to see it. He began trotting toward the commotion, concealing himself as much as possible, still reluctant to have Ryan learn of his presence. He knew Ryan would be absorbed with the happening too and believed he could remain unnoticed if he moved discreetly.

As he moved, he debated what was attacking the deer. Most likely, another large buck had arrived and was challenging King Charlemagne's dominance in the slough. He had heard countless stories of violent buck fights and wanted to witness one firsthand. The thought of harvesting a trophy buck just after it had won a major battle gave him an extra thrill. Then the alternative possibility of a coyote attack crossed his mind, and he took the matter more seriously. After a little reflection, he doubted a single coyote would dare try to take down a buck this size, and he'd never witnessed a pack of coyotes working to kill prey. Other, more far-fetched possibilities popped into his head, such as a mountain lion, bear, or a pack of wolves, but those candidates were quickly dismissed because he believed each to have been eradicated from the state decades ago.

Nevertheless, as he reached the edge of the thicket, he loaded an arrow on his bow and moved forward like a Special Forces soldier advancing into enemy territory. Pumped with adrenalin, the wrestler hustled toward the action, fully intent on watching the battle play out.

* * * * *

DOUGLAS CAVANAUGH

Though King Charlemagne was obviously maimed, the full extent of his injuries wasn't readily recognizable from my position. It was clear he no longer wanted to continue fighting and that running was his best chance of staying alive. As I watched the injured buck attempting to flee, the view through my binoculars was often hindered by low-hanging branches, as well as my shaking hands. I'd become so unnerved by what was happening I could no longer hear anything except for my heavy breathing. The sounds coming from under my face mask resembled those of a panicked scuba diver on the ocean floor or a frightened astronaut on a spacewalk gone awry. I realized the source of my anxiety had transformed from concern for my lost prey to that of my personal safety. In rapid-fire succession, several disturbing and unanswerable questions came to mind, such as what would happen if I was discovered and how I would escape if whatever was attacking the deer turned its attention toward me. Wishing my Grandpa Conrad was around to consult, I remained still and continued watching the action through my binoculars despite my unsteady hands.

After having finally broken free from his foe with a furious head shake and an impressive shoulder thrust, King Charlemagne bounded several times before stopping at the clearing where he'd been eating acorns just minutes ago. I anticipated his plan to bolt up the neglected path, because that trail provided flat ground on which to run. But once the buck stopped to get his bearings, his pathetic physical state became clearer. I realized right away he had little chance of escape because of the degree of his injuries. The deer's entire left foreleg had been torn off below the knee. Heroically, he had managed to run this far on only three legs. Both sides of his antler rack had sustained major damage, and several tines had been broken off completely.

Worse, I could see King Charlemagne bleeding profusely from a nasty gash on the side of his neck, likely the source of the red mist that had followed him through the brush. The broad patch of white fur under his chin was now stained with fresh blood. As the deer struggled to breathe, I could see him favor his left side and could tell that several ribs had been broken, likely the consequence of the onslaught's initial impact. Admirably, the magnificent buck

THE LONG WAY AROUND

continued huffing and puffing, determined to escape.

* * * * *

After hearing the brawl in the woods grind to a halt, Garner stopped to listen to learn where the combatants had moved during his transit. He avoided entering the deepest brush, and instead skirted the edge of the tree line to where he estimated the opponents to be. He purposely stayed out of sight behind the birch trees and scrub, knowing that if he passed through to the opposite side Ryan would be able to see him. He stood still for a few seconds longer and soon heard one of the participants running ahead in the distance. When sounds of its adversary giving chase ensued, Garner plowed into the thicket, not wanting to miss the fight's conclusion.

* * * * *

The moment the deer had taken enough air to continue his flight, he broke in the direction of the derelict trail leading to the river. But he did not get far before he was again slammed to the ground. As opposed to the first collision, I observed the second attack more clearly and was astonished by what I saw.

King Charlemagne was now unable to fend off his enemy. He lay on one side, defeated and defenseless, moaning in misery and shaking from shock. For a second, it appeared he'd regained the wherewithal to return to his feet, but just as his head lifted it was quickly pressed back to the ground by a strong push from above. I vigorously adjusted my binoculars and squinted to improve my vision, but I still could not identify what was holding the deer down in the weeds. Most of the time, I saw nothing, just emptiness, as if an invisible force had the buck pinned on its side. On a few instances, however, I was able to see something moving just enough to discern some living entity was, in fact, there. Not that I was able to define any shape or size, but I was able to determine something had placed itself over the deer and was beginning to devour it alive. As it did, waves of translucent power began rolling down its sides, blurring the terrain around it.

The sight reminded me of when, as a small boy, I'd once blown soap bubbles inside the house and seen a few land on a stack of magazines. I recalled reading the text under where the largest bubble had landed and being fascinated by the opaque letters in the soapy canopy. I'd been amazed by how they were distorted but still legible. Such was the illusion created by the creature tearing into the deer. As I watched from my tree stand, King Charlemagne released a final groan of opposition, and then was silent. I listened carefully for any sounds the predator might make but heard nothing from that distance. Within a couple of minutes, most of the buck's fur had been stripped from its carcass and loads of raw flesh lay scattered and steaming in the cool, autumn air. Before long, chunks of King Charlemagne were strewn about in a semicircle, blood was smeared in all directions, and the animal's internal organs and guts had been ripped out and pushed aside. When the deer's steaming heart was yanked from the chest cavity, a large spurt of blood gushed from the dangling arteries and landed on the transparent creature, revealing its outline to some extent.

I fought the terror I was feeling, but just when I thought I had spied the most gruesome sight of my life, another scene appeared that trumped this one in spades.

* * * * *

Sliding covertly between the timbers and brush, Garner reached the point where the initial attack on the great buck had commenced. He examined the scene and was surprised at seeing the deer's front leg lying in the grass. After observing several splotches of coagulated blood and a long line of smashed tree limbs veering to the right, he followed the path the fight had taken. Readying his arrow, he proceeded another forty yards, sidestepping his way as quietly as possible. When he reached the clearing, what he saw stunned him.

Blood was spilled everywhere, and hunks of venison meat and intestines were spread over the ground. Before leaving his cover, he examined the scene for signs of a mountain lion, wolf, or any other animal which could have mutilated the deer in such a manner. Nothing was obvious. After another minute of waiting, he came out of seclusion to inspect the broken antlers he'd spied in the center of the mess. If the gigantic rack had not been completely destroyed, it could still be valuable for a collector, but the damage had to be assessed close up. He fixed his arrow snugly in the bow slot and inched forward, watching for danger with every step.

When he reached the severed head, Garner scanned the area once more and waited. After sensing no threat to his safety, he set down his bow and removed his knife from a sheath attached to his belt. He bent down on one knee and began cutting the salvageable parts from the mangled carcass.

*****

During the period it took for the invisible predator to skin and disembowel the giant deer, I'd realized it was either unaware of or undisturbed by my presence. I chose to believe it was the former, and when my nerves began to settle, I decided to devise a getaway plan before it might direct its attention to me. I monitored it constantly for changes in behavior, but its lack of visibility made observation impossible. Now nestled against the trunk of a cottonwood tree a dozen yards away from King Charlemagne's remains, the predator was devouring the deer's rear flank. If it were not for the fact I'd seen where it had dragged the slab of meat through the grass, I would have had no idea of its location.

I could not have been more startled by what appeared next.

A lone man dressed in camouflage apparel emerged from the brush with his compound bow loaded and ready to fire. I knew nobody else was allowed on the property, and from the person's clothing and equipment, I was certain it was not Dieter Metzger. Whoever the trespasser was, he was being cautious, as if he knew danger was looming yet was unaware of what kind of trouble lurked nearby. As I watched him advance toward King Charlemagne's head, I studied his size, gait, features, and attire. Since I had seen him just a couple of hours ago, I quickly realized it was Brian Garner. He had evidently followed me to Metzger's Slough, and had unknowingly put himself in grave danger. I had little time in which to act. I thought about how I could warn him without forfeiting my hideout. I considered calling out but decided against it at the last second. In the end, it didn't matter.

As soon as Garner set his bow down and bent forward with his knife, the creature abandoned his meal and moved stealthily toward the hunter. My heart raced and a heightened terror again started running through my veins. I could see that Garner sensed danger approaching, but doubted he was aware of the source. I lost track of the predator soon after, but when I saw Garner drop the deer head and race for his bow, I assumed it was closing in. Letting his buck knife fall to the ground, Garner lifted his bow and searched for something to shoot.

It happened in a flash.

My old adversary was struck in the head and knocked backward, rolling twice on the ground. The bow and arrow, his best chance of defense, fell to the wayside and out of reach. Garner screamed and reached to his eyes. Through my binoculars, I could see a river of blood pouring from a cut on his forehead and dripping down his face through his fingers. I knew he could no longer see. Blinded, he began raking the terrain with his hands in search of his knife. I watched with horror as he clutched at his chest with his left hand, as if resisting something that had taken a hold of him from behind. With a final effort, he found his hunting knife and flailed it around wildly. He struck nothing with his first few attempts, but just as he was about to be thrown down again, his next effort stabbed the creature, which illuminated it for an instant.

As it flashed, I realized it was as unnatural as anything I'd ever seen, and for a brief instant, I caught a glimpse of its form through the brush. The thing appeared to have a rounded head with two circular eyes that bulged out bug-like, like those seen in a child's drawing. At its midsection, a double row of small appendages, each one resembling a spider leg with claws at the end, held the wrestler securely in their grip. The thing had short, powerful legs, thick and wide at the top, and narrow and bony near its feet. There were no other distinguishable features; no nose, ears, hair, nor tail. It was transparent and therefore colorless, except internally, where a pink streak, remnants of blood from the deer meat it had just consumed, ran from its mouth to its center, presumably the stomach.

Before the illumination faded, I caught sight of something resembling a spinal cord and peripheral nerves, which had temporarily lighted up when Garner's knife had pierced it. Considering the

THE LONG WAY AROUND

amount of power the thing generated, it was not as big as I would have imagined. Its compact build would require me to use extreme precision in order to shoot it with an arrow from the distance I was, a most difficult shot even if my hands were fully under my control. I raised my bow and aimed at the mass before the final traces of light extinguished and the target disappeared.

As the final flickers extinguished, the creature lunged once more at Garner, who screamed out in response. Before I could adjust my aim in order to avoid drilling Garner in the back, the thing slashed his chest multiple times with its flailing claws. I released my arrow just as Garner crumpled over into the weeds with the creature clinging to his back. As the last blush of luminance disappeared, my arrow penetrated its underbelly and caused an unexpected result.

All at once, the bright glow reappeared and increased in intensity until the thing burst into miniscule pieces, each one creating a mesmerizing pattern of dazzling sizzles like those seen in a fireworks display. An enormous amount of energy was released in the aftermath. The explosion produced enough heat to warm the slough in all directions, yet the resulting fragments started no fires, produced no smoke, and left no odor before dying out. As each spark fizzled, it was not replaced by another. Soon the scene was still, leaving only the decimated body of Garner and the uneaten remains of King Charlemagne. All traces of the invisible creature had disappeared.

The last of my nerves finally gave out, and it was all I could do to maintain my balance. Had I not been strapped securely to the tree; I surely would have fallen from the platform. I sat down, nestled against the trunk, and somehow found the wherewithal to secure my bow in its cradle. Unable to stop my hands from trembling, I managed to unbuckle my safety harness and decided to climb down to confirm if what I had seen was real or imagined. I knew I had to check if Garner was alive.

I put my arms through my rucksack straps and lifted it onto my back. Inside was a bottle of water, several packets of Kleenex, and a roll of toilet paper, which I thought I could use to stop his bleeding. Still in shock, I put one foot over the platform and onto the top rung of the makeshift ladder. The light wind began to pick up and the little bit of sunlight that had appeared earlier faded behind some drifting clouds. I climbed three rungs down before deciding to take my compound bow with me in case additional danger was lurking nearby.

Instead of climbing back onto the platform, I opted to reach up and lift it from its bracket before pulling it down. As I strained my body the final few inches, the scrap lumber I was standing on collapsed under my weight and sent me tumbling toward the ground. Reflexively, I grabbed for the nearest limb, but my grip was too weak to hold on. I fell like a stone toward the ground, bouncing off several branches along the way. During the last six feet of my plummet, I hit my head on a large limb and was knocked unconscious.

Piled in a heap in the woods, I lay still, unable to hear the forest birds as they resumed their chirping in the distance.

Chapter Twelve
A Decision Must Be Made

Planned Parenthood Clinic
Cedar Falls, IA
Saturday, October 23, 1993, 10:00 a.m.

The coeds had been sitting in the Ford compact for almost half an hour. They had said little to one another during the trip to the clinic. Mary didn't feel like talking, and Dori had nothing left to say that might persuade her friend to change her mind about the action she was about to take. The silence ended in the facility parking lot. It had been drizzling rain for most of the morning, and in minutes the windshield completely fogged up from the nervous breathing taking place inside.

Dori had used every imaginable angle over the last month to persuade her friend not to end her pregnancy, but every attempt had been rejected. A final effort to get her to talk to her parents had fallen on deaf ears, and it seemed Mary was in a trancelike state as she desperately tried to block the reason for her appointment out of her mind. The decision she had made was uncharacteristic of her normal behavior, as she was never known to be selfish or uncaring.

What she couldn't mentally overcome were the long term ramifications of what motherhood presented at this time of her life. It seemed so unfair to her, the fact that she was just about to reach the pinnacle she had dreamed about, the portion of her life that would reflect the results and achievements of all her hard work. Now more than ever, she was frightened of being restricted to a life she was determined to escape, of losing the best chance of earning her place in the world by herself, and of forfeiting the family she wanted to have when the timing was more appropriate.

She had considered the possibility of confiding in her parents on a thousand occasions, but she knew if she did, the idea of the medical procedure she was about to undergo would have been dismissed outright. As a result, her future's path would be forever altered. By not telling them, the option to make the problem disappear remained intact, and the lingering consequences in her conscience would be hers alone to deal with. She felt her parents had worked too hard and for too long to put her where she was today, and she'd decided to resolve this crisis without loading them down with extra burden.

"Mary, there's still time to reconsider. You don't have to go in there," Dori pleaded.

"I know, but the time frame is closing with each passing day. I'm almost three months along right now. The clinic reps told me I have a sixteen-week window where the procedure can safely be performed. There isn't much more time, and if I wait any longer, I will start to show. People will know. If I do it now, nobody besides us will ever know."

Dori could see the tremor in her friend's hands despite the brave front she had on display. Mary hadn't gained much weight over the past weeks as a result of her lack of appetite and morning sickness. "Why don't you call Ryan and discuss this with him? You know how levelheaded he is about things like this. He'll probably be happy about becoming a father. He will definitely be supportive. You're underestimating him."

"This is the most difficult decision I've ever had to make in my life. It may be the hardest I'll ever face again, and I hate that I am making it alone. I really wish I could include Ryan, but if I do, I'll be giving up control of my future. I'd be happy for Ryan to be the father of my child one day, but my God, this is all happening so fast!" she said in a panicky voice. After she'd calmed a bit, she said, "You're right about one thing; Ryan would make a fantastic father. He'd be my perfect choice for a husband, too. But we're so young. There are so many things for both of us left to do before marriage and children. I don't think either one of us is ready yet. A baby now would change everything. The timing has to be right before we plan the next step. I'm sure there would be regrets by both of us down the road."

Dori decided to take a definitive stance. "Mary, if you do this

THE LONG WAY AROUND

today, I can guarantee you'll have a major regret in the future, one you'll never be able to correct."

Mary broke down in tears. She had not cried once over the last seven days, and it was as if all the courage she had mustered to suppress her feelings had collapsed. With that one sentence, Dori had found the key to unlock the true emotions Mary had managed to keep buried.

"I want to talk to him! I need to talk to him! Oh God, I'm so confused!"

Dori took charge of the situation and guided her friend with authority. "Listen to me. I'm going in there right now and canceling your appointment. You must promise me you'll call Ryan today and meet with him as soon as possible. I'll drive you back to Strawberry Point any time you agree to see each other, or you can take my car. After you discuss this, if it doesn't go well, you can always reschedule this appointment and I'll never bring the subject up again. Ever. But you must both decide together, okay?"

Still in tears, Mary nodded in agreement. Dori tried to hug her, but it was awkward in the boxy, undersized car. Instead, she chose to go inside and cancel the appointment before Mary could change her mind. In a flurry of activity, she pulled the key from the ignition, told Mary to stay put, and then opened the car door. After raising her jacket's hood to block the drizzle, she splashed through several puddles as she hurried toward the clinic entrance.

On the way, she smiled from ear to ear, elated she had saved her friend from making a choice she was convinced would be a terrible mistake.

Chapter Thirteen
Along Comes Tim

Rural, northeast Iowa
Saturday, October 23, 1993, 12:50 p.m.

Tim was tired, hungry, and mildly irritated from waiting so long for Ryan to show. After almost an hour of wasted time standing at the pickup point, he decided to walk along the low maintenance road to Metzger's Slough instead of taking a more direct route across a picked bean field and through unfamiliar timber. After a quarter mile trek, he reached a crossroad and turned right on the gravel road Ryan always used so he wouldn't miss him if he were in transit. It wasn't like his friend to be late.

Tim suspected Ryan might be waiting out a dawdling buck and unable to leave his stand, or that he had shot a deer and was having trouble tracking it down. Worst-case scenario, he considered Ryan may have fallen asleep in the tree, as is known to happen to hunters from time to time. In any case, he decided to check on him, even though he had never personally been to Ryan's hunting spot in the slough. However, from their past conversations, he had a good idea of where he had mounted his stand, and Tim knew exactly where Ryan parked his truck each day. He estimated the distance to be around three miles and the time needed to hike to the truck to be under an hour, if he maintained a brisk pace.

Tim set off on foot with his rucksack, hoping Ryan would pull up soon and they could go to town for lunch. Along the way, he cracked pistachios without breaking stride and washed the nuts down with bottled water. About halfway to the Metzger property, he finished the pistachios, rinsed his mouth with water, and opened a can of chewing tobacco, spitting frequently on the gravel as he walked. His heavy breathing pumped hot mist into the cool air, and with no traffic along the way, Tim made good progress. Before long,

THE LONG WAY AROUND

he reached an embankment, which he promptly climbed down, and then crossed a neighboring cornfield, which shortened the distance to Ryan's truck by a third.

When he finally arrived, he wasn't surprised to see the Chevy S-10 parked in its place, and he felt confident his original assumptions were probably correct. Tim studied the truck for signs of mechanical problems, but everything appeared to be intact. He put his hand on the hood; it was cold to the touch and he knew it had not been driven recently. He spit the rest of the tobacco into the weeds, rinsed his mouth a final time, and decided to forge ahead into the woods. He intended to approach quietly so as not to draw attention in case his friend had some hunting action in the works. In order to ensure the surroundings wouldn't be disturbed, he decided to trudge a mile further along the gravel road in order to avoid the thickest brush, and then wander down the sloped cow pasture leading to the slough's side entrance.

Approximately three hundred yards down the line, he was surprised to find a second truck parked inside of the property's alternate access. This one, a decked-out white Dodge Dakota, looked familiar. On closer examination, he remembered it being the truck he saw while leaving the KwikMart that morning, and knew it belonged to Brian Garner. A strange feeling warned him something was wrong, so he picked up the pace in Ryan's direction. By now, the fickle sun had completely disappeared behind heavy clouds, the wind had lessened, and a foggy haze had settled in, limiting visibility from a distance.

On his way across the pasture, he couldn't find an established path to follow so he created his own. After reaching the bottom, he discovered two routes that could lead him to his destination. The first was shorter in distance and presumably faster, though it would entail wading through difficult terrain on the way toward Ryan's stand if he chose to take it. Choosing this path would require dodging limestone boulders and forging through thorny wild roses, black berries, and other shaggy, prickly briars. He debated whether the route was indeed faster or not. The second option consisted of a longer hike toward an adjacent farm, and then another trek along a three-hundred-yard stretch of birch trees running parallel to the Turkey River. The distance was much farther, but the walking conditions would be easier. Since he was already suited in protective hunting clothing, Tim selected the first route and started fighting through the tangled brush.

As he neared the spot he thought Ryan would be, he called out several times, softly at first, and then a little louder with each subsequent attempt. Frustrated by receiving no response, he dismissed the possibility of scaring away any deer and shouted as loud as he could while scanning the forest's barren branches. When he'd almost reached the edge of the timber, he saw a cluster of white oak trees a short distance away and headed toward them. He remembered Ryan telling of the acorn patch he'd been hunting, and as soon as he found it, he backtracked and saw a large elm tree he instantly identified as the one Ryan had been using.

As he headed toward it, he spotted his friend's deer stand mounted fifteen feet above the ground. It was unoccupied. With growing frustration, he stopped to consider the situation. While studying the surroundings, he heard a faint moan coming from some trampled brush under the tree. Tim ran in that direction, calling out Ryan's name. When he reached an open space in the undergrowth, he saw the reason why his calls had received no reply. Ryan was lying under the tree, crumpled like a dirty towel on a bathroom floor. As Tim approached his friend, he noted the bruising on his pale skin and saw a trickle of clear fluid seeping from his right ear. There was visible bleeding and swelling on the right side of Ryan's head. Tim knew from various television rescue shows that head injury victims aren't to be moved until the extent of their injuries have been evaluated, so he bent down over Ryan and listened for breathing. He put his finger on Ryan's carotid artery and was satisfied with what he felt. His friend was breathing normally, and his pulse was strong. Tim pinched Ryan's cheek, and then gently slapped each a few times while repeating his name. Soon Ryan began to stir.

"Come on, buddy. Snap out of it. It's Tim," he said.

Tim tipped the plastic bottle and poured some water over Ryan's lips. He pinched Ryan's cheeks again and his friend began to mumble. In short time, Ryan became alert and recognized his friend. Tim tried to keep Ryan still while he inspected his head. He had already deduced his friend had fallen from the tree and had been knocked out cold. As the minutes passed, Ryan became more aware of his surroundings and sat upright despite Tim's pleas for him not to move. Tim saw that Ryan's eyes looked funny, as if the pupil in his right eye was larger than the left.

Ryan felt lightheaded, dizzy, and sick to his stomach. He was unable to answer Tim's questions about how he had fallen. After a little more time, Ryan remembered the terror from before and tried to describe the event that had happened in a rapid outburst before stopping because of nausea. Tim couldn't decipher most of what Ryan was trying to tell him, but the part he understood seemed incredibly bizarre, and he wanted to get his friend to a hospital as soon as possible. He looped Ryan's right arm over his left shoulder and tried to help him to his feet. Since there was absolutely no way to drive a vehicle into the slough, he was determined to support his friend the entire way back to the truck or carry him if he must. As he stood, Ryan had difficulty maintaining his balance and propped himself against the tree from which he had fallen. With his head bent forward, he held on tightly to a wooden rung and pointed in the direction where Brian Garner's body was lying.

"Go there," he muttered, pointing toward the river. His face was ghostly white. "Check him. He may be alive. Forty yards. Maybe fifty."

Tim couldn't understand his directions entirely. He didn't want to leave his friend alone in the state he was in, yet Ryan refused to leave unless he walked in that direction. Against his better judgment, Tim said, "Alright, I'll be back in a few minutes. Do you want to sit?"

"Just go," Ryan said, resisting the urge to vomit. "Take my bow."

Tim climbed the elm tree, removed Ryan's compound bow from its cradle, and then eased himself back down carefully, paying special attention to the missing wooden rung that had broken free. Ryan had managed to reposition himself and was sitting at the base of the tree when Tim returned. "Don't move. I'll be right back," Tim said.

He loaded an arrow and began walking toward a clearing in the thick brush and birch trees near the river. When he reached the edge, he entered the thicket slowly but saw nothing unusual. Leaving the forest, he first veered left and walked a few yards more before spotting a large quantity of dried blood streaked on the trunk of a young birch. At first, he smiled, thinking that Ryan had shot a large buck that had bolted after being hit. It was probable that, because of excitement, Ryan had fallen from the tree while attempting to pursue his prey. Tim was aware of the great distances a mortally wounded deer could run, but with such an obvious trail of blood to follow, he had little doubt it would be found and collected. Now he began feeling better about being forgotten at the roadside and privately began celebrating his friend's success.

Turning in his tracks, he followed the trail in the direction the blood appeared to be freshest, pushing away the tree branches and heavy brush as he moved. Before long, he saw a broad clearing and turned his head to locate the tree from which Ryan had been hunting. Confirming the line of fire, Tim grinned and shook his head proudly. *Yep*, he thought, *he's done it again!* He moved forward and saw more blood smears. When he reached the last line of birch trees and advanced into the clearing, his proud grin and happy mood quickly faded.

Looking at the scene before him, he was sickened at what he saw. Dark, syrupy blood was pooled in all directions, twisted animal intestines and other internal organs randomly scattered about. Soggy clumps of deer fur were spread to one side of the clearing, while the rancid smell of animal waste choked the air. At first glance, Tim thought maybe one or several coyotes had found Ryan's injured prey and had shredded it in a feeding frenzy. He pulled the arrow back and put his senses on full alert.

As he advanced, he saw an enormous set of antlers in the center of the mess. They were connected to an equally massive deer head, which had been removed from the body. Many of the rack's boney spikes had been broken off. While wondering how that had happened, Tim glanced toward the thicket entrance and was aghast by what he saw. Twisted and distorted, a human form lay mangled and virtually unrecognizable inside of torn, camouflaged clothing. From where he was standing, he could see the front side was drenched with blood. Sticking out from the body's right thigh

THE LONG WAY AROUND

was a carbon fiber arrow shaft, an exact match of the shape, design and color of the one he was holding on Ryan's bow. Recalling the white truck he had seen at the slough's entrance, Tim knew at once the victim was Brian Garner. The circumstances of how he'd been killed were unclear.

He stood still, his mouth wide open, sickened by the sight in front of him.

Chapter Fourteen
Truly at Peace

Intensive Care Unit
Mercy Hospital
Oelwein, Iowa
Sunday, October 24, 1993, 5:30 a.m.

The critical care suite was completely dark on one side and dimly lit on the other. A single patient, his head shaved and bandaged, was lying in the center of the room in a railed hospital bed situated between two unoccupied beds. Though the room had not been soundproofed, very little noise could be heard inside except for an occasional beep from a vital sign monitor and the repetitious swishing produced by a ventilator hovering over the patient's shoulder. A soft shade of blue light emitted from its display. A white curtain hanging from the ceiling on a U-shaped metallic track had been pulled around the foot of the bed to serve as a symbol of privacy. The curtain's mesh material offered the patient sanctuary from the hallway's fluorescent lighting, though it was hardly necessary because of his unconscious state.

Just outside the entrance's glass door, the night shift nurse read a romance novel at her station to help pass the time. Seated on a vinyl couch further down the hall, a uniformed Fayette County deputy sheriff watched cable television and drank black coffee from a throwaway cup. An expression of boredom was obvious on his face.

The room's single window to the outside world was tightly sealed and offered no clue of the day's early hour, but the patient's biorhythms had grown accustomed to his early risings over the last several weeks and had triggered his bodily functions to begin working almost an hour ago. The nurse addressed this promptly, then checked the tube attached to the morphine drip

THE LONG WAY AROUND

before returning to her workstation. The young man's vital signs had stabilized overnight and were much stronger now. Later that morning, the treating neurosurgeon would arrive from Waterloo to make a follow-up examination and decide if the opiates were to be reduced in order to bring his patient out of the induced coma.

In the meantime, Ryan Meyers's brain cells continued firing. For the time being, he could only dream in solitude, oblivious to the world around him.

* * * * *

The quality of the images running through his mind varied drastically between well-defined vividness and nonspecific murkiness. Two themes dominated his thoughts, and both occurred with perplexing irregularity. At times, less distinct visions appeared, and whenever those began to broaden in scope and gain in depth, they were quickly replaced by one of the primary ones that had formed a replay loop in his mind. Only one of the two main dreams, the clearest and the one which appeared most often, carried any measure of familiarity.

It was a replay of a vacation he had experienced just months ago that had been etched in his mind as the most pleasant time of his young life. Even though the event had occurred long before he'd suffered the head trauma responsible for his current state, the vision's clarity was remarkably precise.

* * * * *

Summers had always held a special place in Ryan's heart ever since he was a boy, and the enjoyable memories the season produced intensified as he matured. In truth, each of the four seasons had found their rank in his subconscious based on their respective qualities, and summer had edged out autumn as his favorite time of year, irrespective of the fact bowhunting season never started until autumn was in full swing. But this past summer had been particularly noteworthy. Those hot months carried extra relevance because they were the final ones before he and his best friends were to disband to begin the next phase of their lives.

The season also stood out because it was the first time he

realized he was in love, though he never admitted it to anyone except to the girl who had won his heart, Mary Kelleher. Mary had been his girlfriend for the last ten months, and she had made an impression on him that was irrefutable. After their high school graduation in June, life continued as if it were one big party that would never end. Each in the group had no serious responsibilities for two months, and the time that followed seemed to move at a snail's pace. The days were long, and the seemingly unending string of late nights buoyed their youthful spirits. When July arrived, one final, unexpected party developed about a month before their futures were destined to change forever.

That summer's Fourth of July celebration formed spontaneously after a friend of Conrad Doyle's offered Ryan the use of his summer house and boat ramp on the banks of the Mississippi River near a town named Harper's Ferry. Ryan knew it was a great opportunity and he seized it at once. The house, an A-frame log cabin tucked away in the hardwood forest just above the river's flood plain, offered quick access to the water and was just a short drive to local nightlife that consumed the small town for a few months each summer. Thrilled with his good fortune, he immediately collected Mary and his best friends: Tim Ross, Andy Ludlow, Rory Meeks and their girlfriends for a week of fun on the Mississippi River.

Each morning, the boys rose early and left to fish for crappies, walleyes, and northern pike until lunchtime. After lunch and an afternoon rest, the friends loaded a cooler of drinks into a 1992 Bay liner Capri speedboat they rented for waterskiing on the river channels. When they returned each day, wet, sunburned, and exhausted, they showered and changed, then fired up the grill for their evening meal. Afterward, they sometimes drove to town to play pool and darts at one of the local bars or stayed in the cabin to play cards late into the night. Each subsequent morning, the alarm clock rang before dawn and the process started again, until before long, one day blurred into the next and all track of time was lost.

The seven days of fun solidified their friendships, but it was the evening of the Fourth, after watching a fireworks display that had been fired from the deck of a barge docked on the Mississippi, when a late night romance elevated Ryan and Mary's relationship

THE LONG WAY AROUND

to the next level. That night, the breezeless, humid air was stifling, and the star-filled sky glittered excitedly as the young couple stood on the cabin's deck and stared at the distant lights flickering on the Wisconsin side of the river. Later, after all their friends had fallen asleep, Ryan sat on a sturdy wooden deck chair with Mary on his lap and the lovers discussed a lifelong commitment to one another in a moment of passion. The topic of marriage appealed to both, and Mary proposed the idea of starting a family as soon as she finished college as the logical next step. Mary was certain she wanted to spend the rest of her life with Ryan, and if he would agree to wait for her to finish college, the dream they shared would become reality.

Ryan, resisting a fixed timeframe, promised not to interfere with her collegiate ambitions and gladly encouraged her to pursue her education while he used the time to take care of his ailing grandfather and sort out his future. Maybe in a year or two, he thought, when his life had calmed down, he would join Mary at the University of Northern Iowa. Or perhaps she would join him if he chose another course of study at a university other than the one she was attending. It all seemed so simple, and the two were sure they could overcome any obstacle in the way of their life of happiness together.

The hours passed, and before long, the morning sun was rising over the eastern horizon. In all his life, Ryan had never felt so good.

* * * * *

The second main vision occurred less frequently, was vaguer in detail, and made no sense to Ryan. Its cast of characters remained mostly unclear and that confused him, yet the nature of the dream delighted him each time it appeared. The setting and background scenery were always the same, and though he enjoyed the vision greatly and tried to make it last longer, it always ended at the identical point, which was far too soon for his liking.

The dream began with a close-up view of a boy's face; a toddler of about two years old looking directly at him with his eyes squinting because of the glare of the sun. As the picture panned back from the tyke's face and included the surroundings, it became obvious it was summer because the boy was dressed in only a diaper and T-shirt. He was in the backyard of a country home. It was not the lawn of an extravagant estate, but it was more upscale than many of the farmhouses in that area of the state.

The lad was running barefoot on freshly mowed grass under the shade of a large beech tree. On top of his head he wore an oversized baseball cap, a blue one with a prominent red C showing on front that prevented his blonde locks from swinging freely. In his hands he held a colored, oversized bat he used to swing wildly at a plastic ball somebody out of frame was tossing in his direction. After a several missed attempts, the boy swung hard and ticked the ball before running haphazardly around the lawn. Along the way, his chubby thighs rubbed together, and he giggled hysterically as he moved. Indistinct voices could be heard cheering. A man's shadow closed in on the running child and the toddler was lifted high into the air with his mouth wide open, exposing a mouthful of new teeth through his laughter. After catching the boy, the man's hands gently tossed him high above his head before safely bringing him back down. The boy cackled loudly while being lowered to the ground, and the entire event repeated.

Then, just as unexpectedly as it had begun, the dream ended, bringing other, more ambiguous thoughts back to the forefront of Ryan's mind.

* * * * *

Visitors were not permitted until nine a.m., but Mary showed up early in case extra time would be needed to talk her way past the Fayette County deputy on guard duty. Fortunately, she had known the critical care department's head nurse, Janet Epping, for years. In fact, Janet's younger sister had been in Mary's high school graduating class and the girls had been distant friends since childhood. Mary had called Janet the night before to discuss the chances of her seeing Ryan before other visitors were allowed. Since Janet had known the officer's mother for years and had babysat the deputy when he was young, she offered her help to coax his consent for Mary to see Ryan before the shift became too busy. This suited Mary fine, as she desperately wanted to see her boyfriend without attracting any attention, and without the distraction of other people stopping by.

THE LONG WAY AROUND

When Mary arrived at eight o'clock sharp, Janet came out from behind her nursing station and ushered her into the intensive care suite. There was little time to waste, because in just a few hours the medical specialist from Waterloo would arrive to evaluate Ryan's condition. Mary only wanted enough time to check on his condition. More than anything, she wished she could be there to support and help Ryan through his crisis, because she knew he would be there for her. But she was dealing with a crisis of her own, and Ryan's emergency had only worsened her situation.

Before Ryan's accident, she had planned to share her secret with the father of their unborn child, but now she realized that conversation couldn't happen before her final decision had to be made. Too much time had already passed, and there was no way to know when Ryan's mental state would be able to cope with the dilemma Mary was enduring. When she had first learned of his accident and the bizarre circumstances surrounding it, Mary's spirit had dropped to new lows and she felt the last chance of making a rational decision with the person whose opinion mattered most had been missed. Once again, she was all alone to make an impossible decision, one that undoubtedly would affect the people she loved most and the family she truly wanted to have forever.

Silently, she moved toward the bed and took Ryan's free hand in both of hers. She gripped it firmly and started crying. In a voice just above a whisper, she muttered, "Oh, Ryan, I'm so sorry. I'm sorry to have ignored you for so long and not to have been there for you. I'm so sorry to have excluded you about so many things, important things that will affect your future…our future."

Choked up and unable to speak further, she broke down, tears streaming down her cheeks. Regaining her composure, Mary wiped her face with a Kleenex and stared at the young man she loved as he lay still, his head bandaged, his chest rising and lowering in concert with the respirator swishes. *It's no use*, she thought, *it just wasn't meant to be*. She lifted Ryan's hand up to her cheek and held it tightly. "My God, if you only knew. If you only *knew*," she repeated. She lowered his hand and bent forward and kissed his cheek. With her eyes beginning to swell again, she said, "If *I* only knew."

Her mind a twisted state of confusion, she turned and walked away.

Chapter Fifteen
Conrad Makes a Stand

Mercy Hospital
Oelwein, Iowa
Sunday, October 24, 1993, 1:00 p.m.

Conrad could hear them coming long before they reached his suite. A nurse from the dialysis department had tipped him off that he'd be receiving visitors concerning his grandson. It was about thirty minutes later when he heard shoes tapping down the hallway in his direction. Before they'd reached his room, he'd repositioned himself upright and was trying to eavesdrop on their conversation. When they finally approached his door, their chatter diminished before entering.

Conrad hoped the man in charge was the owner of the voice he liked best, the one that sounded straightforward, experienced, and trustworthy. The other voice was younger, and the man's attitude was overconfident, brash, and contentious. Conrad was in no mood to deal with an abrasive youngster, so he decided to direct the conversation toward the man he thought would be most agreeable with his temperament. After all, these men had come to visit him in order to determine his grandson's fate, and Conrad needed to play his cards right. He was too shrewd to fall for the good cop, bad cop routine, and too experienced to get sucked into a false confidence scheme. He was also determined not to start rambling and say something stupid he may regret later.

For now, he wanted to keep his answers concise and try to put the officers on the defensive. It was crucial for him to learn what the police knew about the case and whether the report Tim Ross had given him earlier that morning was being taken at face value. Incredible as the yarn was that Tim had told, Conrad knew there would be no way to contest his story unless the evidence suggested otherwise, and since there had been no other witnesses around to dispute Tim's account, his testimony would have to carry credence. Nevertheless, because Ryan's hunting partner had clearly happened onto the scene several hours after the actual event had occurred, his testimony couldn't prove exactly what had transpired, and this complicated matters significantly.

As Conrad saw it, there were only two people in the world who really knew what happened during those early morning hours, and one of them was dead. The other eyewitness, his grandson, was lying in another wing of the same hospital in critical condition.

After three firm knocks, the door to Conrad's room opened bit by bit, and then more rapidly when the detectives discovered Conrad was awake. Upon entering, the senior officer made a formal introduction but refrained from shaking Conrad's bandaged right hand.

With a businesslike tone, the older man said, "Mr. Doyle, I'm Captain Terry Erwin, and this is Lieutenant Christopher Gates. We're special agents with the Iowa Division of Criminal Investigation. I'm based at DCI headquarters in Des Moines, and Lt. Gates comes from our field office in Cedar Falls. I think you know why we're here. If you don't, I'll quickly fill you in about why we've been summoned to Oelwein."

"Please do, Captain Erwin. Tell me why you are here," Conrad said respectfully. "But there's no need to be quick about it; you can take your time. I'm not going anywhere," he added. "Since you're from the Division of Criminal Investigation, shall I presume you are here to investigate a crime? Has a crime been committed?"

The young lieutenant, standing to the left and a little behind his superior, let off a short snort. "Unfortunately, it appears that way," he said, stepping forward. "This morning we examined the mutilated body of a dead man whose remains were found yesterday out in the middle of nowhere. Only one other person was in the victim's vicinity at the time of his death, an archer who hunts deer using arrows identical to the one found in the victim's right thigh. We suspect that arrowhead pierced the femoral artery, which could easily have been the victim's cause of death, though we're still waiting for confirmation from the coroner's report. The victim's body was also severely disfigured; multiple lacerations, gouges, and stabbings. Whoever attacked the victim was serious about his intentions."

The older officer raised his hand to stop his subordinate from saying more, but the ambitious lieutenant continued.

"To tell you the truth, I don't know why the Fayette County Sheriff's Department bothered calling us in on this one. Everything appears to be neat and clean. I suppose it's because the victim is a local celebrity, one of Dan Gable's prized recruits down in Iowa City, and they want to be sure this case gets investigated correctly. This kid's death is going to make major headlines across the Midwest, or at least throughout the Big Ten region."

Conrad didn't make eye contact with the younger detective. Instead, he listened in private thought and glared at a spot on the wall above the captain's head. He considered the information the lieutenant offered and compared it with what Tim Ross had told him earlier that day.

The lieutenant continued his monologue. "Mr. Doyle, the arrow found in the body belongs to your grandson. It is an exact match to those found in his possession near the scene of the incident. Our initial investigation indicates that your grandson and the victim had a longstanding rivalry. In fact, the two had nearly come to blows on the same day just hours before the victim's estimated time of death. Two eyewitness accounts can corroborate this. So, you can see where this is going." With a pompous flair, the lieutenant flipped back his sport jacket and left it bunched behind a nine-millimeter pistol he wore holstered on his belt. Then, with his hands on his hips, he began pacing the floor at the foot of the bed.

Seeing the blatant act of showmanship, Conrad could barely restrain himself. Trying to remain cool, he directed his eyes toward the captain. "Listen, Captain, who is in charge here? Is it you, or have you decided to sit this one out?" he said. Glancing toward the lieutenant, he said, "And you, son, put that little peashooter back in your pants. I've seen bigger guns in carnival games."

"Mr. Doyle, I'm well aware of your reputation—" the captain started before Conrad interrupted.

"You mean my deer hunting expertise? You're damn right, and my grandson is on his way to earning his place in the world of bowhunting, too."

The lieutenant jumped in, "No, he was referring to your stint as a soldier. We know you are a decorated veteran. So, for your information, we are a lot alike. I served in an infantry unit during the Gulf War three years ago," Gates stated proudly.

"What the hell is this imbecile talking about?" Conrad fired at the captain. He returned his attention to the lieutenant. "Son, do you mean to tell me that because you were part of that beach party in Iraq you think you and I share some sort of brotherhood? Let me tell you something. Whatever combat you think you saw during your tour in Iraq, even at its worst, couldn't match one day of the hell I saw in the Battle of the Bulge. Like I said, junior, put that little peashooter back in your pants."

Captain Erwin, a Vietnam War veteran himself, turned his head to hide his grin, while Gates maintained a condescending, yet dumbfounded look on his face.

"Oh, I get it, pops. You think the war you fought is the only one that matters; the biggest one, where only the bravest soldiers got killed and the most innocent people suffered. Is that it? And you probably think people back in your generation were better than us folks nowadays, too. Am I right?"

"By golly, son, you finally said something intelligent. There's hope for you after all. As for fighting in any war, a dead soldier is a dead soldier, brave or not. It doesn't really matter what he was fighting for, does it? And yes, it's true innocent people suffer in every war. That's the greatest tragedy of all. As for my generation, of course people from my time were a hell of a lot more decent than folks nowadays. You're *goddamn* right they were! But they weren't perfect either, that's also true. You know what folks in my generation weren't great at? Raising kids, that's what. I do know this; most of my buddies who died in Belgium would be rolling in their graves if they could see what their offspring have done to this country. And the way I envision things, it's only going to get worse as time passes. But that means job security for you, doesn't it? So why don't you go about trying to catch some criminals and leave me and my grandson alone."

Captain Erwin had purposely allowed the conversation to

THE LONG WAY AROUND

continue in order to gauge the character of the man he wanted to question. It was irrelevant that he agreed with nearly everything Conrad had said. What he was trying to learn was how forthcoming the elder would be with information concerning his grandson, how protective he was of the youth, and how mentally stable he was considering the extent of his stress and deteriorating physical condition. Conrad looked at him with surprise when he finally took control of the conversation.

"Mr. Doyle, are you Ryan Meyers' legal guardian?" he asked.

"No," Conrad answered, which prompted the captain's eyebrows to rise. "I was until his eighteenth birthday. The lad is nineteen now. He still resides at my house, however, and he's welcome there until the end of my days and long after."

"Mr. Doyle, as you likely already know, your grandson suffered a very serious injury out in the woods, the result of falling from a tree. Sometime during his descent, he took a helluva blow to his head. We've been informed by the staff physician on duty that his condition was pretty touch-and-go upon his arrival at the hospital. On initial inspection, they weren't sure if he was going to make it. A neurosurgeon was called in for an on-site operation even though this facility is barely equipped for such procedures. The treating doctor didn't feel he could survive the transfer to a better equipped hospital and proceeded to operate here. Are you aware of what I've told you so far?"

"Yes, Captain. I've been informed of this, but I'm waiting to hear the latest update on his condition," Conrad answered.

"As are we, Mr. Doyle. I do know that your grandson's head injury was accompanied with a broken collarbone. Other than those injuries, he checks out okay, which is a miracle if you consider the tremendous plunge he took. It is the fractured skull and resulting hematoma that are the chief threat at this point. After a long surgery, the neurosurgeon put him in a medically induced coma, and he is now under constant observation," the captain added. "He's scheduled to return tomorrow for a follow-up exam and evaluation."

Conrad spoke up. "He'll be fine. Ryan's a strong kid. He's got a soft heart but a hard head, thank God. And thank you for the update, Captain. But my nurse could have told me this, so why did you come to see me? How can I help you gentlemen?"

"As my colleague alluded to earlier, there are some unusual circumstances related to the death of Brian Garner, too many questions that remain unanswered."

"Maybe that's because they are unanswerable," Conrad rebutted.

Gates jumped in. "Mr. Doyle, we realize there are a lot of gray areas in life, but we operate in a world of black and white. We need some hard answers about what really happened at that gruesome scene in the forest. In the best-case scenario, your grandson was a witness to what happened, even if he wasn't an accomplice or the main perpetrator."

"I haven't heard either one of you yet use the phrase 'crime scene.' I believe that's because you're doubtful that an actual crime has been committed, so you've chosen to tiptoe around the subject."

"We have some working theories, nothing specific," the captain said. "What your grandson tells us during our interview will determine the direction in which our investigation will lead. We'll be speaking with him as soon as the doctors think it's prudent to reduce the sedatives to bring him out of his coma. We hope it can happen as soon as tomorrow morning. That is, of course, if the attending physician grants us his permission."

"Nobody will be talking to my grandson without legal representation present in the room. Understand? I want my lawyer, Andrew Gleason, in attendance during your questioning. I repeat, neither of you are talking to my grandson without Andrew Gleason present," Conrad fired.

"Relax, Mr. Doyle," Gates said. "This will be just an informal conversation to help us understand the circumstances surrounding the victim's death. We believe your grandson is the only living eyewitness, therefore it is vital we hear what he has to say."

The afternoon shift nurse walked in to check on Conrad's bandages.

"There'll be no pressure put on your grandson to answer our questions whatsoever," the lieutenant continued. "He'll have as much time as he needs."

Conrad lifted himself forward. "Kylie," he said to the young nurse, whose father he had known for years. "Get the Dunn, Dunn, and Gleason Law Office in Waterloo on the phone for me. Ask for Andrew Gleason. Tell him you're calling on my behalf, and that it's an emergency."

"Yes, Mr. Doyle," she said, and left promptly.

"I repeat, officers, nobody will talk to my grandson without legal counsel present. I want no room left for misinterpretation or false depiction of the answers he gives to the questions you ask. He's been through a lot already, and now is not the time for an in-depth interrogation without supervision," Conrad said.

"That's fine, Mr. Doyle," Erwin said. "Your lawyer is welcome to sit in on the conversation. Believe me, all we want is to get to the bottom of this as efficiently as possible. If you could have seen the victim's mutilated body, you'd understand our concern better. Nobody deserves to die like that."

Gates cleared his throat. "Mr. Doyle, does your grandson ever have rage issues?"

Conrad almost broke a grin. "Listen, sonny, you're barking up the wrong tree. My grandson didn't attack, or kill, that Garner kid. I know this because I know Ryan better than anyone in this world. He just doesn't have a killer instinct, you see. I've been telling him that for years. Look, as good a wrestler as the dead kid was, he was nothing compared to my grandson, and if my grandson wasn't such a goodhearted kid, he'd have been unbeatable on the wrestling mat. There is no way on God's green earth Ryan purposely put an arrow in that Garner boy," he said fervently, though weaker than intended. "Tell me, were my grandson's boot prints found anywhere in the area of that Garner kid?"

"The evidence processing team is doing their job as we speak," replied the captain. "Impression evidence is one factor they'll be looking at."

"I doubt they'll find any prints that didn't belong to the dead kid, unless Tim Ross trampled up the place," said Conrad. He coughed some excess phlegm that had clogged his throat. "Detective, was there any of the victim's blood found on or near my grandson?" he asked, then coughed some more.

"Mr. Doyle," the lieutenant said, "there is already plenty of evidence to pursue an investigation. Did you forget we found your grandson's arrow sticking out of the victim's thigh? With or without boot prints, he could have easily killed that young man from a distance."

"And what about those other multiple wounds the victim suffered? How did he get those? Maybe those were the cause of death. Maybe that arrow found its way into the victim because my grandson was trying to protect that Garner lad."

"But from whom?" asked the captain.

"Or from what?" answered Conrad. "Your team will have to figure that one out. The truth is, Captain, you haven't a clue as to what happened out in that slough. That's why you haven't referred to the scene as a crime scene."

"Like I said," the captain continued, "we'll know more after we talk with your grandson."

"Captain Erwin, how long have you been an investigator for the DCI?" Conrad asked.

"A long time—twenty-two years, I guess."

"And I bet you think you've heard and seen it all by now. Am I right?"

"Yes, I've seen some unbelievable scenarios. Why?"

"Well, hold on to your hat, Special Agent. I have a feeling what you are going to hear from my grandson will knock your socks off. I've been out in these woods for nearly sixty-five years, and I still can't put the pieces of this puzzle together in my head. I have a hunch that whatever happened to that Garner boy isn't the garden variety case you usually experience," Conrad said.

Erwin didn't answer verbally, but rather, he cocked an eyebrow and lightly nodded his head.

Impatiently, Gates said, "Thanks for the heads-up, Mr. Doyle. We'll take that under advisement."

Before they left, Conrad said, "Captain, whatever report Ryan gives you after he wakes, no matter how impossible it may sound, know this: my grandson is not a liar. Take his account at face value. He'll be telling you the truth."

"Thank you for your time, Mr. Doyle. Good day," the captain said.

THE LONG WAY AROUND
* * * * *

Fifteen minutes passed before another knock sounded on Conrad's hospital room door. Surprised by the increased traffic, he called out in a shaky voice for the visitor to enter. As he did, he realized the news story had broken, and that unwanted intrusions were going to happen more frequently in the future. As much as he hated interruptions, he now realized he would have to expect more of them. What he didn't anticipate was the worn and worried expression on the face of Dieter Metzger. He was clearly in shock as a result of the media blitz that had been thrust upon him. It was the kind of news frenzy that can tear a younger, more vibrant man to shreds in short order. For an older recipient, the psychological trauma of the unrelenting pressure can be lethal.

Dieter shuffled toward Conrad's bed. "Conrad, you…you promised me," he stammered. "You assured me I'd receive no grief from my decision to allow your grandson to hunt the slough. What the Sam Hill did you get me into, anyway? My God, there were helicopters circling my property when I left home to come here!"

"I can imagine there were, Sarge, and I'm sorry as hell about it, too," Conrad said. "I had no idea an event like this would occur. How could I? I need you to understand how sorry I am about this happening. Did the police interview you yet?"

"Twice…yesterday. And I'm supposed to be available over the next few days for further questioning."

"What kind of questions did they ask? Anything that sounded unusual?"

"Just normal stuff, like if I was the property owner, how long I've held the deed to the land, how often I venture into the slough. Toward the end of the second interview, though, the DCI detective did ask me two questions that seemed odd."

"What questions?"

"The first was if I ever discovered any livestock mutilated and left to rot in the fields. Well, I've never raised any hogs or beef cattle, and since I quit dairy farming almost thirty years ago, I really couldn't say." Dieter calmed down some and began to sift through his memories. "Oh, Good Lord," he said to himself. "Nah!"

"What is it?" Conrad asked.

"Well, nothing really," Dieter said. "Just some old wives' tale."

There was enough uncertainty in his voice for Conrad to push the matter further. "Tell me, Sarge. It could be important. My grandson's future is hanging in the balance."

"I can remember overhearing my grandfather telling my father a livestock mutilation story when I was a boy. But that was a story my grandfather had heard from his father when he was just a boy, many, many years ago."

"Yet it was enough to keep people out of the slough all this time, wasn't it?" Conrad said.

Dieter didn't answer for a while. "To tell the truth, I don't know why my ancestors were so dead set on keeping folks out. As a youngster, I'd simply been taught that was the family policy, and I was determined to follow it for the rest of my life. I'd completely forgotten about my grandfather's story until just now."

"What else did the detectives want to know?" Conrad asked.

"There was another question that was even more curious. It was if I'd ever seen any powerful lights or hovering aircraft in the vicinity of my farm over the last several years. I thought that was a darn strange question," Dieter said.

"Well…have you?"

"No. Never. Not even once."

"That's what I thought you'd say."

"Do you suppose they're curious about poachers?" Dieter asked.

"I don't have a clue. Like everybody else, we'll have to wait to hear what Ryan has to say about all of this. I expect his story to be a whopper. I hope he has the strength to handle the consequences of his version of the facts. And if his story is anything like I imagine it might be, well…God help us all."

Dieter leaned forward. "That bad, huh?"

"Yes, it'll be that bad," Conrad said.

* * * * *

The Metzger Family Farm
Rural Elgin, Iowa

THE LONG WAY AROUND

Monday, September 29, 1930, 1:30 p.m.

Ordinarily, the old man wouldn't have been able to see the boys playing at that distance because his view would have been obstructed by a towering mound of husked corn in the wagon under his charge. However, he'd just emptied the last load into the wooden crib near the barn and returned the cart to where the rest of the family was waiting in the field. It was lunchtime, and they were taking a break from collecting the ears by hand.

"Shouldn't dem young'uns be in school today?" Otto Metzger growled to all within earshot. He didn't like the direction the children were running. He'd told them dozens of times to steer clear of the slough.

"No school these days, Pa. You know that," Gerhard Metzger told his father as he heaved an armful of ears into the wagon. "All the older children are needed in the fields during harvest. Folks need all the help they can get."

"Well, dem boys aren't helping one bit. Just running wild," Otto rebuked.

"Too much trouble bringing only the youngsters to school," his son replied.

Along the tree line, the two lads were following Lady, the family's German shepherd, which was sprinting ahead. When the dog bound into the forest, Otto began to fret. Reflexively, he lifted his right hand to whistle, but stopped midway after realizing he'd have to use his other hand. The right one was missing its thumb and index finger as a result of a mishap with some farm machinery a decade earlier. Otto's anxieties jumped when he lost sight of the boys. He inserted his left thumb and forefinger into his mouth and wedged them snugly between his lips. At full force, he blew outward and sent a piercing screech over the pale, dry stalks. The family patriarch had taught himself to whistle as a child and had perfected the technique using minimal effort. The blast was so potent it caused the others to cower and cover their ears. The old man was conscious of its power and used his whistle only during moments of urgency. Everybody was aware of the fact, so when the boys failed to respond to his call, he began to panic.

"Out of da way everybody! I need to turn dis wagon around," he shouted. "Gerhard," he alerted his son, the father of one of the missing boys, "climb aboard. We're going after dem."

Just then, the boys emerged from behind some overgrown brush and began trotting through the brown stalks toward the adults. One of the pair, the larger and slightly older one, had a big head covered with thick, blonde hair. His name was Dieter, and he was Gerhard's only child. The other boy's name was Karl Jaeger, son of the Metzger family's closest neighbor to the north.

As the boys approached the wagon, Otto jumped down from his perch. Gerhard called out to him. "Now, Pa, take it easy. They're just boys."

Otto turned to his son. "Gerhard," he snapped, "you still don't know da gravity of da situation. If you did, you'd be a helluva lot more concerned." The old man faced the first graders and stood with his hands on hips. The boys sensed they were in big trouble, yet they were unsure why.

Otto stared directly at Dieter. "Young man, I'm certain I've told you and everyone else in dis family to steer clear of dat slough. Isn't dat so?" he scolded.

"Yes, sir," the boy answered. He avoided looking into his grandfather's eyes. Karl looked at the ground.

"And yet, here I see da two of yuz emerging from dem woods before my very eyes. Dat slough is full of danger, I tell you! When I was a boy, I saw tings dat happened in dat slough which still make me shudder. So, I'll remind you once more: you stay far away from dem woods! Next time you forget, I'm going for da strap, and I'll perform a whipping you'll never forget. Dat goes for you, too, young Mr. Jaeger. Do yuz both get da message dis time?"

"Yes, sir," they agreed in a hurry. Then Dieter spoke up. "But, Grandpa, we were just playing with Lady. We weren't planning to go into the woods until she did."

Just then, Otto realized the dog hadn't returned with the boys. He stepped away and whistled. Lady always responded to his commands at once. This time, she didn't answer. Otto pierced his lips and blew hard again. The screech was deafening. A short time later, a faint yelp sounded from deep in the forest. Soon another

THE LONG WAY AROUND

bark sounded, much louder than the first. Gradually, Lady's barking increased, until she could be seen at the timberline, bent forward and tugging at something with all her might. The rest of the family gathered to look.

Little by little, the German shepherd dragged her found prize toward the group. From that range, nobody could identify what was in her mouth, but it looked heavy, awkward, and something quite unnatural for a dog to be retrieving from the woods. In time, it took the form of a giant clump of weeds or the root ball of a small tree. Stranger yet, the object had a bright red tint that glistened in the sunlight. As Lady brought her booty nearer, Gerhard identified the mysterious trophy with disbelief.

"What in tarnation?" he mumbled. "Deer antlers?"

The others gasped when they saw the majority of the deer's head remained attached to the antlers. The family collected around Lady as she licked at the blood dripping from the severed spine. All of the buck's fur had been stripped away, and the remaining flesh on the skull was completely exposed. Chunks of muscle and fatty tissue were hanging by threads, and both eyes had been ripped from their sockets. Surprisingly, the deer's black nose was mostly intact, and no stench emitted from the meat.

"Goodness gracious," Gerhard said. "The blood's still fresh. That deer couldn't have been killed more than a few hours ago."

After a little more inspection, Otto said, "Leave Lady to enjoy her prize. Everybody back to work. Time is wasting and dere's still plenty of corn to be husked. Clouds are moving in from the west so dere'll be no harvesting by moonlight tonight."

Several hours later, long after the women had walked home to prepare supper, the men quit husking corn as darkness set in. Gerhard sent the older companions home on foot, then he and Otto loaded the boys into the back of the wagon and covered them with blankets. The children were exhausted, and each fell asleep against the hardened, shifting ears.

"What shall we do about Lady?" Gerhard asked his father. Otto had noticed how Lady hadn't budged from the deer skull all evening.

"Leave her be," the old-timer said. "Let her enjoy da marrow.

She'll come home eventually."

Gerhard snapped the leather lines and the horse moved forward over the choppy field. The men sat in silence, but something was brewing inside both of their heads. Gerhard knew his father wasn't going to bring up the topic he wanted to discuss, so he spoke first.

"What did you see in the slough so many years ago that gets you so riled, Pa?" he asked his father.

The men hadn't noticed Dieter stirring in back. He was no longer asleep and was inadvertently eavesdropping on their conversation.

Otto knew Gerhard would be asking about the statement he'd made earlier that day. It was a subject he'd never discussed in detail with his son before because he'd never deemed it necessary. After inheriting the land in his youth, Otto had decided to make the slough off-limits to everyone, including his own family. In his mind, he didn't need to explain the reason why, and that was the final word on the matter. Now, he was cornered, so he decided to tell his son the truth.

"I can't really say dat I witnessed anyting myself," he told his son. "I was no older dan dem young'uns behind us, but I still remember tings clearly. It was my fadder, your grandfadder, who saw da results of what had taken place earlier. He didn't see da events play out firsthand, mind you. Your grandfadder was da original Metzger to emigrate from Germany. He was already quite old when he got here. He'd hunted all his life in da Rhineland, and I remember him telling how he'd never saw nudding like what he saw in da slough dat day.

"What did he see?" Gerhard asked.

"Well, da original homestead was near the spot our house is now. At da time, it wasn't much more dan a log cabin, really. Dis must've been in the late 1860s, I reckon. I remember dere was a barn big enough for some livestock and a big chicken coup built alongside it. It was sometime in autumn, after da crops had been harvested but before da snow had begun to fall. My fadder let out our two heifers and da bull to graze da pasture near da slough dat day, but darkness came early dat evening. Since da skies were clear, he decided to leave da livestock out for da night and planned to collect

THE LONG WAY AROUND

dem in da morning like he'd done many times previously. Only da next day, when he went to fetch dem cows after breakfast, he found a terrible mess instead. Apparently, da two heifers had followed da bull into da tall grass on da edge of da slough for da night. When my fadder finally found dem, only da bull was still alive. Da two heifers had been slaughtered and scattered throughout da weeds. A few bits of bone, some skin, and lots of blood was all dat was left of dem. Whatever it was dat attacked dem tried for da bull, too, but it must have met its match. Dat bull must've put up a helluva fight. It was maimed and gouged and barely able to walk, but my fadder managed to lead it back to the barn, where it collapsed in da hay. For four straight days, dat bull moaned and wailed as infection took hold. On the fifth day, it was obvious it wasn't going to survive so I watched as my fadder shot it in da head wid his rifle."

"What do you suppose killed those animals, Pa?" asked Gerhard.

"I dunno. We never investigated. We'd never seen or heard any signs of grizzly bears back den. I don't think dey ever existed in dese parts anyways. I doubt a black bear, or a mountain lion could make such a mess on its own. And I don't tink just one of dem critters would try to take down a full-grown bull singlehandedly, much less devour both dem heifers overnight. Could have been a pack of wolves, but we'd never had problems wid dose neider."

Otto leaned forward and rested his elbows on his lap where the cotton of his denim overalls had worn thin. "After dat experience, my fadder forbade anyone from entering dat slough. When he died and left me da land, I was still a teen, and I've kept his policy intact ever since," he explained. Otto elbowed his son in the side. "And if I'm unfortunate enough to die in my sleep tonight, Gerhard, it'd be wise for you to keep your family and everyone else out of dat slough, too."

Gerhard nodded his head in agreement and goaded the horse forward with a brisk snap of the line.

Dieter now understood his grandfather's angry reaction much better. He decided right then he'd never enter the slough again, and the matter dropped from his mind.

Chapter Sixteen
Another Missed Opportunity

The Kelleher House
Arlington, Iowa
Sunday, October 24, 1993, 5:30 p.m.

Don and Maureen Kelleher had celebrated their twenty-third wedding anniversary just two months earlier. It was on the Saturday before their youngest of two children, their only daughter, Mary, moved to Cedar Falls to begin her undergraduate studies at the University of Northern Iowa. It was an exciting time in their lives. With their son having graduated the previous spring from the same university and the financial burden for Mary's anticipated four-year program secured, Don had approached his wife early in September about the possibility of upgrading their house for the homestretch of their lives together. The house they lived in now, a small, three bedroom and one bathroom bungalow they'd purchased the year they were married, had served its purpose dutifully, but because the property had no garage, after many years of cleaning snow and ice from his car in winter's early morning darkness, Don was ready to upgrade to a more suitable accommodation. With interest rates low and the local real estate market in a slump, it was an ideal time to buy, and many other factors, most of them financial, were enticing the couple to make a move.

Don's job at the John Deere plant in Waterloo was on firm footing. The farm implement industry was projected to rebound over the next few years, and his foreman had told him he could work as many overtime hours as he desired for the foreseeable future. Though he'd put in an incredible amount of overtime in order to save for his daughter's college expenses, he had started working early in life, and at only forty-five years old, Don felt he could continue putting in long days for another ten years to pay off the mortgage before retiring. Maureen's job as a bank teller was safe, and the future looked bright for the entire Kelleher family.

Once their son, Daniel, was able to find a job and start his career, Don's plan for the family's future would be well established. Danny would be working before long, Don knew, because he was extremely bright, though he was spoiled and lazy enough to not be in any rush to enter the nine-to-five world. 'A smart slacker,' his father often referred to him to his friends. He always followed the comment with, 'But a good kid with a lot of potential.'

Don and Maureen's daughter was a totally different story. Ambitious and goal-driven since she could crawl, Mary had become the apple of her father's eye the instant she was born. In Don's view, Mary could do no wrong, and out of her deep respect for her father, Mary was sure to never allow her father's image of her to be tarnished. Mary had always known exactly what she wanted from life, and Don wanted Mary to have the best in the world, or at least the best he could afford to give her. He vowed to work as much as necessary for his daughter to have the opportunity to achieve the success in life she desired.

Mary and her brother Danny were also close, but the four and a half year age difference between the two created an obvious distance in the relationship. The two shared little in common, rarely discussed their personal lives, and their relationship consisted mostly of the older brother teasing his younger sister, which Mary handled with style. In fact, the petty bickering between the two was so common it was often comical, certainly innocuous. It's how the two communicated best with one another.

The parents knew their daughter had set her sights on leaving the small farming community where they lived, and though the thought of her absence would bother them, they never told her so, and prayed she would change her mind after having been away from home at university. When Mary had fallen in love with Ryan Meyers during her high school senior year, Don and Maureen couldn't have been happier, as Ryan was not only an intelligent and well-mannered young man, he handled himself brilliantly in the limelight, and impressed everyone with how much he'd achieved on his own after dealing with the difficult circumstances life had presented him.

More important to Mary's parents, it seemed as though Ryan had no desire to leave the area, and her parents hoped he would keep their daughter close to them. Mary's family soon accepted Ryan as one of their own, and Don and Maureen believed the couple to be a match made in heaven.

It was about five-thirty in the evening when a small, blue Ford Festiva rolled to a stop on the street in front of the Kelleher bungalow. After switching off the ignition, Mary looked at the only home in which she'd ever lived and immediately felt a sense of relief. She knew her problems were serious, but she felt better dealing with them on familiar turf. After all, this was the place where she had confronted every challenge in her entire life until now, and she'd performed remarkably well with every trial she'd encountered. But the troubles facing her now far exceeded any of those in the past, and she couldn't see how the home field advantage was going to make much difference this time.

There was still about an hour of daylight left when she opened the door and stepped from the car. As she walked up the driveway where her dad's new pickup truck was parked, a sinking feeling almost overpowered her. Full of anxiety, she considered returning to the car and racing away. Suddenly, a gentle force seemed to take hold of her and guide her forward. Mary continued despite her uneasiness.

Sunday evenings had always been reserved for family dinners. Other days of the week were just too hectic and unreliable; as Don's erratic work schedule often conflicted with his wife's, leaving Sunday as the single day where the whole family could be counted on to share a meal. That time slot, however, had suffered over the last five years when Daniel left for college. It didn't take long before the family tradition waned. The discrepancy continued after Mary left for college at the end of August. Though she had called occasionally over the last two months, Mary hadn't visited once since early September. This surprised her parents, though not enough to raise concern.

The day before, when her parents had heard the news of Ryan's accident and the facts surrounding his injuries, they'd called Mary's dormitory several times throughout the day and missed her each time. After Maureen managed to reach Mary's best friend, Dori, she was relieved after learning Mary planned to come home soon. That was the last update they had received, until the front door opened and their daughter entered and hugged them both.

"Hey, kiddo!" Don bellowed. "How's my little girl holding up? Where the heck have you been? We've been dying to hear how you've managed to singlehandedly elevate the reputation of the University of Northern Iowa to a whole new level."

Mary smiled as her father squeezed her; she could feel his love pour into her, but her smile quickly faded. Then Maureen hugged her daughter and told her the latest she'd heard concerning Ryan, how he was recovering wonderfully, and how he was going to be fine. This seemed to please Mary on the surface but didn't lift her spirits for long. Maureen pretended not to notice and quickly changed the subject.

"Dinner is almost ready. You came at a perfect time. Roast beef, mashed potatoes and gravy, fresh homemade rolls, and apple pie for dessert. You can thank Dori for that. When she told me you'd be coming today, I suspected she was going to lend you her car so you could visit Ryan. I made the pie just for you. The roast was Danny's idea. Are you planning to spend the night, sweetie? I'll go fix your room if you are."

"No, I don't think so, Mom. I have an exam on Tuesday to study for," she fibbed. "I stopped to see Ryan already. Janet Epping was working and managed to sneak me past the deputy on guard duty. There was nobody around for me to ask about his condition. Mom, is he really going to be okay?" The relief in Mary's voice was genuine, and the news appeared to snap her out of her doldrums.

"It's still very serious, honey," her father said. "But news travels fast around here, and the last report we heard was very encouraging." Not wanting his daughter to get emotionally distraught, he added, "You better go wash up. Danny is already at the dinner table, and if we wait much longer there won't be any food left for us."

Don, Maureen, and Daniel were seated around the table in the spots they'd been sitting at almost every Sunday for the last eighteen years. When Mary came near, her brother jumped from his chair and hugged her. "Glad you're home, sis," he said. "Sorry to hear about Ryan. He's going to be okay, you'll see."

"I know he will be," Mary said. "God, I hope so."

What Daniel said next surprised the family, Mary most of all. "So, what gives? When I hugged you, you felt a little plump around the middle. Don't you know girls are supposed to wait until the end of the year to put on their freshman fifteen pounds? You need to take it easy in the cafeteria buffet line," he teased.

After an uncomfortable silence, Don shot a nasty look toward his son. Maureen spoke gently. "Daniel, no more teasing. Your sister's been through a lot in the last forty-eight hours. Let's just have a nice, quiet dinner together this evening, all right?"

Mary's mind raced through the possible consequences of Danny's statement. Though she hadn't weighed herself in several days, the last time she did, she hadn't put on any significant weight. She doubted there was any visible change in her appearance, though she couldn't dismiss the possibility since she hadn't seen her family for over two months.

"I was just kidding, Mary. You know everybody has been telling their versions of the stories circulating about what Ryan's grandpa is saying about the large nurses at the hospital. I just don't want you to get put on his list of those he verbally assaults each day," her brother said.

"Listen, Danny," Mary warned. "Conrad Doyle would never be mean to me no matter how bad of a mood he happened to be in. We've become good pals over the last year. Just out of curiosity, though, what have you heard?"

"Get this…," her brother started, passing her the potatoes. "About a month ago, some people I know were visiting one of their relatives recovering in the same wing as Ryan's grandpa. Well, nurse Tammy Lane went into his room on her routine rounds to give him his medication. Conrad was watching something on television he considered important and didn't want to be disturbed. Before long, my sources said, all hell broke loose. The next thing they knew, Tammy was stomping down the hallway toward the head nurse's station, red-faced and with tears flowing down her cheeks. The entire time, she was yelling, 'I will not deal with that man anymore! I will not deal with him anymore!' Other patients could hear Conrad shouting out from inside his room, 'And stay out, you big sow!'"

Though Don and Maureen were able to hold their amusement in check, Daniel couldn't and had to finish the story by alternating his normal speaking with uncontrollable outbursts of laughter.

"I guess there was a big meeting among the hospital administration concerning Conrad's welcome at the facility. A hospital official went to talk to him. Conrad had to apologize to Tammy Lane and promise to stop harassing the nursing staff or he was going to be moved to a private long-term care center. Well, once you check into one of those places you usually don't check out, and Conrad wants nothing to do with that. Even so, the latest gossip is that he continues to pester at will. He even watches the noon agricultural report each day so when Tammy Lane stops in on her rounds he can tell her how much pork bellies are trading for on the Chicago Mercantile Exchange!"

With that, Don could no longer restrain himself and laughed into his napkin. Maureen shook her head. "That Conrad Doyle is the devil himself."

Knowing Conrad Doyle better than any of the others, Mary appreciated the humor in Danny's story, too, but the anxiety she was feeling from her own problems dominated her emotions so completely that she didn't join in the jovial atmosphere. Her mind wandered relentlessly. She had every intention of telling her parents of her dilemma that evening but wanted to wait until the moment was right. *After dinner, I'll help wash the dishes and sit with my parents after things have settled down. When the mood has changed*, she thought, *I will tell them everything.*

When dinner ended and the table had been cleared, Maureen went into the kitchen while Don relaxed with his children at the table. He was extremely proud of them, Daniel for having been the first Kelleher family member to have received a university degree, and Mary for her beauty, charm, and above all else, the achievements she had accomplished until now, and for those which were still to come. Not wanting to dampen the positive energy, Don resisted bringing Ryan's tragedy back into the conversation. Instead, he waited for Maureen to return so he could make a surprise announcement. Before long, his wife returned to the table with clean dishes, silverware, and the apple pie.

"Now that I finally have the whole family together, your mother and I have some big news to share with you," he said. Hardly able to contain himself, Don glanced at Maureen, who nodded approvingly for him to continue. "Things appear to be going terrific for the Kelleher family," he crowed. "Daniel has finally received his degree, it's just a matter of time before he finds a job and moves out of the house, and the expenses for your four years of university are locked in tight, Mary. Based on this, your mother and I have made a major decision to improve our standard of living while there's still plenty of time for us to enjoy the fruit of our labor."

"Is this some sort of a midlife crisis you're both going through?" Danny asked. "What kind of upgrade are you talking about? Are you getting a motor home, or a pair of his and her Harley-Davidsons?"

He, and even Mary, began to laugh.

"No, not a motor home, son. It's better than that. More like a different house that will become our new home," Don answered.

"Seriously?" Daniel asked. "I mean, you've chosen now as the time to get a bigger house, after we've practically left the nest?"

"It will only be slightly larger. Too much bigger and it would require more upkeep," he said. "And I don't have time for that. It will be an improvement, though—a four-bedroom ranch with two full bathrooms on four acres with a two-car garage and matching machine shed. And before you ask, hotshot, the property does *not* have a pool," Don told his son. "Because if it did, you'd probably never find a job and leave."

Danny rolled his eyes but offered no rebuttal.

"You mean you've already decided this?" Mary asked. "Are you sure it's what you want?"

"Honey, it's already official," Don said. "We signed the papers and closed the deal two weeks ago. We plan to move next month. This house goes on the market as soon as we get settled."

"But why didn't you tell us?" Mary asked.

"Well, we were going to, but you weren't around to discuss the matter. An opportunity knocked and we opened the door, just like I've been trying to teach you both to do for the past two decades,"

THE LONG WAY AROUND

her father said.

"That's true, sis," Danny said. "'You snooze, you lose.' He says it all the time."

"Don't worry, Mary. You're going to love it. It's only seventeen miles from here, just northwest of Volga. The house has a gorgeous view of the Volga River valley, and the property line slopes right down to the riverbank. It was owned by the Gerard Casey estate. He was a very successful businessman back in the day," Don boasted. "He owned a grain elevator business in Edgewood, and a real estate company in Elkader during the sixties and seventies. He personally chose the location for that house and designed it himself," their father said, getting more animated as he spoke. "I've had my eye on the property for years, and when I heard it was on the market, Maureen and I jumped at the chance to buy it!"

Don's excitement was now unstoppable and spilled over onto Maureen. Daniel stood up and high-fived his father. Mary feigned happiness, while realizing that her personal problems would remain hers alone to cope with until another day. But time was quickly running out.

Mary excused herself under the pretense of returning to her dormitory in Cedar Falls to study. Darkness had set in over an hour ago, and she didn't want to drive if it got much later.

The family walked her to the curbside and waved goodbye as she sped away. As Don, Maureen, and Daniel walked back to the house, Daniel asked his parents if they'd noticed anything unusual about Mary's behavior. Don, the first to defend his daughter under any circumstances, concluded that with the transition to her new life on her own at university and the stress created by Ryan's accident, a mild depression could be expected. The parents agreed to check on her more frequently until Ryan recovered, and Daniel's inquiry was satisfied.

As Mary drove, she thought about her situation, saddened by the fact she couldn't enjoy her parents' good fortune and the family celebration like she would have under normal circumstances. So many changes had occurred in the last few weeks, and she wasn't sure if she could manage all the factors affecting her life.

Chapter Seventeen
The Heat Is On

Critical Care Unit
Mercy Hospital
Oelwein, IA
Monday, October 25, 1993, 9:40 a.m.

Dr. Brian O'Malley, the neurosurgeon in charge of Ryan's care, arrived at Mercy Hospital earlier than expected because of a sudden change in scheduling. Aware of the significance of his patient's condition in Oelwein, and of the fact there were two officers from the Iowa Division of Criminal Investigation waiting to interview the young man after he regained consciousness, O'Malley headed there directly, expecting extra scrutiny of his medical opinion and prognosis to be forthcoming.

High profile cases such as this were exactly the type many of his colleagues craved, because they were the kind that might get their names mentioned in the newspapers or their faces on television, but O'Malley's ego wasn't in line with those of his peers. In fact, he dreaded cases that attracted additional attention and avoided them whenever possible. Not because of any self-doubt about his abilities to treat head trauma injuries–those were his specialty—but because of demands created by outside sources, which often attempted to pressure him into hurrying his decision-making process, irrespective of the patient's injury and expected recovery time. O'Malley knew that rushed analysis often led to poor judgment, and this ultimately jeopardized patient care.

Despite these additional stresses, he took comfort in knowing that since he had been designated as the treating physician in this case, he had complete authority and the final say on all things related to Ryan Meyers's treatment and recovery. Therefore, all decisions associated with the patient's care, whether they suited

THE LONG WAY AROUND

the investigators' timetable or not, were for him alone to make and nothing could be altered or overruled by any official without a court order. This often clashed with law enforcement officers and other legal entities whose priorities lay in gaining access to the patient's testimony as quickly as possible.

Upon arriving at the hospital, O'Malley was surprised by the lack of attention the case was drawing, especially in the aftermath of the heavy media coverage it had received over the last thirty-six hours. The parking lot appeared to be no fuller now than what he remembered seeing on previous visits, and the reception area was empty and looked unchanged. As he strolled down the hall toward the critical care wing, he saw the county deputy on guard duty, and a bit further along, two plainclothes officers at the nurses' station, whom he assumed were waiting to speak with him.

Before coming into sight, he ducked into the medical staff lounge and quizzed some of the hospital's full-time staff about the latest gossip. He wanted to hear their reports firsthand to prepare himself for what he would be facing before meeting with the two DCI officers. As he talked shop with his colleagues, he changed into his white coat and fixed his tie, prepared his notes and charts, and then headed toward the critical care nursing station, intent on examining his patient.

When the two DCI agents saw the unfamiliar face in the white coat approaching their position, they assumed it was Meyers' treating physician and jumped to attention. Before O'Malley could consult with the head nurse, Lt. Gates moved between them and extended his right hand.

"Excuse me, are you Dr. O'Malley?" asked the investigator.

O'Malley remained relaxed and poised, realizing he had no reason to create friction with the DCI agent. "I am," he conceded. "And to whom am I speaking?"

From the right of the lieutenant, Captain Erwin stepped forward and extended his hand. "We're special agents from the Iowa Division of Criminal Investigation. I'm Captain Terry Erwin from DCI headquarters in Des Moines, and this is Lieutenant Christopher Gates from our Cedar Falls field office. Dr. O'Malley, the young man you operated on two days ago was found near the scene of a gruesome attack that resulted in the death of someone the patient knew. We were requested by the local authorities to investigate the scene and determine exactly what happened in those woods. It is critical for us to question your patient before too much time elapses. In our line of work, time is an extremely valuable commodity. As the treating physician, it's your call when the patient can be brought out of his induced coma so we can question him. We'd like to know when that process will begin."

"I fully understand your situation, Captain," O'Malley answered. "So, let me explain my position so there are no misunderstandings. Yes, the young man in question was operated on for a hematoma as a result of head trauma. He was also treated by a local orthopedic surgeon for a fractured clavicle, which is a minor injury considering the height from which he fell. But his brain trauma is the potentially life-threatening injury, which makes me the treating physician. I am fully responsible for his care, so what I say is what goes. The young man is a strong kid in the prime of his life. Compared to other patients I've treated with similar injuries, I believe he stands a better chance than most for a full recovery, but that will only happen under the strictest protocol for such cases. When my patient is ready, I'll make sure you gentlemen are the first to know, and you'll be able to interview him as much as the law allows. Until then, you'll have to do the best you can by using other resources at your disposal."

Gates turned to the captain and cocked an eyebrow, then looked back to the doctor. "That's the problem. There are very few other leads to investigate. In fact, our only hope of learning exactly what happened in those woods rests somewhere in your patient's mind. Until we can talk with him, we may never learn for sure what happened to the victim."

"Doctor O'Malley," Captain Erwin said, "after suffering such a head injury like the one Meyers has received, what are the odds his memory will be compromised? Will he remember what happened?"

O'Malley considered the question. It was a good question, a fair one, and one he hadn't considered in depth until it was raised. "Unfortunately, the main hematoma occurred near the juncture of the brain's parietal and temporal lobes," he said. "The medial temporal lobe is particularly relevant in the processing of memory, and chance for substantial memory loss may be quite high with an injury to that area."

Gates, unsatisfied with the ramifications of the doctor's answer, demanded clarification. "So, where does this put us in regard to our investigation, for finding out what we need to know from the patient?"

"Lieutenant, I cannot unequivocally state that Ryan Meyers will have recall of the events that played out that morning," he answered. "My main concern now is to stabilize my patient's vital signs, get him breathing without mechanical assistance, and reduce the drug regimen that is keeping him unconscious. After he wakes, we can evaluate his mental state and memory function. In the best-case scenario, he'll be able to recall everything and tell you exactly what you need to know within hours of waking up. But I warn you, it may take longer than you expect, more time than either of you will care to wait. For now, let me concentrate on getting the patient stabilized. When I feel the time is right, I'll let you know. I'm going to examine him right now."

Reaching into his shirt pocket, he pulled a business card showing his telephone and pager numbers and exchanged his for one belonging to Captain Erwin. "If you don't hear from me in the next twenty-four hours, feel free to check back with me the day after tomorrow. Thanks for understanding." With that, O'Malley turned his back and entered Ryan's room.

*****

Conrad Doyle appeared to be resting peacefully when the door to his suite opened. In reality, he wasn't at ease at all, at least not internally. Since the DCI agents had visited him the day before, his mind had been churning and what was left of his once robust nerves, which had served him so valiantly during the most stressful moments of his younger years, had been reduced to a state of stubborn fragility. He detested not being able to stop worrying, and even went so far as to scold himself for behaving like an old woman. Because he had not learned any new information about his grandson's condition in the last twenty-four hours, his nerves continued working overtime as his imagination anticipated the worst.

Conrad knew very well to fear brain injuries after having witnessed firsthand the lasting results of many GIs who had received similar injuries during the war. Some of those soldiers had been reduced to vegetables, mere living shells of what they were before entering combat. Conrad could clearly recollect how many of them had returned stateside unable to speak, and how others would never again be able to function on their own. Some of the soldiers who were hit in the head eventually regained full use of their bodies but changed in personality and were later unable to cope with their altered psyche. Many of those became suicidal. Because of those frightful memories, he had become a nervous wreck, yet he was aware that all the worrying in the world could not change the outcome of his grandson's fate.

Adding to his stress was the fact that his own health had deteriorated so quickly over the past few weeks. His strength had diminished so much he could now barely reposition himself without a nurse's assistance, and the use of a wheelchair was necessary for him to move through the hospital halls. All this left him feeling powerless to aid in Ryan's recovery, and at this time of his life, helping his grandson was the only reason he had left for living. He repeated over and over to anyone who would listen that if the doctors diagnosed Ryan with any permanent, debilitating physical or mental damage, he would die within a week, and he meant what he said. He simply couldn't bear the thought of losing his grandson in any way, shape, or form while knowing the potential Ryan had inside yet to develop.

When the door to his room swung open, Dieter Metzger's familiar face entered to greet him. Before Conrad could open his mouth to ask Dieter about the media onslaught he was enduring, Dieter waved him off.

"Hold your horses a minute. I brought you something." He set two recent issues of the *Iowa Fish and Game* magazine on the nightstand. Reaching into his pocket, he removed a small box and put it on top of the magazines. "I thought you should have these."

Conrad reached for it and raised its lid. Inside, a decorated, oversized wooden rosary was on top.

THE LONG WAY AROUND

"It was my mother's," Dieter said. "She swore it got her through the toughest times in her life, and I'm hoping it will help you even more." Then Conrad removed a small medallion that dangled from a chain made of white gold. "I want you to have one of the nurses hang this around Ryan's neck," he said. "That's Saint John Licci on front. He's the patron saint of head injuries. There's something else in there for you, too."

Conrad scraped at the box's bottom with his fingernails and pulled out a small prayer card. He looked at the print on front and studied it a while. The picture showed a man with a long beard holding a staff. Around his head was a lighted circle, which Conrad understood to represent a halo of holiness.

Dieter said, "That's Saint Benedict. Do you know what he's the patron saint of?" Conrad had never been religious and answered in the negative. "He's the patron saint of kidney ailments. There's a real nice prayer on the card's flipside. Don't be shy, Conrad, put him to work."

"Thank you, Sarge, I may just do that," he said as he began putting the things back into the box. "I'm afraid my time's about up, regardless of Saint Benedict's work ethic. Concerning Ryan's recovery, however, Saint Licci will be getting an earful from me."

Pulling a chair next to his friend, Dieter said, "I want to apologize for the tantrum I threw the last time I was here. I was out of line, still in shock from all the questions the reporters were bombarding me with at the time. I didn't give your grandson's condition enough attention, and that's the reason I'm here right now. My problems with the media will simmer down soon, I suppose. I'll survive against those evils for sure. But now I want to know more about your grandson's struggle."

Conrad lifted his free hand and Dieter took hold of it. They sat quietly and stared into space. Neither man could have imagined how so much stress would hit them at this late stage of their lives.

"I don't have much to tell you, Sarge, and it's killing me. I only know Ryan banged his head hard after falling out of a tree and was knocked out cold for a while. His best friend, Tim Ross, came to see me yesterday to fill me in on the details he knew. He isn't the brightest star in the sky, but he's a good kid. He was the one who found Ryan in the slough. He practically carried him to the truck, and then raced him here. On the way to town, he said Ryan was alert but had a helluva headache, some dizziness, and was puking off and on. That certainly sounds like a concussion to me, and you know as well as anyone what havoc a head trauma can cause."

The old friends were surprised when the door opened again. This time, a doctor Conrad had never seen before entered his room. Conrad was certain he was not one of the kidney specialists who checked on him regularly. The doctor picked up the chart at the foot of the bed and began flipping through the notes.

"Are you Mr. Conrad Doyle?" the doctor asked.

"In the flesh," Conrad answered. "I don't think I've seen you before, Doc, and I suspect you aren't here on my behalf. So how can I help you?" Conrad had a fretful tone, as if he were expecting bad news.

"You are very perceptive," the doctor said. "I am not here to examine or treat you. I'm here on a courtesy call. I want to inform you about your grandson, Ryan. My name is Dr. Brian O'Malley. I'm a neurosurgeon from Cedar Falls. I'm Ryan's treating physician, the one who performed a craniotomy on him two days ago."

The news stunned Conrad. He had no idea his grandson's injury was so severe it required having his skull opened. Reflexively, he squeezed Dieter's hand as firmly as his feeble strength permitted. "Give it to me straight, Doc. Is the lad going to live?"

"First things first, Mr. Doyle. Let me explain the situation so you have a better understanding of where your grandson is in the recovery process. I'll assume you are aware Ryan fell from a tree. Somewhere on the way down, he hit his head about an inch above the right ear and fractured his skull. That's a pretty delicate area of the brain in which to sustain an injury. However, it isn't the area responsible for keeping a person's vital organs functioning. If he had received the same fracture just an inch or two further down and a little behind, then it'd be unlikely your grandson would still be alive. But he *is* still alive, and for that we can all be thankful."

"What's the diagnosis, Doc?" Conrad asked. He liked the doctor and had already placed his trust in his ability to save his grandson.

"Your grandson suffered an epidural hematoma near the

parietal-temporal junction of the brain. As a direct result of the trauma, the middle meningeal artery tore and began to hemorrhage. Gradually, blood accumulated between his skull and the brain's top layer, the dura mater. Little by little, the resulting clot began putting pressure on his brain. If it wasn't drained to release the pressure, he surely would have died after only a few more hours," the doctor said. O'Malley turned his head and put his index figure on the area where Ryan's skull had been cracked. "This is a very complex area of the brain. It's responsible for many functions, memory being one of the most notable. But your grandson was lucky. If the hematoma had occurred here," he said, relocating his finger to the back of the head, "his vital organs would have quickly seized, and he'd already be lying in the morgue."

Dieter removed his glasses and subconsciously began scratching the scar on the side of his head with his fingertips, which O'Malley picked up on at once. "I see my explanation has some extra relevance for you, sir," he said.

Conrad spoke up and introduced his friend. "This is Dieter Metzger. He's the owner of the property where my grandson was found."

"I see," the doctor said, reaching his hand out to shake Dieter's. "It's nice to meet you, Mr. Metzger. I can see the scar on your head doesn't go all the way around, so I will assume your cranium has never been opened. Yet something serious happened. What's the history behind that scar?" As he asked, O'Malley moved over to Dieter and peered more closely at the old wound. Then he palpated the crease with his fingertips once before stepping back.

"Oh, that's just an old war injury. I hardly remember it's there," Dieter said sheepishly. "The wound was superficial—a chunk of my scalp was ripped away."

"Mr. Metzger, were there any lasting side effects as a result of your head injury?"

"None I'm aware of, Doc. I was hit by some shrapnel from a shell fired from a Panzer," Dieter stated with equal amounts of modesty and pride. "Lucky for me, my helmet absorbed the brunt of the impact."

"Good Lord!" said the doctor. "So, I'm talking to a bona fide war hero?"

"I don't think the term war hero is really accurate, Doc," Dieter said. "War survivor seems more appropriate. I never thought of myself as any sort of a hero. Hell, I was just glad to get home in one piece with nothing more than this scratch on my noggin."

After a short pause, O'Malley redirected the conversation. "Mr. Doyle, you asked me earlier if Ryan is going to live. The most honest answer I can offer you at this point is to tell you I cannot be sure. These are complicated cases, and the corrective procedure for injuries such as these carries significant risks. However, surgical intervention was the only option, and the standard medical protocol was followed."

"Okay then, off the record. What are his chances?" Conrad queried.

"My gut feeling is that he's going to recover. My preliminary follow-up exam, which I just performed, was encouraging. He is responding favorably on all levels. His vital signs have stabilized, and he appears almost ready to begin breathing without mechanical assistance."

"Well, when will that be?" Conrad asked.

O'Malley took a moment to think through his answer. "Mr. Doyle, there are some external pressures building for me to bring your grandson out of his coma as soon as possible. However, I won't allow my treatment plan to be influenced by outsiders. If Ryan's vital signs continue improving as I expect, I can begin reducing the sedatives keeping him comatose as soon as tomorrow. It could take a while for him to regain consciousness, though. When he does, I will reassess the situation. Before that time, I cannot accurately gauge the extent of his disabilities, if indeed any exist at all. It would be purely speculation to do so, which could leave room for all sorts of misinterpretation. I simply won't do it," O'Malley said.

"Come on, Doc. I asked you to give it to me straight," Conrad fired back as strongly as he could. "What are the odds my grandson could survive such a fall, crack his skull, have it opened and closed, and not suffer any permanent disabilities? I want to know if it's even possible my grandson will be the same as I remember when all this is done."

THE LONG WAY AROUND

"Mr. Doyle, you're asking me to answer an unanswerable question, at least for the time being. Epidural hematomas are tricky devils. An injury that affects one patient in a definitive manner doesn't always replicate in another. A lot of complicated factors are in play at this stage. I don't mean to alarm you, but some patients never come out of their coma. Other times, they regain consciousness but present with unexpected physical impairments that require long-term rehabilitation and physical therapy. Aside from the worst-case scenarios, less dire, but more common side effects can include personality changes, mood swings, and depression. You grandson may not seem the same as you remember, but even that may be temporary. To some extent, I'm sure Ryan will suffer some post-concussion syndrome—dizziness, headache, and fatigue. That sort of thing. I will go as far to say this: of all the head trauma patients I've treated, those who recovered the best were strong, younger adults like your grandson. Nevertheless, while I cannot make any guarantees, I truly believe your grandson has an excellent chance of recovering based on how he has responded until now. We found the hematoma in good time, the operation went smoothly, and he's a strong kid."

"You're *goddamn* right he is," Conrad said, squeezing Dieter's hand as tightly as he could.

"I will be checking on Ryan's status regularly with the nursing staff tomorrow via telephone. Barring any emergencies, I'll return in two days. Ryan will undergo a new MRI and I'll examine him again after that. If all goes well, I'll likely begin reducing the morphine drip and weaning him off the Midazolam, both of which can be quite addictive. After that, it might be a matter of hours, or days, before he regains consciousness. With some luck, he may be able to communicate soon after. Then I'll know much more. I promise to stop by and fill you in on what I find right afterward."

"Please do that, Dr. O'Malley," Dieter said. "Conrad, I'll be back at the same time in two days. We can wait together for the doctor's visit. Is it a deal?"

"Absolutely," Conrad said.

After the neurosurgeon left, Dieter stayed with Conrad a little longer and the men talked more about the tragedy surrounding

Ryan's accident. Conrad wanted to hear the latest news reports and learn more about the most recent investigative findings. Dieter kept repeating that as far as he knew, the DCI had found nothing connecting Ryan to the dead collegiate wrestler except for his arrow. The latest opinion from the county coroner, as Dieter had heard, was leaning more to the theory that the wrestler was already dead before the arrow had reached him, leaving mass uncertainty about the official cause of death. But that was only a rumor. With the investigation at a standstill, most of the regional news teams were being reassigned to other stories until fresh developments surfaced. The two-day media circus was already on the decline, but nobody could know for how long. Both men now fully realized the pressure Dr. O'Malley was under to bring Ryan out of his coma. Speaking to Ryan was the only way the authorities were going to move forward with their investigation, because Ryan was only one who knew the answer to the mystery.

When Dieter had told all there was to tell, he excused himself and promised to return in forty-eight hours. He was just as curious as Conrad to hear the doctor's report and wanted to be there to support his old friend.

After Dieter left, Conrad lay in bed and stared at the ceiling thinking over the situation, feeling sorry for himself about his failing health, and worrying incessantly about his grandson's fate.

Chapter Eighteen
Conrad Pays a Visit

Critical Care Unit
Mercy Hospital
Oelwein, IA
Tuesday, October 27, 1993, 8:00 a.m.

The gentle swishing coming from the breathing tube was accompanied by a faint hum created by the mechanical ventilator to which it was attached. Conrad, in his pajamas, sat in his wheelchair beside Ryan's bed, marveling at how the contraption worked. He hadn't slept much the night before, and as soon as he finished breakfast, he'd asked to be taken to see his grandson. He'd been pushed there by the morning shift nurse, the one he liked best, and then left alone by his request. Before she left, he had politely asked the nurse to place the Saint John Licci necklace around his grandson's neck.

On initial inspection, he was taken aback by Ryan's appearance. After all, just a few days ago, the young man had come to visit him and looked to be in the prime of his life. Now, the same youth looked broken and pale. Conrad likened his image to that of a malnourished ghost. He tried to convince himself it was only temporary, that before long his grandson would return to his old self, mentally and physically. It had to turn out that way, he thought, there was no other alternative. Soon the old man's frustration turned into anger, partly because of his own helplessness in the situation, but mostly because of the uncertain future Ryan was facing. Mixed emotions attacked Conrad from every angle.

It disturbed him how much his grandson had already battled in his short life, and yet it pleased him how he had always bounced back from adversity with the spirit of a champion. To meet the boy was a pleasure, he'd often been told by friends and acquaintances over the years, and Conrad was never prouder than when he received a compliment concerning Ryan's character. It always impressed him how the positive traits his grandson possessed, which were also present within himself but mysteriously dormant, dominated his grandson's personality and were constantly on display. It seemed as if Ryan's personality was an extension of what Conrad felt inside, but for reasons he couldn't explain, his good nature surfaced outwardly only on random occasions. Now the young man was comatose, and his prized demeanor didn't count for anything.

Conrad found himself observing Ryan's face, curious if he had any awareness about what was happening around him. He wondered if there was a sliver of hope that his grandson felt his presence nearby. More than anything, he wanted Ryan to know he was there for him, just as he'd been there for him since he'd been orphaned as a teen.

The day Conrad took legal custody of Ryan was a day of enormous pride intertwined with great sorrow. The sadness resulted from the loss of Ryan's parents in such a short period of time. The pride came from Conrad's fundamental sense of duty to make certain his grandson's potential was fulfilled, regardless of the bad cards life had dealt him. Conrad knew, of course, that Ryan's future would depend on his ability to overcome the challenges that inevitably arise in life, and he toiled tirelessly to coach the boy how to conquer those obstacles. Crisis management, self-discipline and control, reliability, and awareness of others were just some of Ryan's internal qualities Conrad had worked hard to extract. He was determined to provide the boy with all the tools at his disposal to aid in his success.

Ironically, just as the particular phase of Ryan's life had arrived for which Conrad had been patiently waiting, the point in time when Ryan would begin making his own critical decisions based on his capabilities to react like a man and not as a boy, tragedy struck. His grandson was so close to having his expectations fulfilled, and now this unanticipated turn of events had wreaked havoc on everything for which they'd worked so hard. Just as the moment of truth neared, that fateful time when Conrad was preparing to rest peacefully in eternity, his entire plan had been turned upside down. Once again,

THE LONG WAY AROUND

Ryan's future was in jeopardy, and Conrad knew it was too late for him to start his teaching process over again. The thought made him squirm in his wheelchair. Bitter, almost irrational, thoughts filled his head, which only caused his anxieties to grow.

Good Lord, Conrad stewed internally. If the boy doesn't come out of his coma soon, all will be lost. And if he does wake up and is mentally impaired, which result would be worse? Conrad squirmed some more, then tried to put a positive spin on the situation. He's young, healthy, and strong, and Dr. O'Malley seemed as genuinely confidant as he could allow. Maybe the best-case scenario will prove out. Sure. Why the hell not?

Suddenly, his positive perspective turned negative again when he remembered a statement Dr. O'Malley had made: "This is a very complex area of the brain. It's responsible for many functions, memory being one of the most notable."

That sent Conrad into another mental tailspin. What if Ryan awakes as mentally sharp as ever, but his memory is shot? What if he cannot remember any of the most valuable lessons of life I've taught him? What if he can't remember where my assets are hidden, and I die before I can tell him? Conrad slumped down in his wheelchair, depressed and distraught. How on earth could this have happened?

In time, his nerves settled, and his anxieties diminished. His thoughts drifted to past events, and a flashback of his life-or-death sprint across the open field during World War II resurfaced in intense detail. He could feel the weight of Dieter's body bearing down on him as he hurried to carry him to safety. The same combination of fear, desperation, and panic he had felt then paralleled the emotions which he was feeling now. On that dreadful day, he remembered saying the Lord's Prayer aloud as he trudged, and how his progress steadily improved as he shouted it out between gasps of air. Conrad recalled how, as he progressed, his strength and stamina increased and his will to survive took command of his body. But that glorious memory had disappeared into his subconscious when the Mauser bullet struck him down and had never again resurfaced until now.

Conrad sat a bit longer and thought in silence. After a while, he removed the rosary Dieter had given him from his bathrobe pocket.

Unsure how to proceed, he held the chain, and then repeated the Lord's Prayer, the only one he'd committed to memory, at every bead until each one in the loop had been touched. Gradually, Conrad relaxed, his spirit lifted, and his torment faded. And though reservations about Ryan's situation lingered, a sense of serenity and confidence returned, and his mind was at ease.

* * * * *

Best Western Inn
Cedar Falls, IA
Friday, October 30, 1993, 7:30 a.m.

"So, after sleeping on it last night, were you able to draw any conclusions concerning my examination results?" asked Shane Medley, the polygraph specialist Captain Erwin had contacted to evaluate Ryan Meyers' preliminary statement. "Were the findings useful?"

Erwin scratched the back of his head and grimaced. The two men were drinking coffee from disposable cups in the Inn's breakfast room. The captain was scheduled to drive Medley back to Des Moines that morning. It was Erwin who had insisted his superiors pay extra for Medley to perform the procedure. The two had worked together several times in the past, and on every prior occasion, he had produced superb results. Erwin considered him to be the best in the business, and he felt the Meyers case was too complex to be assigned to an unproven stranger.

"Off the record, Shane," said Erwin, "I'm just as clueless now as to what happened in those woods as I was before your interview. Don't get me wrong, I agree with your data, and I have no doubt that Meyers is telling the truth about what he witnessed. That's the problem. With the head trauma he suffered, and the psychological ramifications the injury may have caused, a terribly vital question remains."

"Which is?"

"Is Meyers telling the actual truth about what he witnessed, or is he telling the truth he *believes* he witnessed? I doubt your equipment can differentiate between the two."

THE LONG WAY AROUND

"Your concerns are legitimate, and both points are well placed."

Erwin took a sip of coffee, then shook his head. "This story the young man told...It all seems so implausible. Paranormal, maybe even supernatural. Yet, based on your results, it cannot be dismissed as a lie. Nevertheless, it'd be nearly impossible to make a murder case stick against him, as I'm required to provide concrete, irrefutable proof to charge any potential suspect. The only evidence we have against Meyers is purely circumstantial. Any way you look at it, we have nothing!"

"There is one fact that is certain, Captain. Based on my analysis, I have no reason to suspect the young man is being untruthful, nor that he intentionally killed the victim. That's what is going into my official report."

The DCI agent tapped his fingernails nervously on his coffee cup's plastic lid. "Point taken and I concur. In fact, I believed his version of the facts as they were being told, even prior to reviewing your results."

"And why was that?"

"Call it professional intuition, a hunch, or whatever term best suits you. I prefer *gut instinct*. The young man's grandfather warned me he'd be telling the truth, and I believed him. The old guy is a straight shooter."

Medley grinned. "I'd probably be amazed by your gut's accuracy. Professional experience has to count for something."

The breakfast room door opened and DCI Special Agent Christopher Gates strutted toward the others. The young officer had a folded newspaper in his hand and a smile of satisfaction on his face. He poured himself a cup of coffee. "Top of the morning to you, gentlemen."

The captain and Medley glanced at one another, then Medley said, "Since we are in your hometown, shall we assume you're in such a good mood because you were able to sleep in your own bed last night?"

"No, sir. That would be an entirely incorrect assumption. The reason I am in such a good mood is because I believe I have solved the mystery surrounding the Garner killing," he answered. With that, the lieutenant plopped the newspaper on the table between the seated pair.

Erwin raised his eyebrows. "Well, what do we have here? Last evening's edition of the *Waterloo Courier*. Is there something specific you'd like me to review?"

"Page three, bottom half, on the right," answered the lieutenant.

Erwin flipped the front page, while Medley maneuvered around and leaned over the table to see. In the center of the page was a photo of a large black bear. Next to it was a headline which read:

Rural Postville resident spots stray bear meandering through Clayton County.

Medley leaned over Erwin's shoulder and the men began reading the accompanying article simultaneously. The story started with the journalist describing rare occurrences of transient black bears native to Minnesota and Wisconsin entering Iowa by happenstance, usually during mating season or before the winter hibernation period. A quote from a regional Iowa Department of Natural Resources agent stated it was an abnormally large, male black bear, which weighed around five hundred pounds. He added it had likely wandered beyond its normal range in search of high protein and high carbohydrate food sources it would use to get through its winter dormancy period. The agent added that black bears are usually not dangerous if left alone, and that there was no cause for alarm.

Sensing the men were finished reading, Gates perked up. "Did you notice the location? Postville. That's only a thirteen-mile drive from Elgin, and a fifteen-mile hike from Metzger's Slough. A mature black bear could easily cover that distance in a day or two, and this article was written six days after the attack."

Erwin stared into space, calculating logistics. Medley spoke first. "Was there any evidence at the scene indicating a black bear had been present?"

Self-assured, the lieutenant fired, "There was plenty of evidence, Mr. Medley. For starters, how about a slaughtered white-tailed buck sprawled next to a dead college wrestler?"

Erwin cut off his impatient subordinate. "Mr. Medley meant less obvious evidence, Lieutenant Gates, such as bear tracks or fur that can be analyzed to prove whether or not this particular bear was in the vicinity. If there were any droppings, we could test to see if it contained deer residuals and then proceed from there. I don't recall any of those remnants being found nearby."

"Look, the MO fits perfectly," said the lieutenant. "After reading the article, I did some research. Despite what the *Courier* journalist misreported; black bears do not hibernate. Rather, the term used for their winter sedation period is called torpor. In preparation for that, the beasts must gain an incredible amount of weight in the fall. They feast mostly on berries and nuts, but this time of year, they gorge on acorns—white acorns. The area where that Garner kid was killed is chock-full of them. You don't need Sherlock Holmes to deduce that the deer and the wrestler stumbled across a ravenous bear in the forest and got mauled as a result."

"Nonetheless, we're going to need physical evidence, something substantial to pursue," replied Erwin. "But I won't discount your theory at this point. Good work, Lieutenant, we have our first lead."

"Aw, come on, Captain. It's practically a slam dunk. At the very least, it's the only scenario that makes any sense. This just saved our butts. We had no other prospects before this. Just some wild story told by a nineteen-year-old recovering from brain surgery. And he even admitted that whatever killed Garner was transparent, as in *invisible*, meaning he didn't see what killed Garner. It must be the bear. It couldn't be anything else."

"If I'm not mistaken," Medley said, "we all just officially settled on one very important detail." The other men looked at him questioningly. "It seems we have a consensus that Ryan Meyers most likely did not murder Brian Garner."

The DCI detectives traded looks with one another. "Indeed, it does, Mr. Medley. Indeed, it does," said Erwin.

Chapter Nineteen
A Voice from The Past

Strawberry Point, IA
Thanksgiving Day
Thursday, November 25, 1993, 7:00 p.m.

Tim Ross had been lying on his parents' couch for most of the afternoon. His mother was a fantastic cook, and he had overeaten during the family's traditional Thanksgiving dinner. Groaning with discomfort, he reflected about why he did this to himself every year and never learned from past mistakes. The main reason for his idleness, however, was because two NFL games had aired on television that day and each had commanded his attention. The first game featured the Chicago Bears against the Detroit Lions. Tim loved watching pro football, and for him, nothing was more enjoyable than watching the Bears play. This game ended favorably for his favorite team, as they squeaked out a 10-6 victory. The Dallas Cowboys played the Miami Dolphins in the late game. That game ended excitedly too, with an extra dose of controversy surrounding its outcome. With the game's final moments marred in chaos, the announcers were thrown into a state of boisterous debate so loud that Tim didn't hear the telephone ringing in the kitchen. It took several tries by his mother to redirect his attention to answer the call.

"Hey, Timo! What's going on, buddy?" came a voice from the past.

"Rory? Is that you?" Tim replied. "Are you back in town?"

"No, pal, I'm still in Texas."

"I was just thinking about you while watching the Cowboys suffer an agonizing defeat," Tim said.

This caused Rory to laugh, as he'd correctly assumed his friend would be watching football all day. "Yeah, a friend of mine had the game on, too. I saw it all. What have you boys been up to? What's new back home? I tried calling Ryan a couple of days ago but got no answer. Is he in Cedar Falls with Mary these days?"

Realizing Rory was unaware of the calamities that had occurred in his hometown over the last five weeks, Tim cautiously steered the conversation in that direction. "Hey, Rory, you probably haven't heard the bad news about what happened here last month, huh?"

The response wasn't what Rory was expecting, and he froze in anticipation of a terrible report. An incredible sinking feeling overtook him as he sensed he was about to hear something awful that was going to affect him for the rest of his life. "No, I've been out of the loop. I haven't talked to anyone recently, not even my folks. What happened? Did Ryan and Mary break up?"

"Yes, they did, but that's just the tip of the iceberg. It's much worse than that," Tim said.

"Timo, what is it?" Rory asked as he melted onto the couch. At this point, he was prepared to hear something dreadful, a genuine tragedy, because he had learned over his lifetime that nothing newsworthy ever happens in small towns that isn't associated with tragedy.

Tim stretched the cord of the kitchen telephone as far down the hallway as it would reach and stepped into the food pantry for privacy. Then he described to Rory, to the fullest extent possible, the events of the last few months, leaving his friend shocked and bewildered.

With a knot in his stomach, Rory said, "I've got to talk to Ryan as soon as possible. Where can I reach him?"

"It won't do you any good. Ryan's awake and alert, but his recovery is dragging on. If you call him at the hospital, you won't be put through. Besides, he might not even know who you are. Maybe if you visited in person it would be better. I mean, he knows me most of the time," Tim said. "He's able to speak, and at times he seems like his old self. Then, the next thing you know, he drifts away, and you can't get him back. Sometimes, he seems agitated and says he doesn't want me coming around to visit him. From the look on his face, I'm certain he means it. The nurse told me this is common. She said his therapy is progressing, and she sees improvement daily.

Sometimes I'm not so sure."

"There's no way all of this could have happened in such a short time. We were all partying on the river just a few months ago!" Rory calmed down enough to think through the situation. "What about Mary? Does she know?"

"I think so. I mean, she must know. I don't know how she couldn't. But I'm not sure because I haven't talked to her since August. None of us have."

"Come on, Tim, tell me you're kidding. This has to be a joke."

"It's no joke, Rory. Life here has been turned upside down. You should come back and see for yourself. Man, I could sure use some help here putting all the pieces together. Are you coming home for Christmas?"

Rory didn't say anything for a few seconds. He already knew he wouldn't be returning and needed to come up with a credible explanation as to why he wouldn't. "Well, the football season is just winding down and I doubt we'll be allowed to travel for the holidays."

"Why not? North Texas is a Division I-AA football program, right? There's no bowl game in the picture, and you're not in the playoffs. Besides, I figured you were redshirted this year because we didn't hear any news about you. So why can't you come?"

Rory knew Tim was well informed on all things sports related, and that college football was one of his specialties. He needed to change the subject before his excuse was exposed as a lie. "You don't understand how things work, Tim. I don't make the rules, and I have to follow the program as if I was the starting tight end. No exceptions. Now, tell me more about Metzger's Slough and Brian Garner. I know Ryan had nothing to do with Garner's death. So, what do the authorities think happened?" Rory had big news to tell, too. But for now, it was still a secret. His update was the kind he wasn't proud of. Shame was the primary reason.

"No one knows for sure. Not the police and not even the Iowa DCI. So far, an official cause of death hasn't been announced. Rumors are circulating it was from a bear attack, yet Ryan was the only person at the scene.

"Ryan isn't a suspect, is he?"

THE LONG WAY AROUND

"Well, he was the only suspect for a while."

"What kind of stupidity is that?" Rory raged. "There's no way Ryan would do something like that!"

"You're exactly right, except for one thing," Tim replied. "One of his arrows was found sticking out of Brian Garner's leg. That arrow clipped an important artery and could have been the cause of death. That's why he's still a suspect."

Rory was quiet for a few seconds. "This is weird, Tim. Is Ryan even aware of what's going on?"

"I'm pretty sure he is. He has been interviewed several times by the DCI. They even hooked him up and performed a lie detector test. It was against his grandfather's wishes, but Ryan had a lawyer present, so he consented. He passed with flying colors."

"I knew he would. Ryan Meyers ain't no liar," Rory said with a newly acquired, Texas twang. "So when can I try to call? I'd sure love to talk to him."

"Now that I have your number, I'll call you," Tim said. "There's talk he may be released from the hospital soon. Once he gets settled at home, I'll let you know."

"Ah, Timo, I may be changing my telephone number, so don't call me. I'll call you again in a couple of weeks, okay?"

This time, it was Tim who stayed quiet for a few seconds. "Rory, is everything okay with you? I mean, you sound a little edgy."

"Oh, hell yeah!" Rory fired back. "I'm fine, buddy. Top shape. This awful news has me confused and upset, but I'll be fine. I'll keep in contact and get an update soon. You take care of Ryan, okay? Tell him you talked to me and that I'm pulling for him to recover quickly."

"I'll do that," Tim said. "And don't forget to call. Let me know what's going on with you, too."

After the call ended, Tim returned to the living room and television. *The Simpsons* were on, and he settled onto the couch to watch. His conversation with Rory had left him feeling troubled. He clearly sensed something wasn't right, but since Rory was in another part of the country, and because he had bigger problems concerning Ryan to deal with, he brushed the conversation aside and stretched out on the cushions under a quilt his grandmother had made for him years ago. Soon, Homer Simpson said something funny, which distracted his attention long enough for him to forget about his friend in Texas.

Chapter Twenty
Something Goes Awry in Texas

University of North Texas
Denton, TX
Thursday, August 19, 1993, 5:00 p.m.

The north Texas sky had been cloudless for days, allowing the hot August sun to bake the practice field's synthetic surface brick hard. After many seasons of exposure to the elements, the artificial turf was so faded and hardened that many patches felt like the team was practicing on concrete.

Head Coach Denny Paulson had ordered evening workouts to beat the one hundred-plus degree temperatures that had made afternoon scrimmages impossible. There were just two weeks left before his team was scheduled to travel to Lincoln, Nebraska, for the season opener against the University of Nebraska Cornhuskers, and the coaching staff had yet to finalize the status of several key positions in the starting lineups. One position under intense scrutiny was tight end. That slot had been vacated when Justin Webb, who had played the position so admirably for the past three seasons, graduated in June.

With Webb's absence, Coach Paulson had a major void on his offensive that needed to be filled. His scouts scoured the nation for the best tight end available, but most of the top prospects had already committed to Division I schools. Since the University of North Texas was a Division I-AA, the country's top-tier athletes would be difficult to sign. Yet Coach Paulson knew plenty of talented players were overlooked each year by the majors, and many of those lightly recruited athletes would be happy to play football for his team after visiting the University of North Texas campus. It was a recruiter's job to single out which of those talented, less sought-after prospects would fit best into his program, and it didn't take long for two strong candidates to emerge.

The first was a surprisingly nimble, powerful brute from a small town in northeast Iowa named Rory Meeks who had paid a visit to the university campus that spring. Meeks had instantly become Coach Paulson's top contender for a scholarship because he was the spitting image of Justin Webb. The second prospect, Odell Dupree, had arrived on the scene later. Dupree was from Tyler, Texas, a city east of Dallas and similar in size to Denton. Initially, Dupree had been heavily recruited by most of the major universities within the state, but the youth carried a lot of baggage, which caused the top teams to lose interest over time.

Most serious for the incoming freshman, Dupree's history of academic and personal problems had raised red flags. On the playing field, he had decent size, phenomenal speed, and great hands, everything the tight end position required for the program Offensive Coordinator Lee Leander wanted his offense to pursue. Off the field, the antics and poor decisions made by the eighteen-year-old chipped away at his football-playing value. He was regularly in trouble with the law, so much so that all the Division I universities eventually dropped him from their lists of recruits. But Leander loved what he saw in the young athlete and pushed hard for Paulson to reserve a place on the roster for him. As a result of his persistent pressure, and his promise of taking full responsibility for the new recruit's off-field behavior, Paulson relented and signed Dupree to the program.

From that point forward, Rory Meeks, the top prospect from Iowa, fell out of favor of the coaching staff, and his play on the practice field came under sharp criticism. But it was just days before the season opener that slanted the Iowan's relationship with the team, and his attitude toward the sport in general, in a direction which could never again be realigned.

* * * * *

University of North Texas
Denton, TX
Thursday, August 26, 1993, 7:00 p.m.

THE LONG WAY AROUND

The final summer practice started like all the others. Until then, two-a-day drills had been the normal routine, but over the last four days the relentless heat had reduced the schedule to one workout daily.

Battling for the starting tight end position had been distressing enough for Rory without the unexpected strain added by Coach Leander. To Rory, it seemed obvious the decision to instill Odell Dupree as the starting tight end had been made by the offensive coordinator during summer camp. No matter how well he performed, it was never good enough for Coach Leander, and regardless of how mediocre Dupree's play was during practice, extra praise was heaped on the recruit.

After having moved to Texas nearly a month and half ago, the eighteen-year-old was alone, vulnerable, and subject to the will of an assistant coach who hadn't promised him anything. To Rory, the writing was on the wall, as he realized only one freshman tight end would be allowed to play during their first season. The second would be redshirted so an extra year of eligibility could be squeezed out of the two high-caliber recruits. Rory hadn't moved to Texas so he could watch the games from the sidelines. All practice without playing time wasn't his idea of fun. If there wasn't any fun in the picture, there was no reason to attend school in Texas.

In the last days before the regular season was set to begin, Coach Leander announced the opening game's starting line-up at the end of practice. Before leaving the practice field, he stated in front of the entire team that Odell Dupree would be playing tight end and that Rory would be red-shirted, making him ineligible to play for another year. Upon hearing the news, Rory's heart pounded vehemently, more from disappointment than shock.

Rory walked alone to the locker room. Along the way, a couple of offensive linemen attempted to console him. A few even walked beside him and tried to comfort the freshman by telling him that everything would be okay, but Rory just waved them on. Some of the other players studied the Iowan's face, expecting to see frustration and anger. They were surprised when they saw neither. Rory felt fine. He realized an important decision was awaiting his attention, and the quicker the decision was made, the faster he could get on with his life. He decided to sleep on it and think things over in the morning after his head had cleared. Yet the issue kept burning in his subconscious, steering him in a direction he had been contemplating for weeks, and his heart was offering little resistance. Rory was determined to fight the feeling for another day, to delay drawing a premature conclusion that might jeopardize his entire future until every angle of his decision had been thoroughly considered.

By the time the last of his teammates had showered, changed, and exited the locker room, only the student equipment manager and Rory remained. Rory snatched a folding chair from the trainer's station and sat near his locker. There, he propped his feet on the wooden bench he normally used while changing. Still wearing his pants, a sweaty T-shirt, and socks, he stared at the University of North Texas Mean Green logo painted on the concrete wall opposite him. Over the white paint base, large letters in bright green read: NORTH TEXAS. Alongside the text, in matching green, was a huge ferocious-looking eagle swooping down with its wings extended and talons spread. The image reminded Rory of the logo he remembered seeing as a kid used by the Iowa Hawkeyes football program during the 1970s. As his mind drifted, he considered the difference between hawks and eagles and the similarities of the designs, then wondered if there was some hidden meaning to the coincidence. In the end, he figured it didn't really matter, and then thought some more about his problem.

Thirty minutes later, the training facility cleaning crew entered the locker room and found Rory alone, showered, and dressed from the waist down. He was slumped forward in the same chair with his elbows resting on his knees. A white towel was draped over his wet head. Even though he had promised himself to get a good night's sleep and not make a final decision until the next day, he continued contemplating his options. The circumstances facing him were not the sole result of his own doing, and his football-playing future was still in his control. Rory's mind kept repeating that it was his life, choice, and destiny in question, and he didn't need to satisfy anyone other than himself. That's the way he liked it.

Yet, he wished he had a trusted friend from back home with him to discuss the matter and help make such a difficult choice. He certainly couldn't talk about his predicament with his parents, as the choice he was about to make would break their hearts. In the end, he would have to decide alone and stand or fall by his decision. After all, he had chosen to move to Texas without anyone's guidance, and he alone would have to choose his future going forward. And then, as if an invisible presence had put the answer in his head, it came to him. The relief that accompanied his decision was exhilarating. Tomorrow, Rory would quit the University of North Texas Mean Green football team, vowing to never look back.

After some more thought, he figured he would stay in Texas for a while, find a job, and experience life outside of Iowa. He didn't have the guts to disappoint his family and friends, who had been so proud of him the year before. He planned to fade away and disappear into obscurity for a while until people back home no longer remembered his promising football career, and for that matter, his college education. He thought that Texas was far enough away that he could defer any inquiries indefinitely, making excuses and alibis unnecessary. After enough time, he figured, people would realize his football career had died a quiet death and stop asking about it. If worse came to worse, he could always claim some career-ending injury had forced him to quit the sport.

Then, one day, he would return to his hometown on his own terms, and no one would even remember his football past.

Chapter Twenty-One
A Final Gleam in Conrad's Eyes

Mercy Hospital
Oelwein, IA
Tuesday, December 07, 1993, 7:30 p.m.

Meals had become harder for Conrad to digest. In the mornings, his stomach could only tolerate oatmeal and egg whites, and on the rare occasions when his appetite resurfaced later in the day, he enjoyed soups and broths the hospital dietician prescribed the kitchen staff to prepare for him. Meat was no longer on offer, and he didn't miss it anyway. In fact, he had developed an aversion to eating anything from his former favorite food group, though he couldn't remember exactly how or when that had happened. Over the last few days, he'd reasoned that because he'd been reduced to consuming what was essentially baby food, it was a telltale sign that his life's end was drawing near.

Conrad's appearance was now more haggard than ever. His hair had grown to lengths which, over the last fifty years, would have been unimaginable, and his face exhibited a constant five-day stubble, the result of his skin being too sensitive to shave because of an obstinate irritation and itchiness. More menacingly, other end-stage kidney failure signs had developed, such as swelling in his hands and ankles, shortness of breath, and an unrelenting fatigue that had grown stronger each day over the past few weeks. Conrad knew it was just a matter of time before his kidney shut down completely, which left the hospital's mechanical filtering system in control of his fate. But differing from other patients in the similar stage of kidney failure, Conrad's mind was remarkably clear, and his grandson's recovery dominated his thoughts. He checked on Ryan as often as possible, regardless of the fact the young man's mood and attention span varied drastically from visit to visit.

THE LONG WAY AROUND

* * * * *

Ryan Meyers had awoken from his coma just over a month ago. His physical rehabilitation and mental acuity were progressing steadily, though not nearly fast enough for his grandfather's satisfaction. He was now able to sit, stand, and could almost walk the hospital halls without assistance. He also had been able to speak for several weeks, but the rate and clarity of his speech was inconsistent, and the quality of their conversations suffered greatly consequently. That's what bothered Conrad the most. He needed to be certain Ryan's life was returning to normal, that he was healing both physically and mentally, before his soul could succumb to nature's call and leave this world in peace. Regretfully, it appeared Ryan's recovery was going to take longer than Conrad's kidney could hold out. One thing working in his favor, though, was that Ryan's initial interviews with the law enforcement agents had gone well, leading Conrad to believe his grandson would not face any charges concerning Brian Garner's death.

Conrad was sitting alone in his room watching television when his favorite nurse opened the door and poked her head in to announce a visitor. The old man's eyes were glued to a news story that had broken earlier that day—a report of a mass killing on a commuter train on the Long Island Railroad in New York—and he barely turned his head to notice who dared to disturb him. When he saw that it was his grandson, he muted the television's volume.

* * * * *

"Well, howdy, young fella," my grandfather said to me in a weak voice. He looked frail, and even speaking had become a chore. His face was pale from anemia. "If I'd known you were coming, I'd have dressed for the occasion."

I didn't smile like I normally would have before my fall. In fact, over the last several weeks, I'd shown little emotion and displayed virtually no facial expression at all. Not because I didn't want to, but because I couldn't. I could feel my mind clearing with time, however, and my therapists were heartened by gains in my long-term memory. In contrast, my short-term memory was a lingering problem. It had been severely impaired, and improving it was my therapists' primary goal. Still, even with the progress I had made over the past couple of weeks, I could sense my grandpa study me suspiciously, as if he was skeptical that I was the same person he'd known before. The specialists had preached to him over and over to allow me the necessary recovery time, but Conrad Doyle was notoriously one of the world's most impatient people.

"What are you watching?" I asked.

"Nothing," he snapped as he clicked the television off with the remote control. "Just some more depressing garbage the world doesn't need. Some passenger went berserk on a commuter train and killed a bunch of innocent strangers on their way home from work. I tell you, Ryan, there are moments when I don't even care that my days are numbered. This is one of them. This great country is facing some serious problems that need to be addressed, and frankly, I don't see any changes on the menu. It's just steady as she goes until the whole shooting match goes up in smoke."

"That's not too optimistic, Gramps," I responded. I had heard him repeat this rant countless times since childhood. "It definitely wasn't the pep talk I was hoping to hear."

"I know, son. I'm sorry about that. I'm glad you're here, but you picked a bad moment to drop by. These kind of news events always put me in a sour mood," my grandfather said. I doubted ever hearing him apologize for anything in my entire life. "You know what?" he asked. "I've had a radical change in my personal philosophy over the past three months. Going forward, when your recovery is complete and you're out on your own, remember this; aside from your immediate family and a very few of your closest friends, make sure to care only about yourself in this world. That's the opposite of what I would have taught you a generation ago. Not anymore. Above all, pay attention to protect only yourself, your wife, and your children, if you should ever have any. You won't be able to count on the kindness of strangers like during the Great Depression, and the government can't be relied on to protect its citizens anymore either, not like in the good old days, anyway. Take notice that I didn't say *support* its citizens, so let me be clear about that," he said, pointing his swollen index finger at me. "Ryan, you just look out for number one going forward, and if you aren't sure who *numero uno* is, I'll clear up any confusion; it's you. Don't forget this advice, promise?"

"I'll remember, Grandpa," I answered. I was uncertain if I really would, but my response was convincing enough to permit my grandfather to change the subject.

"Do you feel up to reviewing other important matters we've discussed in the past?" he asked. "Maybe a little refresher course concerning your future?"

"Sure, if you keep it brief," I answered. The stoic expression on my face reflected my level of seriousness.

My grandfather's lips cracked a smile. "Sure, it'll be short. I don't have the stamina like I used to, either," he said with a grin. "I do need to revisit a few important topics we covered over the last year, however, just to be sure you have things under control after I'm gone."

He directed the conversation toward my financial future and refreshed my memory about my inheritance, what he intended to leave me, and where he had hidden the assets he did not want taxed by the government. Then we discussed my wrestling career and the prospects of it being revitalized going forward.

Sometime during the recap of my state title match, I spotted the rosary Dieter had given him resting on the nightstand. I reached for it, picked it up, and played with it a bit. "I remember this," I said. "I think it helped a lot."

"No, son. I don't think you've ever seen it. That would have been impossible. You see, since you came out of your coma, it hasn't left this room."

"I meant that I remember you having this when you visited me before I woke. I can remember you praying the same prayer over and over. The Lord's Prayer, right?"

My grandfather didn't answer. He was caught off guard by the revelation and was unsure of the appropriate response to give. "Well, I'll be damned," he said. "Is there more you were aware of while you were out?"

"I had a few visitors, none of whom I can remember, and lots of doctors and nurses. I don't remember much, but I absolutely remember you sitting with me."

A tear developed in his right eye, formed a bead, and rolled down his cheek. "Yes, son, I was there for you, just like I've always been, and just like I always will be. You can count on that."

"I know, Grandpa," I said without expression. I'm sure it appeared as if I had no emotions at all, or if I did, that I was unwilling to show them. It was like the expressive part of my personality no longer existed. "Although I don't feel like I know too much at the moment, Gramps, I'm certain you'll be there for me, just like always."

As I finished my sentence, I winced from a pain in my head that was growing stronger with each passing second. My hands jumped to cover my eyes, I leaned forward in spasm, and let out a prolonged howl–a cross between a muffled moan and an exaggerated whimper. It was loud enough to alarm my grandfather. I hadn't a clue what was happening, but the pain behind my eyes was so intense that it soon became unbearable. As it progressed, a flash in my mind's eye revealed a moment of terror from my memory—a brief clip of the mighty buck being mauled by the invisible creature. As it continued, my brain activity surged while the horror in the forest replayed in my head. Bent forward in agony, the vision continued as I remembered how frustrated I'd been not having my grandfather near me to consult as the deer was being slaughtered. Suddenly, the vision's subject matter changed and a rerun of my spiraling fall from the elm tree seized my consciousness. Then, just as quickly as it had begun, the vision disappeared, leaving me short of breath, dripping in a cold sweat, and clinging firmly to the wheelchair armrests.

"Are you okay, son?" my grandfather asked. "Shall I call the nurse?"

By the time my panic attack had ended, the awful scenes had vanished from my mind. After I'd caught my breath, the lingering feelings left me more confused than ever. *What had I done to deserve this? How many of these horrible flashbacks were still to come? When they did come, would they be more intense than what I'd just experienced? When would this insanity leave me?*

My grandpa understood immediately what had happened and tried to comfort me. He rallied the strength to say in a firm, but compassionate voice, "It's going to take some time for the cobwebs

THE LONG WAY AROUND

to clear, son. A traumatic experience like the one you suffered doesn't just disappear in a few days. Ryan, do you remember me telling you how I wasn't able to sleep so well after the war? Well, that situation continued for years. I wouldn't be surprised if you have to go through a similar healing process."

Still in shock, I remained stone-faced. Inside my head, anger had taken over, and the accompanying bitterness easily found its way into the darkest crevices of my mind. More than anything, I wanted to return to my old self and regain control of my previous life. Simultaneously, I felt what few emotions remained inside of me were rapidly slipping away. My shoulders began to tighten, and my hands squeezed the wheelchair siderails reflexively.

"Take it easy, son," my grandfather said, as if he knew exactly what was swirling around in my head. "Everything will work out fine in the end. It might take weeks or months, maybe even longer. You need to explain all of this to the doctors and therapists so they can get you back on track."

After my nerves had calmed, I decided I wanted to return to my room and sleep. I promised my grandpa I'd visit again in the morning to resume our conversation because, for reasons I couldn't explain, I'd never fully appreciated the significance of what we were discussing until the vision had reminded me how dependent I was on my grandfather. I would be alone soon, and it was now abundantly clear that relearning everything I needed to know to survive after his death should be my top priority. I suggested he put together a list of some trusted individuals I could consult if any emergencies arose in the event, God forbid, he died before I was ready to take care of myself.

"You bet I will," my grandpa said proudly. His face lit up like a grade school student who knew the correct answer to a question posed by the teacher. "That's what I was hoping you'd suggest. That's the first step, son. Your thinking process has just taken a giant step forward," he said with a beam. "I'll mull it over right now and dictate the names to my nurse the first thing tomorrow morning."

When the nurse came to take me away, my grandfather turned the television back on but left the volume muted. As I said goodnight,

DOUGLAS CAVANAUGH

I noticed the joyful mood he was in. It was as if the single reason he had to remain alive was to figure out how to continue helping me after he was gone.

Chapter Twenty-Two
How Quickly Life Changes

Rural Strawberry Point
Northeast Iowa
Thursday, January 06, 1994, 9:00 a.m.

My Grandpa Conrad died the day after Christmas. Thirty-six hours later, at ten o'clock on a frigid, Wednesday morning, a funeral Mass was held for him at St. Mary Catholic Church in Strawberry Point. He was buried in the church cemetery two hours later. The routine was quite familiar since I'd twice undergone the identical process for my parents' funerals a few years ago, except this time, my grandfather's casket was draped with an American flag as the parish pastor delivered the homily. Another difference occurred when a group of seven veterans from the VFW chapter in Manchester performed funeral honors for my grandpa's service in World War II at the conclusion of the ceremony. As the squad lifted their rifles, I saw Dieter Metzger move closer to the casket, stand at attention, and salute.

Though it should have been the saddest day of my life, I was apathetic during the whole event, and immediately after, as I walked prudently down the icy path to my truck with the folded flag under my arm, I wondered why so many visitors were weeping as the bugler played "Taps" after the honor guard finished firing the traditional, three-shot volley.

Most of the mourners left me alone after passing on their condolences, though several volunteered to drive me home in their warmed up cars. I didn't recognize all my grandfather's friends and distant family members who came to pay their last respects, even though I may have known most of them very well before my injury. Many faces simply didn't register in my brain. Tim Ross was at my side the entire time, and when the last of the guests had said goodbye, I declined his offer to have lunch at his parents' house. Against my doctor's wishes and my therapist's advice, I drove my old Chevy over the snow-packed roads to where I wanted to be most—at home and alone.

As I left the cemetery parking lot, I didn't notice the compact blue Ford parked behind a privacy hedge in the distance, nor did I see the two young ladies bundled in woolen winter coats walking arm-in-arm over the grit-laden sidewalk in the same direction.

* * * * *

Only one of the ladies had come to pay her last respects to Conrad Doyle, albeit from afar. She was the shorter of the two, and the one whose abdomen was disproportionately large in relation to her slender, athletic frame. Her companion, who had tagged along for moral support, was markedly taller and broader in shape than her friend. She had the kind of build that no young lady desires; the type that made her realize early in life she'd been betrayed by bad genetics. What she lacked in natural beauty, however, was generously compensated for by her intelligence, positive attitude, and pleasant disposition. Despite her physical shortcomings, the sturdier companion was a gifted, driven, and proud young lady. Dori was an excellent choice for a best friend, and Mary considered her as a sister.

As the two walked gingerly over the walkway's dubious surface, Dori noticed a change in her best friend's mood since she'd seen her just a few days ago. After having found one plausible excuse after another to avoid coming home over the last two months, Mary had managed to delay the inevitable until the point where further evasion would have caused massive suspicion by her parents. Missing the holidays at home would have been unprecedented and inexcusable, especially since her folks had worked overtime decorating their new home in time for the holiday season. So, just five days earlier, on Christmas Eve day, Dori drove to Cedar Falls, picked her up, and brought her home.

Mary hoped the excitement caused by her maiden visit to her parents' new place would divert their attention from her expanding waistline. She'd intended to break the news to them about her pregnancy after sensing the perfect time, but she knew she couldn't stall any longer; nature was set to give her secret away at any moment. If confronted about why she had not confided with them sooner, she would explain how the shock of Ryan's tragedy, combined with the surprise of the new house, had complicated matters and resulted in the postponement. It was the truth, though her personal shame, embarrassment, and bruised ego also played major roles in her decision to wait.

Mary managed to delay telling her parents until after Christmas morning Mass, though she almost panicked and blurted out the truth while gazing at the church Nativity Scene. There, a couple of elderly ladies whom Mary had not seen since the previous summer commented that she had appeared to have gained weight. That close call prompted her into spilling the beans earlier than planned, first with her mother while they prepared Christmas dinner, and then again with her father and brother during the feast. Once her secret was out, her family's reaction could not have been more receptive.

Her father jumped from the table and danced across the dining room on his way to hug his daughter, and then his wife. Even her brother, Daniel, bolted over and squeezed his sister tightly. When the last tears of joy had been shed, an intense family discussion about what to do next ensued. Mary was stunned by her parents' enthusiasm to the news. Her father was acting like a child who had asked Santa Claus for a grandchild only the night before. Her mother was equally excited and drilled Mary with questions about her health during her pregnancy's first trimester. As the conversation progressed and the history of their daughter's situation unraveled, her parents were amazed how maturely Mary handled her problems while still achieving perfect grades in her first semester.

Eventually, they focused on the unborn child's father, Ryan Meyers, and considered how he would react to becoming a father at this stage of his recovery. They debated the best time to tell him and discussed how they could keep the pregnancy secret until he would be better suited to find out. Don and Maureen doubted whether they could keep the matter under wraps in the rural community, yet they needed time to contact Ryan's therapists to discuss the situation professionally. Mary thought her parents' concerns were misplaced.

She thought Ryan would be ecstatic about the news and wanted to tell him immediately. Still, her parents cautioned her about the personality changes associated with traumatic head injuries and warned it would be better to avoid surprising Ryan with any major psychological stress.

After a period of consideration, Mary agreed, and the family planned to find Ryan's doctor and schedule a consultation. Then, with the guidance of trained professionals familiar with his case, Mary would meet with him and share the details. If all went accordingly, they estimated Ryan would learn about his fatherhood in the spring, sometime around Easter. In the meantime, Don and Maureen thought it was imperative to keep their daughter's pregnancy hidden.

Next, they began plotting a strategy for Mary's second semester of school. Mary would meet with her faculty counselor before the spring semester started to consider her options for the rest of the year. If necessary, she offered to take a break until the following fall, but there was an obvious look of reluctance on her face. More questions arose that required answering, and the family spent the next several hours gathered around the dining room table in deep discussion.

* * * * *

After the funeral, the days passed quickly, with each day blending into the next with few clues to differentiate the time. I stayed at home as much as possible, venturing out into the cold only to attend my therapy sessions in Oelwein. Tim called often with offers to visit, and he repeatedly tried to get me to go along with him to a local sports bar, but I wasn't interested in shooting pool or watching football, so he left me alone by my request.

The depression that had me in its grip was intensifying, and my former easygoing personality had undergone a radical reversal. As a result, the more my mood worsened, the less I wanted to be around people, and my self-imposed isolation pushed me further into the abyss. Against my will, I'd become trapped in a vicious cycle that was spiraling downward. I could see no relief on the horizon, so I avoided contact with everybody and sulked, hoping my situation

THE LONG WAY AROUND

would improve on its own over time.

Almost two weeks after my grandpa's funeral, after watching a *Late Show with David Letterman* rerun, I went to bed planning to get a good night's sleep, which I hoped would rejuvenate my exhausted spirit. In bed, my head resting on my favorite pillow, a familiar pain quickly developed behind my eyes. It was the pain that had first appeared in my grandfather's hospital room, only this time, it was broader and much more intense. New symptoms accompanied it, and soon, not only was my head raging in agony, an irrepressible dizziness was making the room spin wildly, and a tenacious throbbing began to pound in my ears.

Resisting panic, I managed to sit upright, and then methodically slid myself to the edge of the bed. Once there, I bent forward at the waist and waited. With my hands firmly pressed against my eyes, I pushed the palms deep into the sockets, trying to gain some relief. Just as before, visions of the horror I'd witnessed in the forest popped into my mind, and I began to hyperventilate as the brutal attack on Brian Garner and the deer replayed in slow motion. My cotton pajamas absorbed the excess sweat and were soon drenched, and I pounded my forehead in a futile attempt to bang the thoughts from my mind. As the pain intensified, I dropped to the floor and crawled over the hardwood to an empty spot in the corner. I pressed my spine between the adjoining walls and pulled my knees against my chest as if I were protecting my chest and abdomen from the invisible beast that had killed Garner.

In time, the visions dissipated, my body relaxed, and my breathing slowed. I sat petrified, ashamed and angered from the fear that was overwhelming me. When the vertigo finally subsided, I staggered to my dresser in the dark and took a dry sweatshirt and a pair of sweatpants from the bottom drawer. After peeling off my soaked pajamas, I dressed, then pulled the blanket and a pillow from my bed. Still shaken from the flashbacks, I returned to the corner, wrapped myself in the blanket like a cocoon, and plopped down on the pillow. In my haze, I stared at a small streak of light on the ceiling that had entered the room through a crack in the curtains. It came from the streetlamp my grandfather had paid the county extra to install on the premises many years ago.

DOUGLAS CAVANAUGH

A fierce wind was whipping outside, provoking the branches of a nearby silver maple to sway and alter the light's trajectory. Through tired, swollen eyes, I considered how the flickering resembled a strobe light affect I'd seen at discos in the movies. Twenty minutes later, as my body relaxed, my attention drifted to more serious matters concerning my future and how it was being affected by my past. As hard as I wished, my desire to sleep never arrived, and I sat helplessly throughout the night with nothing to do except think. With little to distract my attention other than the wretched thought of more terrifying flashbacks, I reviewed my life since waking from my coma.

Many of my most recent memories were well defined and clear. Others were unnervingly vague. I could recall most of the details from early December and after, but several important matters that happened in November remained ambiguous. Burying my grandfather was the topic I reflected on first, and if I hadn't been in shock since he died at my side, I would have recalled his entire funeral in concise detail. On that day, I made an extra effort to mentally record the event, knowing that when my normal emotions returned, I could mourn like a regular person who had just lost their best friend. But on that day, I felt indifferent, as if I was attending the funeral of a complete stranger, and I knew in my heart that my grandfather deserved better from me.

The second important matter that gripped my thoughts while I sat in the corner was the series of DCI interrogations in mid-November. Those took place just days after Dr. O'Malley had reduced my meds in order to wake me from my coma. My grandpa and his lawyer from Waterloo were present for the interviews, but neither contributed much to the proceedings, and I doubt if their attendance was necessary. It was my grandpa's distrust in the modern legal system that spurred his instinct to protect me from myself, especially since I was in such a vulnerable mental state.

But the questions the agents peppered me with during those meetings were less accusatory in nature than my grandfather had anticipated, and even though I was slow in answering many of their queries, all I had to do was tell the truth because I knew the truth was on my side. At first, I didn't even mind the contemptuous look

THE LONG WAY AROUND

on the younger DCI agent's face as I described what I remembered seeing in the forest that day, but eventually his arrogant, disbelieving expressions got the better of me, and I began to wonder if he was acting out some malicious strategy to provoke me into veering from the truth. I didn't like him, and when I became annoyed by his suspicious glances and flippant scoffs, I looked right at him and told him so. The veteran agent's character contrasted starkly with his subordinate's attitude. His expression reflected a fair degree of skepticism of my account as well, but only because my account was so implausible from anything he had ever experienced in his entire law enforcement career, and life in general. He was simply unable to accept my story as fact, and yet, I sensed he sympathized about what I'd endured. And though he never said so, I recognized he truly wanted to believe me, but I suspected the distance between his perception of reality and mine were spread so far apart it prevented him from accepting my account at face value.

A few days later, I underwent a polygraph exam performed by a DCI technician from Des Moines who accompanied the agents. When the expert said I passed the interrogation, I sensed the older agent no longer doubted my credibility. Even still, I could tell the younger agent was unwilling to concede, and that bothered me. It was at that moment I became aware that for the rest of my life a significant portion of the population would never believe I didn't kill Brian Garner. That fact ate at me viciously, and as a result, it deepened my depression.

Analyzing the situation all night only worsened my mood, and with each passing hour, my anxiety level elevated to a point I'd never thought possible. By dawn, a fiery rage was burning in my mind, and when the morning sun finally brightened my room, I decided to do something bold. I was going to confront the demons that had overtaken me and return my life to normal or die trying. One way or another, my mental torture was going to end, and though I didn't know the proper way to challenge my past, I knew sitting in the bedroom corner each night was not going to solve my problems. The time to settle things was now, before my mental state sank deeper into the crater it had fallen into. In a moment of courage brought on by fear and frustration, I decided to convert the boy I'd been living as into the man I needed to become. I had nothing to lose, and no other options.

I turned the living room television on with The Weather Channel showing on cable. It was the main channel I'd been watching since being released from the hospital, and the only one I could tolerate viewing, as the competing news channels were breaking two obnoxious stories currently in progress—one about a female figure skater who had been maliciously attacked before her championship qualifications, the other covering the renewed shelling of Sarajevo in Yugoslavia. Both were dismal stories, which wouldn't help raise my spirits even if the media could refrain from overkill.

The local forecast reported the temperature outside would remain bitterly cold all day despite the sun dominating the sky. A harsh winter storm front was passing over the Midwest from the Rocky Mountains but wasn't scheduled to hit Iowa for another day. For now, the wind had already started to lessen, leaving me with no legitimate reason to abort my plan and stay home. Through my depression, I trudged around the house in search of the appropriate gear for my excursion. I pulled my long underwear and woolen socks from my bedroom dresser, then went to the basement in search of my insulated hunting clothes. To my amazement, I found my heavy woolen stocking cap and gloves on my first try, even though I had no idea where Beverly Hayes, the part-time housekeeper my grandfather had hired to clean the house after my grandmother died, had put them. I spotted my fur-lined, rubber boots under the steps. I mumbled to myself that I hoped they still fit as I began trying them on. Satisfied with the results, I walked around confidently, knowing they would suit me better than my ankle-high hunting boots while walking in deep snow.

I shook my head repeatedly as I dressed, partly as a result of my growing anxiety, but mostly because my plan wasn't really a plan and I didn't know why I had decided to act on the idea I'd become fixated on. I only knew that confronting my past seemed to be the logical way for me to reset my future in the proper direction. Inside, I was afraid, not only of what I may discover still lurking in the woods, but also of what I might not find: the answer to my troubles and the pathway to getting my old life back. I feared what I might do if my problems appeared to be unsolvable and my future hopeless.

When I had collected everything I needed, I pulled out my high school wrestling duffle bag and stuffed my snow pants and coat inside, then left the gear at the front door. As soon as I stepped onto the porch, I realized I was underdressed for the weather, but my truck was parked close enough for me to start the engine before completing my plan's final details. By now, the wind had mostly died, though a sneaky breeze continued blowing, which caused the temperature to feel colder than the thermometer showed. I sprinted back into the house and searched for a pen and notepad as my hands warmed. I planned to write a note to Beverly informing her where I was going, and in the event I did not return, I instructed her to tell the authorities where they'd likely find my body. I signed the letter and rushed from the kitchen before I could change my mind and chicken out.

I hustled back down into the basement and pulled the metal tab dangling from a string attached to a light bulb mounted on a wooden rafter near the bottom step. I moved around in the dim lighting and found my grandpa's WWII footlocker buried under a lifetime's worth of junk that had been collected by a survivor of the Great Depression. After unlocking it, I blew some dust off the lid and raised it. The container was filled to the top and had been neatly packed by my grandpa before his health had deteriorated. In his hospital room, I remembered him explaining to me the importance of this footlocker, how it had a false bottom where had he stored dozens of gold bars and silver coins, which he liked to refer to as 'the tip of the iceberg.' He joked about how the box would only be heavy if I tried to lift it, and suggested I store it in an out-of-the-way spot so it wouldn't need to ever be moved. Gold bullion wasn't the reason I was rummaging through the box now, however. There was something else I intended to find tucked away inside that I thought would either help fix my problems or end my pain.

From the top, I removed an oversized envelope containing magazine articles and newspaper clippings from regional publications featuring my grandfather's deer-hunting achievements. I glanced at a few in the faint lighting before digging deeper. When I came to his army uniform, I lifted it out and placed it on the concrete floor beside me. On top of the folded olive drab pants rested a thin, purple case with gold trim running along the outer edges. Gold lettering in the center advertised the contents inside, and when I opened it, I saw the Purple Heart he had received for being wounded during the Battle of the Bulge. As a kid, I was aware he had received the medal, though he never offered to show it to me, and I'd always presumed it was because my mother had instructed him not to. Now it was right in front of me—a striking profile of George Washington in gold mounted on purple backing and attached to a purple ribbon. The medal rested on a soft yellow material lining the inside, leaving the award looking shiny and splendid like the day it was made. But its significance hardly seemed relevant without my grandpa around to tell me about it. As beautiful as it was, I thought about the reason it was given to him and how he probably wished he had never earned it. In retrospect, it was hardly compensation for a kidney, especially since it was the only fully functioning one he had. I put the box on top of his uniform and reached back into the footlocker.

This time I found what I was after. Wrapped securely in an oily, cotton cloth was his Army-issued Colt M1911 semiautomatic pistol. A leather holster with the letters US pressed into its cover flap was next to it, along with an empty magazine and a box of .45 caliber bullets. I took all four items and put everything else back into the footlocker before returning upstairs. Once in the daylight, I loaded a magazine with bullets and inserted it into the gun. Then I holstered the pistol and set it in the duffle bag before turning off the electricity, water, and gas furnace in case I didn't return.

While zipping my jacket, I spied the wooden rosary my grandfather had received from Dieter Metzger hanging on a key hook near the front door. I grabbed it and pulled it over my head, gently at first, and then a little stronger after flattening my ears with my thumbs. With the crucifix snug against my chest, I zippered my jacket to the top, locked the door, and hustled out into the cold.

Chapter Twenty-Three
Will Lightning Strike Twice?

Rural northeast Iowa
Thursday, January 06, 1994, 9:45 a.m.

I pulled my stocking cap over my ears, stepped off the front porch, and raced through the cold to where my truck was idling. After skidding to a stop on the snowy ground, I opened the door, tossed the duffle bag onto the passenger seat, and then took a quick look back at my house in case I never saw it again.

Now more determined than ever to solve my problems, I put the clutch into gear and stomped on the accelerator. I cruised down the lane and plowed over some ice and snow en route to the county highway running perpendicular to the property. When I reached the intersection, I glanced at the mailbox before turning. The flag was raised, indicating the postman, Roy Weber, with whom my grandpa had arranged a delivery system, had already stopped. I pulled over and rolled to a halt, then hurried to retrieve the mail.

The steel bin was stuffed full, so I pulled the bundle out in a roll, lowered the flag, and scampered back to my truck. I wedged the mail between the passenger seat and my duffle bag without sorting through it. I had a good idea what it encompassed. The familiar heavy glossiness of hunting magazines was mixed among a large manila envelope and several smaller white ones, which were probably bills. The bundle also included an abundance of junk mail and flyers, advertising nuisances that had always irked my grandfather to no end—nearly as much as telemarketers, who customarily call at dinner time. The most dogged of those pesky salespeople who let the phone ring until answered were invariably sorry for their persistence after my grandpa finally picked up.

I turned right on another county highway and sped in the direction of Elgin; the town closest to Dieter Metzger's property. I didn't notify Dieter I was coming because I didn't want him to try to dissuade me from my mission.

I purposely drove the exact route to Metzger's Slough I'd used every time before. As I drove, I noticed something seemed different about the scenery this time. I attributed it to the most obvious reason that the cornfields had been harvested and were now buried under a crusty layer of old snow. It was a clear, sunny day and I'd forgotten to bring my sunglasses. On several instances, I was struck by snow blindness, and as a result, the brightness forced me to squint to the point of discomfort. Even after having driven only a few miles, a powerful headache developed around my eyes. The stronger it grew, the more I worried I became about another panic attack striking, and my chest began to tighten as a result. Beads of sweat appeared above my brow, and I removed my gloves to hold the steering wheel more securely in my hands. As time passed, the other symptoms didn't appear, and I soon realized my imagination was playing tricks on me. After turning right on an adjoining highway, the sun shone to my back, lessening the glare significantly. I felt better at once.

When I reached the gravel road leading down to the Turkey River, I tapped the breaks frequently to avoid skidding on some ice patches the road crews had been unable to remedy. The slope seemed much steeper than I remembered, and soon my truck was swerving against my will. As I neared the bottom, the road veered left just in time to keep me from sliding into the ditch and rolling into the river. By the time I had regained full control, I'd reached the pasture access where I'd parked my truck nearly every day during the previous October.

I pulled to a stop on the shoulder, taking care to avoid the deepest snow. I killed the engine and sat in solitude for a full minute before moving. A light wind was blowing, just strong enough to shake the barren tree branches in the surrounding timbers. I reached into my duffle bag and removed my heavy clothing. After putting on the snow pants and camouflage coat, I pulled my rubber boots over my wool socks. Then I took out the Colt and slung the leather holster strap over my left shoulder. Before I could outthink myself, I got out of the truck and inhaled several breaths of frigid air. My cheeks quickly numbed from the biting cold. This left me wondering

THE LONG WAY AROUND

which expression would be showing on my face if I'd had full control of my emotions. Fear? Anger? Hatred? Raw determination, or false courage? More than likely, it would have been a revolving combination of each.

When all my gear had been organized, I headed into the slough in the direction of my tree stand. I had no idea if it was still in place, but I definitely knew where it had been mounted, and could adjust my bearings once I spotted the tree. The snow's depth lessened some in the thickest woods, and I heard nothing other than the rhythmic swishing of my nylon pants, an occasional dead branch snapping under my weight, and my heavy breathing as I walked. Wherever there was an area of open ground, the snow had amassed more, making the hike more laborious. As a result, I fatigued much sooner than I would have just a couple of months ago. Eventually, I neared the grove of oak trees in the area of my former perch. I pulled out the Colt and racked a round into the chamber. The apprehensions I had experienced earlier were gone and had been replaced by anger, frustration, and fierce determination.

As I advanced, I spotted the elm tree in the distance and moved toward it with the pistol pointed forward. I squeezed it tightly in my right hand as I cleared away low-hanging branches and brush with the other. I tried to move quietly, but the snow and underbrush made it impossible. About every twenty feet, I took a break to look and listen for danger. I half-expected a strong headache and dizziness to appear to commemorate my fall, but the symptoms didn't appear. In fact, I felt fine, and my pounding heart and sweaty palms were merely the result of the cardio workout and increased adrenaline pouring through my veins.

Suddenly, a short distance away, I heard the trampling of a small herd of deer flanking my position. They had probably smelled my presence long before I saw them, and each maintained a trot-like pace as they passed. They didn't seem to be bothered by my company. I presumed the herd had some better place to be and the deer simply ignored me out of eagerness to get there. Most likely, they were in search of food, as the blizzard forecast for tomorrow would leave them hungry in the days to come. I leaned against the nearest tree and watched as the group passed. Each was normal-sized like those I'd been accustomed to seeing over the last seven years. Still, I couldn't help fantasizing if another incredible buck like King Charlemagne was among them, so I studied them until the last one had disappeared. The herd's lack of concern for their safety boosted my spirits. My right hand relaxed around the pistol, yet I kept it pointed forward, never dismissing the possibility of another invisible creature like the one I'd encountered a couple of months ago stalking nearby.

I was more resolute than ever about reviewing the kill zone in order to prove to myself I had done everything possible to change the incident's dreadful outcome. I trudged toward the elm tree with the desperate hope of finding clues that might relieve my doubts, end my pain, and restore my personality back to normal.

When I reached the elm, I rested against its trunk and looked up to see if my stand was still in place. It wasn't. It had been removed, along with the scrap-wood rungs I'd used to climb up. I stood bewildered, wondering when this had occurred and why the scene of an open investigation had been altered. Incredulously, I stared at the empty void where my stand had been and estimated the trajectory of my fall. I speculated about the angle and speed of my descent, and which limb was responsible for almost killing me. After a brief contemplation, I decided it was a miracle I'd survived. This increased my depression, as I felt it would have been better to die in the forest that day than to survive in my current state. I began worrying I'd be forced to carry on with an altered personality and be plagued by nightmares for the rest of my life. This caused my anger to grow stronger.

Since there was no way for me to climb the tree, my intention to survey the attack scene from where I'd originally witnessed it collapsed. Instead, I rerouted my path toward the clearing where Brian Garner had been killed. With the elm tree at my back, I moved forward cautiously, trying to remain aligned with it in order to maintain my sense of direction and field of vision. I continued stopping periodically to scan for signs of trouble. As I approached the spot where I remember Garner lying face down, I slowed my pace to a crawl. When I got to the place where the attack had occurred, the reality before me was so disheartening that the last glimmer of hope to fix my dilemma extinguished before my eyes. It may have been that my expectations were set too high. I had envisioned discovering some important clues about the case, vital details only I could have known the significance of and which the investigators had overlooked. Naively, I'd imagined the clearing would be marked off with yellow tape, and the surrounding brush cleared by chainsaws.

In fact, the only sign of any human presence was a trodden pathway through the highest weeds leading to the scene, which was now buried under snow. Other than that, there was absolutely no sign the star athlete and record-size deer had been killed near where I was standing. No indication of a police investigation or any sign of a struggle for life and death. There were no bloodstains and no inkling of the invisible creature that had exploded and vaporized before my eyes after having been pierced by my arrow. Nothing. Just an open patch of snow-covered ground in the middle of the forest that looked like every other clearing in a thousand-mile radius.

I gauged the spot I recalled Garner's body being keeled over and wandered over to it. Then I turned around and singled out the elm tree I'd been sitting in when he was killed. I was amazed by the distance between me and the tree. It now looked much farther than when I had aimed my arrow at the creature's obscure shape. In fact, it was probably the longest distance from which I'd ever attempted to fire an arrow from a tree stand.

The two burning questions I wanted answered for my peace of mind were if I could have saved Garner if I'd released the arrow sooner, and because I hadn't, was it because I was more concerned about saving my own hide rather than helping my nemesis in his time of need? It wasn't just me that had been asking these questions. During the investigation interviews, the younger DCI agent had implied that possibility repeatedly, though he never directly made any accusations. As much as it hurt, the question was a legitimate one, and a smidgeon of suspicion was unintentionally provided in my official account. After rehashing the subject over and over during the last few weeks, I considered that if the detective could conceive such a ridiculous notion, then others might draw the identical presumption, too. And that's what bothered me most.

DOUGLAS CAVANAUGH

After studying the scene in person, it was now abundantly clear that my best chance to redeem my future had been destroyed, not by what I'd found, but by what I hadn't. I stood at a loss, debating my next move. A flash chill rippled through me that wasn't a result of the cold. My protective instincts told me to look around, check that the pistol's safety was off, and proceed cautiously, but my conscious mind decided against it. I no longer cared if I lived or died. If I were attacked by another creature at this very moment, I would not resist my assailant. Rather, my spirit would submit to what fate had in store for me. I had lost all desire to continue living.

I was breathing more heavily now, and I watched the steam pour from my mouth into the cold. My exhalations evaporated about an elbow's distance away. Finally, I began the return trek to my truck, but my exhaustion made it difficult to maintain a steady pace. I forced myself through the snow and quickly fatigued. When I reached the elm tree, I rested my back against it, then slid down trunk and sat in the snow. There were no tears in my eyes, nor was there any expression on my face to reflect the despair in my mind.

Light gusts of wind were shaking the branches above, and some sent snow crystals fluttering down around me. The falling flakes glistened in the sunlight, and those that landed inside my collar were unwelcomingly cold. The sensation reminded me that I was still alive, and I resented the annoyance even more. When the calm returned, I considered the peacefulness of the scene around me and how thrilled and honored I'd felt to be here just a couple of months ago. Right now, it seemed more like hell frozen over. I looked at the pistol and my thoughts began to wander. I could have never imagined such a horrible thought circulating within my mind as the one I was considering just then.

I looked up to the sky—there wasn't a cloud in it. It was almost noon, and the sun shone straight down, though its rays were too weak to melt the snow on the branches above me. My cheeks and right hand had numbed in the subfreezing temperature, and the Colt's cold steel exacerbated the discomfort. I removed the glove from my left hand with my teeth and transferred the weapon into it before stuffing my right hand into my coat pocket to warm. I saw no reason to move, there was nowhere else I needed to be, so I sat

THE LONG WAY AROUND

in seclusion. A few birds chirped in the background, but over the next hour there was little other sound in the forest.

At one o'clock, I grew tired of waiting and decided to act. I looked again to the sky and noticed bunches of thick, white clouds rolling in from the west at a brisk clip. Within minutes, a significant breeze picked up sending the wind chill even lower. I sensed a storm front approaching and decided that whatever I was going to do, it would be better not to wait much longer. I glanced over to the attack scene again, my mind full of hate and disgust. My life was in shambles as a result of what had occurred there, and nobody, not even my therapist, could tell me when or if I would ever return to normal. My frustration was growing stronger and it would soon morph into anger, and then into rage. At that point, I knew I would want my pain to end.

I returned the pistol to my right hand and pulled the glove back on the cold left one. While making the switch, I felt something dig into my sternum and was curious as to what was stabbing me. I unzipped my coat and reached under my sweatshirt to identify the annoyance. Dieter's antique rosary was hanging around my neck. I pulled out the bulky crucifix, brought it to my chin, and held it firmly in my clenched fist. I sat some more and thought while the wind whipped and sent snowflakes flying throughout the forest.

* * * * *

I returned to my truck at a faster pace after being reenergized by the break. The blizzard wasn't predicted to hit for another day, but the sky had already darkened, light snow flurries were zipping past me, and a distinct scent of moisture was in the air—all precursors to what was forecast to come. When I finally reached my truck, my grandpa's pistol was hanging from its holster around my shoulder. Both of my hands had warmed inside their gloves, making it easier to scrape the ice from the windshield.

I got in and started the engine, then I let the motor idle and waited for the cabin to warm. As I sat, I blasted the defroster, organized my gear, and picked through the roll of mail. The large manila envelope caught my attention first, so I pulled it from the wad and flipped it over. It was addressed to me. Initially, I was wary when I saw the sender's name.

Iowa Department of Public Safety
215 Hoover Street
Des Moines, Iowa 50328

In short order, however, my curiosity was aroused. I found a pen in the glove compartment and pried clumsily at the envelope's thick, yellow flap. Inside, there was a single page that displayed the State of Iowa's Division of Criminal Investigation seal at the top. I read the text slowly in order to absorb each word, as if I were trying to memorize it. Letters as important as this are received perhaps only once in a lifetime, and I wanted to leave no room for misunderstanding. When I finished, I lifted my eyes and looked outside. As usual, no emotion showed on my face, but I was overjoyed and relieved inside. The news could not have been better.

The letter stated that no criminal charges were being brought against me by the State Attorney General's office for the death of Brian Garner. In fact, no charges were being filed against anyone. The letter continued to say that the case had not been officially closed but had been deactivated indefinitely as a result of a lack of evidence. Unless new evidence surfaced, it would remain dormant until further notice. Most importantly, it informed me that I was free to leave the state any time from this date forward. The letter concluded with an apology for any inconvenience the investigation had caused and included a telephone number for me to contact if any further information about the case came to light.

My instincts tried to cajole a smile on my face. Competing emotions told me to cry, to release tears of joy, sorrow, or some strange mix of the two. In the end, neither reaction ensued. Instead, I put my truck into gear and stepped hard on the gas pedal in celebration. As my S-10 climbed the hill leading up from the Turkey River Valley, I pounded the steering wheel with my right fist and vowed never to return to Metzger's Slough again.

Chapter Twenty-Four
A Voice from the Past - Round Two

Rural Strawberry Point
Northeast Iowa
Thursday, January 06, 1994, 6:00 p.m.

The full brunt of the blizzard wasn't expected to hit until after midnight, but frozen rain was already bouncing off the windowpanes. I was stretched out on the couch watching an old sit-com, fighting the urge to sleep under a quilt my mother had made for me the year before she died. Drowned out by the clamor of the icy pellets, wind, and my television, I barely heard the telephone ringing in the kitchen. I forced myself to move and answered just before I sensed the caller was about to hang up.

"Hello? "I said in an exhausted voice.

The caller hesitated, and then cleared his throat. I pictured his mind racing to decide whether he had dialed the correct number, what he should say next, or if he should respond at all. After regaining his composure, he asked, "Can I speak to Ryan, please?"

"This is Ryan," I said. "Who's this?"

"Really? You don't know who this is?" Again, the caller took pause. Finally, he said, "Ryan, this is Rory. Rory Meeks."

"Oh, hey, Rory. Sorry I didn't recognize your voice. It's been a while. Besides, my concentration has been erratic lately," I confessed.

"So I've heard. I had a long talk with Tim on Thanksgiving Day. It sounds like we have a lot of catching up to do. Are you busy now?"

"No, but I'm not much of a talker these days. So, where are you? Are you back in the area?"

"No, I'm still in warm, sunny, south Texas, and I'm not missing the Iowa cold, I must admit," Rory said.

I agreed with him. "There's an ice storm in progress outside as we speak, so don't be surprised if our call gets cut off. A full-blown blizzard is scheduled to hit later tonight."

"So where are you exactly?" I asked. "You said south Texas, but you attend the University of North Texas. That's near Dallas, right? You're a long way from home. Did you take a trip on your holiday break or something?"

Rory knew he couldn't keep his secret forever, but he wasn't ready to reveal the truth considering Ryan's state of recovery. Yet, he also knew he had to answer his friend's question with something convincing or risk having the truth exposed. In the end, he decided to share a portion of his story and hope his plan would remain intact.

"Yeah, Ryan... Well, you know, there have been some changes in my life, too. Nothing as serious as what you've been going through, that's for sure. I'd love to discuss the details, but the phone bill will be enormous if we both tell our stories at once. I think it would be much better if we talk in person," Rory said.

"Okay, sure, that'd be great," I agreed. "When are you coming home? Anytime soon?"

"Well, no, it won't be anytime soon. In fact, I was hoping you might want to escape the winter weather and come down to see me. I'm sharing a house with a friend right now, so you'd have a place to stay for a few weeks. What do you think?"

My initial reaction was to decline the offer on the grounds of absurdity. I still had several therapy sessions and estate lawyer meetings to attend over the next few weeks, and the farm needed to be rented to a new tenant before planting season arrived. But after a little more deliberation, the idea began to appeal to me.

Yeah, sure, I thought. I could use a break from here. What do I have to lose? Absolutely nothing. All the meetings can be rescheduled, and there is no pressing farm work that needs to be done for a couple of months. And now that I'd received official permission from DCI to leave the state, there's no legitimate reason for me not to go except for my own reluctance.

"So where are you exactly? Which city are you in, Austin or Houston?" I asked. Those were the only two cities in south Texas I could think of except for Galveston, which I was familiar with only

THE LONG WAY AROUND

because I could remember Glen Campbell singing about it on the radio when I was younger. I seriously doubted he was there.

"Neither," Rory said. "Right now, I'm way down in Harlingen on the Mexican border, but by the time you arrive, I'll be in San Antonio, where I've been living for the last few months."

The revelation presented all sorts of questions that needed answering. Before I could ask the first of them, Rory cut me off. "I know what you're thinking, buddy, but it's a long story that you're not going to get to hear until you're with me in Texas."

"Do you want me to ask Tim if he wants to come along?" I said, hoping he'd tell me not to.

"It would be great to see both of you guys, Ryan, but I'd prefer if what I plan to share with you is kept quiet around home. You know how much Tim loves to gossip. I'd rather you come alone. In fact, I'd prefer it if you didn't tell anyone you were visiting me. What do you say?"

I didn't have to think it over very long. "Okay. I think I'd rather make the drive by myself anyhow. I could use the quiet time. I'll explain to Tim where I was when I get back. I doubt I'll be away long anyhow. He may not even miss me," I said. "What do I need to bring with me? And how much money should I take along?" The questions poured from my mouth as the road trip's intrigue began to overwhelm my sense of reasoning. "Tell me everything I need to know," I said. "I only have a few hours head start on the storm, and the roads are already dicey."

"Just pack a jacket, some jeans and a few shirts. It's never Iowa-cold here, but you should take a heavy coat to wear until you get far enough south not to need it. Travel light. Time will pass quickly, and you won't need a bunch of extra junk. Bring enough money for gas to Texas and back, maybe thirty dollars per day for food, and some spending money. I'm making some good coinage now so there shouldn't be a problem with incidentals," Rory added.

It was another revelation I knew better than to inquire about now. *How much was good coinage?* I wondered. *What kind of job was he working?* He detested helping his dad with chores on the family farm. I never knew Rory to have any skill set except for catching game-winning passes and throwing lightning bolt-like blocks as a

178

high school tight end. But he was far away from being professional caliber. *Had he quit college and joined a semi-pro team that was paying him nicely? Was he even good enough to sign a hefty contract?* The answers to the mystery would have to wait for a couple more days.

    I don't remember the exact moment I officially decided to go to Texas. My excitement wasn't so much from the idea of traveling to a new destination as it was escaping my current environment and trying to break the grip of whatever was holding me in place. It was clear that a change was needed at this point in my life. I was at rock bottom mentally, and I couldn't imagine how my personal situation could sink lower than where it was right now. Yes, a change was necessary. For better or worse, I was going to hit the road and visit my friend in Texas.

    After Rory gave me his contact information and some directions of where to find him once I reached San Antonio, I said goodbye, and for the second time that day, I hastily began to pack my duffel bag for the trip ahead.

Chapter Twenty-Five
On The Road

Strawberry Point
Rural, northeast Iowa
Thursday, January 06, 1994, 8:00 p.m.

It didn't take long for me to organize my affairs and collect what I needed to bring with me on my trip south. I turned off the natural gas line, closed the water valve, and drained the pipes so they wouldn't freeze while I was away. Besides clothing, money, and something to eat and drink on the road, the final details I could think of before leaving were to snag a road atlas from the hallway bureau and check The Weather Channel forecast for the direction I intended to travel. The report looked dismal, and if I planned to beat the foul weather, I had to move fast. As an afterthought, I reached for Dieter's rosary sitting on the kitchen counter and hung it around my neck before locking the front door behind me.

Blizzards rarely hit Iowa without adequate warning, and this one was no exception. The National Weather Service had been preparing the upper Midwest for heavy snow for days, and if the unexpected call from Rory hadn't clouded my judgment, I would have bunkered myself in the house until the coast was clear. The radar showed a cold front from Canada colliding with a span of warm, turbulent air heading east over the Rocky Mountains, putting the Dakotas, Nebraska, and most of Iowa directly in the storm's path. More disturbingly, the front appeared to be gaining in strength with each tick of the clock. Live weather alerts showed the major roads in northwest Iowa already under siege and emphasized the dangerous driving conditions and lack of visibility.

Upon closer scrutiny of my road atlas, I decided not to take to most direct route to Texas. Rather than driving west to Des Moines before heading south on Interstate 35, I planned to outfox Mother

Nature and continue southbound from Iowa City on smaller highways until reaching Missouri. Once in The Show Me State, I'd follow the local highways until hooking up with Interstate 70 heading west. By the time I'd skirted Kansas City, I imagined, the driving conditions on I-35 would improve considerably, which would get me to San Antonio none the worse for wear. My preliminary calculations revealed I should reach Rory's house in about sixteen hours, and except for the fact I'd be driving on unfamiliar roads through a snowstorm in the middle of the night, it all seemed simple.

I'd been on the road for only forty minutes when the first indications I'd need to revise my plan became obvious. The weather had turned nasty just north of Cedar Rapids, and I could already feel my neck and shoulders tightening from the chore of keeping my pickup under control. I decided the best chance of reaching my destination was to push forward at a slower speed with the hope that the interstate highways had been cleared and salted for ice.

As I forged through the heart of Cedar Rapids, I realized I was trapped in a tremendous whiteout, and it was too late to reverse course. Yet, like many other instances throughout my life, I stubbornly resisted the urge to quit, and continued based on my confidence the storm would relent before I would.

Staring into falling snow through the headlights' glare eventually began playing havoc with my eyes, and a nauseous feeling in my throat and stomach grew stronger with each mile I drove. At times I felt dizzy, and my anxieties increased in response to the threat of another panic attack. Of all the times I could least afford to be distracted by my fragile nerves, it was now, and I felt certain if I diverted my attention from the road, even for a second, I could lose control and end up in the ditch.

As I neared Iowa City, I passed a few automobiles abandoned at the roadside with their hazard lights flashing. At the rate I was going, I estimated I was already a full hour behind schedule. Trying to remain optimistic, I calculated how I could regain lost time on the country highways further south, which I knew would have little traffic at this hour. But as I neared my turn-off, the snow fell harder, the wind strengthened, and my pessimism increased.

I had been to Iowa City several times, and I knew the I-380

cloverleaf interchange well. I never liked the outdated exit, and found it difficult to navigate even on clear, summer days. I could see the glow of the streetlamps in the distance, and I sensed I was getting close to where I needed to be, so I slowed even more and studied the path carefully for signs of the off-ramp. As the snow pounded down, reflections of swirling lights could be seen ahead. I advanced diligently, assuming an accident had occurred, and emergency assistance had arrived on the scene. As I crept forward, I saw a semi-trailer truck lying on its side. It was completely blocking the exit, and consequently, the entrance into Iowa City that I wanted to take. Two heavy-duty wreckers with yellow lights spinning on their rooftops had just arrived. When I reached the crash site, a figure in a fluorescent vest waved me over with a wand-style flashlight. I assumed it was an Iowa State Trooper, and when a cruiser with the light bar flashing appeared alongside the crashed eighteen-wheeler, my hunch was confirmed.

There were not any headlights in my rearview mirror, so I rolled toward him with little concern of being rear-ended. As he shuffled toward me, I saw he was dressed in full winter gear. On his head, he wore a wide-brimmed hat fastened snugly by a chinstrap. Its crown was coated with snow. Underneath his reflective vest he sported a winter coat that looked thick, warm, and official. A pair of fur-lined boots kept his feet toasty and dry while he performed his duty. My window was down by the time he was within earshot.

"Where are you headed, son?" he asked. A stream of mist poured from his mouth as he spoke. The trooper looked to be in his late forties. His nose was red and dripping, and some snot droplets were frozen to the tips of his moustache.

"Texas," I answered.

His eyes opened wide and he took a step back as if astonished by my response. "Texas? In this weather? Sheesh! What's her name?"

"Huh?" I said. A split second later, I corrected my inappropriate response. "I mean, excuse me, sir, I don't understand. What's *whose* name?"

"The girl in Texas you're going to see. I've known plenty of young men like you who were both brave and dumb enough to drive through storms like this, but only if a beautiful girl was involved. So, what's her name?" he shouted through the wind.

"I'm going to see a high school buddy who plays college football there."

"You're driving all the way to Texas, alone, in the middle of a blizzard, to visit a high school buddy? Sheesh!" he repeated. "And I thought I'd heard it all. Well, in that case, you correctly chose not to go west on I-80. There's no chance of that happening. Driving south through Iowa City is out of the question, too. There are two big rigs out of commission over there," he said, pointing his glowing wand. "One is jack-knifed, and the other is completely overturned. This exit will be blocked for at least a couple of hours."

"Do you have any suggestions?" I asked.

The trooper bent forward; his eyebrows scrunched together. "Look, son, as I see it, you only have two options. First, you can follow Interstate 80 east and try to beat the storm to Davenport. I hear they aren't getting blasted too badly yet. From there, you can drive south to St. Louis before turning west, or you can choose the second option; the wiser choice."

"Which is?" I asked.

"You can drive to the next interchange a few miles east of here. Take that exit, and when you come to the traffic light, turn left and then cross the overpass. You'll see a Days Inn Hotel. Do the smart thing, son. Get a room for the night and start out again tomorrow after the storm has passed and the roads have been cleared."

I had to make some quick calculations in my head. "How far is Davenport from here?" I asked.

"Under normal driving conditions? A little more than an hour. But with the roads in the shape they're in now, you could double, maybe triple that," he warned. The trooper then circled my truck and inspected my tires. He returned and said, "Your tires aren't very good, but at least your truck has four-wheel drive. Do you have any snow chains?"

"No, sir," I said.

"Hmm," he responded, then stood still in thought. "I see you have Clayton County on your license plates, so I'll presume you're no slouch when it comes to driving in snow."

"No, sir," I replied again. "I'm pretty experienced on winter roads."

"Son understand I'm not telling you what to do. If you're determined to press on, be sure to keep your gas tank full. Once you leave Iowa City heading east, if you run into trouble, there is only one rest area and, of course, the big truck stop right before Davenport where you can take refuge. Watch out for other drivers, both from the front and behind. With such poor visibility, it can seem like other vehicles will appear out of nowhere. And remember, lots of folks on the road right now do not know how to drive in snow. Take care."

"Thank you, sir. I'll be careful," I said.

The patrolman wished me luck, turned his back, and moved to another automobile that was closing in from behind. I rolled up my window, touched lightly on the accelerator, and turned the steering wheel in the direction of Davenport.

*****

Incredibly, the snow fell harder the further east I drove. It didn't matter that I'd rejected the option of spending the night at the hotel the state trooper suggested, because I missed the exit that would have taken me there anyway. In fact, I didn't even realize I'd passed it until I'd driven down the road an additional five miles. At that point, I had no alternative. It was on to Davenport.

For the time being, I was taming Interstate 80 with ease. As I plowed forward with the annoying sounds of ice and snow clumps bouncing against the undercarriage, a form of highway hypnosis took over. Soon my attention drifted to things other than staying on the road. Brief glimpses of long-lost memories reappeared from nowhere, and each impulse generated new pathways for my mind to wander. Fragments of certain thoughts took precedence, though odd recollections from my past resurfaced randomly for no explainable reason. Mixed among the ponderings, I wondered about where the interstate cleaning crews got the salt they spread to battle the ice. Certainly, it wasn't produced in Iowa, as I'd never known or heard of anyone who worked in the rock salt business.

A flash memory of a giggling toddler in a Cubs cap being hoisted above his father's head emerged, then disappeared as quickly as it came. Ordinarily, the joy on the boy's face would have put a smile on mine, but as I drove through the blowing snow, I felt no emotion at all. My thoughts switched in a second, and I recalled the time I was sitting with my grandfather on the wooden deck behind our house one Indian summer evening. It was mid-September, well over a year ago, the sky was clear, and the temperature was unseasonably warm. My grandpa had invited me to listen to a baseball game between our favorite teams on the radio after dinner. The sun had disappeared an hour earlier, and we left the lights off to avoid attracting mosquitos. Two innings into the game, we heard trumpet music playing in the distance. My grandfather turned off the radio, and we listened to our neighbor, a high school band member, practicing in his barn for an upcoming performance. I saw my grandpa smile in delight as the music played, and when the tune had finished, we sat and chatted while listening to his St. Louis Cardinals defeat my Chicago Cubs.

Now, as I drove through the winter slop in a daze, the piece the neighbor kid had been playing on his trumpet returned into my mind. But it didn't take long before it morphed into the bugler playing "Taps" at my grandpa's funeral. All at once, my heart sank toward my stomach and dropped into my abdomen. The feeling was an unnatural, deep wave that bore at my nerves from within, and after a few seconds, it spread throughout my body and into my limbs. An overwhelming feeling of sadness dominated my thoughts, and a strong urge to cry came and went. I tried to shake the feeling by concentrating on the road, but I had trouble focusing. The next instant, the impulse disappeared, and I was again emotionless. But another memory quickly surfaced.

It was a vision of me standing on the champion's podium after having won the state wrestling tournament. As I'd listened to the award presentation over the PA system, I recalled scanning the crowd in search of the person who meant the most to me in my life except for my grandfather—my girlfriend, Mary Kelleher. I remembered spotting her cheering face and absorbing the special pride she had for me that day. Then a different kind of sorrow overcame me as I realized how she had also disappeared from my life several months ago. Mary had been my first and only love, the girl I'd secretly hoped to marry and spend the rest of my life with.

THE LONG WAY AROUND

Now, for all practical purposes, and for reasons I never understood, she'd vanished, and I doubted whether I'd ever know why.

*****

A vast dome of light shone upward along I-80 in the distance. I doubted the lights were glowing as powerfully as they would under normal weather conditions, yet the sight made me wonder if I was nearing the outskirts of a major city or approaching some farming community in the middle of nowhere. I flipped on the cabin light and dragged my finger over the road atlas spread out on the passenger seat. When I found Davenport, I traced I-80 westward and pinpointed the oasis I was nearing. I calculated around twenty miles were left before I would reach my St. Louis turnoff at Davenport.

As I extinguished the light, a warning signal appeared on my dashboard showing the engine was overheating and the temperature gauge needle jumped accordingly. I thought at first it was a glitch; maybe a fuse had blown or some sort of electrical flaw in my nine-year-old truck. I reduced my speed and waited to see if the light would turn off. It didn't, so I decided to take the next exit and check it out, hoping that any township along the interstate highway was large enough to have a twenty-four-hour service station. As I exited the interstate, I saw a cloud of steam seeping out from under the hood. Initially, I reasoned it was the result of snow melting from the engine heat, but then my truck began losing power.

As I coasted down the off-ramp, my truck's motor continued sputtering and I saw more steam pouring out from under my windshield. My palms began sweating and my heart pounded harder as I brainstormed what to do next. My attention became distracted by an impressive sight before me.

Under a canvass of snowflakes blowing across the horizon, I saw scores of semi-trucks parked in neat columns behind a large structure. Around the complex periphery, several fast-food restaurants encircled the main hub. Though alight inside, most were empty. Where the semi-trucks were parked, several towering poles with giant floodlights mounted atop illuminated the lot through the storm. Some of the idle eighteen wheelers had their engines running and their chrome side stacks pitched black plumes of diesel exhaust into the night. Most had their marker lights shining, and the sight looked fantastic against the white backdrop. Zipping around the parking lot, a fleet of four-wheel-drive pickups with snow removal blades fixed on front were pushing snow into massive piles in order to make room for even more truckers seeking sanctuary from the storm.

Propped upon a metallic arch stretching over the building's front entrance, a huge display reading IOWA 80 shined brightly in red neon, while another impressive sign standing further to the right boasted WORLD'S LARGEST TRUCK STOP. That sign had yellow lettering over a blue backing, and it boldly defied the blowing snow. After reading it, I knew for certain I'd reached the Walcott truck stop the Iowa State Trooper had spoken of back in Iowa City.

Separate and a way to the left of the main building, an Amoco gas station stood empty and aloof with its lights on. Adjoined to it, multiple gas pumps were bolstered under an overhang that protected them from the storm. The pumps looked bored and lonely as they waited for customers who were unlikely to come. I was hopeful the facility had car parts and mechanic on duty, so I steered in that direction. My truck's motor suddenly died, and I rolled to a stop, stranded in ankle-deep snow about fifty yards short of my destination. I hit my emergency flashers, put on my coat and stocking cap, and got out to assess the situation. I felt the hood to test its warmth, not wanting to lift it in case boiling water was ready to spray out from underneath. As the steam dissipated, I pulled the hood open an inch with my gloves before peeking inside. Things looked safe, so I lifted it higher and leaned in to inspect. Even in the dark I identified the problem immediately. A quarter-sized gap had opened in the radiator hose, which had caused the coolant to leak and the engine to overheat. The hose needed to be replaced and the radiator refilled before my truck would go another inch. I zipped my jacket to the top and ran toward the Amoco station.

A brown-haired woman with glasses was manning the cash register when I walked in. No other customers were in sight. The cashier was middle-aged, broad in the shoulders, and had a powerful build, though she carried her physique gracefully as she moved behind the counter. She snapped her gum as she tried to

THE LONG WAY AROUND

make herself look busy, yet I sensed that if I hadn't appeared, she would be reading the romance novel that was lying spread eagle behind the counter.

"You can't leave your truck parked there," she barked when I said hello. "The plows are going to be working all night, and they'll need to clean our lot often."

"Yes, I realize that," I said. "But I didn't pick that spot by choice. Can't you see the hazard lights flashing? I'm having radiator problems."

"Well, you're still going to have to move it," she replied with another snap of her Dentyne. A name tag pinned to the lapel of her smock announced her name was Lorraine.

I stared at Lorraine in disbelief. "Or what? Are you going to call the police? I don't think they'll be in any hurry to come from Walcott to cite me." I regretted the direction our conversation had started and decided to soften my stance. I had a hunch she would be more accommodating if I kept the dialogue friendly. "Look, Ms. Lorraine, I'm in a huge jam. If there is anyone around who can help me out, I'll be happy to move it. Is there a tow truck available at the truck stop that could pull my pickup to a mechanic?"

Lorraine relaxed when she sensed I wasn't going to give her a hard time. Obviously, she was under stress from the havoc the blizzard was causing. She said, "Oh, okay, hon. I'm sorry. I'm stuck working a double shift because of the storm, you know. I'll ask my manager to call the administration office and see if the maintenance crew can help push it out of the way."

Lorraine picked up the phone behind the counter and punched some numbers. I listened to her explain my situation to the person on the other end. After hanging up, she said, "The manager will be here soon."

"Thanks."

After about five minutes of wasted time, Lorraine screamed out toward the rear of the store. "JAMES! Are you going to get this young man some help to move his vehicle or not?"

From the back, a tall, lanky guy emerged from a door I didn't realize was there. He had wavy hair, a goatee-style beard, and wore a sweater vest over a button-down shirt. The shirt's top two buttons had been left open under a loosened necktie. If I'd seen the fellow in a different setting, I'd never have guessed he was a truck stop gas station manager, but rather, a starving artist or poet. The first words out of his mouth made a positive impression, and I decided immediately he was a good guy.

"So, your truck died, huh? On a night like this? Good grief!" He hustled past me and slipped his right arm through the sleeve of his winter coat. His snow boots were already on. At the entrance, he pulled a stocking cap over his head, then grabbed a shovel that was propped against the doorframe. "You couldn't have picked a worse night to have a breakdown. Let's go see what the problem is."

I followed him out into the blizzard. As I hurried after him, I shouted, "I already know what the problem is. There's a big hole in my radiator hose. I just need some help moving my truck to a better spot."

"And that's why I have the cavalry on the way. Let's go take a look."

By the time we reached my Chevy, James had eyeballed the surroundings and formed a plan in his head. He made a half-circle motion with his hand and called out, "We need to move it around to the other side of the station. Once there, it can sit for as long as necessary until it's repaired."

When I looked back toward the truck stop grounds, I saw a top-of-the-line Ford pickup with a blade on front racing in our direction. A light bar on its top displayed two rotating yellow lights. It skidded to a stop about five yards from us and two unshaven brutes got out. Each was wearing insulated coveralls and rubber boots. Both greeted James and seemed genuinely happy to see him. I couldn't imagine three more unlikely characters being friends. After a short introduction, I gave them a condensed version of my problem. The guys smiled and told me not to worry, that I'd called the right men for the job.

"The situation is under control, buddy," James said. "Don't worry about a thing."

I relaxed and took comfort in knowing that, though I was five counties from where I lived, I was still in Iowa, and among people I could depend on.

THE LONG WAY AROUND

The pair jumped back into their truck. The driver lowered the blade and began clearing a path to where James wanted my truck moved. After cleaning the pavement, they returned and directed me to sit behind my steering wheel, where I waited patiently for them to decide the best positions from where they should push. Soon, I was moving, and my helpers were chasing my truck's rear bumper as it rolled forward. A slight decline allowed easy access to the gas station and my Chevy advanced nicely along the path to the structure's far side.

In celebration, I took the guys inside the gas station and bought each a hot chocolate. All too soon, the snow removal team was summoned back to work. So much snow had fallen in the last twenty minutes that a huge section of the lot just recently cleared needed to be re-plowed.

James, Lorraine, and I stood at the counter making small talk and watching the snow fall.

"Do you sell car parts here?" I asked with high hopes and low expectations.

The corners of Lorraine's mouth turned downward. "Headlight bulb replacements, motor oil, windshield wiper solvent, and ice scrappers are all we have in stock."

"What about over at the truck stop? Do they have an auto parts store? Any chance of a mechanic on duty?"

"I'm not sure about *car parts*," she answered. "Now, if you were asking me about semi-truck parts, I know for a fact they have everything you'd ever dream of, and then some. You'll likely have to tow your pickup into Walcott for repair, but I doubt any local mechanics will be working an early shift tomorrow," she added.

"I was afraid you were going to say that."

I stood perplexed while trying to figure out my next move. I decided to make a break for the truck stop in search of a solution. Before leaving, I went to my truck and grabbed my bag from the cab. Then I returned inside the gas station, thanked the staff, and left the key to my truck with James, stating that if I didn't return, he was welcome to fix the radiator himself and use my vehicle until I did. I ran recklessly through the snow toward the sprawling main building with my bag slung over my shoulder. Near the door, I admired the rock-wall facade and log cabin-style trim. A metal placard mounted on the side read: 1988, and I realized the entire structure was just a few years old.

The wind forced the glass door shut behind me, and I stomped the excess snow from my shoes and walked toward the main lobby. I was surprised by the size of the building and the amount of businesses and attractions it contained. Hordes of stalled truckers were milling about, and I walked past a few old guys who looked as though they'd spent decades behind the wheel of an eighteen wheeler. I needed to collect some useful information fast, so I approached a janitor mopping chunks of melted snow and water near the entrance. He looked like a local who was nearing retirement age. This was the guy, I figured, who could help me the most.

"Excuse me, sir, I need a little help. Do you have a minute?"

He stopped scrubbing the floor and rotated his head slowly, as if he were surprised anyone was addressing him. As he straightened his posture, he seemed agreeable to be of assistance. "What can I help you with?" he asked with a slight smile.

On closer inspection, I saw he was younger than I'd originally estimated. He was unshaven, and his hair was salt and pepper colored and in need of a trim. His skin tone was some exotic mix, and I had difficulty judging if he was black or white. His teeth slanted inward at odd angles, and there was a hole at the top of his smile where a tooth had once been. The one next to the opening was stained brown from cigarette tar. The janitor's enthusiasm faded, and I sensed him withdrawing his hospitality after just a few seconds.

"I'm in need of a truck part, a radiator hose. And a mechanic," I said as an afterthought. "Is there somewhere I can find these here?"

"Are you kidding me, boy?" he snapped. "This is a truck stop! The world's largest, just like the sign says. You can find everything for an eighteen wheeler here."

"I know, but I drive a pickup truck; a Chevy S-10."

"Hmm," he said. "Now that's a whole different ballgame. You'll need to go talk to Teddy Bear about that."

"Who's Teddy Bear, and where do I find him?"

The janitor inhaled deeply and shot a look of contempt in my direction. Additional truckers had entered, tracking more slush

THE LONG WAY AROUND

across the section of tile he'd just mopped. This obviously perturbed him, and he cursed to himself in a mumble. Then he said, "You'll find Teddy Bear down in the main truck parts center. The store is huge, but you can't miss the Teddy Bear. You'll know him the second you see him. Oh, and if he scowls at you, just ignore it. He don't mean nothing by it. That's just Teddy Bear's way. Go straight through the open hall, and then turn right down the steps."

We parted company and I followed his directions. In the process, I realized I now had more questions needing answers than before I had stopped for information. Along the way, I weaved between loitering truckers from every part of the country. They came in all shapes, sizes, and colors, and they were dressed in all fashions imaginable. I saw cowboy hats, boots and belt buckles as big as Frisbees, truckers with pork chop sideburns and Harley-Davidson motorcycle attire, and war veterans sporting military haircuts and desert camouflage. Several truckers reminded me of Evangelical preachers I'd seen on television, while others looked like inner-city gang members I'd seen in movies. There were some Mexicans, Asians, and one truck driver I guessed to be from Africa, because he didn't dress like the black guys I'd seen in Waterloo. I couldn't imagine a more diverse crowd of Americans all congregated in one place, and yet, the mood inside was merry, as if each in the crowd was enduring the same hardship and making the best of the situation.

I studied the faces as I moved, and soon spotted a sign pointing to the staircase I needed to descend to find Teddy Bear.

Chapter Twenty-Six
Planes, Trains, Automobiles...and *Semi-trucks?*

I-80 Truck Stop
Walcott, Iowa
Thursday, January 06, 1994, 11:45 p.m.

I'd been running on adrenalin for most of the last five hours. Inside the truck stop, I warmed quickly, and my muscles relaxed in response. Suddenly, I was famished. A huge restaurant appeared on the right, and the glorious odor of cooked food invited me inside. I glanced into the dining room, and though it was full of truckers, plenty of open tables were available. Even still, I resisted the temptation to eat, knowing if I stopped now fatigue would overwhelm me and delay my mission indefinitely.

In defiance of the food's allure, I stayed focused on getting my truck repaired and side-stepped through a congregation of truckers in search of the truck parts store. With my duffle bag slung over my shoulder, I began my search for Teddy Bear.

Teddy Bear? What kind of man goes by the name Teddy Bear? I wondered as I dodged a lanky driver presumably from Tennessee because he was wearing a white ball cap with an orange 'T' on front. Trying to remain optimistic, I considered that even if I couldn't get my truck back on the road, I was going to meet a grown man named Teddy Bear, and that convinced me my effort would be worthwhile.

I passed a food court opposite the main lobby and cut through a gift shop en route to the staircase leading down to the truck parts store. The gift shop had the usual souvenirs for sale, mostly Iowa-themed trinkets and knickknacks such as refrigerator magnets shaped liked corn cobs, grain silos, and tractors. There were also racks of postcards and ceramic coffee mugs featuring cows, pigs, and pheasants. As expected, I saw stuffed animals and a lot of clothing available. T-shirts were plentiful, many displaying farm animal caricatures and barnyard humor. Other attire offered designs boasting the colors and emblems of the state's major universities. Off to the side, some standalone racks held sunglasses, bracelets, and other items that were easy to ignore. I headed toward the staircase and bounced rhythmically down each one to the lower level.

Halfway to the bottom, I became aware of the store's vastness and stopped to study its layout. The floor tiling was checkered black and orange, and in the center of the retail space, a brand new semi-tractor was parked inside as a promotional display. Its marker lights were blinking and the excessive chrome trim around the frame was polished and shiny. In the adjacent aisles, there were hundreds of tools and supplies targeting employees of the trucking industry. I saw racks of denim and leather apparel, rap, rock, and country music CDs, work boots, and cowboy hats. Other shelves were flush with rain gear, safety equipment, and road atlases. Decorating the walls around the periphery were huge photos of smiling professional truck drivers and their happy families. It had never occurred to me how enormous the transportation industry was, nor how thousands of drivers across the nation support their families by transporting parts, products, supplies, and inventory in need of delivery.

At the service desk, a cluster of younger drivers was huddled around a lone store employee. I didn't understand the attraction until, through a crack in the swarm of onlookers, I caught sight of the pages of an accessory catalog being flipped by the worker's chubby fingers. Apparently, the employee was searching for some rare chrome accessory one of the truckers was interested in fitting to his rig. In a boisterous voice, the staff member informed the trucker of the unit price and the installation cost of the part in question, and the crowd around the prospective customer erupted in laughter at its outrageous expense. Soon the assembly broke apart, and the mob of drivers drifted aimlessly around the store. Only then did I get a good look at the guy in charge, and I decided immediately I had found Teddy Bear.

Seated on an ergonomic chair pressed against the service desk, a stocky, barrel-chested man in his early forties continued flipping pages of a truck parts catalog. I hovered over the counter and waited to catch his attention. The man had long, reddish-brown hair that he wore in a ponytail pulled tightly against his scalp. A blue bandana fitting snugly over his mane was fastened in back by a knot. The man's complexion was pinkish-red, and he kept his face well hidden under a five-day growth of beard. His facial hair continued the whole way down his neck and blended with an abundance of chest hair jutting out from the top of his undershirt. I imagined there was ample back and shoulder hair to match the excess fur sprouting from his collar, and I realized the origin of his nickname. The worker was wearing a solid blue vest over a blue and white flannel work shirt. A patch sown into the material over the heart read *Teddy* in red, cursive lettering. A bulky, stainless steel chain connected his wallet to a belt loop. A single gold earring clinging to his chubby left lobe completed the image I saw before me.

When I rested my elbows on the countertop and yawned, he slammed the parts catalogue closed with a thunderous bang and looked at me with an expression of displeasure suggesting my presence was bothering him.

"How can I help you?" he said with a mild snarl.

In an equally serious tone, I said, "I'm in need of a radiator hose and a good mechanic who works in blizzards after midnight."

He nodded. "Aren't we all?" Then he stared into the distance as if in deep thought. I did not get his point and was confused by his reaction. A moment later, he cracked a smile, and I realized he was joking. When he asked what kind of rig I was driving, I understood that Teddy Bear was on my side, an obliging guy who was willing to help me if possible. I announced it was for an older Chevy S-10 and he scratched at his beard. While doing so, his smile morphed into a grimace.

"I don't usually deal parts outside of the semi realm, but that doesn't mean I can't get what you need," he said. He reached for a different catalog and began flipping the pages of the one he'd selected. "Timing is going to be a problem," he added. "How soon do you need it?"

With a dash of hope on my face, I answered, "How soon is now?"

"Like the song by The Smiths," Teddy Bear said. "I like your style, son. But seriously, late tomorrow morning would be doable

THE LONG WAY AROUND

under normal conditions, but because of the storm, noon Monday is the best I can promise. Where are you headed in such a hurry?"

I was so engrossed with solving my problems, I didn't realize another customer had approached and was inadvertently eavesdropping. I sensed a nervous fidgeting to my right but decided to ignore the nuisance until my business had concluded. "San Antonio, Texas," I said. "And I'm already behind schedule."

With that, a voice with an odd accent chimed in over my right shoulder. "Shoot, buddy. I'm on my way to New Orleans in about ten minutes. I can deliver you to St. Louie in a matter of hours. From there, you can catch an Amtrak train to San Antone. It won't cost me much time, and I'll drop you off at the train station doorstep. I know right where it is."

I turned to examine the person who had made the generous offer. The driver was about my age, or maybe just a year or two older. He had straight, black hair that he kept tucked under a baseball cap advertising Louisiana State University. His face was thin, angular, and finely featured, and his nose was large and slanted. Oddly, his skin tone had a distinct color that suggested he'd recently been exposed to an abundance of sunshine in recent days. In the middle of an Iowa blizzard, that detail stood out. The guy was at least three inches taller than me and had a wiry yet muscular frame resembling that of a college basketball player. As he waited, he shifted his weight often in an antsy fashion, and used hand expressions as he talked.

"It seems you have an unexpected option, Mr. Chevy S-10," said Teddy Bear. "And a good one, too. I sense this gentleman's in a hurry though, so I wouldn't waste time weighing his offer."

"Oh, I'm in a hurry all right," the truck driver said. "I'm fixin' to hightail it back to Louisiana. I've got to put some miles behind me and this crazy weather. I don't know how folks in these parts put up with this each winter. I mean, geez...just three days ago I was on a boat in the Gulf of Mexico. What a switch!"

Teddy Bear kept his attention focused on me. "So, are you going to accept the offer? And if so, what shall I do about the radiator hose?"

"I left my truck over at the Amoco station," I answered. "Do you know James and Lorraine who work there?"

"Sure do. Everybody knows everybody out here."

I removed my wallet from my inside coat pocket. "Go ahead and order the part. I'll pay for it now and leave some extra money for the repairs. When the hose arrives, if you'd be good enough to contact James and tell him what I've done, he'll take it from there." I glanced at Teddy Bear from the corner of my eye. "You look like a trustworthy character," I stated with a crooked smile. "Do you have an envelope handy?"

Teddy Bear returned the grin and nodded. "Good choice," he said. "Once again, I like your style."

The truck driver tapped my shoulder. "So, what do you say? Am I going to have some company on the way to St. Louie?"

"Do you have any experience driving through blizzards?" I asked with legitimate reservation. "I mean, I know you're not from around here, and I doubt you got that sunburn on a Montana ski slope."

"Yeah, friend. Driving in hazardous weather like this isn't for rookies," Teddy Bear agreed.

"Shoot! This little dusting," the trucker said. "I've been driving through slop like this since my first haul." He moved closer and leaned on the service counter, fully enjoying being the center of attention. "I mean, you can hold on to the cab roof and close your eyes if you like, but you might feel silly by the time we get to the Missouri state line," he added with a chuckle.

With that, I reached out and shook his hand. "It's a deal. I accept your offer. I'll meet you at the back door in a few minutes."

"Just one thing," he said. "You don't smoke, do you? I mean, my daddy is a heavy smoker and I learned early in life I can't stand being cooped up in a truck cab with cigarettes stinking up the place. I won't drive any smokers anywhere, not even my daddy."

"I don't smoke. Never have, never will."

"Good answer. See you around back in a bit," he said.

A short time later, the Louisianan and I were dashing through seven inches of snow between rows of eighteen wheelers. Finding his truck in the blizzard was not easy, as there were at least twenty-five columns, each parked twenty deep. A constant shuffle of moving trucks, more incoming than outgoing, hindered our sprint.

THE LONG WAY AROUND

When we reached his, I looked for the cab's make and model, which was buried under several inches of white powder. As the owner cleaned the windshield and engine hood with a broom, I saw the make he was driving was a Peterbilt. Before climbing in, I scanned the side of the trailer attempting to identify a company logo. So much snow had stuck to the side panel it was hard to make out a design. In the secondary light of a passing truck, I caught a glimpse of a large shrimp claw poking out near the top.

*****

"I'm Ryan Meyers," I said while buckling my seat belt. "I'm from a small town in northeast Iowa called Strawberry Point. You ever heard of it?"

"Nope," the driver said.

"Are you sure?" I continued playfully. "It's the home of the world's largest strawberry—a fifteen foot, fiberglass one."

"Nope," he repeated, unimpressed, as he turned east bound onto the I-80 ramp.

I scanned the cab's interior and spotted a small, plastic figurine affixed to the dashboard. It was a miniature statue of a robed man with a staff in his right hand and a baby on his left shoulder. I had a good idea of who it was supposed to represent but decided to ask the driver anyway.

"Who's that?"

"That there is Saint Christopher," he said. "He's the patron saint of truck drivers. Lots of truckers take Saint Christopher along for the ride. Many others don't but should. Saint Christopher is popular around New Orleans. A lot of Catholics down there," he added. "You a Catholic?"

"Yes," I answered, with no intentions of elaborating.

"Do you know anything about the patron saints?"

"I know a little about a few of them," I said, wanting to change the subject. "I've never been to New Orleans before. Is that where you're from?"

"Nope. Officially, I'm from Belle Chasse. It's a smaller city south of New Orleans."

"Is it in the bayou?" I asked, stretching the limits of my

geographical knowledge.

"Not quite," he said. "But it's on the way there."

"So, what's your name?" I queried.

"Tomislav Novak. But you can call me Tommy."

"Tomislav? That sounds regal. I've never heard that one before. Are you royalty or something?"

"Royalty? Do I look royal to you?" he fired. "I said you could call me Tommy if it's easier."

"I'd bet a dollar you're the only Tomislav in Louisiana."

"Well, then you'd lose your money, Iowa boy," he said, matter-of-factly. "I personally know of at least four others. It's a popular Croatian name. A lot of Croats ended up in Louisiana over the years. I was named after my great, great, great grandfather. He was a fisherman from Dalmatia, one of the first Croats to immigrate to the New Orleans area. He chose it primarily because it was familiar to him. He was a Catholic and could make a living by fishing. He couldn't speak a word of French or English when he arrived, though. He even fought for the South in the Civil War in the 10th Louisiana Infantry, otherwise known as Lee's Foreign Legion. I'll bet he gave them Yanks hell, too." The trucker shifted gears as he finished the sentence, and as he did, I could see a look of pride beaming on his face.

"Croatia's in Europe, right? Is it a country or a region?"

"Gee whiz, Iowa! Don't you watch the nightly news? There's been a war going on over there for the last three years."

"I thought the war was in Bosnia?" I countered, much to his surprise.

"Well, yeah," he responded. I could see the shine on his face begin to fade. "That's what's on the news *now*. But Croatia declared independence a few years back, so you should have known about their war first."

"I didn't care much about the news or world events three years ago. I was still in high school," I said. "Now that I think about it, I don't care much about world events these days, either."

"Well, I do. That's the Croatian flag right there," he boasted, pointing to a red and white checkered crest swinging from a decorative string spun through a hole above the windshield. "In

THE LONG WAY AROUND

fact, I've been thinking about flying over there to help my people's fight for independence. I'm in contact with some distant relatives on the Dalmatian coast. They're having a rough time of it nowadays."

"You aren't a Croat," I protested as we neared Davenport. "You're an *American*, at least five generations removed from your Croatian roots. So why get mixed up in problems that aren't your own? Do you even speak their language?"

"Well...not really."

"Not really or not at all?" I asked.

"Not at all," he confessed reluctantly. "But what do you expect? I'm from Louisiana. I don't speak good English neither," he joked.

With that, something broke free inside me and I laughed aloud for a few seconds. Tomislav's humor hit home because his statement sounded exactly like something my buddy Tim would have said. It was the first time I could remember showing emotion since being released from the hospital, and it felt wonderful. But when the humor waned, the attempted reset of my emotional state fizzled along with it. I asked Tomislav if he was seriously considering going to Croatia to fight.

"I might. I'm twenty-one years old so no one can stop me," he answered. "My father said I could go if I wanted, but we have a successful, century-old, family business to run that requires my presence."

"A trucking business?"

"No. This truck is for delivering our product to the customers. Seafood, Iowa. That's our specialty. Shrimp and oysters. I just delivered a massive order of frozen crustaceans to some restaurant chain in the Twin Cities area. Have you ever eaten at the Minnesota Fish Fry and Steak House? There's a huge one next to the Mall of America by the Minneapolis airport."

"No. I've never been to Minnesota," I said.

"Shoot, Iowa. You've got to get out of the house more. You're nearly as old as me, and I've been all around the country. What do you do with your free time, anyway? Are you a student? What college do you attend?" the southerner fired in rapid succession. "I'll bet you're an Iowa State Cyclone, ain't you? If I went to college in Iowa, that's where I'd go for sure. I always considered myself to be a natural born *cyclone*," he said with a Louisiana drawl, making the word sound more appealing than in my local pronunciation.

"Well, I could have gone to Iowa State if I wanted. They recruited me and offered a scholarship, but I rejected their offer last spring. I wasn't ready to go to a big university just then," I told him.

"You passed up a university scholarship? *Gol-ly*! Are you kidding me? *Cho! Co!*" he said, which I presumed to be in Cajun dialect. "A scholarship for what? You don't look like no Einstein to me. You're too puny to play football or basketball, that's for sure. So, what was the scholarship for? You must be a cheerleader or in the marching band," he said with a laugh.

"Ha-ha," I answered. "I know I'm not in condition at the moment, but I was a pretty good wrestler in high school."

"Just a pretty good one? Iowa State University offered you a scholarship and you call yourself a *pretty good* wrestler?" he questioned. "I'll bet you were better than pretty good. You must have been a first-rate."

"Well, my grandfather thought so. I always considered it just a recreation."

"Listen to me, Iowa. There are probably thousands of high school grapplers around the country who would love to wrestle at Iowa State. Their program is famous nationwide. So how on earth could you have turned them down?" he wondered aloud.

"It wasn't difficult. No harder than turning down the others."

Tomislav's eyes widened. "Others? You mean you had multiple offers? *Gol-ly!*" he said again. "What other schools recruited you? Don't tell me you rejected Dan Gable and the University of Iowa?"

"No, I never had an offer from Dan Gable. I defeated his prized recruit in the Iowa High School State Tournament championship match though. The other scholarship offers I refused came from the universities of Oklahoma and Northern Iowa."

"Holy smokes, Iowa! You must have been a high school wrestling sensation!"

"I did all right, I suppose."

After a bit of reflection, Tomislav said, "Still, you didn't answer my original question. Since you ain't wrestling in college, what do you do with your free time?"

THE LONG WAY AROUND

I didn't want to answer explicitly, as I wasn't sure what kind of reaction I'd receive. I decided to choose my words carefully. "Oh, I've kept myself busy over the last six months," I said. "The last three incredibly so."

"Do you work?" he asked.

I saw the direction the conversation was taking and sensed it was going to be a long ride to St. Louis. Tomislav had purposefully invited along someone to chat with as he drove, and he was determined to get a return on his investment. He had an unending number of questions to ask, and I estimated about five hours more in which to ask them. Yet, I didn't mind entirely. I was finally starting to relax, and I enjoyed talking with someone other than my therapist.

"I worked some odd jobs last summer."

"Doing what?" asked Tomislav.

"I primed and painted a huge barn. And that was no easy task. Including some major repairs I helped make, the whole project took about six weeks to complete working ten-hour days."

"So besides wrestling, you know how to work with your hands. I'm impressed," he stated.

"I know it must appear that I'm a multi-talented physical specimen to a simple truck driver such as yourself," I kidded. "But I consider myself to be more of a dormant intellectual."

Tomislav grinned widely and we laughed for a little while, but the break didn't last long before the barrage of personal questions resumed. The return of my sense of humor was encouraging, and an elusive hope was being kindled that my old personality was on the mend. After the third attempt of avoiding the subject of my life over recent months, I decided to tell the trucker what he was itching to know. I had become comfortable talking with Tomislav Novak, and I began to think of him as a friend. I decided to let the chips fall where they may and suffer or celebrate the consequences once my story had been told in full. I'd leave it to him to accept or reject the parts of my story he couldn't handle.

After skirting Keokuk, we crossed the Missouri state line and the snow vanished almost magically, though darkness, fog, sleet, and slick roads continued to hinder the driving. Tomislav commented how he and US Highway 61 were like old friends, and claimed to know every bump, twist, and turn between the Iowa-Missouri border and St. Louis. Yet, I noticed how his haughty tone fizzled and the frequency of his questions dissipated as he steered through the thickest patches of gloom.

By the time we'd reached Hannibal, I'd revealed most of my personal history from August of last year until the tragic day in October. At Hannibal, I took a break from my narrative leading up to the grand event which preceded my fall. Against Tomislav's wishes, he allowed me to change the subject to discuss Mark Twain. It seemed appropriate since we were both familiar with the writer's most famous books and knew the settings of each were inspired by the river town we were passing through. That discussion ended before its time, however, as Tomislav cunningly switched the topic back to my original story after just a few minutes.

Two hours and eighty-seven miles later, we entered the St. Louis city limits just as I concluded my tale. Tomislav had been engrossed in my story, and except for some well-timed expressions of astonishment such as '*Gol-ly!*' '*What in tarnation?*' and '*Well, I'll be!*', which I imagined to be popular in his part of Louisiana based on the frequency in which he used them, his only interruptions were to ask a few pertinent questions concerning details I'd neglected in my report.

Tomislav looked at the clock on the dash. It was now after six o'clock in the morning. Sunrise was still an hour away. Bright streetlamps came into view along Interstate 70, and after he steered the truck onto it, we sat quietly as he drove into the heart of St. Louis.

"There's just enough time to beat the morning traffic. I'll take the I-270 bypass, and then connect with I-64, which will take us downtown. After dropping you at the train station, it'll be easy for me to join I-55 direct to New Orleans."

"Sounds good. And thanks a lot. Not just for the ride, but for listening to my story. I hope it didn't bore you," I said with a grin. "So, do you believe it?"

"What can I say, Iowa? You just dropped a bombshell on me. I'm dumbstruck. Seriously…words fail me," the southerner said in

THE LONG WAY AROUND

response. "But, yeah, I believe it. *Gol-ly!*"

I was expecting more questions, but he asked few over the next twenty minutes. Instead, he sat with his eyes trained on the road. I took that to mean he was sincere with what he'd said, and he was considering all that I'd been through. Then, just as we approached the train station exit, he asked me, "So what are you going to do now? Ain't there folks in Strawberry Point who will be missing you?"

"I don't know. I didn't really think about it. I needed some time away and left on the spur of the moment. I'll return when I'm ready I suppose, maybe sooner rather than later. For the time being, I doubt anyone will even notice I'm gone."

The train station came into view and he pulled the eighteen-wheeler over to a spot that would make it easy for him to return to the highway. "You can hoof it from here. Hustle through the underpass and cut across the parking lot until you see the station entrance. Then it's just a matter of buying your ticket to San Antonio and waiting for the train to board. You'll be fine."

"Got it," I said.

Tomislav took a business card from a compartment under his armrest and handed it to me. "If San Antonio doesn't work out and you need a job, call our office. I'll warn the staff to be expecting your call, but it's your choice. I'll be driving and delivering the rest of this month, and then back to shrimping and fishing in February. Have you ever worked on a shrimp boat? I'd be glad to have you aboard."

I gave his card a look. It read: Novak and Novak Seafood Delights – *"We deliver from coast to coast - No order too shrimpy!"* The motto made me laugh "No order too *shrimpy*." I said.

"Yeah, that was my idea," he said. "Sounds silly, I know. But you wouldn't believe how popular it is. People from all around the country get a kick out of it."

"I'd be honored to be associated with an outfit like that," I answered, slipping the card into my wallet.

"You'd be welcome, Ryan Meyers," he answered, addressing me by my real name for the first time. "Just call."

We shook hands, and I pulled my bag from behind my seat. I

thanked him again and lowered myself onto the damp pavement. A minute later, I had breached the underpass and entered the train station parking area. About halfway to the entrance, I heard a blast from the Peterbilt's horn and turned to wave to my new friend as he veered onto the road heading home.

Chapter Twenty-Seven
A Real Trip

Amtrak Texas Eagle
Northeast Arkansas
Friday, January 07, 1994, 11:45 a.m.

Embarking on a cross-country train ride would have been one of the highlights of my life just six months ago, but any excitement I felt now was dampened by uncertainty and exhaustion. The single joy I'd relished after boarding the Texas Eagle four hours ago was finding the seat next to mine empty. When I'd paid my fare at the ticket counter, I chose a seat in coach, as the extra expense of a sleeper car seemed unnecessary. The poster on the train station wall showing the seating alternatives made the coach seats look plush and roomy. They felt as comfortable as advertised, and the abundance of leg room was appreciated. The fact that the seat next to mine was unoccupied was a huge bonus. And better yet, this leg of the trip was not in high demand on this day, probably as a result of the poor weather and time of year.

At first, I thought I'd have the entire car to myself, but that prospect faded when, just as the train pulled away, a pair of ladies plopped down in seats one row ahead and across the aisle from me. It seemed odd they picked seats so near because the whole car was vacant, yet I didn't care enough to consider the matter in depth. I simply assumed those seats were issued by the ticket agent and the women were sitting where they were assigned, even though they could have chosen any others. Weariness overtook my senses and I barely had the strength to set my ticket on my food tray and lift my coat to cover my eyes. Almost instantly, I was asleep, oblivious to any distraction.

After about three hours of travel, the train was rolling through the southernmost portion of Missouri. When my eyes opened, I lowered my coat and peered out into the daylight. The Missouri landscape looked brown, hilly, and dreary; all characteristics of winter quite familiar to someone from Iowa. Minus the recent snowfall in my part of the state, the countryside reminded me a lot of home. The route we were traveling wouldn't pass through the heart of the Ozarks, and this left me disappointed because the wives of many retired farmers I knew had told me of the wonderful scenery they'd seen while vacationing in the area. Their husbands usually rolled their eyes, and then boasted about the great live music they heard in the Branson theaters performed by many old-school country stars they'd been listening to for decades. The map on the pamphlet that came with my ticket showed the train would eventually pass through a section of the Mark Twain National Forest, so I'd be able to catch a glimpse of the region after all, which cheered me up mildly.

When we stopped at Poplar Bluff to exchange passengers, I got up to stretch my legs and find something to eat and drink. Just as I returned to my seat, the train jolted forward and began moving again. In my absence, a young family consisting of a mother, father, and toddler had taken seats at the front of the car. I guessed the parents to be not much older than I, and I paid attention to how well they managed to travel with a small child in tow. They were organized and efficient, and the wife looked to be prepared for any change in circumstance. At this stage of my life, I imagined, there was no way I'd be able to handle marriage and fatherhood, at least not as well as the young father up front was handling it.

Before long, we reached the Arkansas state line and fatigue again overwhelmed me. I lifted my coat over my face to block out the light and began to dose off. The chatter of the ladies across the aisle woke me. Only then did I realize they had not known each other before the trip's onset. Fate had seated them together, for better or for worse, and though I tried to avoid eavesdropping on their conversation, I couldn't help but listen in on some of it.

Even though the women had boarded together, from what I understood, they were bound for different destinations. I hadn't a clue how well they'd gotten along during the trip's first leg because of my comatose state. As their conversation progressed, I suspected evasion of boredom was the primary motivation keeping them

THE LONG WAY AROUND

together rather than desire for companionship or a sense of kinship.

I estimated the lady next to the window to be in her late sixties. Her name was Lucinda. She was black, smartly dressed, and wore stylish reading glasses fixed to a chain around her neck. She constantly worked at something in her hands. I couldn't tell if it was a crossword puzzle or if there was a sweater on her lap she was knitting. She had a pleasant disposition and was probably the most patient and tolerant human being I had ever encountered. I concluded she was very religious, because she often responded to her companion's long-windedness with phrases such as, "Dear, Lord, child," "Bless you, child," and "Lord Almighty, have mercy!" Lucinda was from St. Louis and on her way to visit family in the Dallas suburbs.

Lucinda's seatmate was named Carlene. Her destination was a town in northeast Arkansas named Walnut Ridge. From the map in my hand, I saw it would be the next scheduled stop in about one hour. Carlene was white, in her late fifties, and built like an NFL offensive lineman. Physically, she was a sight to behold, but not solely because of her robust features. She possessed a specific, audacious style like no woman I'd ever seen, even on television. Some people might describe her as gaudy; others might say that adjective didn't scratch the surface. I've seen a few women with similar taste to hers who were able to pull it off, but it's a tough sell, and Carlene's character didn't have the finesse to make it work.

She wore bright, flashy colors, as if attracting attention from anyone in her vicinity was what she craved most in life. Her hair was doused in gel and many wisps jumped out in random directions. She caked on excessive makeup, and the cobalt-blue eye shadow and scorching red lipstick made her appear clown-like. But it didn't stop there. Her speech and mannerisms were equally over-the-top, which killed any chance she had of seeming normal, or perhaps even sane. The more I listened to her exaggerated ramblings, the more amused I became, but it was cheap amusement I didn't enjoy, and it was mixed with a dash of revulsion. Paradoxically, I sensed Carlene had a good heart, which I supposed she rarely, if ever, received credit for having. Certainly, she wasn't mean-spirited, and her biggest faults may have been that she was out of tune with the world around her.

DOUGLAS CAVANAUGH

By the time I'd gathered the power to pull my coat collar below my eyes to peek at the pair, Carlene had her left knee bent and her massive leg draped over her right thigh. Her boot was off, and her left foot and beefy calf were dangling in the aisle. Suddenly, she winced in pain and began massaging her foot as if she were suffering an agonizing spasm. The fuzzy sock she wore was fluorescent yellow, and the material was reminiscent of what they might use to make Muppets.

For the next several minutes, I listened in on their banter. Carlene spoke so raucously; I had no choice.

* * * * *

I forced myself to concentrate on other things in order to block the ladies' conversation from my consciousness. I glanced at my watch. It was nearly twelve-thirty p.m. The train would stop in Walnut Ridge in about twenty minutes. When the journey resumed after the break, I estimated five hours would have elapsed since I'd left St. Louis, which meant I still had twenty-one hours of travel time before reaching San Antonio. Once again, I covered my face, planning to sleep through Walnut Ridge entirely.

More than two hours later, I awoke feeling alert and refreshed. I looked left expecting to see Lucinda alone and Carlene gone. Instead, I found both were absent. I raised myself to have a better look around the car. It was still mostly empty, and I could see no new passengers had boarded at the last stop. After leaning further forward, I spotted Lucinda curled in the seat in front of me, snoring just loud enough to alert me of her presence.

In the process of repositioning myself, I noticed a pair of blues eyes staring at me from the aisle. The toddler from the front of the car was standing there holding the armrest of the seat next to mine. He had wavy blonde hair, a dimple in each cheek, and a mouth full of teeth in varying stages of development. I presumed he'd either escaped his parents' supervision, or more likely, had been allowed to wander freely throughout the car to relieve his growing boredom. I caught his mother's eye and waved to let her know he wasn't bothering me. After she acknowledged me, I refocused on the youngster. His company was a welcome distraction, as the

THE LONG WAY AROUND

scenery outside had become boring to view.

Over the years, I had heard many jokes and remarks concerning the tediousness of traveling across Iowa. And while I can understand why a visitor might think staring at never-ending corn rows and soybean fields for consecutive hours to be mind-numbing, excluding Iowa's winter season, I consider my home state to be one of the more picturesque in the country, especially the part from which I hail. Yet, because I hadn't traveled out of the state, I never defended its attractiveness against the opinions of others who have traveled more. Nonetheless, the landscape in southern Arkansas and eastern Texas I'd been observing through the train window over the last several hours simply couldn't compare. I conceded that winter was likely amplifying its ugliness, like how the season has the same depressive effect up north. Still, I couldn't imagine how the cotton growing region in which I was now traveling could hold a candle to the rolling hills of Iowa, especially in summertime.

I traded funny faces with the boy for a short time, and then instigated a game of peek-a-boo. He responded exactly as I expected and hid behind the empty seat to his right. Mere seconds passed before his ability to resist temptation dissolved. I stretched forward and waited for him to peer around the corner. When he finally committed, I caught him by surprise, and when I blurted out peek-a-boo, he erupted in laughter. Then we did it a second time, and he laughed even louder. Lucinda stirred in her seat and I remembered she was sleeping. Ashamed, I'd completely forgotten about her and hoped we hadn't woken her. I tried to calm the boy by changing games, but he wanted to continue what we'd been playing. I attempted to distract him and lighten his mood, but he started crying instead. Thoroughly frustrated, I asked him his name and he wailed even louder. Just as I had reached my wit's end, Lucinda saved the day.

"That's all right, boys. You go on having fun," she said with a warm smile.

"Sorry, ma'am," I said, embarrassed.

"Don't worry, child. It's a long way between here and Dallas. I'll have other chances to rest. You two just enjoy yourselves."

"Thank you," I responded.

Before our game could resume, the boy scooted down the aisle and climbed onto his mother's lap. Therefore, for the next several hours, I had no choice but to stare at the drudgery outside for entertainment.

I nestled back into my seat and let my mind wander. I thought about Rory and what condition I'd find him in when I got to San Antonio. I wondered how he'd been making a living, and how he was adapting to his new environment. In any case, it was just a matter of time before I'd see for myself and find out. Soon, I dozed off and wild thoughts about my past resurfaced. Not the most haunting ones, thankfully, but others resumed that continued to make no sense to me. When the vision of the small boy in the baseball cap being lifted above his head by his father ended, I woke and looked to see if there was a resemblance to the father and toddler with whom I had been playing. After a series of short glances, I decided that there was no connection, and that the mystery would remain unsolved.

Chapter Twenty-Eight
Hope Springs Eternal

Rural Clayton County
Northeast Iowa
Saturday, January 08, 1994, 11:00 a.m.

Mary spent the entire morning pretending to enjoy her free time. She'd slept later than everyone else in her family, and then relaxed in her maternity pajamas, slippers, and bathrobe near the bay window in her parents' living room. There, she drank orange juice and watched her father and brother clean the snow off the driveway. Mary was no stranger to operating a snow blower and had volunteered to help. Her father instantly rejected her offer. He was adamant about not letting his daughter exert herself during the final trimester of her pregnancy, and this made her crazy. As a result of her father's overprotectiveness, combined with the travel restrictions created by last night's blizzard, she felt trapped and had become restless. Monotony had set in, and she still had three months more to wait in seclusion. Mary hated being cooped up and began searching for excuses to escape her confinement.

After the men had finished the job and come inside, she stayed seated on the couch and watched the forest birds that had gathered to eat at the feeder station. Before the storm hit, her father had filled the plastic tube with sunflower seeds and hung it from the branch of a young maple tree in the front lawn. Now, the sun was shining brightly, and the blue jays, cardinals, chickadees, and finches took turns flaunting their colors against the glistening, white backdrop as they pecked at the seeds in the tray. It had been a long time since Mary had enjoyed such a simple sight, but it was exactly the type of nature's artistry she would have devoured prior to dealing with all the stress her unexpected pregnancy had produced.

At least Mary no longer viewed motherhood in a negative

light. In fact, over the recent weeks, she had warmed to the idea of becoming a mom and was delighted by all the attention and support her family was giving her. Her parents filled the spare bedroom almost daily with supplies and accessories a newborn baby would require, and most of the distressing thoughts she'd had of the birthing process were beginning to fade away. Lamaze classes at the county health facility were scheduled to begin next week, and she reasoned that any further apprehensions she'd have about the process would be alleviated by the clinic support staff. Then, suddenly, sadness struck when she realized she would be attending the program with her mother and not the baby's father.

Despairing thoughts overtook her as she considered how Ryan wasn't being allowed to participate in the experience of the birth of his first child. She considered how the circumstances were no fault of his own and dwelled on how it all seemed so unfair. As many wonderful memories of Ryan filled her head, an abundance of guilt was resurrected. Her face felt flushed, her ears began to burn, and a menacing tingle ran down her spine. Uncharacteristically flustered, Mary broke out in a cold sweat and fought off an urge to cry.

Ever since the blizzard ended in the day's early hours, the county snow plows had been running without a break to clear the rural roads. Because this was the Kelleher family's first winter at this location, nobody knew how long they'd have to wait before the road to their house would be passable. About an hour later, just before noon, a bright orange truck with a flashing yellow light on top rolled down their street and pushed the excess snow into the ditch. An hour later, the high sun had melted the remaining frozen film, and the pavement began to dry. Mary didn't waste the opportunity to ask her father if she could borrow his new pickup to visit Dori. Although her father was reluctant, he consented to the use of his four-wheel drive vehicle on the condition she only used roads which had been cleaned. Mary agreed, and then dressed in appropriate post-blizzard attire. She rummaged through the closets and found her heaviest coat and boots she'd worn in past winters. Leather gloves, a thick scarf, and matching cap completed the set. She promised to be home long before darkness arrived.

Twenty-six miles of county roadways separated her parents'

new house from the farm Ryan had inherited from his grandfather. Under normal driving conditions, she could expect to be there in about twenty minutes. This day, however, she allotted a full hour in case some roads were inaccessible.

Mary had called Dori to let her know what she was plotting. Dori knew she couldn't stop Mary from seeing Ryan, but she reminded her there could be unforeseen consequences for her actions, that even the best intentions could backfire and cause more harm than good. Nothing she said could deter Mary from informing Ryan of the impending events that were destined to alter their lives forever. Irrespective of Ryan's state of recovery, Mary didn't want to live another minute shielding him from the fact he was going to become a father. In fact, she felt she knew Ryan so well, she was convinced the news would serve to expedite his recovery.

More than anything, she wanted to level with Ryan, to right her wrongs and apologize to him for the way she'd handled the situation from the beginning. He had done nothing to deserve her maltreatment, and she was ashamed of her behavior toward him since she had moved away last summer. She hoped he would understand her conduct and the reasons why she had acted as she had. It was so very confusing how her life had reached this point, but she knew there was still time to correct her past mistakes. *If only she could sit with him and explain everything,* she thought over and over along the way, *then everything will be fine in the end.*

Somewhere along the journey, Mary considered how Ryan would already be participating in the fatherhood process, and how they'd still be together as a couple planning their future as a family had it not been for his tragic accident. But, the more she thought about it, she decided this was senseless speculation. That thought didn't make her feel any better, and she dismissed it with a subtle shake of her head.

Mary slowed her father's truck to a crawl as she neared the lane leading to Ryan's farmhouse. The paved county road had already been cleared, but she was unsure if the crushed gravel lane leading to the house would be open. Fortunately, Ryan's neighbor had been out with his tractor a few hours earlier and had cleared a path so Ryan could exit if he needed. Mary couldn't see any tire tracks in the lane, indicating there was an excellent chance he was home.

But when she parked in the spot where Ryan always parked his truck, she could plainly see the house was empty. The curtains were drawn, no smoke was leaving the chimney, and the walkways remained covered in snow. Mary left the truck's engine running so the heater would continue working and blazed a trail to the porch. At the top step, she whisked the excess snow from her boots with an abandoned broom, then stepped carefully over the icy wooden planks on the front porch. She glanced to the right and saw the porch swing wavering in the breeze. A few small icicles hung from its armrests, and a thin dusting of white powder was pasted to the frozen seat. Mary reminisced about the many evenings she and Ryan had spent together on the swing last summer, and how the young couple had shared their most private thoughts while sipping lemonade and swinging back and forth. She pondered about how those times were the best of her life, and how badly she wished for those moments to continue.

When she reached the front door, she stood on her toes to peer through the decorative glass window. From that position, she couldn't see anyone moving around, nor did she see any lights on. There were no sounds coming from the television, or any other sign suggesting someone was inside. She rang the doorbell twice. After ten seconds of waiting in the cold, she removed a glove and knocked as hard as she could, first pounding on the door with her clenched fist, and then on the glass windowpane with curled knuckles. After getting no response, she tried pushing, pulling, and shaking the door handle. It was no use. It was locked and wouldn't budge. Obviously, Ryan wasn't there. And since there were no footprints leading away from the house down the walkway, it could only mean he'd been gone for at least a day, maybe more.

She backed away from the door and brushed the snow from the swing with her glove. She sat down and thought about where he could be as she swung back and forth in the cold. She began to worry something awful may have happened to him, or possibly, that he'd been readmitted to the hospital. Certainly, if that were the case, her friend on the nursing staff would have contacted her by now. It occurred to her how, after so many times of trying and

THE LONG WAY AROUND

failing to speak to Ryan, she'd yet again been unable to inform him of the impending news. It was as if a strange force was interfering with the situation, as if what she was preparing to reveal was being suppressed by a powerful entity that was denying the process in order to achieve a different outcome. With each passing day the baby's due date grew closer, and Mary realized this moment may have been her last chance to see Ryan in person before the baby was born. Then, just as had happened earlier that day, her ears began burning and an unpleasant chill ran down her spine.

Dazed and confused, she left the porch and retraced her steps back to the truck. Once inside the toasty cab, she sat in silence, doubting if the situation could ever be resolved to everyone's satisfaction. When her nerves had calmed, she backed up and then steered toward the highway. As she regained her senses, her spirit returned, and she started feeling better. After double-checking for traffic, Mary turned in the direction of Dori's house and thought about the important topics she wanted to discuss with her best friend when she arrived.

Chapter Twenty-Nine
A Lukewarm, Texas Welcome

Rory's house
San Antonio, Texas
Wednesday, February 02, 1994, 8:20 a.m.

It was a beautiful, sunny day outside from what I could see from the window. Rory and his roommate, Lee Randall, with whom he shared a large ranch house in an upscale part of the city, had left for work over an hour ago. They worked together at a landscaping company in a neighboring suburb. I rose early, too, and drank coffee with them before they left. As they were preparing to go, they told me about the project they were working on and some of the problems they faced each day. They also talked about some of the fun they had on the job. But when I asked about their paychecks, they glanced quickly at one another before changing the subject.

Rory looked no different than when I'd last seen him in the summer. The fact he'd quit playing football hadn't changed his physical appearance at all. He kept his hair short, but now wore a beard and moustache combination in the style many pro athletes were wearing. Being as big as he was, I expected him to have gained weight, but he hadn't. He was quick to tell me that working long hours under the hot, Texas sun made it easy for him to burn calories.

Rory's roommate, Lee, was one hundred percent Texan, or at least as Texan I'd always imagined a person could be. He was a cowboy at heart and wore denim jeans and boots wherever he went. He often sported multi-colored, striped, buttoned down shirts as casual wear, and usually kept his jeans secured by a belt with an oversized buckle. Outside the house, he alternated between wearing cowboy hats and baseball caps, depending on his destination. My first impression of Lee was a positive one, and the more I got to know him, the more favorable my opinion of him grew. He was

THE LONG WAY AROUND

a good guy, mild-mannered, even tempered, and quick to throw some wry Texas humor into our conversations. For me, that was a welcome change.

After the guys had left for work, I sat on the couch and watched *The Today Show* while trying to battle boredom. The program's weatherman, Willard Scott, stated the temperature across south Texas would be unseasonably warm, with an unlikely eighty-six degrees for the high. Back home, in early February any temperature above freezing is considered unseasonably warm this time of year, and I considered the contrast. Eighty-six degrees sounded ridiculous, and it would surely set a record in any part of Iowa.

Unwilling to take Willard's word for it, I walked outside behind the house and strolled around the swimming pool and fenced yard. It already felt like summer. It was an unbelievable, unnatural sensation, and yet I adjusted to the heat quickly. Soon, I found I didn't miss winter at all. I returned to the house.

When the weather report ended, and the program resumed after a prolonged commercial break, Bryant Gumbel and Katie Couric introduced a segment about a groundhog somewhere in Pennsylvania that had seen its shadow before scurrying back into its hole. As the cohosts blathered on, they began complaining about an additional six weeks of winter people in the northeast were destined to suffer based on the groundhog's exploits. I took another look out of the nearest window and figured there must not be groundhogs near San Antonio. I mused for a moment if armadillos were used to predict the weather patterns in Texas, and if so, why Rory had never mentioned it. Over the last three weeks, he'd filled me in on nearly everything else he'd learned about living in The Lone Star State, but he hadn't mentioned a word about armadillos substituting for groundhogs.

Other than being an unofficial holiday celebrating a large rodent, the day had begun like all the others since my arrival, and I started getting antsy for a change of scenery. Over the past few weeks, I'd had several chances to talk with Rory about life, more about his than mine, and I realized his personal problems were affecting him more than mine were bothering me. Though my mood swings had leveled off, I hadn't really felt any better about my future since coming south. Just the same, I was glad to have come to Texas, and all the attractions I had seen in San Antonio had definitely lifted my spirits, at least temporarily.

These included whirlwind visits to the Alamo and the San Antonio River Walk one balmy Saturday afternoon, followed by our attendance at my first rodeo later that evening. The next day, we visited the historic San Fernando Cathedral, and then lunched at an authentic Mexican restaurant run by a family of genuine, Spanish-speaking Mexicans. For some reason, that meal left an impression on me that I wouldn't soon forget. More recently, Rory and I went to the newly opened Alamo Dome and watched an NBA game between the San Antonio Spurs and their intrastate rivals, the Houston Rockets. All these adventures were features of big city life I would never have enjoyed had I stayed in Iowa, and for that reason, I was happy to have made the trip.

But a disturbing conversation I'd had with Rory just days ago doused my enthusiasm and convinced me it was time to leave.

* * * * *

Rory's house
San Antonio, Texas
Sunday, January 30, 1994, 5:30 p.m.

The end of the football season is a sad time in Texas, and today would have been no different if the Dallas Cowboys had not won the NFC championship game and earned a spot in the 1994 Super Bowl. Super Bowl parties are a Texas tradition regardless of the participating teams, and extra interest was garnered since the Cowboys were playing. Like most football fans across the country, Rory and Lee decided to celebrate the occasion. The house where they were living was spacious and an obvious choice to entertain guests while watching the iconic Texas team play. So lavish was the house, it left me wondering how they could afford the rent. Each time I questioned Rory about his expenses, he either changed the subject or answered vaguely. But the monthly rent wasn't the only expenditure that stirred my curiosity regarding his income. Other recent acquisitions, such as the expensive new truck he was driving

THE LONG WAY AROUND

and the fashionable clothes he wore, left me wondering how large the paychecks of manual laborers were in the local landscape industry. Everywhere we went, money was never a problem for Rory.

It wasn't until the second half of the Super Bowl that I suspected something dubious was going on. Whether it was legal or not was the question. I had known Rory since grade school, and I doubted he was involved in something illicit. But after some serious deliberation, I decided this Rory wasn't the friend I remembered. Something in his character had changed since last summer. This Rory was out of his element, as if potential trouble had found him and he was either too greedy or naïve to see what was going on.

A group of guests arrived during the pregame interviews—mostly Lee and Rory's coworkers—and since Lee had grown up just a couple of blocks away, a few of his personal friends had also been invited. Soft drinks and beers filled the fridge, and plenty of food had been catered—mostly Tex-Mex dishes upon my request. Country-western music was playing loudly in the background, drubbing out the voices of Dick Enberg and Bob Trumpy on the television as the duo took turns peppering players and coaches with questions they hoped viewers would find interesting. Of the fifteen people at Rory's house, only three were women, two of which were wives and one a girlfriend of my hosts' coworkers. The rest were diehard, football-loving landscapers who had waited patiently all season for this annual, testosterone-fueled event.

When the game finally started, everyone filled their plates, grabbed a beverage, and sat around the television to cheer on the Cowboys. The banter was fast and furious, and entire conversations were crammed between the network announcers' calls. I couldn't have found myself in a more jovial atmosphere. For a little while, I became a Dallas Cowboy fan, not because I cared if they won or lost, but because the Texans around me were enjoying the action so much I didn't want to spoil the fun.

As is popular and readily found in Texas, I'd been drinking iced tea for most of my visit. Sometime during the game's second quarter, as I returned to the kitchen to refill my glass, one of Rory's coworkers blurted out, "Going for more of that sweet tea, ain't you Iowa!" The group erupted in laughter, and as a result, I earned a new nickname. For the rest of the day, I became known to everyone as Sweet Tea. I didn't put up any resistance, because I found it amusing, though I didn't let it show. Not that it would have helped anyway. Once the female guests began calling me that, I knew it was official. Among the San Antonio crowd, I had officially become Sweet Tea.

It was just after the second half kickoff when the doorbell rang. At the time, I was closest in the kitchen, so I volunteered to answer it. A collective, "Thanks, Sweet Tea!" sounded out over the game from the living room as I headed toward the foyer.

When I opened the door, I was surprised by what I saw waiting. Three Mexican guys were standing there with mixed expressions on their faces. The largest stood in front. He had on jeans, work boots, expensive sunglasses, and a white button-down work shirt with advertising on back that I couldn't recognize. Though serious and businesslike, he maintained a friendly expression on his face. Behind him were two smaller companions. Both looked like trouble. They seemed shifty and appeared to have bad attitudes. Nobody inside had announced they were expecting guests, and this made me uncertain about how to proceed.

"*No hablo español*," I said, trying my best to remember what Rory had taught me to say to the waitress in the Mexican restaurant a few days ago. Before I could close the door, the big guy in front smiled and said, in good English, "Wait a second, *amigo*. My name is Carlos Reyes. I'm here to see Rory. I'm his boss."

"Oh. Sorry," I said, sneaking another glance at his two friends. The group didn't seem like an even match. The two smaller guys wore dirty, wrinkled pants and had shabby shoes. Each had tattoos on their necks jutting up from under the collars of their T-shirts. More tattoos in dull green, which appeared to be homemade, were stenciled across the backs of each finger. I couldn't tell if they were letters or symbols, nor did I care to find out. I only knew that I wanted this encounter to be over. I couldn't imagine what business Rory had with this gang.

"These are my associates, Pedro and Jose Luis," Carlos stated. "They're visiting from Mexico. They will wait here while I talk to Rory."

THE LONG WAY AROUND

"Rory has guests now. Wait here a minute while I see if he is available, okay," I said, politely.

"No problem, *amigo*," Carlos said.

I closed the door and retreated to the living room. I caught Rory's attention and waved over him to the kitchen. He looked surprised and asked me who was at the door.

"Well, I'm not really sure. Three guys want to talk to you. One of them speaks English and says he's your boss. His name is Carlos Reyes. The other two look like they swam the Rio Grande last night to get here. They don't speak English."

"Carlos is here? Why didn't you say so?" Rory said as he hustled toward the door. I followed him with a confused look on my face.

Rory swung the door open. "Hey, Carlos! Come on in, man!" in a voice that sounded as if he'd been expecting his employer, when he hadn't. The two shook hands and Carlos introduced his friends from Mexico. Once inside, Rory invited them to join the Super Bowl party, but Carlos declined even though he knew almost everyone in attendance. "I don't have time today, *amigo*, but *gracias* anyway," he said. "I want to talk to you about something in private."

"Yeah, sure," Rory answered before looking my direction. "Hey, Ryan, could you get Carlos' friends some beers from the fridge and anything else they want?"

"Okay, sure. No problem," I answered. And except for the language barrier, it really wasn't a problem, because the minuscule interest I had in the Super Bowl had been easily replaced by my new interest in what Rory was up to.

I led the Mexicans into the kitchen and opened the fridge. "*Cerveza?*" I asked. Both nodded in the affirmative. There was Mexican and domestic beer from which to choose. "Tecate or Lone Star?" I offered. To my surprise, though I wasn't sure why, they both chose Lone Star. After opening the bottles, I motioned them over the game on the television. They declined and pointed toward the front door. I peered out back and saw Rory and Carlos circling the swimming pool behind the house. Carlos was doing all the talking as Rory looked at the ground and walked. Occasionally, he nodded his head in the affirmative.

I returned to the front steps where the Mexicans were waiting.

They spoke to each other in Spanish and gulped their beers. The ice in my glass had melted long ago and the tea was warm. I sat on the step and daydreamed. Before long, the front door opened and Carlos came out alone. He seemed to be in good spirits. His friends quickly finished their beers and handed me the empty bottles. They all said *adios* and got back into the company truck. I went back inside the house well before they were out of sight.

When I returned to the game, Rory was sitting with his friends and laughing. He'd somehow managed to squeeze his massive frame between two coworkers on the couch. He gave no indication anything was wrong. The third quarter was winding down, and the Cowboys looked to have the game under control. Everyone inside was happy and satisfied. I refilled a glass of iced tea and sat on the last available seat, an armrest of the couch. The party was still going strong, and I decided to rejoin it.

* * * * *

Super Bowl XXVIII had ended a couple of hours ago, and the party disbanded soon after. I helped Rory and Lee clean up the mess. Nobody said much in the process. Lee was tired, and I could tell something was on Rory's mind. Before long, Lee went to bed, and Rory and I stayed up and watched television.

"Did watching the game make you regret quitting football?" I asked.

"Not even a little," he said. I believed him.

"Are you ever going to tell me what happened at North Texas? I mean, when they recruited you, the coaches were beaming like they'd won the lottery. And your signing was featured in headlines of all the Texas newspapers. What gives?"

I could almost see Rory's blood pressure start to rise. "Yeah," he said with a scoff. "Do you remember that headline in the *Dallas Morning News* sports page claiming my signing was revenge for North Texas losing Hayden Fry to Iowa?" He began laughing. "I even believed it myself! Do you know how difficult it is to resist reading headlines about yourself? What a joke!"

"So, what happened?"

"I think their intentions started out sincere enough. Then they landed a star recruit from Tyler, the one they really wanted. I got demoted to second string quick. But I didn't move to Texas to ride the bench. In fact, I wasn't even given an opportunity to win the position. It was a done deal, so I left and never looked back. Not once."

"Fair enough. At least now I know the truth." I decided to change the subject while Rory was in the confessing mood. "So, Carlos owns the company where you work?"

"Carlos? Nah. He's just the main foreman of the different crews our company has scattered around at any given time."

"How did he get that job?"

"I suppose he started out as a crew member and got promoted as a result of longevity, experience, and merit. The same way as anyone else probably. Why?"

"I was just wondering what your business meeting with him was about during the Super Bowl."

"It's too late to talk about that stuff now. How do you like your new nickname, Sweet Tea?" Rory said with a cackle.

It was a weak attempt to change the subject. I decided I wasn't going to let him off the hook this time. "I don't mind it. What kind of business meeting was it?" I persisted.

Sensing he couldn't avoid my queries any longer, he said, "Well, Ryan, if you must know I do some moonlighting for Carlos on the weekends. So does Lee sometimes. It pays great, and the work is easy."

"What kind of moonlighting? Easy money for doing what?"

"We use the company trucks to make pickups and deliveries in the region," Rory said.

"Why does that pay so well?"

"Because it's done on weekends, it takes all day, I'm dependable, and I have the right look," my friend answered.

His response begged the next logical question. "What kind of look does someone need to drive a delivery truck?" I asked.

Rory was starting to get annoyed by my persistence. "The trustworthy, All-American kind of look," he said. "You know, young, clean-cut, Caucasian. The description least likely to get pulled over."

"What are you delivering?" I said.

"Mostly plants and shrubs from Mexico, I guess" Rory said. "I've never had a look inside the cargo van, and that's the beauty of it. I don't have to check the inventory or help load the truck when I arrive or unload it upon delivery. It's all been prepared for me. I only need to start the engine and drive to the San Antonio drop-off point determined by Carlos. Like I said, easy money," he said with a smirk.

"Which kinds of plants are so valuable that having them delivered safe and sound pays so well?" I asked, obvious suspicion in my voice.

Rory just stared at the television, as if he were looking right through it. I could tell he'd been so enticed by the lucrative pay he'd never considered the situation in full. Eventually, he said, "I don't know. The usual landscaping plants and trees, I guess. Agaves, cactus, palms. Maybe avocado plants for local growers. I don't really care. What are you, my mother?" he snapped.

I ignored his irritation. "What exactly does Carlos have you doing? And what is your business arrangement?"

Rory didn't answer right away. For a moment, I thought he wasn't going to respond at all. Then he said, "It's all legit, Ryan. I wake up early and Carlos picks me up. I don't know the final destination until we're halfway to it. Usually, we end up in some border town along the Rio Grande, but I never cross the border and go into Mexico. The towns are usually just small specks with a few houses and a gas station. I doubt most are even on a map. If I didn't know better, I'd guess half of them don't even have electricity or indoor plumbing. On some runs, we travel to bigger cities, too. I've been to Brownsville several times and Laredo once. It's usually around noon when we arrive. Carlos always takes me to lunch. After we order, he finds a payphone and makes a call. By the time we've finished eating, the van I'm hired to drive is loaded, ready, and waiting. I don't waste any time when we get there. I jump in, start the engine, and follow the directions straight to the delivery point. After delivering the cargo, I hand Carlos the keys to the company truck and he gives me an envelope stuffed with cash. And I'm not talking about Mexican pesos, my friend. The compensation varies, but I have yet to receive less than a thousand dollars per run,

THE LONG WAY AROUND

sometimes more. To date, I've made nearly thirty runs, and I've saved almost all my earnings."

"Thirty runs? You're playing with fire, Rory," I warned.

"Look, Ryan, I'm in a good situation. I found a sweet spot by pure luck. I've got a three-year plan, and now all I have to do is work my plan. At this rate, I can return to Iowa in a couple of years and buy a farm with a house included! And when I do, I'll be coming back a success instead of a disgrace for quitting school."

"So that's what this is about? You won't go home because you quit playing football?"

"I didn't just quit football, I quit *college*. A free ride. I was supposed to be the first in my entire family to earn a college degree. Now, I'll be just another farmer. But that's okay. I decided there's nothing wrong with that as long as I succeed on my own terms."

"Look, pal, you don't even know what you're hauling around in those trucks. It could be drugs for all you know. Bales of marijuana, or worse! Or maybe you're transporting Mexicans brought here illegally. If you wind up in jail, you can forget about a shameless return home."

This stalled Rory's rebuttal. "Don't start messing with my head," he said. "My plan is too simple, and the money is too easy. You don't know that the trucks aren't filled with agaves and cactuses."

"Did you forget what my Grandpa Conrad told us at least a dozen times?" I asked. I intentionally brought my grandfather into the discussion because Rory always had great respect for him. "He always said, 'If something sounds too good to be true, it's because it probably is.'"

Rory continued staring at the television in silent protest.

"Rory, I'm your best friend. I just want to help sort things out so I know you'll be okay."

"No need to worry about me, Sweet Tea. I'm a big boy, all alone down here in Texas and doing fine. In just a couple of years, I plan to come home for good. By then, I should be able to buy one hundred acres of prime crop land with *cash*. Then I can live my life how I always imagined I would at the end of my football career. Life is funny, Ryan. Circumstances change quickly, and you must figure out solutions to your problems as you go. It's not like it was back in high school."

I resisted the urge to roll my eyes at his lecture. Instead, I thought, *you're telling me?* "In that case, I don't expect you to come back at all," I said. "You might as well face it."

"Sure, I will," he said with a mixture of disbelief and spite in his voice. "Why wouldn't I?"

"In the event this side job *is* legitimate and continues, you'll get too comfortable with the lifestyle you're living, if you haven't already. Just look at yourself—only nineteen and renting a great house with a pool, a brand new truck, and some good friends. All that's left is for a beautiful girl to enter the picture and then you won't have any reason to leave Texas."

This gave Rory another reason to think before speaking. Before he opened his mouth, I cut him off.

"But I doubt your side job is on the up-and-up. You could run into a whole bunch of trouble, so maybe when you do return to Iowa, it'll be with your tail between your legs."

Flippantly, Rory brushed my concern aside. "You always did worry like an old woman," he said with a grin. "I don't know whether I'll continue calling you Sweet Tea or start calling you Old Mother Hen."

"You better hope you don't have to call me *correct*," I answered. I could tell he had no intentions of taking my advice, and I wasn't going to belabor the point and wear out my welcome. However, I did want to express my concerns in case problems with the law were in Rory's future. That way, he could never say I should have warned him.

We changed the subject and started talking about other things. Through all our conversations, I noted how Rory had never bothered to ask me about my troubles. He never brought up my grandfather, and only mentioned our mutual best friend, Tim, to warn me not to tell him about anything we'd discussed. I considered this may have been as a result of selfishness, or that he purposely didn't want to rekindle my delicate emotional state. Nevertheless, by the time I'd gone to bed, I knew my visit in Texas was winding down. It was time to leave, but I still didn't have a desire to go home. I decided to stick around a few more days to plan my exit strategy.

THE LONG WAY AROUND

* * * * *

Rory's house
San Antonio, Texas
Wednesday, February 02, 1994, 10:30 a.m.

After *The Today Show* ended, I became even more restless and anxious. Flipping through the plethora of cable channels with nothing worth watching had become tiresome, and there were still six hours until Rory and Lee came home from work. Maybe the warm temperature was causing my blood pressure to rise, or maybe at night the stars in the Texas sky had aligned in some perverse configuration, but whatever the reason, I suffered my first panic attack in weeks.

This one hit without warning and, consequently, rattled me more than usual. It struck while I was in the shower, so I was not able to feel the customary burst of perspiration at the onset. Rapidly, my sense of balance became overwhelmed by dizziness, and I had all could do to support myself against the wet acrylic to keep from falling on my face. In time, visions of the brutal attack I'd witnessed in the forest recurred, and I slid down the shower wall until I was sitting under the deluge of water with my elbows propped on my knees and my head in my hands. Through split fingers, I strained to breathe through the torrent of water, and my eyes immediately swelled. I reached to my chest for the rosary Dieter had given my grandfather. I'd been wearing it continuously since leaving Iowa, but it wasn't in place at the moment. As fate would have it, I'd removed it for the first time in weeks before entering the shower.

Seconds turned into minutes before my blood pressure dropped and my breathing normalized. When my nerves steadied and my strength returned, I noticed how good the pounding water felt on my neck and shoulders. After a short time, my muscles relaxed and I wanted to stand, so I turned off the water and climbed to my feet. After drying off, I stepped out and wiped the foggy mirror with my towel. At the sink, I slapped cold water in my face, then leaned in closer to the moist glass.

Staring at my reflection, I thought long and hard about what I should do next, realizing I was just as confused about my future as the day of my first nervous breakdown. The obvious choice was to go home, to get back into a familiar atmosphere and routine, and to continue with my therapy sessions. But it was a disappointing choice. I'd begun to notice some improvement over the last few weeks, and except for the growing need to rent my farm before the spring planting season, I was in no hurry to get back to Iowa. On the other hand, I didn't want to stay at Rory's house any longer. I still thought of Rory as one of my best friends, but the position he'd put himself in raised enough alarm for me to recuse myself after my attempted guidance had been rejected. I didn't need more time to deliberate on the situation before deciding to leave.

Once dressed, I packed my clothes into my duffle bag, and prepared to head out. I found the phonebook and searched out a taxi in the yellow pages. While waiting for it to arrive, I wrote Rory a note at the kitchen table informing him of my decision to leave. In the letter, I tried to persuade him to visit Iowa in the summer and hang out with me for a few weeks so I could return the hospitality. I even swore to him I wouldn't inform anyone he'd be coming, hoping that once he was back in familiar surroundings his sensibilities would be revived. Lastly, I tried to lure him back with a fishing trip on the Mississippi River, his favorite recreation in the world. In the end, I suspected he'd refuse the offer.

Before our conversation after the Super Bowl, I never realized the extent of the shame Rory had over quitting college, nor the humiliation he felt about returning home in disgrace. He'd decided to gamble away his future, all-or-nothing, in favor of a chance at personal redemption, and I knew he wouldn't show his face back home until he'd regained his self-worth and esteem. At this point, I could only hope he achieved his goals before the hammer fell and his life was ruined forever.

*****

San Antonio Train Station
Wednesday, February 02, 1994, 2:30 p.m.

I had never had any luck traveling on short notice, mostly because cheap fares and sufficient scheduling to destinations I wanted to go never seemed to align. Not that I had a long list of places I wanted to visit anyway. Lack of money and bad timing had always restricted my adventures to within a two-hour drive of my grandfather's house during summer breaks.

As I stood at the San Antonio train station ticket counter, it came as no surprise that organizing my return trip to Iowa would be a fiasco. The Texas Eagle did not depart to Galesburg, Illinois, the closest available drop-off point to my destination, until seven o'clock the next morning. This left me flustered as I debated my options while the ticket agent stood glaring at me. I could feel a line of impatient people behind me shifting their weight, crossing and uncrossing their arms, and hemming and hawing in annoyance.

"So, do you want a seat on the Texas Eagle tomorrow morning or not?" the lady asked gruffly through a hole in the window separating us.

I calculated there wouldn't be enough time to return to Rory's house before he had read my note telling of my leaving, and if I did manage to beat him to it, I certainly didn't feel like defending my position concerning my decision to leave the next morning. Rather, I decided to buy the ticket and camp out at the train station all night in order to catch the morning train to Galesburg.

"How much is a roomette?" I asked. I'd learned my lesson on my trip south from St. Louis. The extra privacy and a cot to stretch out on would improve the journey, especially since I had further to travel north than I'd experienced on the first leg of the trip.

"Three hundred and ninety-nine dollars, unless you're a student," she said, catching me by surprise with her initiative. "Then you're eligible for a fifteen percent discount. Do you attend school full-time?"

"No, ma'am," I said, checking my wallet to count the available cash inside. "I took this year off, so I guess I don't qualify." After flipping through the bills with my fingertips, I tallied seven hundred and fifty-eight dollars. For renting a bunk bed in a sleeping compartment, the price seemed steep, and left me unwilling to part with the extra money. Instead, I asked, "How much is the fare to Galesburg for a regular coach seat?" Before she could answer, I added with a smile, "Without a student discount." I could tell she received my attempted humor but offered no sign it was appreciated.

"Eighty-nine dollars," she replied without expression.

As I hunted through my wallet, I saw the business card with the large shrimp claw on front I had tucked away last month just before boarding the Texas Eagle in St. Louis. An idea struck me, and I told the agent to help the next customer while I took care of another matter. The lady stared back in disbelief. I ignored her scowl and meandered around the train station in search of a payphone. In the hallway leading to the public restrooms, two phones were mounted on the wall and waiting for use. On a touch-tone dial pad, I punched in the number printed on the business card, followed by more numbers from my AT&T calling card.

A few seconds and two rings later, a female voice with a slow, southern drawl answered. "Novak and Novak Seafood Delights. This is Dixie. How may I help you?"

It then dawned on me I should have prepared an appropriate explanation about why I was calling. Since I hadn't, I tried my best to stammer out a clear, concise reply.

"Hello. My name is Ryan Meyers, and I'm a friend of Tomislav Novak. He said I could reach him at this number. Is he available to speak?"

"Oh, are you the young man he drove to St. Louis through a blizzard a few weeks ago?" she asked. "He told us office girls you might be calling."

I enjoyed Dixie's Louisiana accent very much. She sounded like a genuinely kind person. "Yes, I am," I answered.

"You're in luck, Mr. Meyers. Mr. Novak is in the office today. If you can hold, I'll track him down immediately."

"Thank you, Dixie. I'll hold."

Less than a minute later, a familiar voice appeared on the line. "*Where y'at*, Iowa?" Tomislav chimed.

"Hello, Tomislav. I'm in San Antonio, but I don't think that's what you want to know, is it?"

"No, not exactly," Tomislav said with a chuckle. "But it would have been my next question. How are you?" And before I could respond, he asked, "And when are you coming to Louisiana? My offer to work on a fishing boat still stands you know."

THE LONG WAY AROUND

"That's why I called. I'm at a crossroads at the moment, and I'm considering my options. I don't feel like going home yet."

As much as I tried to disguise it, Tomislav could sense the depression in my voice. "I hear you, buddy" he said. "Don't worry, that homesick feeling will return before you know it. But don't even think about going back until you first come visit me and we have some fun on the Gulf!"

Tomislav's Louisiana accent was much stronger now than I remembered it being on the road from Iowa to St. Louis. I took it to mean he was more comfortable on his own turf and was treating me as one of his own. And though it was unnecessary, he reassured me several times that his offer to hire me as a deckhand was still intact. It didn't take long for me to agree and commit.

"Then it's settled," he said. "You can use the spare bedroom in my condo until we ship out Monday morning. On the shrimp trawler, there'll be a berth waiting with your name above the door. I'll show you the ropes the first couple of days, and before you know it, you'll be a first-rate shrimper."

"It's that simple, eh? Okay. What time in the morning do we leave?" I asked.

"Dark-thirty a.m., sharp. Just like in your old deer-hunting days," he said, before realizing he might have put his foot in his mouth. In fact, I barely noticed, and when Tomislav sensed his poor choice of phrasing had caused no harm, he moved to the next topic. "Have you ever been out to sea?"

"Um…no. Why?"

"Do you think you might easily become seasick? You know, because of your dizziness."

"I've been fishing on the Mississippi River and never had a problem before. If you don't take me into a hurricane, I think I'll be fine."

"That's what I was thinking, too. Okay, it's a deal. Call me when you know your arrival time in New Orleans, and I'll be at the station to pick you up. This trip is going to do you a world of good. You'll see, it'll be fantastic!"

I began feeling better the instant Tomislav said that. I was ready for a new experience and another adventure. I hurried back to the ticket counter after our conversation ended.

"A one-way coach ticket, please," I said to the same agent I'd been dealing with before.

The lady remained stone-faced. "No student discount, right?"

I understood her humor but gave no sign it was appreciated. "When does the next train to New Orleans depart?"

"*New Orleans?*" she asked with surprise. "Folks in Galesburg are going to be very disappointed, I'm sure," she stated with Texas sarcasm. She tapped some numbers on some sort of keyboard. "It usually leaves at six twenty-five a.m., but you're in luck because this month a second daily is running on a trial basis. The outbound to New Orleans begins boarding in an hour," she said.

"Great! I'll take a ticket for that one," I replied. The good fortune painted a smile on my face, and I handed my money over with delight.

The agent punched in the codes and a ticket ejected from the electronic dispenser. As she slid it under the window, she smiled and said, "Have a nice trip."

Chapter Thirty
A Trip to the City

Crossroads Mall
Waterloo, Iowa
Saturday, February 05, 1994, 11:15 a.m.

Maureen Kelleher had been planning a shopping excursion with her daughter on different occasions over the last few weeks, but winter storm warnings had forced them to cancel each time. Mary was now seven months pregnant, and the last thing either lady wanted was to be stranded on the highway in the middle of a snowstorm. However, many last minute items for the baby's arrival remained to be acquired. And although Mary felt fine, her mother cautioned she would fatigue more easily the closer her April delivery date neared, and that she would not feel up to shopping later on.

"You can plan on being less active during March and April," she advised Mary. "I don't think I moved from the sofa the entire last month I was pregnant with your brother. It's better that we take care of the final details as soon as possible."

The streak of nasty weather had ended abruptly in the previous few days. Clear, sunny skies were forecast for the entire week ahead. Temperatures were beginning to warm, and many massive snow drifts had already begun melting in the sunshine. As she drove, the glare was so strong Maureen was snow blinded, and in reaction, she developed a throbbing headache around her eyes from squinting. When Mary suggested her mother put on her sunglasses, Maureen informed her she had broken hers and hadn't replaced them, nor did she plan to until after all the baby expenses had been settled. Mary was reminded of the sacrifices her parents had endured for their children over their lifetimes. She considered how fortunate she was to have been born to them and promised to herself to repay her parents for their love.

DOUGLAS CAVANAUGH

Maureen turned into the Crossroads Mall shopping center in Waterloo and parked outside the entrance of their favorite department store. The ladies smiled at one another as they entered, just as they had so many times before. It was eleven a.m. and they had the entire day free.

* * * * *

Tim Ross despised shopping and avoided anything to do with it unless it was a store selling sporting goods or hunting and fishing equipment. Being from a rural community, time and distance aided him in avoiding outlet centers and shopping malls, yet many of his friends enjoyed spending time in the larger cities on weekends, and roaming shopping centers was a regular occurrence for them. This made complete evasion impossible for Tim. More often than he liked, he was forced into wasting time in one store or another whenever one of his friends drove to Waterloo and his presence was included. This day was different though. Today, Tim was alone and strolling through the Crossroads Mall on his own accord and unashamedly enjoying the experience.

Inside his coat pocket, Tim carried an envelope containing a Christmas present from his favorite aunt. It was a gift certificate for a pair of sunglasses he'd seen advertised in a hunting magazine. Through some personal research, which consisted of asking a few friends and acquaintances if they knew where he could find that brand, Tim learned one of the kiosks in the mall carried the style. This pleased him enormously, and it took all the patience he could muster to wait until the cold spell snapped so he could race to Waterloo and buy them.

* * * * *

Mary and her mother were strolling leisurely down the mall, their hands heavy with bags full of maternity outfits, baby pajamas, and supplies for a newborn. Neither paid attention that Mary's secret was exposed for the eyes of the world to see. It was rare that they ever ran into anyone from their hometown while in Waterloo. However, Mary's parents were still not prepared to surrender the secrecy of their daughter's pregnancy, even though Maureen's pride

THE LONG WAY AROUND

of becoming a grandmother was growing daily and aching to be released.

Mary was ecstatic with her parents' decision to allow her to go shopping. Being cooped up over the last few months had made her stir-crazy, so she was prepared to deal with any consequences her pregnancy's revelation might produce. Questions, she knew, were certain to arise if she was seen, and she had decided to answer each truthfully and sincerely if asked.

*****

Tim was happy to see there were no other customers at the mall's sunglasses kiosk. He timidly greeted the attractive young lady working the stand. He estimated her to be a year or two older than him, probably a college student working a weekend shift to earn some extra money. She was a bit taller than him, had shoulder length, brown hair, and matching brown eyes. The young lady carried herself with a calm style and manner that he liked immensely. Next to Mary Kelleher, the girl behind the counter was the most beautiful he'd ever seen. He now regretted putting a pinch of chewing tobacco in his bottom lip before approaching the kiosk.

"Hi. Can I help you?" she asked confidently when Tim came near. A name tag pinned to her blouse read *Mandy*.

Tim felt flustered. The earlier thrill he'd been relishing from the thought of owning new sunglasses was quickly overshadowed by the more pressing one created by the gorgeous girl waiting on him. He straightened his posture and said, "Hi, Mandy," as if he'd known her all his life. That made her smile. Tim resisted an urge to spit tobacco juice in the plastic cup he held at his side. He said, "I hear this kiosk carries Costa Del Mar Outdoor Elites. I received a gift certificate for Christmas *especially* for a pair of Outdoor Elites."

"Hmm," Mandy said. "I know we carry Costa Del Mar, but I'm not sure about the Outdoor Elite edition. I'm only here on weekends, so let me check if new stock has arrived in the last five days." With that, Mandy circled the kiosk and opened a series of locked cabinets under the cash register. Tim watched her walk away, excused himself, and told her he'd be right back.

While Mandy was searching for the Outdoor Elites, he hustled twenty meters down the mall to an oasis of fake plants surrounded by some benches used primarily by elderly visitors who congregated to watch the passersby. Behind an artificial banana leaf extending from a planter made from synthetic wood, Tim spotted a garbage can. On the sly, he swiped at the tobacco in his lip with his tongue and spit the contents into the cup he was carrying. As he tossed the cup into the trash, he vowed to quit the filthy habit, and as if to make a show of good faith, he removed the round canister from his back pocket and threw it in, too. When he returned to the kiosk, he saw Mandy leaning against the counter and smiling at him. On top of the display case, a box advertising Costa Del Mar Outdoor Elites rested between her elbows. "I have some good news," she happily reported. "I found what you're after."

Tim's eyes were brightened by his good fortune. A jolt of adrenaline raced through his veins, and he fought a powerful urge to ignore Mandy and focus on the sunglasses. Instead, he decided to ask Mandy some personal questions about her life. The more he asked, the more receptive Mandy seemed. To Tim's surprise, he learned they were the same age and had graduated from different rural high schools within the same conference. He also discovered the sunglass kiosk to be her part-time job on weekends, and that she worked full-time during the week as a receptionist at a dental office in a town not far from his. Tim decided to back off a bit, reluctant to risk being too forward. In the process, he redirected his attention toward the sunglasses. Mandy took the box and unpacked it carefully. While she fiddled with the inner cardboard packing and pulled at the cloth protective sheath, Tim read the advertising on the box cover aloud. "Bronze-colored, plastic, polarized lenses. UV protection. Perfect!" he said excitedly. "Only twenty-three percent light transmission, with increased contrast. Excellent!" Mandy smiled at his enthusiasm. "And they have wraparound, camouflage frames. Awesome!"

"If you'd like to try them on," she said, "there's a big mirror on the corner display."

"Would I ever!" Tim said. Together, they side-stepped a short distance and Tim slid on the sunglasses. He then adjusted his posture and looked straight into the mirror.

THE LONG WAY AROUND

"So, what do you think?" asked Mandy.

"I don't know why they named them Outdoor Elites. They should have called them *Swashbucklers!*" he answered, proud of his uncharacteristic confidence.

That made Mandy giggle. "Does that mean whenever you put them on, you'll think yourself as a modern-day Errol Flynn?"

That tamed Tim's newfound cockiness. "Who's Errol Flynn?" he asked.

Mandy was amused by his sudden seriousness. "You know, the actor from the thirties who played the hero swordsman in those black and white movies?"

"I don't really know much about black and white movies," he said plainly, hoping she wasn't an old movie buff.

"Oh, he played Robin Hood, too. I think that film was in color," Mandy added casually.

"Well, back in high school, I was one of the Three Musketeers." Then he reflected for a second. "Don't ask where the other two are now. I sort of lost track of them," he said. "Maybe Outdoor Elites works better after all. In any case, they fit great and look excellent. I'll take them."

"I thought you might," Mandy said. "And just so you know, they do look great on you."

Tim felt a heavy fluttering in his stomach. *God, please don't let me ruin this.*

* * * * *

When Mary and her mother had bought everything they needed, and some additional items they didn't, they returned to the department store they'd originally entered. Maureen was exhausted, and the store lighting only strengthened her headache's intensity. Mary found a comfortable chair near the shoe department and sat her mother in it. There was something she'd forgotten to pick up, she told her mother, and it wouldn't take long for her to find it. She instructed Maureen to wait for her and charged off toward the mall entrance, intent on finding one last thing to buy—a gift for her mother that would not only make her look good, but make her feel better on the drive home.

DOUGLAS CAVANAUGH

*****

Tim had just exchanged the gift certificate for his new pair of sunglasses when a young lady approached the kiosk from the opposite side. Mandy excused herself to greet the potential customer. Tim's mind raced as he debated between wearing his new shades out of the mall or putting them on after he was in his car. He reopened the box and slid them on, then admired himself in the mirror while Mandy guided the customer around the corner to the women's glasses near where Tim was standing. Tim heard the customer say she was looking for a gift for her mother. Soon, the ladies were discussing her mother's style, taste, and the fact new sunglasses were needed to fight the blinding, winter brightness on their drive home. When Tim had enjoyed enough of his new image, he turned and faced the ladies, wanting to say goodbye to Mandy. As he did, he was surprised by the pregnant woman standing just a couple of feet away.

"Mickey?" he said. "Where have you been?"

Mary recognized the face behind the sunglasses instantly. Impulsively, she leaned to hug Tim as tears swelled in her eyes. Her mixed emotions were overwhelming, and the tears fell from a combination of happiness, shock, confusion, and shame. "Oh, Tim! I'm so sorry I lost touch with you guys!"

Tim was noticeably disturbed by the distended abdomen pressing against his belt buckle. He wanted to ask about it but didn't know the proper protocol involved. Finally, he said, "I see you have some news. I mean…if you want to tell me."

"Of course, I want to. I've been dying to tell someone, Ryan especially," she volunteered. "But because of circumstances beyond my control, almost nobody knows," she added, wiping away salty drops on her cheek.

Mandy eavesdropped on the conversation and tried to put the puzzle pieces together.

"You mean Ryan's going to be a father?" Tim asked with a wild expression of excitement and disbelief. He put both hands on top of his head. "Mickey, this is incredible! We have to talk about this. Let's go over there and sit on that bench."

THE LONG WAY AROUND

As Mary walked over, Tim hustled back to Mandy. In a controlled outburst, he explained how the situation was an emergency, and how he needed to go. Before leaving, he regained the courage to ask Mandy for her telephone number. Mandy wrote it on the back of Tim's receipt. She smiled and said she'd be home tonight if he wanted to talk. "Believe me," Tim answered, "after the conversation I'm about to have, I'm going to need someone to chat with later on." They smiled at one another and exchanged goodbyes.

*****

Tim drove extra slowly the whole way home. It wasn't because the weather had turned poor—the whole day had been gorgeous. The roads were clean, safe, and dry, and the traffic was almost nonexistent the further he motored away from Waterloo. Nevertheless, his driving was distracted, and he had trouble focusing his attention on the matter at hand.

The saga of Mary's pregnancy concerned him deeply. Tim felt terrible for what she'd been through, and he sympathized with her unsuccessful attempts to meet with Ryan to discuss the matter in person. Likewise, Tim's account of Ryan's accident was an eye-opener for Mary. She'd dismissed the sordid details and accompanying accusations that had been circulating about the event as malicious rumors. Now that she'd heard the closest thing to an official story directly from Tim, her heart sank to a new low as she tormented herself with guilt. The pair had sat on the bench for a long while—long enough for Maureen to be worried about her daughter's absence.

When Maureen finally found Mary talking to Tim, she realized their family's private matter was no longer a secret. She made Tim promise to keep Mary's pregnancy under wraps and explained how Ryan's recovery could be adversely affected if he found out before the time was right. She described how they'd met with Ryan's doctors and decided to inform him according to a plan. Tim agreed not to say a word to anyone until Mary had informed Ryan personally. The biggest problem was that Ryan was nowhere to be found.

On the way home, Tim considered every possibility where Ryan might be. Until now, he'd seen no reason to be alarmed about his lack of contact over the past few weeks. He'd presumed his friend would find him when he was ready, and that he was probably visiting relatives or trying to heal in solitude. But a lot had changed that afternoon, and he suddenly thought it odd Ryan had avoided him for so long. Tim considered how he could find Ryan to check on his health without interfering with his recovery, and simultaneously realized how difficult it would be for him to keep Mary's news a secret.

Normally, he would begin his search by calling Rory, but Rory wasn't readily accessible either. He decided to stop at Rory's parents' farm before going home. Maybe Rory's folks had been in contact with their son and could give him a lead to where he could be reached. It would be a long shot if Rory knew of Ryan's whereabouts, but it was solid place to start, especially since there were few other options.

Chapter Thirty-One
Out to Sea

Hurricane Bay Marina
Grand Isle, Louisiana
Monday, February 07, 1994, 3:30 a.m.

Truth be told, I never cared much for being on the water, and even less for being in it. Even all the fun I'd had fishing, boating, and waterskiing on the Mississippi River after high school came with some private trepidation. My insufficient swimming ability is the primary reason for my feelings on the matter, though it isn't the only factor. And it isn't as though I can't swim at all because I can. In fact, I've been told I possess excellent form and technique. The main reason for my concern is that my body has a tendency to sink rather than float, though most people don't believe me when I tell them, so I don't discuss it openly and try my best to remain on *terra firma*.

I can clearly remember one instance when Mr. Timmerman, my high school wrestling coach, accused me of slacking off after witnessing me finish several lengths behind the next-to-last member on our wrestling squad during Saturday morning workouts at the local pool. Slacking off isn't in my vocabulary, and when I discussed my poor performance with him confidentially, we concluded that my dense muscle mass was causing havoc with my buoyancy and hindering my progress. At the end of our conversation, he confessed his chewing out was only intended to motivate the underachievers on our team by showing that his star grappler didn't get special treatment. Then, with a kind smile, he told me not to take his scolding to heart and made me promise not to try out for the swimming team. After that conversation, he never hollered at me for my last place finishes, and the matter was never brought up again. Looking back, I respected my coach for his honesty even more after our talk and remember working harder to win as a result.

Another reason for my aversion to water developed as a result of reading frequent reports in our local newspaper about fishermen and boaters who drowned each summer. Boating accidents can happen in seconds on the Mississippi River, and powerful undertows are always present and unpredictable. Learning from the mistakes of others was heavily preached by my grandfather, and these lethal events served as regular reminders to respect the water while having fun.

It may seem odd that as Tomislav and I walked down the dock toward the shrimp trawler in the early morning hours, I did not rethink boarding even once. I knew he had worked hard to convince his father to hire me—a complete novice to the shrimping industry—and both were risking their company's productivity as a result. I intended to prove my worthiness as a deckhand, and like most other tasks I set out to accomplish that I am unfamiliar with, I was determined to learn the ropes quickly and excel.

As we walked, a gentle breeze blowing in from the Gulf was trying its best to circulate the musty air, but it was of little use. Several shrimp trawlers were moored in the marina. A few already had their engines running and deck lamps glaring as their crews prepared for a day of shrimping, while others remained darkened, locked, and empty. About a quarter of the way to our vessel, he pointed at another. "See those big, folded, metal arms? Those are the outriggers. They'll be lowered to stabilize the craft after we leave the harbor. Then, when we reach the shrimping zone, nets will be attached to them. Do you see those flat wooden boards stacked alongside?"

"Yes."

"Those are the doors," he said.

"Doors?"

"Well, they aren't really doors, but they look like doors," he explained. "They get lowered the same time as the nets. They skim along the bottom on their sides to keep the nets open and stir the shrimp inside."

I could tell Tomislav was proud of his knowledge. This was a job he'd been working with his father since childhood and it showed

THE LONG WAY AROUND

in his confidence. I had to admit I was impressed with his expertise.

"So you skipper shrimp trawlers on the Gulf of Mexico and drive semi-trucks around the country at only twenty-one years old? You are multi-talented, my friend. Very impressive."

"Twenty-two," he said. "I had a birthday the week before you arrived."

At the end of the dock, one of largest trawlers in view was waiting for us, its bowline tied to a wood piling. In back, its deck lights were shining just brightly enough for the two crewmembers already aboard to begin preparations for a day at sea. Before stepping onto the gangplank, I strolled a ways further toward the front of the boat, wanting to see the name painted on its side.

"*The Rebel Yell,*" I read aloud.

"What do you think of it?"

"Not too shabby," I answered. "Not bad at all."

Tomislav smiled, then boasted, "I chose it myself the day we took possession of her when I was ten. I named it after my great, great, great grandfather; the one I told you about who fought in the Civil War."

"You mean your family's original immigrant from Yugoslavia?"

"Croatia!"

"Sure, I remember. The ancestor you're named after, right? So why didn't you name her *The Tomislav?*"

He shook his head and grinned. As he turned to the trawler, he muttered under his breath, "Rookies," and then climbed aboard.

*****

By one o'clock that afternoon, I had learned the basics of netting and sorting shrimp. I spent most of the time with the two other deckhands: Maurice Fontenot, a stout, middle-aged, Cajun guy everybody called Mighty Mo, and Rusty Livermore, a lifelong shrimper with a freckled complexion, small, babylike teeth, and a big heart. Mighty Mo didn't talk much. He was wearing shorts, tennis shoes with their laces untied, and an oversized T-shirt with both sleeves cut off at the shoulders. Rusty was wearing faded jeans, a T-shirt, and a camouflage baseball cap with an imprint of an alligator on front. The cap's bill was grimy and stained by greasy fingerprints. The men had been working together for years, and each had been trained by Slim Mathers, the fellow I was replacing.

Slim had retired the same day my grandpa had been buried a couple of months ago. A lifelong deckhand, he had been employed by Tomislav's father's company for decades. He'd stopped working at the age of fifty-four. When I asked Rusty if being a shrimp trawler deckhand was so lucrative a guy could retire at such a young age, he frowned and told me Slim had barely saved any money at all, and that his retirement had been forced because of health reasons.

Most of my first day on the job was spent following the deckhands around, absorbing their advice, learning the lingo, and practicing some tricks of the trade the others insisted I learn. Most of it was easy, but I sensed I was going to have to devote some serious effort into mastering a few rope-tying tactics. Other than that, my coworkers ordered me to stay out of the way and avoid any winches, cables, or other moving objects I might disrupt or could cause me harm. My real chance to shine was when the nets were retrieved, and the catch was spread onto the sorting table. Sorting shrimp was a job I learned quickly and enjoyed.

Tomislav remained at the helm the entire time, sitting in an elevated bucket seat while monitoring his course and watching the gauges and dials. On the counter above the steering wheel, a plastic figurine of Saint Peter, the Patron Saint of Fishermen, stood tall. Along the helm's wood trim, old Polaroid photos of large catches of shrimp, flounder, and mackerel were pinned in a circle, and another taped in the center showed Tomislav in his youth holding a red snapper that was nearly as big as his tiny frame.

Now, Tomislav was drinking orange juice and talking into a radio handset. He was sporting a navy blue captain's hat, and not only did he appear confident, I was convinced he was more than competent enough to skipper *The Rebel Yell*. Before long, my seafaring apprehensions faded entirely.

Tomislav emerged from the cabin early that afternoon. After a brief consultation with Rusty and Maurice, he decided to call it a day. The other deckhands showed me how to collect and stow the gear, then Tomislav turned the trawler around and we relaxed in the shade until reaching the marina.

THE LONG WAY AROUND
*****

Aboard The Rebel Yell
Gulf of Mexico
Friday, February 25, 1994, 2:30 p.m.

It seemed my nerves had stabilized over the last few weeks, yet I could not be sure if I was headed down the road to recovery or if the progress I'd been making was a temporary phenomenon. I chose the optimistic viewpoint because I was feeling better day by day and happy to be active and working. Even though our relationship was more businesslike than friendly, I got along well with Mighty Mo and Rusty, and I sensed they were pleased with my output. Back on shore, after the catch had been unloaded and delivered at the end of each day, the others went home to their families, while Tomislav and I stayed aboard the trawler in two cabins. One day blended into the next and losing track of time became routine.

During this period, I still experienced some occasional nerve-racking moments, but I suffered no anxiety attacks like the one I'd endured the day I'd left San Antonio. I attributed the lull to the fact I was directing all my mental energy toward improving my job performance. Yet, there were sporadic moments when I felt some familiar twinges from my past resurface, as if to remind me that my mental healing was a work in progress and my demons had not disappeared forever. Nonetheless, I was encouraged with my gains, and my worries about another breakdown had been pushed into the distant corners of my mind. That glorious break lasted until the middle of the current day's shrimping run.

Aboard a shrimp trawler, while the nets are down and the vessel is trolling, about four knots per hour, there isn't much for a deckhand to do once the prior haul has been sorted and put on ice. After the nets are lowered and the deck scrubbed clean, the crew has plenty of time to kill, and I've read books, slept, and talked my way through lots of empty hours. I wasn't feeling much like chatting this day, so I took refuge in a shady spot alongside the wheelhouse and leaned against the guardrail to watch the seagulls and pelicans following our wake.

It was a perfect day. There wasn't a cloud in the sky, and

even with my sunglasses in place, the glare off the water caused the muscles around my eyes to contract in spasm. A shifting wind was gaining in strength as the morning sun arched higher in the sky. Before long, *The Rebel Yell* began rolling as white-capped waves broke against her sides. Out at sea, a heavy rocking motion isn't uncommon, and I'd become accustomed to the sensation over the last three weeks. This day was different, though, and I soon began feeling nauseous and dizzy. In response, my pores opened wide and beads of sweat started to roll down my ashen face. As I took hold of the rail to maintain my balance, two colossal waves collided right before me. Millions of water droplets burst into the sun's reflection, creating a spectacular, lustrous spray brighter than a comet's dust tail. Instantly, a replay of the invisible creature exploding in Metzger's Slough surged through my mind, causing my body to convulse in response. I released the rail to cover my face, then lost my balance and crashed hard against the wheelhouse with a tremendous thud, startling Tomislav and the others inside.

By the time they had rounded the corner to discover the cause, they found me thrashing wildly on the deck with blood streaming from my nose, which had banged hard against the deck when I fell. Tomislav and the others sat me up. After a quick inspection, it appeared my injuries were minor. Mighty Mo held a rag that smelled of shrimp and diesel oil over my nose to stop the bleeding. For a while, I couldn't speak. I sat motionless on the floorboards with swollen eyes, embarrassed by the spectacle I'd made.

"All right y'all, we're quitting early today and heading back to Grand Isle to get Ryan checked by a doctor," Tomislav said while popping a lens back into the frames of my sunglasses, which had bounced free when my face hit the deck.

I waved Tomislav's decision off with a vehement sweep of my hand and stated that I'd be up and ready for work in a few minutes. The good mood I'd been in for weeks quickly disappeared, and I became bitter and angry as I wondered when my mental torture would end. The lingering depression I'd begun to shake free of had me in its grip again, and I sat on deck with my head in my palms as the rest of the crew watched over me. Gradually, my nerves calmed, and fifteen minutes later, I was on my feet trying to stammer out an explanation of what had happened. In time, I returned to my senses, and the others began to relax, too. Soon it was back to business as usual, and we joked and laughed as we brought the nets up and sorted the catch.

Even so, I could not help noticing some occasional awkward glances and concerned expressions by the crew, as if they assumed my spells were going to return at any moment and they wanted to avoid witnessing a tragedy at sea. I felt like all the goodwill I'd built up over the last few weeks had been destroyed, and that prospect depressed me even more. Fortunately, their worries subsided, and in a couple of days, the team was working better than ever.

* * * * *

Hurricane Bay Marina
Grand Isle, Louisiana
Monday, February 28, 1994, 6:30 p.m.

Back on shore after the final catch had been sorted, packed, and delivered, I watched Tomislav from afar as he chatted with Rusty and Mighty Mo outside the marina's main office. It wasn't unusual for me to be excluded from business conversations with the full-time staff, as my employment was provisional until either Tomislav's father found a suitable candidate for Slim's full-time position or I decided to leave on my own accord. As their discussion continued, I could see mixed expressions on the workers' faces, ranging from apprehension to disappointment to satisfaction, and when the meeting ended, each shook Tomislav's hand and patted him on the shoulder. A change was coming, I sensed, but nothing that seemed to leave the deckhands overly disturbed.

When the group separated, Rusty and Mighty Mo walked to their pickups, and Tomislav waved me over to the marina restaurant. We took a table on the outside terrace overlooking many tethered cabin cruisers and recreational boats and ordered Cokes and burgers. Zydeco music was gently playing from speakers mounted on the restaurant walls. Seagulls circled overhead in the distance, and several pelicans, perched in succession on wood pilings, watched us eat with envy.

"What's going on? Is everything all right?" I asked between bites.

"Nothing major," he answered. "Well, nothing unexpected, anyway. My father just got word a slot opened in dry dock. *The Rebel Yell* is overdue for maintenance. She's going to be out of action for a couple weeks. That's all."

"What does that mean for the crew?"

"Well, Mighty Mo and Rusty are on a fixed salary plus percentage pay scale, with the percentage part generating the lion's share of their income. They're on paid vacation as of right now, though the salary is just enough to make ends meet for a few weeks. It also means you are on a two-week unpaid vacation." With this, he finished his burger, tipped his head to one side, and studied me with concern. "I'll have your February paycheck ready for you tomorrow. Unless you want to return to Iowa, you can stay with me, expense free, until we're back in action. Then our deal resumes—you can work with us if you like or until my father finds Slim's replacement. How does that sound?"

Had my mental health not suffered a major setback just days ago, I probably would have decided to return to Iowa. Not because I was unsatisfied with the terms, but because tasks requiring my presence back home were waiting for me and time was becoming an issue. Also, I was starting to become homesick. But my head wasn't as ready to return to Iowa as my heart was, so I told Tomislav I'd stick around for a while longer. As soon as I'd finished my sentence, he cracked a smile, clapped his hands once, and briskly rubbed his palms back and forth. Beaming brightly, he said, "That's what I hoped you'd say!" After rattling the ice cubes at the bottom of his glass, he finished his cola with one large gulp. "Come with me, buddy. I've got something to show you."

I admit to being filled with curiosity. "What is it?"

"Geez, hold your horses, will you? You never were the patient type, Iowa," he teased. "We'll be there soon enough."

Tomislav guided me along a path leading to another area of the marina, a portion with limited accessibility where several extravagant yachts and high-end sailboats were moored. In a small cabin at the gated entrance, a guard was on duty to check us in.

THE LONG WAY AROUND

"Hey, Lamar," Tomislav said to a black man dressed in a security uniform. "Slip twenty-nine."

"Good evening, Mr. Novak," he replied. The guard was in his mid-forties and had short, frizzy hair with a bald spot in back. He moved slowly and limped a little on his right leg.

Tomislav looked at me. "This here is Lamar Bastion. He was a very famous running back for McNeese State University in Lake Charles back in the early 1970s, but you probably never heard of him since you're a *Yankee*." He and Lamar began giggling, as if they were sharing a joke on me of which I was unaware.

"Sorry, Mr. Bastion. I've never heard of you, not because I'm from up north, but because your career was over before I was born."

With that, Lamar let out a laugh and patted my shoulder. "It's okay, son," he said. "All that recognition down here didn't get me anything except for six free knee operations and this security guard job. I ain't complaining though. It has its benefits, thanks to good folks like Mr. Novak and his father. All that complimentary seafood they bring me keeps my family well fed." Lamar returned his attention to Tomislav. "Are you off to see your new baby girl?"

Tomislav cut the security guard off with a wave of his hand. "Now, Lamar, you can't be giving all my secrets away." I could see the joy on my friend's face increase with each passing second.

"Okay, I get it. You fellas just put your John Hancock on the dotted line, and you can be on your way," the guard said.

After we each signed the security log, Tomislav led me along the docks until we reached one with a sign advertising slips twenty-one through twenty-nine. As we stepped onto it, his pace quickened, and I had to hurry to keep up. When I finally caught him, he was staring at the last in a long line of sailboats. Tomislav now had an obvious glow on his face. The surprise he had for me was right in front of us and was it ever a sight to behold.

"It's the latest model built by Hunter Marine!" he said. "Well, what do you think?"

"She's beautiful!" I said. "Is she yours?"

"*Damn straight, she is*," Tomislav answered. "She's a birthday present from my dad. A thirty-footer delivered only a few days ago. We must wait for the registration papers to be finalized in the next couple of days, or we could take her for a spin right now. I can hardly wait, let me tell you. Let's take a look inside."

Before boarding, I repositioned to an angle where I could read the name that had been recently been painted on the boat.

"*Domagoj*? What in the world is a *Domagoj*?"

"It's a traditional first name in Croatia," my friend answered.

"A male or female name?"

"It's a man's name, Iowa! Man, you need to get out of the house more," he answered.

"Tomislav and Domagoj. *Sheesh,*" I said. "I'm afraid to ask what traditional girls' names sound like in Croatia."

"Very funny. Domagoj translates to something like a home healer or nurturer. I interpret that to mean a 'family man.' I have a cousin over there somewhere named Domagoj."

"Why didn't you name it *Tomislav* instead?"

Once again, Tomislav shook his head. "Rookies!"

Laughing, we boarded the vessel and Tomislav proceeded to show me around. The sailboat was brand-new and very impressive. The cabin's interior had all the amenities imaginable, and it even possessed an aroma like that of a new car.

"This must have cost your dad a fortune," I said. "I'll bet he thinks the world of you."

"Of course, he does. He and I have a great relationship. But don't forget, we run the business together as a team. We're partners. He knows how hard I work to make it successful. Even still, this didn't cost as much as you might think. My father knows the local dealer and saw him at last year's annual boat show up in the New Orleans Superdome. This baby was the showroom demo model of the Hunter 29.5 model, so technically, it isn't brand-new, and it isn't a thirty-footer because it's just twenty-nine and a half feet. Because of this, my father was able to negotiate a fantastic deal."

After a while, Tomislav's excitement began tempting his mind into considering all the possibilities his new sailboat could offer. "Hey, I just decided something. You and I, we're going to make the best of things and pass a good time," he said, slipping in some Louisiana jargon. "We're going to Mexico! We can leave as soon as the registration papers are finished and return when the *Rebel Yell* is ready. What do you say?"

I sensed now wasn't the time to break the news about my general dislike of being on the water, so I deflected his proposition by telling him I didn't have a passport. Undeterred, he said, "No problem. We can go to South Padre Island, Texas. It's practically Mexico anyway, at least on a map, and there's no passport required to go there. And it'll be cheap. We can sleep onboard. How does that sound?"

I'd already used my single, viable excuse to dodge a trip to Mexico, so I said, "Wouldn't you rather stick around here, maybe spend a few weeks sailing the *Domagoj* around the Louisiana Gulf coast until you get all the kinks worked out?"

Tomislav shot me a look that suggested he thought I may be intellectually impaired. "What's there to see around *here*?" he asked.

I didn't answer.

"The correct answer is oil platforms, refineries, and shrimp trawlers. That's it. I've already seen a lifetime's worth of those in my twenty-two years, and I'll be seeing a lot more. No sir, we have got to go somewhere special. Someplace neither of us have ever been. That place, I've decided, is South Padre Island. So, are you in or not?"

"Look, Tomislav, you should know something. I'm not too keen on the idea of sailing on the open sea. I mean, I can handle the shrimp trawler gig because it's a huge boat and I can usually see land from where we're shrimping. But heading out to sea in this little sailboat, as beautiful as she is, doesn't really interest me. I'm just not a fan of being on the water."

Tomislav was unfazed. "Not *yet*, you aren't," he said. "But once we set sail, your whole perspective on life will change. A brand-new world will open to you, and you'll have me to thank for it. And believe me, I'll be happy to tell you, *'De rien.'*"

We toured the boat some more, admiring all its features. Had my feeling about open water not been preordained, I would have jumped at the chance to embark on such an adventure. Yet, with my reservations firmly rooted, it took extra effort from Tomislav to prod me forward.

"What's all this *not a fan of open water* nonsense? You just spent a month aboard a shrimp trawler and didn't mention it once. And you know my abilities as a captain are first-rate. If it helps, we can sail along the coast and keep close to the harbors along the way. But it will have to fit our allotted time frame. Remember, we have only a few weeks before the *Rebel Yell* is ready to resume shrimping."

I didn't respond immediately. Rather, I stood with my hands in my pockets and continued examining the boat's interior. Everything looked so new and exciting.

"Admit it, Ryan. This is a chance of a lifetime. A short sail across the Gulf of Mexico, and then a week of fun in the sun. And it will cost us next to nothing. What do you say?"

"I'll sleep on it and let you know tomorrow," I answered.

Tomislav sensed I was ready to capitulate. "I'll chart a course tonight and check the weather forecast. We can gather supplies first thing in the morning. Once the official paperwork is approved, we'll set sail immediately."

That night, I stirred restlessly in bed while considering my options. In the end, none of them were as appealing as setting sail to south Texas, regardless of my aversion to water. I awoke early the next morning, and when I saw Tomislav moving about, I told him to count me in.

Chapter Thirty-Two
The Pain Ends Today

Aboard the Domagoj
Somewhere in the Gulf of Mexico
Sunday, March 06, 1994, 10:30 p.m.

It was smooth sailing during our voyage's first day. I spent a lot of time chatting with Tomislav from a stern rail seat while watching him maneuver the *Domagoj* between the buoys and oil rigs scattered throughout the Gulf of Mexico. Just before sunset on the second full day, however, indications of brewing trouble appeared on the horizon. A massive, gray cloud was bearing down on us ahead of the coming night sky. In its wake, bright bolts of lightning shimmied across the blackened canvas, and further in the distance, beyond a lonely, deep-water oil platform alight like a centurion's birthday cake, thunderclaps rumbled as the lightning disintegrated into nothingness. We could smell the electricity in the air, but from our position, it took concentration to hear the storm's growls. It wasn't difficult to imagine how ferocious they sounded to anyone in closer proximity judging by the lightning display we were witnessing. Quite simply, our future sailing conditions looked treacherous. When the wind increased and the air pressure suddenly dropped in tandem, they *felt* treacherous, too. The Gulf of Mexico started to roil beneath the *Domagoj's* hull, and I knew it was only a matter of time before enormous waves would begin crashing against her sides. I looked at Tomislav, who was braced against the stainless steel wheel at the stern. He was trying his best to project confidence and disguise the gravity of the situation.

Around ten p.m., it became obvious we'd be overtaken by the squall and he barked at me through the growing wind. "Hurry below deck, Ryan! Get the storm jib from the stowage compartment! It's bundled in a bright-red canvas sleeve. We're going to try to outrun the heavy stuff!"

I swallowed hard as I hustled below deck, sensing it was already too late.

"Bring my life jacket, too!" he hollered. I had been wearing mine since waking that morning. "And prepare the safety harnesses!"

I knew exactly where to look, since Tomislav had given me a crash course in the boat's safety equipment while waiting to receive the registration and insurance paperwork. During the downtime, he had intensified his pressure on me to take a more direct route to Texas in order to recover lost time. Rather than hugging the Gulf coast as originally agreed, I consented to sailing across open sea, even after he'd revealed a winter tropical depression was developing southeast of where we were heading. After granting my approval, I recall thinking how I might regret the decision, but he assured me we'd beat the storm by two full days. To sweeten his sales pitch, he forecast we'd be basking on a beach in the South Padre Island sun as the turbulent weather proceeded northward. Then he guaranteed it. Now, I realized his calculations were misguided, and judging by the look on his face as he stared at the ominous clouds bearing down on us, I knew he realized it, too.

"The Gulf temperature has been too warm all winter," he fretted aloud, shaking his head.

"Huh?"

"The Gulf water temperature hasn't fallen enough this winter. Hurricane season doesn't officially begin until June," he said.

"Hurricane season? What are you talking about? Who said anything about a hurricane?"

"See for yourself," he said, pointing at the control panel. "Look at the wind speed gauge. If it reads seventy-four miles an hour or less, it's only a tropical storm. If it's stronger, we're fleeing a category one hurricane!"

On the digital display, the wind speed registered sixty-two miles an hour, still twelve miles an hour less than hurricane force, which was mildly comforting.

Bobbing and weaving with the motion of the sea, I squeezed the fiberglass frame and descended the steps to the below deck. Suddenly, I heard huge raindrops pounding against the cabin ports

THE LONG WAY AROUND

from inside.

"Bring the rain gear up also!" Tomislav hollered down to me. "Hurry, Ryan! There's a lot of work to be done and not much time. We've got to reef the mainsail and attach the jib. To do it right, I have to turn the boat into the wind before the sea gets any rougher!"

I could tell Tomislav had never sailed through such volatile weather before and was operating on a combination of instinct and knowledge his father had shared with him. I felt his proficiency was stretched to its limit. As I fumbled around below deck, I turned on the radio and tried to decipher the banter. The *Domagoj* began to pitch and roll. Several times it felt like Tomislav's new sailboat would break to pieces from the pounding its hull was absorbing. I tried to imagine the mayhem a category four or five hurricane could produce.

Though I was determined to assist my captain through the emergency, I admit to being staggered by fear. More than once, I clasped Dieter's rosary cross in my hand and said, "Dear Lord, don't abandon me now." Gratefully, I hadn't felt any symptoms of my prior panic attacks. It was as if the current crisis was developing at such a rapid pace there wasn't time to jumpstart my anxieties. In my state of alarm, all the sailing terminology I'd recently learned began to slip my mind, and I had to repeat Tomislav's instructions over and over so I wouldn't forget the details. Finally, I found what I'd been sent to retrieve.

I put my raingear on and slipped into the safety harness. Leaving the storm jib and Tomislav's gear near the cabin door, I returned to the helm, intending to steer the boat while he changed. In my absence, the conditions had deteriorated to the point that we could barely hear one another's shouts through the howling wind. In just minutes, the wind had risen to seventy-nine miles per hour, well within the category one hurricane range. I took the wheel and Tomislav pointed in the direction for me to aim before scurrying below. Proper steering was wishful thinking, as it took all my novice ability to keep the *Domagoj* from heeling over, or worse.

A short time later, Tomislav emerged from below looking ruffled and haggard. Bundled under his right arm was the storm jib that needed to be mounted in order to better control the boat.

"Should we send a distress call?" I shouted.

"Not yet," he answered, "because we aren't in distress yet. We're in for a tough slog though. If things worsen from here, that's next on the list. In case I'm unable to reach the VHF DCS radio, you'll have to do it. Do you remember how I taught you?" he bellowed.

"Mayday, mayday, mayday!" I said.

He nodded in the affirmative. "All the important data is next to the radio."

"I remember," I said.

"We're in deep water, so that's good," he yelled to me. "There's little chance of us hitting rocks like in the shallows. I'll trim the main sail now. We're going to have to lie ahull and drift while you help me attach the jib. Then I'll lower the sea anchor. That will help keep the bow pointed into the waves. If all goes to plan, we can heave to, lock the helm, and take refuge below deck!"

I didn't understand all his sailing jargon, but it sounded promising. And it was reassuring to hear him taking command of the situation.

"Trimming the jib windward will be extremely difficult in these conditions," he hollered. "But it's our best chance to ride out the storm. You'll have to watch my back and lend a hand whenever I need help. For now, stay at the wheel and turn on the anchor light in addition to the masthead light so I won't be working blind. Stay put until I'm ready for you. When I signal, lock the wheel and advance carefully. Don't dawdle; we need to get it done as soon as possible!"

I turned on the anchor light as instructed and returned to the wheel. The waves were unruly and angry, but the cockpit monitor showed the wind speed had leveled off at seventy-eight miles an hour, still below category two hurricane speeds. Fighting the torrential rain, it took about an hour for Tomislav to reef the main sail by himself, during which the *Domagoj* was floating wildly around the Gulf of Mexico. Sometime around eleven-thirty p.m., he signaled for me to help backwind the jib, a burdensome chore that even experienced sailors have trouble performing in more favorable conditions. In the ravaging conditions at present, it would be a grueling, exhausting, and nearly impossible task to complete.

I lashed the steering wheel the best I could and unhooked the tether securing my life jacket to the stern. I half walked, half crawled along the side deck intending to reattach my safety harness to the jack line further ahead, but the incessant rain, wind, and motion of the waves knocked me off balance before I could refasten the tether. I rolled hard and caught hold of the lifeline surrounding the boat's perimeter. I took some time to catch my breath. The vicious weather was impairing visibility to just a few feet in each direction. Tomislav's attempts to fasten the jib by himself were futile, his efforts continuously disrupted by the driving rain, which required him to stop and cover his eyes with his forearm. He shouted directions often, but the noise of the storm was so deafening I couldn't hear his message. When I'd collected my senses, I pressed the crucifix once more into my chest and thought, *Let's do it*. Then I continued shuffling forward along the side deck. In the confusion, I neglected to secure my tether before scampering toward my friend.

The gusts began blowing harder when I reached the foredeck. To improve his view, Tomislav had a small Maglite clinched between his teeth. He held the unfolded storm jib against the anchor locker with his knees. With his hands, he alternated between fixing it to the jib sheet and grabbing hold of the bow rail to steady his balance.

When I got to within earshot of Tomislav, I sprawled myself flat against the deck and held tightly to whatever I could reach while the incessant, breaking waves washed over us. Tomislav was drenched and exhausted. I wanted to ask how I could assist but there was no point. Even if he could hear me, I doubt he would have answered. I could see the competing expressions of concentration and frustration on his face, and in all that time, he had made minimal progress. The fact I hadn't been there to help would not have mattered. I looked across the bow and saw the waves growing larger.

I felt a punch on my shoulder. It was Tomislav getting my attention. "It's no use! The wind is too strong. I'm exhausted. We must get back to the cockpit. We can lie ahull until the heaviest winds die down, and then try to mount the storm jib later. We'll switch off between steering duties taking shelter below deck. Let's get going!"

I sensed our contingency plan wasn't an ideal scenario in the kind of storm in which we were fighting. As I squared my body to retreat sternward, I thought again to ask if I should place a distress call. I never got the chance.

"Hold on!" Tomislav screamed.

When I glanced his way, I saw the reason why. A humongous, twenty-five-foot wave was rolling toward us. As the *Domagoj's* bow raised to meet the swell, her trajectory spun in the current and the boat was struck broadside by an incredible force. The sailboat nearly breached like a whale before heeling over onto its side.

On deck, Tomislav and I were overpowered by the water. Because my harness hadn't been tethered, I was swept overboard and pulled deep under water. With a sense of urgency bordering on panic, I kicked and heaved until I reached the surface, where I gulped a big breath of air before being dunked again by the next colossal wave. With the aid of my life jacket, I quickly resurfaced, and then managed to stay afloat long enough to see the *Domagoj* on her side and drifting away. Tomislav was clinging to its hull and riding the waves with the boat. I heard him call to me, but my laggard swimming abilities were doubly hindered by the raingear, which stuck to me like glue.

By then, I had swallowed so much saltwater I could only vomit when I tried to respond to his calls. Another wave lifted me high, and I spotted the *Domagoj's* mast light still glowing about six feet or so beneath the surface. I swam toward it with all my ability in hopes of catching the aluminum beam, but the next large swell pulled me even further away before dragging me under. The last image I recall of the *Domagoj* was the mast light shining defiantly under water but fading by the second.

I was alone in the Gulf of Mexico, engulfed in total darkness.

* * * * *

With the aid of his tether, Tomislav pulled himself back to the *Domagoj's* hull and maneuvered himself toward the stern. He did not want to be poorly positioned if the boat was able to right itself with the help of a well-timed wave. He shouted out to Ryan and tried to formulate a rescue in his head. His shouts were useless and thoroughly drowned out by the roar of the storm. He had no

THE LONG WAY AROUND

idea which direction Ryan had drifted in relation to the boat. The waves were far too powerful to do anything except hang on for dear life. Analyzing the situation, he doubted his new boat would sink. He was certain the hatch had been fastened tightly and the inner compartment was watertight and secure. It was imperative for him to be prepared for the ballast to pull downward and reverse the *Domagoj's* position. He hoped this would happen at any minute but considered that hours might pass before the Gulf of Mexico showed any sign of mercy. He pressed his nose close to his watch. The fluorescent hands read twelve-forty a.m.

*****

I fought valiantly for another hour to keep from drowning. Just when I thought I was through the worst of it and the waves seemed to have leveled off, the back end of the storm appeared and punished me dearly for my optimism. I managed to ride to the top of two consecutive tall waves and tried to scout for some sign of the *Domagoj* at the crest of each. I couldn't see anything through the dark and rain, and even if Tomislav had managed to sound a whistle, I wouldn't have been able to hear it through the wind. I considered that my death was near. The water wasn't frigid, but hypothermia was setting in. I was exhausted and starting to shake. I sensed an anxiety attack would appear soon, and if it did, it would likely finish me off. I tried thinking of what my Grandpa Conrad would advise if he were with me. I imagined him telling me to 'fight like hell, son!' I knew if he were watching, he'd already know I'd been giving everything I had. Then, unconsciously and spontaneously, a prayer spouted from my quivering lips. "*Our father, who art in heaven, hallowed be....*"

That was as far as I got before another immense upsurge in the cycle of waves came crashing down on top of me. This one's thrust was more powerful than all the rest combined. It pushed me deep under water, and my saturated life jacket was no match for the undertow. With the last of my strength, I flailed and kicked to reach the surface but the force holding me down wasn't about to release its grip. As my oxygen depleted, I began to lose consciousness.

I felt strangely at peace and no longer struggled to hold my breath. I could feel my body being pulled by the current, but I made no effort to swim to the surface. It was all I could do to keep the Gulf of Mexico from pouring into my mouth and filling my lungs, though if it had, I would not have resisted. My ease was disrupted when the invisible creature from Metzger's Slough appeared in my mind to kill Brian Garner. I writhed and thrashed from the terror, trying frantically to save him whereas I had failed before. My senses were overwhelmed, and the salt water breached my lips and began trickling down my throat. I didn't gag, only because I couldn't. Instead, I drifted beneath the sea with my eyes wide open, yet completely unable to see. It was then I heard a voice so succinct and soothing I thought I must have died.

The pain shall end today. It was a delicate, female voice. *The pain shall end today*, she repeated.

Under the waves, a shining entity appeared in the blurry form of a woman. I could not define her features, but her silhouette resembled that of a statuette of the Virgin Mary in my hometown church that I'd stared at many times while growing up. Seeing the light, I was overcome by a feeling of euphoria and jubilation.

The pain shall end today, the voice repeated, and then the illumination began to fade. *Ryan, she is waiting for you.* Just before vanishing completely, she said, *Go to her, Ryan. They are waiting for you.*

Then everything went black.

* * * * *

I was awakened by an intense light. Sunlight. Bright, beautiful sunlight that nearly singed my retinas before I could look away. I was lying crumpled on my side, dry, and floating on a craft of some sort. The Gulf of Mexico was calm. I was thirsty, my lips were cracked, and my tongue was swollen. My throat burned from overexposure to vomit and sea water. Masses of tiny salt crystals clinging to my clothes irritated my skin as the sun's rays bore down on them. I had no idea what time it was, where I was, or how long I'd been there. I assumed it was late morning.

Steel. Definitely steel, I thought about the surface beneath me. From the corner of my eye, I could see it was painted a lively yellow. There was an annoying, continuous buzzing nearby, an odd,

THE LONG WAY AROUND

pulsed humming that never ceased, and an occasional bellow that sounded whenever the sea produced a wave large enough to move the platform in any direction. A strange, screeching noise, more animalistic than synthetic, broke the monotonous mechanical drone at irregular intervals.

I couldn't muster the strength to lift my head, so I stayed still and reviewed events the best I could. I thought about Tomislav floating away in the hurricane clinging to his capsized boat and wondered if both had been lost at sea. Then I pondered the mysterious woman's voice that had spoken to me with such tranquility and tried to decipher her message.

The pain shall end today. She is waiting for you. They are waiting for you. What did it mean? Whose pain shall end today. Who were waiting for me?

It was all very mysterious and dreamlike, yet genuine and real. I was certain I hadn't imagined it, so I decided to take it seriously, and if I survived this ordeal and my life returned to normal, I wanted to find the answers to these questions.

As the morning passed and the sun rose higher in the sky, I gained the power to sit and examine my situation. While repositioning my body upright, a single seagull took to flight from above. It had been sitting on some rigging overhead and my unexpected motion had scared it away. It was obviously the source of the squawking I'd heard earlier. I looked around and discovered I was on a buoy, though how I'd gotten there left me baffled. It was a weather buoy, I determined, because an identification marker reading National Data Buoy Center was stenciled in black paint near where I was sitting. In the center of the platform, a steel pillar jutted skyward. I rotated a few degrees and pressed my back against its side, which offered me a thin strip of shade.

As I regained my senses, I considered how to secure rescue, realizing I had neither food nor drinking water, and my thirst was growing stronger by the minute. When my head cleared some more, I began studying the panorama around me. To my astonishment, I spied an oil platform over the horizon, although to the naked eye, it was difficult to judge the distance from the buoy on which I was floating. It was too far away to swim to, maybe a couple of miles, perhaps more, but I figured the weather buoy had been purposefully positioned close enough to remain in its view. With that in mind, I schemed how to draw attention in case the oil rig personnel could be alerted.

The buoy's center pillar had a steel ladder welded to its side. The ladder led up several feet to the fixtures on which the seagull had been perched. From below, I spotted a flashing beacon light and other rotating instruments that spun in directions only the wind and current could determine. Other, unidentifiable sensors and equipment were rigged atop also, and I decided the best way for me to inspect them was to climb up and have a look around. I was still quite unsteady, so I first stretched my joints before scaling the metallic rungs. As I neared the pinnacle, the buzzing I'd been hearing increased in volume.

On closer examination, the equipment appeared much larger than from the buoy deck. I snooped around and considered which component would be best to vandalize in order to alert the oil platform. The warning light was the most obvious and first on the list. I unfastened my belt buckle and slid the leather band out from the loops, then I inserted two fingers through the metal buckle and began punching at the lamp's casing. After a frustrating minute of wasted time, I realized the glass was reinforced and better tools would be required to crack it open. Fortunately, I spied where the salt water and humidity had loosened the screws holding the casing in place and managed to wedge the buckle prong into the groove. Gritting my teeth, I torqued my thumbs against the wedged prong, and to my satisfaction, the screws loosened easily. I then removed the glass casing and smashed the bulb with the buckle. Mission accomplished, I examined the other sensors and contemplated which I'd destroy next if the missing warning light remained undetected. My strength depleted, I climbed down the pillar and fell in a heap in the strip of shade. I was dying of thirst. I lay wondering how long it would take before someone from the oil rig would notice the missing beacon light.

About two hours later, I heard a dull thumping in the sky in the distance. It was a helicopter nearing the oil rig helipad, likely shuttling crewmembers or supplies to and from the mainland.

THE LONG WAY AROUND

Before long, the helicopter landed and the noise it created ceased. I squinted through the sun's glare but was unable to see much from that distance. About thirty minutes later, the rumble started up again, and then grew louder as the chopper flew in my direction. It didn't take long before it was above me. I rose to my knees and began waving my arms madly. The helicopter dropped in altitude, circled twice, and then flew away to the north. I was reluctant to celebrate, yet I was certain I'd been seen.

I sat back down in the shade to await my fate.

Chapter Thirty-Three
A Not-So-Subtle Change

John Sealy Hospital
Galveston, Texas
Tuesday, March 08, 1994, 8:30 a.m.

"**G**ood morning, sunshine," the nurse said as she pulled back the curtains. She spoke with a slight accent and had a big smile on her face. "You have an examination scheduled in an hour. I'm here to get you ready."

My eyes were slow to open. I didn't feel any major pains, but my body ached all over and I was extremely fatigued. It was easy to assume I was in a hospital. The familiar smell, the nurse, and a bag of clear fluid hanging next to my bed with a tube leading into my arm were dead giveaways. "Where am I?" I asked. "And what time is it?"

"It's eight-thirty Tuesday morning, March eighth. You're in the recovery ward of John Sealy Hospital in Galveston, Texas."

"What kind of shape am I in? Is it bad?"

"Not a scratch on you. Just some dehydration. You are a very lucky young man," she said. "The doctor will check you over in a little while. He'll decide whether to keep you here longer or if you're fit to be released this afternoon."

I'd spent enough time in a hospital over the last four months and didn't want to spend one minute longer than necessary in this one.

"How did I get here?" I asked.

"Don't you remember? You were brought here by helicopter. The US Coast Guard picked you off a weather buoy in the Gulf of Mexico."

All at once, everything hit me like a ton of bricks. The last twenty-four hours ricocheted to the forefront of my mind. "Our

THE LONG WAY AROUND

boat! You must send help. The *Domagoj* capsized! The captain is still with her. Call the Coast Guard. You have to hurry!"

"Easy does it, Mr. Meyers. Don't you worry. Your boat was found. Mr. Novak was successfully rescued. He was miles and miles from where they found you yesterday. He's in a hospital in Corpus Christi."

"Is he going to be okay?" I asked.

"You were in better condition than he was upon admittance. He suffered from severe hypothermia, but all indications say he'll make a full recovery. I doubt he'll be released from the hospital for several days," she said. "Would you like some breakfast?"

"Yes, please. I'm starving."

"I'll place an order to the kitchen. You rest a bit, and I'll be back to prepare you for your exam," she said before leaving.

I sat up and looked around. The television was off, but I didn't want to watch it anyhow. I considered how no one would come to visit me, but it didn't matter. My mind was alert and my head was clearing. Even though the food hadn't been delivered, I began feeling better and more energized by the minute. I glanced at the nightstand and saw Dieter's rosary on top of it. I grabbed it, slid it over my head, and let the wooden crucifix dangle in the spot it had been resting for the past two months.

The food came before long, and just as the nurse returned to take away the empty tray, a staff doctor stopped by to check on my condition. We chatted a bit before my examination, and he took my medical history. I explained my last four months to him as thoroughly as possible, but many of the details were becoming fuzzy. When I mentioned my head trauma and subsequent brain surgery, he had a difficult time disguising the concern on his face. I felt the need to assure him I was fine.

"Really, Doc. You'll see. I'm in excellent condition. In fact, I haven't felt this good since last summer, before my accident." And it was the truth. As the food digested in my stomach, I became reinvigorated. My head was crystal clear, my fatigue vanished, and my mood shifted from my previous state of depression to only positive thoughts.

When my examination ended, he told me I was physically fit

with an expression of surprise on his face. Based on that, he decided there was no reason to keep me under observation and signed a form granting my release. My clothes were brought to me clean and dry. I noticed the only two personal items left in my possession were the wooden crucifix around my neck and my wallet, which was still soggy from salt water. I carried it in my hand as I walked down the hallway to the elevator leading to the administration offices. I had plenty of paperwork to fill out and hoped the health insurance policy I had under my grandfather's supplemental plan was up to date. Inside the elevator, I opened the wallet and checked the contents. Everything inside was exactly as I remembered.

I reached the billing office and talked with the department head. She took my personal information and told me the amount due and billing process. I thanked her and asked to use a telephone so I could plan my next move. She sat me in her chair and told me to call whomever I liked. She found the telephone number of the hospital in Corpus Christi where Tomislav had been admitted, and I called there first. To my disappointment, I wasn't allowed to speak with him, but the head nurse on his floor informed me that his condition was stable and improving. I left a long message for her to deliver to him and wished him a speedy recovery.

It was at that moment I realized I didn't have a plan, so I formulated one on the spot.

Iowa. Home. I was going home. The time had come, and I was ready. My head was in a different state than when I'd left, and I would be returning to the place I wanted to be and at the right time. I was reminded of what Rory had described about going home when he was ready and on his own terms. I understood his position much better now, and as his best friend, I decided to support his stance so long as he stayed out of trouble. The understanding came to me as a great relief. Mentally, I felt even healthier as a result, and concentrated all my energy on getting home as soon as possible.

Chapter Thirty-Four
Never Better Than This

The Ryan Meyers Farm
Rural Northeast Iowa,
Saturday, April 09, 1994, 1:00 p.m.

Since arriving home, I'd been too busy tending to matters concerning my farm to do much socializing, and the only interaction I'd had were of the business variety. My life seemed to be improving day by day. I'd even been waking before dawn each morning to catch up on chores that had been neglected while I was gone. Oddly enough, I'd grown accustomed to rising early, and I no longer dreaded starting the day in the dark like I had before. Physically, my strength was improving, and I was in excellent spirits mentally. I was happy to be home.

Over the last three weeks, I'd met with many different lawyers and accountants, and interviewed a half-dozen farmers interested in renting my land. *My land.* Those were two words I had trouble saying after a lifetime of referring to the property as *my Grandpa's farm.* Now it was mine, and I wanted to make my grandfather proud about how I handled the financial side of things.

I decided not to rent simply to the highest bidder. Rather, I wanted a tenant who lived nearby and whom I could trust to farm my property responsibly, as if it were his own. Three other things I considered important for the prospective tenant to possess were previous experience renting farmland, solid references from other farmers from whom they've rented, and a personality I thought would be most affable in resolving any disputes. In the end, the tenant I selected was Francis Recker, my neighbor to the north. There wasn't much time until planting season, so I spent many hours over several days with Mr. Recker sorting out final details in order to ensure this season's crop would be profitable.

DOUGLAS CAVANAUGH

In the course of our conversations, Mr. Recker informed me of all the happenings that had taken place in Clayton County during my absence. One tidbit he shared intrigued me significantly. He told me a beautiful lady had stopped by my house shortly after I'd left in January. He'd spied a brand new pickup exiting my lane and turning in his direction. From the barn door, he saw a woman driving and said she looked like my old girlfriend, Mary. Mr. Recker had met Mary at my high school graduation party, and I didn't doubt his description, but I held reservations about his accuracy. What confused me most was why Mary would stop, if indeed it was her. In the end, I decided my neighbor had been mistaken. Yet, the possibility the former love of my life had wanted to see me caused some nervous tension in my stomach and happy thoughts began to stir.

During our business meeting over the following days, I noticed Mr. Recker studying me on the sly so I asked him why.

"You know what?" he asked.

"What?"

"You look different each time I see you," he said.

"Maybe you need to get your glasses checked," I teased. "What do you mean?"

"Well, every time we meet, your face changes. But in a good way. More like it looked before your accident. Now you look exactly like I remember, only a little older. Your mood is better, too," he said.

I didn't know what to say, though I had also noticed some strange physical deviations over the last week. For instance, since my return, the scar tissue under my hairline had stopped itching and pulling. Stranger yet, when I looked in the mirror to examine the area, there wasn't a trace of a suture line anywhere on my scalp. In fact, to the naked eye, it appeared as if I had never undergone a craniotomy just five months ago. And one day last week, while Tim was driving me to Walcott to retrieve my pickup truck from James, the manager at the I-80 Truck Stop gas station, he commented how he almost didn't recognize me since seeing me just a few days before. Several times along the way, he shook his head and told me how much my looks have changed for the better over the last couple of weeks. But there was something else peculiar about our conversation during that two-hour drive.

Knowing Tim so well, I sensed he was privy to some important information he was withholding. When I quizzed him in depth, he stated I was being paranoid and switched subjects. For the rest of the trip, we discussed his new job at the Oelwein Farmer's Co-Op, and just before delivering me at the truck stop, he let it slip that he had a new girlfriend. This was unusual for Tim, a twist I hadn't been expecting, so I allowed him to fill me in on the details at his own pace. I wanted him to savor the moment and encouraged him to gloat if he wanted. My earlier suspicions of something more devious died on the spot.

* * * * *

Spring was finally in the air. The days were becoming warmer and longer, but it rained almost constantly. Easter Sunday and Major League Baseball's opening day had already come and gone. The farmers were antsy to get to work in their fields, but the wet conditions were not accommodating.

Last Sunday, I'd gone alone to an early morning Easter Mass in Strawberry Point, thankful of all the good fortune my life had received in the past several weeks. At its conclusion, I decided to go to Mass more often, but I still desired to avoid people as much as possible. As I left, I didn't pay attention to the subtle glances by a few parishioners in attendance who knew me. I assumed they were happy to see me in church after such a long time away.

Immediately after, I went to the local diner for breakfast. I was the only customer inside, and I read the Waterloo Sunday morning paper after ordering my food. A front page article explaining the ongoing fighting in southwest Bosnia and Herzegovina made me think of Tomislav. I finished reading the story to the end. The more I read, the more I realized the article wasn't about the war, but rather, it was a feature telling of an extraordinary religious spectacle occurring in the same region. It described a village called Medjugorje that had been made famous by recurring apparitions of the Virgin Mary over the previous thirteen years. As I read, I realized many details described in the article were like my experience in the Gulf of Mexico, yet I could not make a definite connection. I thought it over as I sipped my coffee, then decided to keep my ordeal to myself.

Needing a distraction, I opened the sports page and skipped over the more mundane sections like the classified ads and the page announcing local obituaries, marriages, and births. Had the waitress not delivered my food when she did, I might have received the shock of my life.

* * * * *

Six days later, and after an extremely busy week, I had a free Saturday morning with extra time to kill. I called Tim to see if he wanted to do something, but he was not available. Francis Recker hadn't stopped by to discuss business as planned, and I supposed he was waylaid by chores around the farm. At twelve-thirty p.m., I turned on the television hoping to catch the first pitch of the Chicago Cubs home opener, but play was delayed by rain. I was searching for something to occupy my time when the telephone rang.

"Hello?"

There was a brief pause. "Hello, Ryan. This is Mary."

I almost couldn't believe it. Her voice sounded faint and unsettled. "Mary Kelleher?" It was all I could think of to say.

"Yes, Ryan," she said with an insecure laugh. I sensed she was uncomfortable and trying to break the ice. "I heard you had quite a trauma. I tried to visit you, first at the hospital, and then at your home. How are you feeling?"

I realized my neighbor had been correct, and I was sorry I'd doubted him. "Lots better. Thanks," I said. "How are you? Is everything going well at university?"

"Yes, school is fine, but like you, the last several months have been crazy for me, too," she answered. "Ryan, I'd really like to see you in person and talk to you sometime soon. I mean, if you're up to it."

My brain felt like it would explode from the excess emotions running through it.

"Yeah, sure I'm up to it," I said, a bit defensively. "Are you in town? My schedule is wide open today."

THE LONG WAY AROUND

"If you don't mind, Ryan, I'd rather meet tomorrow. I don't know if you know this, but my parents moved to a different house in the country last fall. If it's agreeable with you, they'd like to pick you up and bring you for Easter dinner."

That made me chuckle. "But Easter Sunday was last weekend," I said.

Mary laughed a little, too. It was the same adorable laugh I'd heard many times before. "I know it was last week, but we had some other important family obligations which delayed our Easter celebration until tomorrow. So, what do you think? Would you like to come for dinner? My family and I would love to see you."

With that, my heart skipped a beat, but I didn't want to let it show. "Sure, why not?" I said. "But I'd like to follow them in my truck. It'll be easier for everybody when I want to leave. Is that fair?"

"It's a deal. They'll be at your doorstep at noon. And Ryan… I'm really happy you're coming. I can't wait to see you."

"Goodbye, Mary," I said before hanging up.

I felt weak all over. I returned to the Cubs game, which was just underway, but I could only stare at the screen without interest in the action. A bit agitated, I turned off the television and sat in silence. After a while, I put my head in my hands and rubbed my eyes. I was in shock.

*****

"Hello, Ryan," said Maureen with a motherly voice.

"It's certainly good to see you," added Don while his wife leaned forward to hug me.

Mary's parents and I always got along extremely well, and after a hug and a handshake on my front porch, when they told me how much they missed seeing me over the last several months, I believed them. I was happy to see them, too. On several occasions during my senior year, they'd acted like surrogate parents.

They didn't try explaining away their daughter's irregular behavior toward me, which I appreciated. Instead, as we walked along the path to our vehicles, they talked about how life works in mysterious ways and assured me that things usually work out for the best in the end.

As I followed them in my truck through the countryside, I still hadn't figured out the reason for my attendance in their family's Easter dinner. Then again, I'd never understood Mary's decision to break up with me after leaving for college last summer, so I confess to being motivated to learn the truth. I was up for the adventure.

The drive to the Kellehers' acreage was farther than I'd expected. I'd never imagined Mary's parents to be the country living type, but as I followed them down the lane leading to their house, their relocation made perfect sense and created a lasting impression. Their purchase was exemplary, and I saw at once what Don and Maureen had envisioned when they became the owners. The rustic atmosphere, privacy, location, and grandiosity of the property were ideal. I'd always known her parents to be down-to-earth, hard-working people, and I could clearly see how their blood, sweat, and tears over the last thirty years had been rewarded.

I parked in the driveway. The garage door was open, and I saw a shiny, four-wheel drive pickup truck inside. *Mr. Recker was right,* I thought again.

Don and Maureen waited for me to exit my truck, then we walked to the front door, where Mary stood waiting. We entered, and before I could say 'hello,' she threw her arms around my neck and hugged me tightly. I could tell she was holding back tears.

Maureen said that Mary's brother, Daniel, would be coming before long, then excused herself before disappearing down a hallway. Don spoke up. "Well, I think there is still plenty of time before dinner will be ready. Ryan, a tour of the house is waiting for you after we eat. For now, you two can catch up. I'll go help in the kitchen." Mary's dad turned and left.

"He usually gives the tour first," Mary said with a smile, wanting to lighten the mood. She took my coat, and then took my hand and led me to the couch near the bay window. I sat down and caught sight of some cardinals picking sunflower seeds from a feeder hanging from a tree in the front lawn. "They've been coming since before Christmas," she said. "I've seen them every single day."

"How can that be?" I wondered aloud. "Haven't you been away at school?"

THE LONG WAY AROUND

"Oh, I'm on a hiatus," she said.

"But you're a freshman; it's just your first year," I said.

"I've taken this semester off."

"Why? I mean…are you okay?" I noticed she looked weak. She was dressed well and made up as usual, but the mascara didn't hide her tired eyes and fatigued spirit. I started exploring alternative reasons for my invitation to dinner. I began to worry about her health.

"I'm fine, Ryan. But there have been some changes in my life since last summer, some drastic changes that affected my academic schedule. That's why I've been trying so hard to meet with you these past several months." Mary leaned forward and put her hands on my knees. "But I couldn't, you understand. Because of your accident."

Nothing seemed clear to me, yet I sensed a measure of gravity in her tone. "Mary, I didn't hear a peep from you after you left for college. You never returned my calls, and that was long before my fall. What did I have to do with disrupting your university schedule?"

She didn't answer right away. Mary sighed and shook her head, as if convincing herself to be brave and stay on course. "Because, Ryan, the reason for these extreme changes affecting me and my academic calendar will also be affecting you."

I sat in wonderment, plainly not understanding the direction the conversation was going.

She added, "But as a result of your accident and recovery, we were advised to wait to bring you up-to-date."

"I feel fine now," I said.

"Great! Because today is the day you get to hear the big news," she said with a smile on her face.

"What news?" I asked, still perplexed.

Just then, a baby's cry rang out from the hallway, followed by a stream of full-blown wailing.

Mary took my hands in hers and squeezed them. "Ryan, I want you to meet your son," she said calmly. "You and I are the parents of a beautiful baby boy."

As if on cue, Mary's mother walked out of the hallway holding a crying bundle in her arms. The baby was wrapped in a soft, blue blanket. Mary squeezed my hands again and stood, wanting to lead me to him.

"Slowly, dear. This is a lot for Ryan to absorb," Maureen said to her daughter. "Ryan, stay seated." Maureen's face was alighted with the look only a proud grandmother could have. She uncovered the baby's forehead and planted a small kiss on it.

There was no chance of me sitting still. I sprang to my feet and raced to see the baby. Mary followed, her excitement matching mine. "But when? How?" was all I could stammer. I looked into his blue eyes and almost melted. He was so tiny. "Is he really ours? Am I really a father?"

Mary wrapped her arms around my waist. "Yes, Ryan. You're his father. He's really ours! Are you happy?"

"Of course, I'm happy," I answered. In fact, *happy* couldn't begin to describe my feelings. It barely touched on my emotions.

Then we kissed for the first time since last August.

*****

I drove home in a daze, but an energetic, satisfied daze. Easter dinner had been great, just like past dinners I'd remembered with the Kelleher family. Mary and Daniel still traded barbs, and Maureen cooked as good as ever, except this time, the ladies jumped every time the baby stirred or made a noise.

On the way home, my thoughts drifted to the newspaper article about the apparitions of Mary I'd read the week before. Suddenly, it dawned on me. My changing looks and the puzzling disappearance of my scars and mental depression, the timely phone call from the love of my life, and my newborn son—it all happened merely weeks after my mysterious rescue. It had to be more than coincidence.

I mouthed the words I remembered the voice repeating while I was under water in the Gulf of Mexico: *The pain shall end today. Ryan, she is waiting for you.* And just before vanishing completely, *Go to her, Ryan. They are waiting for you.*

It all made perfect sense now. In some unexplainable way, I'd been saved and healed and guided while drifting in the Gulf of Mexico. My life had meaning again, and I clearly sensed the direction I was supposed to take. Instantly, I felt in control without any doubt about my future, purpose, or the beginning of my new

THE LONG WAY AROUND

family. Then I wondered if my Grandpa Conrad had something to do with it, and I pictured him watching me from above, sitting in heaven, cackling out loud with a wide, satisfied grin on his face. As I pondered things further, I decided I had been redeemed from my suffering and given a fresh start. Life was good again. In fact, it was never better than this.

Chapter Thirty-Five
In Celebration of a Fine Year

The Kelleher House
Rural northeast Iowa
Sunday, June 16, 1996, 5:30 p.m.

"The burgers are almost ready! The steaks are going on next," my father-in-law called out through a plume of smoke rising from the grill. The group of young men scattered around the backyard hardly took notice. On the patio, a few of the women sitting on lawn chairs sprang into action and begin preparing the tables for eating.

Mary's dad liked to refer to this weekend's barbeque as the Second Annual Kelleher Family Cookout of Success. The inaugural event took place the previous June in lieu of a bachelor party before our wedding, and Don thought it would be righteous to continue the event each year thereafter. It was his way of gathering his family in the same place for at least one weekend every summer, as life had scattered us in many directions. My brother-in-law, Daniel, had landed a job in Des Moines and moved there more than a year ago. Mary and I were currently attending university full-time in Cedar Falls, and we split our time between residing there and Mary's parents' house with our son, Reid.

Last year, Mary's mother, Maureen, retired from her bank job in Oelwein and assumed the responsibilities of an around-the-clock grandmother, nanny, and caretaker for Reid while we are away. To have Maureen available was a blessing beyond imagination, as Mary's drive was pushing her to make up on lost time working toward her degree. As such, her grueling schedule was tighter than recommended, and mine was chasing hers. I was a year behind my wife academically, but my recruitment by the university wrestling team provided a scholarship and some valuable assistance with our living accommodations. I wasn't one to abuse our good fortune,

THE LONG WAY AROUND

and I worked doubly hard to perform well for my team. Though I didn't compete my first year, I came on strong over the past winter and won the NCAA Division II championship in my weight class. The season passed quickly, and I had a personal goal to repeat my performance next year.

As honored guests at the barbecue, we were permitted to invite whomever we wanted, and the picnic had no restrictions on the amount of people allowed to attend.

While my friends tossed Frisbees, footballs, and played other yard games, I stayed nearer the house with our son and pitched wiffle balls in his direction while Mary and her best friend, Dori, chatted and watched. It was a humid summer day. Reid was stripped down to a diaper and white T-shirt. On his head, he was wearing a Chicago Cubs ball cap, which covered his blonde curls and shaded the evening sun from his eyes. Mary had purchased it especially for this day on a recent shopping trip to Waterloo. The rest of us were in summer wear, too; shorts, T-shirts, and sandals.

Reid already had an idea of what he was doing, and when the plastic ball ricocheted off the big, red, plastic bat at his side, he bolted wildly toward a shade tree near the property line. I laughed at how his chubby thighs rubbed together as he ran and sprinted to catch him before he reached the slope leading down to the riverbank. The ladies cheered him as he scooted across the grass in his bare feet. From behind, I snatched the boy under his arms and lifted him above my head as the women applauded. Then I faced him toward me and repeated the performance three times in succession. Reid's laughter's was palpable, and when I stopped, he began squealing for more.

As I hoisted him again, I was overcome with the eerie sensation that I had experienced the identical moment sometime in my past but couldn't recall when. A bit rattled by the *déjà vu*, I set him down and led him to his mother. Then I poured myself a glass of lemonade. After a moment, I remembered having visualized the exact sequence before, only this time, I wasn't intimidated by the flashback. I took it as reassurance I had made the correct choices in my life, and I was relieved more than anything else. I felt refreshed and magnificent. Life, indeed, was a wonderful thing.

Reid stayed in his mother's arms only a short time before squirming away. Mary released him, but Maureen was quick to regain control. It was time for him to eat, which he agreed to do only under protest.

As Maureen supervised her grandson's meal in his highchair, Mary watched them with a sparkle in her eyes. Spontaneously, she turned to Dori. "Thank you so much, Dori. I mean it. Thanks a million. I don't know if I can ever repay you."

"For what?"

"For being there for me when I needed you most. For stopping me from making the biggest mistake of my life. For being my best friend."

"That's what friends are for, right?" she said. Dori flashed a smile, and then hurried to put her sunglasses on and turned away, wanting to hide the tears of happiness in her eyes. "Let's get some food. I'm hungry," she said in order to change the subject and hide her emotions. The ladies rejoined the party.

After the guests had filled their plates at the buffet table, everyone took seats at one of many picnic tables set up banquet-style on the patio. Decorative Tiki torches were burning around the perimeter. As they began to eat, Don stood with a glass of lemonade and thanked everyone for coming. I sensed he'd intended to make a speech, and I tried to coax him into delivering one, but modesty got the best of him and he chickened out in the end. He wished everyone a great summer and lifted his glass for a collective, 'Cheers!'

Just then, two additional guests arrived from side entrance along the garage—my best friend Tim and his girlfriend, Mandy. Mary and I got up to greet them, and the rest of the company shouted salutations from their seats.

"That was a powerful speech, Mr. Kelleher," Tim ribbed my father-in-law. "And a very inspiring one for the 'Cookout of Success.'" Feigning shame, my father-in-law lowered his head and smiled. Some of the guests cheered, others booed teasingly. Maureen brought Tim and Mandy something to drink.

"If it is okay," Tim said, "while Don has everyone's attention, I'd like to steal his thunder and make two important announcements."

THE LONG WAY AROUND

The crowd granted their attention.

"First of all, since we know practically everyone here this evening, Mandy and I would like to announce our engagement. We plan to be married next spring!"

There was a grand applause from the gathering. Mary and I raced to congratulate our friends, with Mary hugging Mandy and Tim and I shaking hands and exchanging high fives. When the moment ended, Tim said, "And the second announcement: we have another guest visiting who we're all very proud of. It's been a long time since many of you have seen him, so say hello to Big Rory Meeks!"

Another round of cheers came from the group as Rory joined the party from around the corner. I couldn't be happier. My last conversation with Rory was a few months ago when I called him in Texas to invite him to our summer celebration. He avoided committing by saying he'd think about it, and I'd doubted he would show. Now, he was here in the flesh, and I was astonished to see him. Rory wasted no time greeting everyone, and he lifted Reid up on his shoulders in no time. My son couldn't have been more pleased with his high perch.

The party grew stronger as the evening progressed. As the sun was beginning to fade, people were scattered all around the premises, and another surprise emerged. A loud blast from a semi-tractor's horn sounded from the county highway near where it intersected Don and Maureen's lane. Maureen saw it first and asked her husband what he had ordered. Don stared at the logo on the trailer. "Certainly not a truckload of shrimp! What in the world is this all about?"

Though I could barely believe my eyes, I knew exactly who the latecomer was. I grabbed Don's elbow and said to my in-laws, "Don't worry, I've got this one under control."

The truck stayed parked on the shoulder of the highway with its marker lights blinking. The driver climbed down from his rig as we reached the end of the lane.

"Hey, Iowa!" Tomislav called out.

I hurried to my friend and gave him a handshake and a half-hug. "I can't believe you actually came!"

"And I can't believe how much you've changed! Good golly, I almost didn't recognize you," he said.

"Tomislav, let me introduce you to my new family. Don and Maureen, do you remember when you told me I could invite anyone to the cookout? Well, this guy traveled just as far as Rory Meeks to be here. This is Tommy Novak, and he came all the way from Louisiana to join our party."

Tomislav took off his ball cap and shook hands with my in-laws. Don said, "Any friend of Ryan's is a friend of mine." He and Tomislav hit it off well. By then, Mary had arrived with Reid and I introduced them next.

"Are you hungry, Tommy?" Don asked. "There's a steak and a whole lot of food waiting for you if you are. Come on up to the house and meet the others."

Tomislav accepted and we discussed what to do with the truck. "Leave it there," Don said. "I'll keep an eye on it and handle any inquiries. You kids go have some fun."

It was dark soon, and most of the group remained seated at the tables talking well into the night. I got to catch up with the lives of most guests one at a time. Mary left the gathering several times to get Reid washed and ready for bed. Tomislav was the hit of the party, and he got to share his version of our boat's capsize in the Gulf of Mexico with the group that remained, most of whom had heard only the abbreviated version I'd been telling for years. Everyone was enchanted with Tomislav, not only from the tales that he told, but with his Louisiana accent, which he exaggerated for effect. I could tell he enjoyed his time with us and hoped his first experience in Iowa had left a memorable impression. Too soon, he announced he had to leave. His refrigerator trailer was empty, and he had more product in Louisiana awaiting delivery. I expected he would be driving most of the night but recalled how he knew every turn in the road on the way home. I walked him to his cab and wished him well. Tomislav and I promised to keep in contact.

After Tomislav left, the other partygoers drifted away a few at a time. Tim and Mandy left at midnight, and by one a.m., Rory and I were the last remaining under the Tiki torch shimmer. We recapped our lives since our final face-to-face conversation in San

THE LONG WAY AROUND

Antonio. When it was Rory's turn to fill me in on his life, he burst into a broad smile.

"Well, I did it, Ryan," he said. "Just like I said I would, buddy. I'm coming home for good."

I didn't sense any smugness or pretentiousness in his statement. His expression seemed to be one of relief.

I didn't respond right away.

Impatiently, he said, "I reached my goal. I'm going to start shopping for a farm to buy before land prices rise any further."

"And you didn't run into any problems with the law?" I asked.

"Not even once. Why would I have? I told you, the job was legitimate," Rory insisted.

"What was in the trucks, Rory?"

"I have no idea. I never asked, and Carlos never said. It doesn't matter now. I quit my job and I'm leaving Texas, for good. I'm coming home, Ryan. And I'm not sad about it either, even though Texas was good to me. I made a lot of friends there, you know."

"I know. I met many of them. I liked them, too."

"But you know what? I never felt Texas was *home* for me like here in Iowa. Plus, my parents aren't getting any younger, and my closest friends and best memories are here, too. I see how good life is going for you, Mary, and Reid, and now with Tim and Mandy about to tie the knot, I figure I should put down some roots. Only now, I can do it on my terms."

Rory and I chatted for another hour. When the last Tiki torch died out, he said goodnight and went home. Still full of adrenalin and unable to sleep, I remained in my lawn chair and pondered life a bit longer.

I was happy for Rory. In an odd way, he had succeeded exceptionally well. He had made a plan, risky as it was, and then worked his plan to perfection. Now, he was ready to implement its next phase. I no longer doubted he would succeed. *"Life is funny, Ryan,"* I recalled him telling me in San Antonio. *"Circumstances change quickly, and you must figure out solutions to your problems as you go. It's not like it was back in high school."*

How hilarious that statement seemed right now. And, simultaneously, how true those words hit home.

Chapter Thirty-Six
Dieter's Demise

Manternach Funeral Home
Elgin, IA
Saturday, May 03, 1997, 10:00 a.m.

I hadn't been to Elgin in years, but it wasn't difficult finding the town's only funeral home. The farming community resembled any other in Middle America. It had one main artery running through the center, and several side streets branching perpendicularly from it on both sides. In the background, there was a domineering water tower announcing the name of the municipality. Along Main Street, a few gas stations were positioned at the town's entry points, and in between those, a couple of restaurants and taverns, small businesses of the mom and pop variety, filled in the remaining landscape. Several churches of different denominations were distributed along the side streets, and a post office, a bank, a public library, and a small city hall gave credence to the downtown. Around the town's periphery, a Co-Op with multiple grain silos disrupted the horizon, two competing car dealerships straddled a regional hotel franchise, and a high school with an accompanying football field completed the picture.

Three days earlier, Mary and I had been in our campus apartment studying for final exams when we received a call from Mary's mother. She had seen the obituary page in the local paper announcing Dieter Metzger had died the day before. Maureen read the notice to me over the phone, and I cleared my schedule so I could attend his funeral on Saturday. Dieter and I had always gotten along well, and he was the closest friend my Grandpa Conrad ever had. I hadn't seen him since before my tragic fall on his property, though I remember my grandpa telling me he'd come often to the hospital to check on me while I was unconscious. Paying final respects to him

THE LONG WAY AROUND

in our family's name was the least I could do considering the history he and my grandfather had shared over their lifetimes.

I parked my truck on a side street and entered the funeral home expecting to see a gathering of family and friends in somber moods and dressed in black. Instead, the visitation parlor was empty except for the shiny casket in which Dieter's body lie. I rechecked the board at the entrance to be sure I had arrived at the correct time. When I returned, I found the funeral director hustling across the floor. I caught his attention and asked if I'd erred on timing for the Dieter Metzger visitation.

"No, you haven't," he answered in a hushed voice. Since we were the only ones in the room, I figured he spoke in that manner out of habit. "Visitation is from nine until noon. A Mass for the deceased will follow at one o'clock, and the burial service at the cemetery will take place immediately after. Mr. Metzger was a US military veteran, and the VFW in Oelwein will be providing a military honor ceremony that'll take place after the religious ceremony. That will entail a flag folding presentation, and a three-volley salute. A bugler will even play 'Taps,'" he said, almost enthusiastically. "We don't have many spectacles like this around here. Military funerals can be quite popular with folks in these parts, so get there early."

"Where is everybody? It's after ten o'clock and we're the only ones here."

"Sadly, Mr. Metzger lived alone," he whispered, before adding, "Hi, I'm Bill Manternach." The funeral home director shot his right hand forward for me to shake. "As I understand it, Dieter had only a handful of distant relatives, who are scattered around the country. A couple of them arrived yesterday to take care of some funeral arrangements, and a few more may arrive in time for Mass later. You're the first visitor today, and aside from some neighboring farmers and another local or two who may eventually show up, I don't expect many others. What did you say your name was?"

I purposely hadn't told him my name, nor signed the registry. "I'm Ryan Meyers."

"Say, are you the young fellow responsible for all the television news crews in town a few years ago? Dieter was something of a celebrity back then. Wasn't that something? An incredible tragedy that happened right here in our own back yard," he mused.

"A tragedy it was," I said, not confirming or denying my involvement in the ordeal.

Sensing the conversation was going no further, the funeral director said, "Well, there are still many details in need of completion. I'll leave you alone to pay your respects. If you need anything, I'll be in my office. It's right around the corner, and my door is always open."

"Thank you, Mr. Manternach," I said.

I approached the casket and looked Dieter over. He appeared practically as I remembered when I last saw him nearly four years ago. His white hair was still full, and someone had decided to leave his plastic rimmed glasses on for the funeral. I leaned forward and spotted the crease on the opposite side of his head. *An authentic battle scar*, I thought. *Dieter Metzger was the real deal.* I picked up a prayer card from a rack placed near the casket and read it silently. After a while, I heard footsteps scampering about behind me. It was the funeral director positioning a wreath of flowers that had just been delivered. When his job seemed to be complete, I backpedaled a few steps and caught his attention.

"Mr. Manternach, could I make a request for Mr. Metzger to be buried with something special?"

"Perhaps. What are you thinking about?"

I reached under my shirt collar and removed the wooden rosary I'd been carrying for years. "This was originally Mr. Metzger's mother's rosary. He gave it to my grandfather, and I inherited it from him. I'd like for Dieter to be buried holding it in his hands."

"I'll arrange it myself. No further explanation will be necessary."

* * * * *

I left my truck parked where it was and walked along Main Street heading into town. I had a little time to kill before the funeral Mass started so I entered the bowling alley and sipped on a root beer. Two separate groups of women, each wearing matching shirts, were at the bowling lanes farthest away. They looked to be competing teams in a league. The ladies were of mixed ages, and several were noticeably overweight. That detail made me think of my grandfather, and I shook my head and grinned. Ignoring the clatter of the bowling pins, I sat at the bar and watched the first inning of the Mets-Braves game playing on the east coast.

After Mass, I followed the procession to the cemetery. I stood far back and away from the small gathering, hoping nobody would recognize me as the deer hunter who had fallen on Dieter's property. The attending priest kept the ceremony brief, and the VFW honor guard performed their routine flawlessly. After they'd presented the folded flag to one of Dieter's relatives, three members of the squad fired blanks from their rifles, and the reports echoed loudly against the nearby bluffs along the Turkey River. A small crowd had gathered to listen to the bugler, and when "Taps" had been played to the end, I returned to my truck.

I reminisced as I walked, realizing how much I missed my grandfather. I hoped he was happy and enjoying Dieter's company in heaven.

I drove back to Mary's parents' house at a lazy speed. My concentration wasn't at full capacity as I was in a state of mixed emotions. I was in no hurry anyway; there were no deadlines for me to meet, though I was eager to see my wife and son. I decided to play with Reid the rest of the day and take it easy tomorrow. Regardless of next week's heavy schedule of final exams, I was in no mood to study.

Chapter Thirty-Seven
Worth Every Minute

Meyers Chiropractic Office
Oelwein, IA
Thursday, June 10, 2010, 8:30 p.m.

The day at work had been grueling. After the last staff member had said goodnight and left, I locked the office entrance and plopped down at my desk. I was exhausted and wanted to go home to my family and eat, shower, and relax, but I was too drained to move. Instead, I loosened my necktie, tipped my chair back to its limit, and propped my feet over a desk corner. The joints of my fingers, hands and shoulders were sore from adjusting patients all day. In Oelwein, Thursday is when the local shops and businesses stay open later than usual, and my office hours reflect the trend. It is also the day that consistently produces my heaviest workload. I sat in silence with my fingers interlocked behind my head and stared at a photo collage standing on the desk in front me. The picture frame was set next to a golden name plate that reads: Dr. Ryan Meyers – Chiropractor.

My attention strayed to the full-length mirror hanging to my right. I marveled at my hair, where just recently, patches of gray have sprouted at my temples. I am thirty-six years old and still in good shape, but my body feels the wear and tear from my wrestling career and the fifteen-foot tumble and subsequent head trauma I suffered after high school. Harkening back to my wrestling days, I reflect on the three consecutive NCAA Division II national titles I won in college. I'm very proud of each, but not nearly as proud as I am of the bachelor's degree my wrestling career helped me achieve in 1998, and far less proud than I am of the Doctor of Chiropractic degree I earned in Davenport in 2002. Both diplomas hang on the wall behind my desk.

THE LONG WAY AROUND

Superseding everything else, of course, I am proudest of my wife and family, which has grown by one since my graduation eight years ago. My second son, Adam, idolizes his older brother, Reid, who turned sixteen a couple months ago. Both boys do well in school and enjoy sports, but only recreationally. Neither has ever wanted to wrestle, and that's been fine with me. My wife, Mary, earned a finance degree from the University of Northern Iowa the year before I received my bachelor's degree. She worked to help pay my way through Palmer Chiropractic College and liked her job so much in Davenport she almost did not want to leave when I graduated. It took some extra coaxing from her parents to convince her that returning to Oelwein was the wise move to make, and I thank them every chance I get for their persuasive abilities. After a successful transition, Mary now works as a manager at the same local bank where her mother had worked as a teller for so many years.

By happenstance, Oelwein's longtime chiropractor, Dr. Oestermann, required an additional doctor in his office about the same time I graduated. I began working with him to gain experience soon after receiving my license. Just a few years later, my mentor retired, and I bought his practice and building. It was a great deal that worked to both of our benefits. Occasionally, the old-timer stops by the office to visit, and I'm always happy to trade adjustments and discuss life with him.

Mary's parents, Don and Maureen, are doing well. Since her retirement, Maureen evolved into a phenomenal full-time grandmother, and Don's career at the Waterloo John Deere plant is winding down. My in-laws stop to visit us at least twice a week and spend a lot of time in Des Moines visiting their son, Daniel. As hard as it is to believe, my brother-in-law has already lived in the state capital for fifteen years. We'll get to see all of Mary's family this weekend at the Fourteenth Annual Kelleher Family Cookout of Success.

Tim and I are still close, although work and family life prevent us from seeing each other as often as we'd like. Tim has climbed the employment ladder at the Co-Op and is now a shift manager. I'm extremely happy how he found his place in the world. He and

Mandy have been married for twelve years and have three children.

As fate would have it, Mary's best friend, Dori, married an insurance salesman from a town just thirty miles away from ours. He's a few years older than the friends in our circle, but a great guy with a broad sense of humor who fits in well at our family gatherings. At almost every occasion, Mary and Dori reminisce about how they dreamed of leaving northeast Iowa while in high school, and then laugh about how they both currently live within a short drive of the homes in which they were raised. Gratefully, neither has any regrets about how their lives turned out.

Rory delivered as promised. He bought a two-hundred-acre parcel not far from his parents' farm and rents it to another farmer nearby, though he ended up moving to Cedar Rapids and marrying a girl he met at work. I see them four or five times a year.

Tomislav and I lost contact quite some time ago, then out of the blue, I received a Christmas card from him last December. Inside, he scribbled a note saying he'd stop to visit me when his delivery route brought him near. I've had no contact from him since, but I haven't given up hope. I expect to see him standing at my office door when I come to work one day.

These days, our family spends a lot of time enjoying the outdoors. I'm my team's left fielder in the local softball league, and I help coach my youngest son's Little League team whenever my schedule allows. We also enjoy canoeing the rivers of northeast Iowa, taking family hikes with our Irish setter, and weekend picnics at a few of our favorite state parks. In the spring and fall, Reid, Adam, and I sneak off to fish the local trout streams every chance we can.

I believe my parents and grandfather would be proud of what I've accomplished in life so far, and the direction in which it's heading. Life's choices are many, and every decision varies in its level of significance and difficulty. Each choice can affect the outcome of one's future, and though I've made mistakes like everyone else, my most important decisions have all been rock solid and were based on the wisdom and experience passed on to me by those whose influence earned my greatest respect. It's that firm foundation I hope to pass along to my sons in order to ease life's burdens and ensure their time in this world is as rich and fulfilling as mine has been. After all, life is good, and worth every minute.

During my lifetime, I'd been the recipient of some of the worst luck and best fortune any man has ever known. Between those extremes, I owe much of my success to good genetics, a strong will and fortitude, common sense, and the unwavering love of an imperfect grandfather who guided me through the transition from boyhood to manhood. I'd also been blessed to marry into a family with strong family values and who accepted me into their unit from the very first day.

In addition, I have always sensed some unknown force, an entity far more powerful than my grandfather's presence, has been watching out for my well-being since I can remember. And though I could never identify it, I was wise enough to accept its existence, and then later to believe, trust, and respect the guidance it offered the older I got.

Two fair questions for anyone to ask are if I still bowhunt for deer, and if I have ever introduced the activity to my sons. The answer to both of those questions is no, although Tim always tries to entice me along on his annual hunts. I would not be opposed, however, to instructing my boys in the basics of bowhunting if one or the other ever wanted to pursue the recreation in the future. In fact, depending on their level of seriousness, I would be honored to teach them all of my Grandpa Conrad's secrets and techniques that I can still remember. Until now, I have only informed my oldest, Reid, of my deer hunting past, including the event that nearly cost me my life. I plan to wait until Adam is a little older before sharing the details with him.

As for Metzger's Slough, I've heard it hasn't changed much after all these years. After Dieter Metzger passed away, the executor of his will had the property auctioned off to the highest bidder, exactly as my grandfather had predicted would happen. In the subsequent years, word spread that the new owners were going to clear a major portion of the slough to grow crops, but I cannot confirm if there was any follow through on the rumor. I haven't been anywhere near the property since Dieter's funeral, and it's unlikely I'll ever pass that way again. And if my attendance were ever required on the opposite side of the tract, I would certainly detour it en route to my destination.

In fact, I'd gladly take the long way around.

Author Douglas Cavanaugh would love to hear from you!

Readers of *The Long Way Around* are encouraged to share their thoughts and comments. The best way to do this is by giving a rating and review on **www.amazon.com** and **www.goodreads.com**. It only takes a few minutes, and the author would love to know what's on your mind. Your input is valued and appreciated.

Also, be sure to check out Douglas Cavanaugh's first novel, the spy thriller *Into Hell's Fire*. Of course, a rating and review are encouraged for this classic, too.

All inquiries and author correspondence can be directed to this official email address:

croauthor@yahoo.com

Acknowledgements

Certain individuals deserve recognition for their assistance while this book was being written.

Bruce Wessell, author of the hilarious Las Vegas comedy-thriller *Double Down,* was inspirational in helping bring this project to completion. Bruce offered some great advice and was integral in choosing *The Long Way Around's* cover design. Be sure to check out *Double Down* today.

Christian Ebenhan is a German friend of the author who now lives in Croatia. Christian provided colorful detail for the chapter centered on World War II.

Mike Winger, an American expat residing in Croatia, contributed his time and insight helping me to complete this story.

Kyle Krier of Bettendorf, Iowa, did a fantastic job designing *The Long Way Around's* cover.

Much appreciation goes out to Elizabeth A. White for editing *The Long Way Around*. Elizabeth's splendid eye for detail took my writing to another level and helped make my book something of which I am extremely proud. Elizabeth can be found at: www.elizabethawhite.com.

And finally, Brian Broderick of rural Iowa City, Iowa, deserves my gratitude for finding the time to proof-read this novel despite his busy schedule.

About the Author

Douglas Cavanaugh is a native Iowan who grew up in Davenport. After living in two rural northeast Iowa communities (Dyersville and Oelwein) in the early 1990s, he expatriated to Croatia, where he has lived for more than twenty years.

"I had often imagined writing a novel while living in Iowa, but the rural settings in which I lived left me uninspired. It wasn't until after moving abroad that my intentions became a reality, when the post-war setting in Bosnia and Croatia stirred me to write my first novel, the spy thriller *Into Hell's Fire*. Based on that book's success, I returned to my Iowa roots to write *The Long Way Around*. I hope my pride of being from Iowa and the fond memories I have of my home state are reflected in the story."

Made in the USA
Middletown, DE
25 September 2021